WE THAT
WERE YOUNG

To
Bobbin

WE THAT WERE YOUNG

A Novel by
Irene Rathbone

With the original preface by E.M. Delafield

Introduction by Lynn Knight
Afterword by Jane Marcus

THE FEMINIST PRESS
at The City University of New York
New York

We That Were Young was first published in Great Britain by
Chatto & Windus in 1932
© 1932 by Irene Rathbone
Introduction © 1988 by Lynn Knight
Afterword © 1989 by Jane Marcus
All rights reserved.

Published 1989 by The Feminist Press at The City University
of New York, 311 East 94 Street, New York, NY 10128, by arrangement
with Virago Press Ltd.

Distributed by The Talman Company, 150 Fifth Avenue, New York,
NY 10011

Printed in the United States of America

91 90 89 88 6 5 4 3 2 1

Library of Congress Cataloging-in-Publication Data

Rathbone, Irene, 1892–1980.
     We that were young.

     1. World War, 1914–1918—Fiction.   I. Title.
PR6035.A73W4   1988   823'.912   88–31029
ISBN 0–558–61001–4
ISBN 0–558–61002–2 (pbk.)

This publication is made possible, in part, by public funds from the New
York State Council on the Arts.

Cover photo by Horace W. Nicholls. Reproduced by permission of the
Imperial War Museum.

Preface

ALMOST thirteen years to a day, after that November morning on which England went mad at hearing that the Armistice had been signed, this book came into my hands.

In thirteen crowded years, with life in England growing a little more difficult with each one that passes, Englishwomen have—not so much forgotten as, almost of necessity, put away— the memory of their side of the War. And things put away are apt to grow dim.

When I read Miss Rathbone's faithful and unromanticised story of women's war-work, I felt: Here is one who has remembered.

Impressions and emotions that I thought I had forgotten poured over me. It was like the feelings that one has—those of us who grew up or were grown up in war-time—when the mass-singing of 'There's a Long, Long Trail' comes through on the wireless, or on hearing the sound, that is no longer a frequent one, of many feet marching in rhythm along a road.

The significance of this book seems to me to lie entirely in its careful absence of exaggeration, and its successful recapitulation of an atmosphere. The characterisation is of less value. Joan, Betty, Pamela are simply the Every-girl of 1914–1918. The men they love, and who love them, are the men of the khaki-clad throngs that passed through streets, and stations, and country houses, and hotels, and theatres, and hospitals, and restaurants—for ever moving on, for ever being replaced by others—all indistinguishable from one another except by a small handful of women and children and old people left behind.

But that very absence of individual identification is characteristic. So is the definitely sentimental colouring that attaches to some of the emotional episodes in the book. War-time does, amongst other things, breed sentimentality, for sentimentality is one of the most powerful narcotics in the world.

To a very great number of middle- and upper-middle-class young women—myself amongst them—the War brought release. We had been brought up in the tradition that a girl did not work: she was worked for, by a male relation, usually her father. Her aim in life was to find another man who would take upon himself this obligation by marrying her. In return, she became his housekeeper and the mother of his children.

To some young women this ideal was satisfying: to others it was not. Only the bravest and most honest-minded failed to conform to it, for the usual alternative was to be 'the daughter at home.'

Women who were girls in 1914 will understand what that meant. Those who are girls in 1931 will not—and never can. And it is in great measure to the war-workers, as we called them—the Joans and Bettys and Pamelas of this book—that these girls of to-day owe the freedom of which the large majority are making such fine and splendid use.

I am glad that Miss Rathbone has written her sober, accurate and moving account of those incredible years, seen from the angle of 1914's young womanhood. I am glad to contribute to her book, even by so little as a page of writing. I believe that her contemporaries and mine will read it and remember. I hope that those who stand now where we stood then, will read it—and realise.

Elizabeth M. Delafield

Introduction

THROUGHOUT the literature of World War I the keening of a devastated generation insists on being heard. That it was a decade or so before many accounts of that period were published is not surprising. One wonders whether its survivors could ever exorcise the ghosts of a war that wiped out almost three quarters of a million men and irrevocably changed the fabric of a nation.

Descriptions of trench warfare and of casualty clearing stations make vivid the unimaginable; at the root of those literal accounts is an overwhelming sense of an experience that mocked assumptions of humanity. One sentence in Mary Borden's *The Forbidden Zone* (1929), a volume of sketches, stories, and poems based on her years as a nurse with the French Army, underlines the contrariness the 1914–1918 years encompassed: "It is the whispering of the grass and the scent of new-mown hay that makes me nervous."[1] In its quiet simple tone it captures the essence of that time, when the ordinary could no longer be relied upon and the horrific became commonplace, when personal testimonies of loss that would seem implausible in fiction, formed the basis of the everyday. Concomitant with this emotional chaos was the way in which the war ricocheted through society, shaking its foundations and realigning, albeit temporarily, the roles of the sexes. For as men became ciphers of militarism, numbers in a platoon stripped of autonomy, women acquired greater economic and social freedom than at any earlier point. These circumstances, with all their myriad contradictions, form a backdrop to *We That Were Young* (1932).

A semi-autobiographical novel, its historical accuracy allies it with the more famous *Diary without Dates* (1919) by Enid Bagnold and *Testament of Youth* (1933) by Vera Brittain. But, unlike those first-person narratives, *We That Were Young* provides not only one of the broadest spectrums of women's work that the literature of the period produced, but also a valuable *social* portrait of the age. For its heroine, Joan Seddon, modeled on her creator, is not a solitary figure. Her progress through the war is accompanied by that of her companions, among them Pamela Butler, based on Irene Rathbone's good friend Ruby Wyld, and Barbara Frewen, a fictionalized portrait of her cousin Marion.[2] Through the minutia of their daily existence, their conversations, companionship, and their relationships with men, Irene Rathbone presents both a multifaceted vision of the lives that breathed beneath the machinery of war and a blueprint of World War I womanhood.

The novel begins appropriately in 1915 (the year in which the popular conception of women's contribution to the war effort was changing) with Joan's decision to quit bandage-rolling for more substantial activities. At the outbreak of the war, the "angel in the house" ethic still prevailed, supported and ennobled by the press. According to one patriotic article, "The foundations of national glory are set in the homes of the people, and they will only remain unshaken whilst the family life of our nation is strong, simple and pure."[3] Having incited men to enlist, women were to devote themselves to good housekeeping ("The tables that today are laden with luxurious food belong to enemies of the Commonwealth"[4]); the knitting of "comforts" (whose recipients were said to use these unwanted articles for rifle cleaning); and the maintenance of femininity ("Advice to women during the War. Do not neglect your appearance. At times like the present the country should see their women-folk looking their best"[5]).

By the spring of 1915, however, it was less feasible for this image to be promoted. Britain's intervention in the European crisis could no longer be viewed as short term, and economic realities began to hit a nation ill-prepared for sustained warfare. Dissatisfaction with the conduct of the war under Prime Minister Asquith led to a Coalition Government, and a weapons shortage led to the creation of the Ministry of Munitions to coordinate and increase the production of armaments. This movement from laxity to professionalism necessitated a tonal shift in the government's response to women, with the Ministry of Munitions actively encouraging their enrollment in industry. In March of 1915 a register of women willing to do industrial, agricultural, and clerical work was compiled. Forty thousand put their names forward, a response no doubt elicited as much by a desire to escape the monotonous and routine lives society prescribed for them, as by patriotic fervor.

Irene Rathbone was twenty-three when this register was created. She had no need to grasp war service as her only bid for independence and indeed viewed it as an interruption of her own and her friends' careers. The Rathbones, a well-known merchant family, were regarded as advanced by their Liverpool contemporaries. Irene's father George had stood as a radical in a local council election and her younger brothers Reginald and Benson were educated at Bedales (then extremely pioneering). While Irene's education was not unorthodox—she attended a small, private "dame" school and later a south-coast boarding school—her freedom of movement thereafter was. Prior to the war she had shared a flat with her cousin, pursued a theatrical career (she appeared in one of Noel Coward's plays and was for some time a member of the Frank Benson Shakespeare Company), and was a dedicated suffragist.

In a later novel, *When Days Were Years* (1939), Irene Rathbone fictionalized what was clearly a contented middle-class childhood. What also emerges is the picture of a young girl already responsive to and responsible for others, with a strong sense of propriety, qualities that Joan of *We That Were Young* also exemplifies and that Irene Rathbone was to call upon throughout her life. She described the heroine of *When Days Were Years* as "of the temperament that prefered to agree than oppose," appropriate words for a woman whose anxiety as to her parents' response prevented her from translating her suffrage convictions into suffragette action. It was some years before she was able to claim her political convictions with impunity.

Three wartime occupations underpin *We That Were Young*. For the vivid recreation of the Y.M.C.A. camps and the work of a Volunteer Aid Detachment (V.A.D.) nurse, Irene Rathbone looked back upon her own experience; for the munitions section of the novel, Ruby Wyld provided the details that enabled her friend to write as if she were not only conversant with the manufacture of weaponry, but also knew the rhythm and pace of a factory. The positioning of these occupations within the novel is as a mirror to the mood of the war: from heady pageantry through relentless drudgery and desperation to careless fatalism.

At the Ostrohove camp in Boulogne (where Joan's war service begins) and at St. Valery-sur-Somme (where it ends) Joan is a canteen worker. The Ostrohove tents are the last site of civility en route to the front. Here, the women workers dispense cheer along with cups of tea and cigarettes before waving battalions "into France and silence." St. Valery, a rest camp at which troops arrive in fortnightly rotation, fleshes out their role as hostesses: in addition to cooking and waiting upon the men, they invite select officers to tea, and they sing in the entertainments tent.

These camps, although under the jurisdiction of the army, are superintended by members of the nonconformist ministry. Joan and her colleagues, as other accounts of World War I testify, are regarded with suspicion by both military and religious personnel who, resenting this intrusion into male territory, merely tolerate but do not sanctify their presence. That the women have no official status adds to their difficulties. Whether as members of the Women's Army Auxilliary Corps (W.A.A.C.) or aligned to the Y.M.C.A., women trod warily with an officialdom that could obscure its fundamental resistance to their involvement with allegations of immorality, which, if substantiated, would bring their war service to an end. And the Y.M.C.A. banner lent a deeper note to the proceedings—religious services were interwoven with entertainments, for such camps were also to offer moral and spiritual sustenance to the troops.

In childhood, Irene Rathbone had dreamed of doing great deeds for Christ, but although the war extinguished any residual faith, she nevertheless accepted wholeheartedly the role of the Y.M.C.A. During her stay at St. Valery, she kept a diary that runs into three volumes and that forms the basis of this part of the novel. Threaded through its detail is a certainty of the anchor these camps provided. In one passage, notable for its naivete, she describes the exhaustion of cooking endless quantities of food, but concludes:

> Provide enjoyable meals for them and drunkenness will fall away; after that they will listen to you, and are happy to sit in solid rows and have their souls informed. Viewed in this light . . . "fish and chips" take on spiritual values, and all of us little blue six are indirectly helping by this . . . to keep up the morale of the British Army—There is a thought![6]

In the novel, in order to ensure that their women workers behave with appropriate decorum, the ministers pursue their loco-parentis role with a vigilance that is often overbearing. But Joan's contempt for the "Christians" goes beyond the irritation of being supervised. They are despised for insulting manhood by not risking their lives, and for preaching a faith that has no place in the maelstrom of war. This prejudice was not uncommon and, after publication of *We That Were Young*, Irene Rathbone received a courteous letter from one such Christian who understood this view (and who was grateful that his predecessor, rather than himself, was the butt of her scathing remarks).

For the most part though, the tendentiousness of the Christians did not mar what was for Irene Rathbone the most enjoyable period of the war. She wrote in her diary, "for years I have not been so completely free and happy."[7] As a smokescreen to the reality of battle, with precarious gaiety at a premium, St. Valery is representative of that peculiar coexistence of hedonism and danger that war creates. The camps offered a sense of release and adventure and the opportunity to participate without witnessing the consequences of warfare. Unlike ambulance drivers or nurses at the front, these women were on the sidelines. As Barbara remarks, "It was rather like being behind the scenes at a play, and seeing only scene-shifters and call-boys."[8] Irene Rathbone wrote her own sense of respite into this, lighter, section of the novel, but her ease was initially tempered by guilt; the unpleasant duties of nursing had seemed a more pertinent contribution to the war effort than the conviviality of the St. Valery camp. While she welcomed her return to France, she could not forget her experiences as a V.A.D.

By 1916 the extent of mutilations and serious injury was far higher than had been anticipated, resulting in an acute shortage of both soldiers and nurses. In May, Universal Male Conscription was introduced, and the demand for nurses soon became insistent. A July article in *The Times* appealed for recruits and "the middle-class, home-sheltered girls of England felt, at last, that their existence was not wholly futile" (194). With her starched uniform and devoted servitude, the nurse is a classic icon of World War I. The reality was far from glamorous. The enthusiasm of those "home-sheltered girls" who enlisted for that most traditional of female roles was easy to exploit in a national emergency. The Voluntary Aid Detachments, which were to supply 23,000 nurses and 18,000 orderlies during the four-year period, flung nurses into hospitals regardless of experience. The difficulties of working for long hours with inadequate facilities, under regulations that often seemed designed to impede rather than promote efficiency, were compounded by the resentment with which V.A.D.s were viewed by some of the professional nursing staff. The recruitment procedures, like those for the camps—via selective interview and referees—were designed to attract the middle and upper classes. Professional nurses, who had earned their way into the hospital hierarchy, understandably viewed these wartime do-gooders with suspicion. As Irene Rathbone demonstrates, that suspicion sometimes tipped over into open hostility, which V.A.D.s were powerless to combat.

Although initially appalled by the mess and stench of serious injury, Joan of necessity becomes inured. The exactness with which Irene Rathbone describes the treatment of various wounds could grace a medical dictionary and is not for the faint-hearted. Other

wartime accounts of nursing are far less explicit. Was she attempting to quash forever the image of the V.A.D. as a genteel soother
of brows? Or to emphasize the horrific results of war, the gap between ideal and actuality? Nursing was one of the nearest approx-
imations to male experience of battle and Irene Rathbone has
ensured that its trials have not gone unrecorded. Several nurses
thanked her for presenting their wartime service so vividly.

The hospitals too have their share of a feigned jocularity:
"Nobody must appear, for a moment, to be seeing beneath the
surface, to be envisaging the tragedy, and not the comedy, of
wounds" (152–153). And there is always the opportunity—though
strictly disapproved of—to socialize in off-duty moments with convalescent soldiers. Joan sees the popular show 'Chu-Chin-Chow'
countless times and Pamela meets her fiancé Ian while nursing.

Pamela's decision to leave the wards and become a "munition-
ette" is prompted by revengeful despair. As the daughter of a
county family, her action is regarded as unsuitable by her aunt.
Between 1914 and 1918 the number of women and girls over ten
employed in industry increased by approximately 800,000, but the
majority of these were drawn from the working class, deemed to
be more suited to the monotonous and physically unpleasant work.
Factories were often poorly ventilated and without adequate health
and safety provisions. Accidents were not uncommon—two are described in the novel in graphic detail. There were also the hazards
of working with TNT, nitro-glycerine, and other explosives. Several hundred women were killed by accidental explosions during
the course of the war. Newspaper reports applauded "munitionettes" for their stamina, ignoring the fact that heavy labor was not
new to working-class women. But along with the praise, popular
opinion held that they were overpaid, extravagant, and immoral,
the most popular accusations leveled at women who stepped into
male roles during those years.

Initially employers used the crisis as an excuse to introduce long
hours, low wages, and to break the prewar Factory Acts. The Women's Interests Committee, headed by Mrs. Millicent Garrett
Fawcett of the National Union of Women's Suffrage Societies,

(N. V. W. S. S.), agitated to counteract exploitation, and the Women's Trade Union League under Mary Macarthur encouraged unionization and negotiated an alliance with the engineering unions to legitimize women's work and to attempt to eradicate the fear that it would jeopardize the postwar industrial economy.

The intense concentration and automaton-like work of the munitions factory suit Pamela's single-minded purpose. When forced to leave through ill-health (unlike working-class women, Pamela is not dependent upon her wages), her decision is supported by her aunt who "saw no point in competing with the lower orders in physical endurance" (276). While a touch of irony underlies this comment, Irene Rathbone herself was less progressive than she believed. She writes of the camps, "in practice we are all socialists here," yet she prepares rhubarb and custard for the Tommies and strawberries and cream for the officers, without apparently noticing the discrepancy in the menu, and she is relieved to hear "the nice voices" of officers. Middle and working classes worked alongside one another, but the war did little to knock down barriers and generally reinforced them. At Staple and Studd's munitions factory, Pamela shares a bench with a shop assistant's daughter and an ex-kitchen maid, but the woman she singles out for acquaintance is a vicar's daughter: "In work hours the other girls treated them in a friendly, natural manner, neither with suspicion nor jealousy, neither with undue reserve or undue familiarity; in off hours they left them tacitly alone" (264). From this sense of writing across a void, as if of another species, here and elsewhere in the novel, Irene Rathbone states the prejudices of her time that she shared, but did not acknowledge as her own.

The war threw most middle-class women into the company of large groups of men, unchaperoned for the first time. And, for the majority of women who became nurses, the war also gave them, in anodyne surroundings, their first sight of a male body: "She was a nurse in uniform, and he was a wounded soldier; the gulf between them was fixed and rigid. And yet across that gulf, unrecognised and certainly unheeded by either, stretched the faint sweet fingers of sex" (212–213). If Irene Rathbone was not new to independence, she was nevertheless as confused by potential sexual relationships as many of her contemporaries. Though vivacious and popular, she was no coquette and the emotional passages of her diary are striking for their gaucheness. Motivated by an earnest desire to be a "decent" woman, she did not cultivate her sexuality—though, unlike Joan, she admitted the temptation: "Oh, if only one hadn't to be respectable, what a time one could have!"[9]

For Irene Rathbone, looking back upon that diary and remembering her younger self, it must have been tempting to erase some of the contradictions she embodied. Instead, because she wrote those same uncertainties and inhibitions into her heroine, one of the novel's attractions is Joan's "girlish" attempts to unravel her responses to men as she matures. Joan is a romantic whose bookish nature provides her with "modern" opinions on relationships and sex, including those more murky areas of prostitution and venereal disease, about which she is ignorant and which are essentially at odds with her idealism. Her relationship with Colin is based on Irene Rathbone's relationship with Mansfield Priestley Evans, a Liverpool man; the relationship was to last for over five years, albeit intermittently and at a distance.

From an adolescent friendship founded on a mutual interest in poetry, Joan and Colin appropriate the imagery of courtly love to outline their steps towards emotions neither is certain of. Through the motifs of chastity and chivalry, Joan is relieved of a sexual pressure she prefers to avoid and Colin is granted the hope that, when he has earned her love, Joan will be his. Colin as potential war hero glamorizes Joan's ideal, but their relationship must remain platonic. She imagines them as "the greatest and happiest friends that ever were" in a relationship "where flesh scarcely counted."

As Colin evolves from "embarrassed boy-lover" to "a man among men," with the war as a yardstick to his masculine stature, their relationship necessarily changes, but the appearance of Paul Wentworth suggests that Joan's insistence on the platonic is a safety catch. Excited and flattered by his attentions, she spends some time telling Paul she is the emancipated woman she would like to be, but consistently reinterprets their conversations in order to give her sexual attraction a respectable framework.

For Joan the contradictions between theory and desire are never really resolved. Prior to the Wentworth debacle, she condones sex without marriage, but for others, not for herself. While disapproving of Pamela's wish to be someone's slave, she feels "a slender thread of disappointment that [Colin] did not show more possessiveness, that he did not—in all senses—grab hold of her and shake her into feeling she was his" (109). But a Victorian moral education laced with poetry weighs far more heavily than the enticement of a sexual one.

If Paul excites Joan, her brother Jimmy symbolizes the man she would like to love: "Oh, Jumbles, I really only want you—only you—ever!" (28). Based on Irene Rathbone's own beloved younger brother Benson, whose death in 1919, while in Germany with the army of occupation, devastated her, Jimmy is the one man with whom Joan feels entirely comfortable. When she fantasizes about her future, Colin as her husband, has a peripheral role, but "Jimmy, as a grown-up brother, was not at all shadowy. In fact the house seemed to consist primarily for him" (133).

Colin remains a shadowy figure, a pale youthful ideal. He conforms to a fantasy whereas Paul disrupts one, and each is a stereotype. But probably the blend of fact and fiction here prohibited Irene Rathbone from creating a convincing hero. Like many women of her generation, Irene Rathbone's marriage was prevented by the death of her fiancé. Mansfield Priestley Evans was killed in Iraq in 1920—his death, like her brother's, coming at a time when she had ceased to expect those dreaded telegrams, gave a further bitter twist to her former notions of heroism: Benson died of pneumonia; her fiancé was killed in a small village uprising. In writing We That Were Young, Irene Rathbone decorated the memory of that relationship, colored now by years of loss and regret, with sentiment. She was to receive other proposals of marriage, but accepted none.

"The Great War" was to be the war to end all wars and the population acceded to the nation's demands with self-righteous gusto. Embodying the ethos of their time, Joan and Colin speak of "the justest war there has ever been, and the finest cause since the Crusades" (4), and the *Oxford Book of Verse* accompanies Colin to the trenches "in the very spirit of 1915—that year of the 'enchanteds,' to whom poetry and the war were one, and the war still worth the winning (48)." For men engaged in combat and women in frontline occupations, that glorification was difficult to sustain and patriotism increasingly became a remote and threadbare concept. Conversely, a civilian population continued to promote a war whose brutalities it need not witness: Robert Seddon, Joan's uncle, regrets his inability to enlist and envies the younger generation their "splendid burden." As the war progressed, such cant and hypocrisy appalled and astounded those required to sacrifice their youth and/or their lives for a war not of their making, and be grateful into the bargain: "What was the use of winning the war, Joan cried to herself in sudden despair, if none of the men who won it were to live? The papers were for ever quoting 'Who dies if England lives?' But after all what *was* England?" (227)

As Joan and Colin's emotional relationship is played out through courtly love, Joan's movement from patriotism to awareness is figuratively upheld by literature. When Brooke-ish sentiments are no longer so easy to swallow, she progresses to Shelley's *Defense of Poetry*, clinging to the notion that order can spring from chaos, and finally turns to the Russian classics, to Samuel Butler and H.G. Wells. Yet Joan's acknowledgment of dwindling patriotism is an uneasy one, generally overruled by an implicit faith in the cause, and she tends to excuse her own doubts through illness or exhaustion. Her one friend who does not enter the war with an eager patriotism is significantly "a man already rooted in his career . . . not a boy just down from the university" (78). His denunciation of war is also justified—as a consequence of neurasthenia.

A perverse collusion existed between the civilian and combatant population. Jack Seddon (Robert's son) will not disabuse his father: "the war's too sacred to him." "Youth understood youth in those times, the old had to be protected and cheered." And levels of consciousness were graded still further. Women's experiences, however bleak, could not parallel those of the trenches: "Men in war-time moved behind a mist. Men you cared for, men you thought you were intimate with—brothers, lovers, friends—all, all, were fundamentally, were pathetically, alone" (312).

For many the Armistice sounded a mocking, futile note, a signal to come to terms with the grief those extraordinary years had obscured. For some that grief became sacrosanct; others were haunted for years by the detritus they tried to forget. The postwar lives of Joan and her circle of friends have a muted tone, their accomplishments tinged with a sense of the second-best. The "ghostly glamour" of the years that burned up their ideals and their enthusiasms clings like camphor.

Peace was to bring poverty, unemployment and retrenchment. Having fluttered her wings, the angel was expected to return to the kitchen sink. The *Daily Graphic* summed up general opinion: "The idea that because the State called for women to help the nation, the State must continue to employ them is too absurd for sensible women to entertain."[10] But the war had highlighted the inadequacy—and the hypocrisy—of earlier concepts of women's capabilities; governmental assertions of their inequality were less plausible. The United Suffragists and the Women's Freedom League had remained active throughout the war, the N.U.W.S.S., which had concentrated its energies on social and economic issues during the previous four years, now resumed its agitation. In 1918 wives of householders and female householders over thirty were granted the franchise, though ten years passed before that right was extended to all women.

In 1918 Irene Rathbone set up a Chelsea flat with women friends, one of whom was Dorothy Wadham of PEN. Rathbone's writing career began almost by accident: friends and family, impressed by the letters she had written when visiting her brother Reginald, by then a captain stationed in India and China, felt that her work should be published. Thus the first of eight novels, *Susan Goes East* (1929), was born. By 1930 the manuscript of *We That Were Young* was complete. Richard Aldington, with whom Irene Rathbone had corresponded—perhaps she had complimented him on the bestselling *Death of a Hero* a year earlier— and who was to have an important role in her life, was instrumental in the novel's publication. At Aldington's suggestion, she approached Chatto & Windus.[11]

Appearing as it did in that cascade of war literature the late 1920s and early 1930s produced, *We That Were Young* was not as successful as Irene Rathbone had hoped, and she envied the acclaim accorded Vera Brittain the following year. Although they did not meet at the time, both women had worked at the First London General during the Somme offensive. Replying to a letter from Irene Rathbone, Vera Brittain was pleased that *We That Were Young* corroborated her own memories of the Camberwell hospital and said, "I read the story with deep interest and sympathy, realising, as you say, how similar was the spirit behind both books."[12] Brittain decided that her signed copy of Rathbone's novel would sit on her shelves alongside Sassoon, Blunden, Graves, and Aldington, in whose company it belonged.

The press response to *We That Were Young* was mixed. Storm Jameson, who later became an enduring friend, gave the novel a lukewarm review, but on discovering its autobiographical nature, felt it should have been applauded regardless of defects.[13] And the novel's detractors could flex their critical literary muscles, for the treatment of episodes such as Pamela's love at first sight is hackneyed and the dialogue, which at times veers toward exclamatory staginess, can be embarrassing. As a social documentary, however, *We That Were Young* merits a place in the canon of war literature. Not only is it unusual for recording a variety of women's war work, but also for providing the details—of clothes, theatres, books read—and the sense of what it was like to be young in those war-torn years.

The letters Irene Rathbone received were unanimous in praise of the novel's realism and sincerity. Several found it impossible to forget, including Winifred Holtby who in 1934 wrote, "*We That Were Young* still haunts me."[14] The reviewer and military strategist B. H. Liddell Hart thought it "should go in the slender list of books that are really necessary for an understanding of the World

War,"[15] while Richard Church wrote, "I find all my critical powers hypnotised . . . You have done something wonderful." Yet he also added, "Feeling, passion, personal faith in human beings, is taboo. Your book is therefore unfashionable at the moment, but it will come into its own."[16]

Irene Rathbone felt that the success of *Testament of Youth* was in part due to its publication as straight autobiography, but perhaps Richard Church's comment rings true, for cynicism was the mood of the day and *We That Were Young* presents, but does not vilify, that 1914–1918 wasteland. Irene Rathbone reserved those sentiments for *They Call It Peace* (1936).

During the 1930s Rathbone's political beliefs gathered strength. Appalled by the mess to which the nation's "heroes" had returned, she felt that her generation had been duped for a cause whose justice had been obscured and whose agony had been prolonged by the greed of profiteers. By the time of *They Call It Peace*, Irene Rathbone's politics were passionate. Anti-fascist, pro-Republican Spain, and heavily involved in the Social Credit movement, she created a novel damning those who cherished economic above human needs. Ranging from April 1914 to Remembrance Day 1934, it chronicles the lives of the Berington family, owners of a small publishing company, and their employees. Taking in the political and national events of those years and their social repercussions, the novel is the work Irene Rathbone most valued.

Irene Rathbone thrived on the bohemian flavor of Chelsea; she enjoyed its political and literary atmosphere, was a great conversationalist and, with good friends around her, including Olga Millar ("Sagitarrius" of the *New Statesman*), she was in her element. The 1930s were her most productive period—six novels appeared during that decade—and they were also the setting for what was probably the most agonizing relationship of her life.

In 1931 Irene Rathbone met Richard Aldington in the South of France where he lived with Brigit Patmore. They soon became lovers. Conducted behind the scenes, their affair continued until Aldington left Brigit Patmore for Nellie McCulloch in 1937.[17] As the invisible "other woman," the recipient of Aldington's attentions only when he visited London, and the partner whose involvement was the greater, Irene Rathbone was in a painful situation. How many times they met is unclear, but they shared one brief idyll in Provence, which she later fictionalized in *Was There a Summer* (1943). In a prose poem where emotional content outweighs literary value, every passage underlines her depth of feeling. The relationship ended as it had begun, with a letter out of the blue, this time from Aldington—asking forgiveness and bidding Irene goodbye. There were other love affairs, but Aldington remained significant; when she was in her seventies she left flowers at his Sury-en-Vaux grave.

Irene Rathbone spent much of World War II caring for her ageing parents in Chipping Campden. As the only daughter and a single woman, she assumed familial duties without question. Earlier, when her widowed brother Reginald was overseas, she had cared for his young son. But the Chipping Campden years were of a different order. She hated being incarcerated in the country and, used to independence, it seemed like an exile. Her father died in 1952; her mother survived him by twelve years. Though Irene visited London and holidayed in France—she was a frequent visitor to her good friend Nancy Cunard's Dordogne house, whose tranquillity provided an essential interlude—she had committed herself to a self-sacrificing arrangement that lasted far longer than she could have foreseen. During this period her last book *The Seeds of Time* (1952) appeared. The critical reception of this novel, which she had agonized over and whose political content she had cut back at Storm Jameson's advice, distressed her deeply.

On her return to London in 1964 Irene Rathbone picked up the strands of her life and became active in PEN once more. But a bitterness could be glimpsed beneath, a sense of outrage at those lost years, lost opportunities, and a resistance to growing old and her single state. "Oh, you *mothers* and your children!" she once exclaimed to her niece.

The last four or five years of Irene Rathbone's life were spent in nursing homes near Oxford, with her brother and niece as frequent visitors. Her mind had begun to fail and she could no longer live alone. If she had known that *We That Were Young* would be republished, would finally "come into its own," she may have felt that her efforts had not been wasted, for she has bequeathed her youth to a generation for whom World War I is history. "At the time, you see, the war was so ordinary—it was just our life. Yes, we hated it, and loved it, both. Loved it only because we gave so much to it, and because it was bound up with our youngness. . . . It was *our* war, you see" (465).

Lynn Knight
London 1988

Notes

1. Mary Borden, *The Forbidden Zone* (London: Heinemann, 1929), p. 52.

2. Private correspondence with the Estate of Irene Rathbone.

3. "Making Home Life Attractive," *The Lady*, 6 August 1914, p. 4.

4. *The Queens Newspaper*, quoted by Mrs. D. C. Peel, in *How We Lived Then 1914–18* (London: John Lane, 1929).

5. Advertisement for The Adair Ganesh Treatment, *The Lady* 20 August 1914, p. 23.

6. Irene Rathbone, *Diary of 3rd Army Rest Camp, St. Valery sur Somme*, Vol. I, private collection, the Estate of Irene Rathbone.

7. *Diary*, Vol. I.

8. Irene Rathbone, *We That Were Young* (London: Chatto & Windus, 1932; reprinted New York: The Feminist Press, 1989). Subsequent references to *We That Were Young* are indicated by page references in the text.

9. *Diary*, Vol. I.

10. David Mitchell, quoting the *Daily Graphic* in *Women on The Warpath*, p. 266, Jonathan Cape, London, 1966.

11. Letter from Irene Rathbone to Chatto & Windus, private collection, the Estate of Irene Rathbone.

12. Letter from Vera Brittain to Irene Rathbone, private collection, the Estate of Irene Rathbone.

13. Letter from Storm Jameson to Irene Rathbone, private collection, the Estate of Irene Rathbone.

14. Letter from Winifred Holtby to Irene Rathbone, private collection, the Estate of Irene Rathbone.

15. Letter from B. H. Liddell Hart to Irene Rathbone, private collection, the Estate of Irene Rathbone.

16. Letter from Richard Church to Irene Rathbone, private collection, the Estate of Irene Rathbone.

17. Interview with the Estate of Irene Rathbone.

PART ONE

1915

'Life is the rose's hope while yet unblown ;
The reading of an ever-changing tale ;
The light uplifting of a maiden's veil ;
A pigeon tumbling in clear summer air ;
A laughing school-boy, without grief or care,
Riding the springy branches of an elm.'

Chapter One

ON a late Sunday afternoon in the spring of 1915 Miss Florence Seddon was crossing the hall of her home in Hampstead to give an order in the kitchen about supper. She paused for a moment at the half-open door of the drawing-room, and her kind eyes blinked at what they saw.

At the far end, in the bay-window, their faces turned to one another, were seated her niece Joan and her niece's friend, Colin Paley. Their forms were dark; but the April sunshine, which made the garden beyond a luminous fairy-land of yellow-green, outlined their profiles, and threw dusty aureoles about their hair. Seen like that they reminded Miss Seddon of figures in some favourite Watts or Burne-Jones picture; there was the same sort of pathos about them, the same unearthly radiance. With a smile and sigh she left them undisturbed, and passed on down the passage.

But to each other those two in the window-seat were anything but unearthly; they were palpable breathing realities. What Joan saw, a foot or two away from her, was the red-brown skin of Colin's face, the stiff waves of his bronze-flecked hair, and the shape of his shoulder under his khaki tunic. What Colin saw was a pale face shell-tinted in the middle of the cheeks, a short freckled nose, and eyes like a boy-angel's whose clear and serious gaze could only be forgotten when the wide mouth (more full of promise to a lover than the eyes) broke into a smile.

Colin sat bent a little forward, as though the diffident love he felt for the girl had somehow subdued his strength. Joan, white-collared and blue-jerseyed, sat with heels tucked under her, elbow on sill, the very ease of her attitude denoting the coolness of her blood. Perplexity hovered over their faces, and at the same time that sort of exaltation that comes to the young from the lengthy discussion of personal feelings. Their united ages came to very little more than forty years.

'You are "The Shepherdess without a Heart," ' said Colin ruefully.

'Perhaps I am—perhaps I am. But I'm not cruel, you know. It's just that I can't feel anything—in your way.'

'You could; but this war prevents my having time to make you feel,' he muttered. 'It's damnable luck. No time for all those things that—well, that *need* time so much.'

'But surely the war would have helped, not hindered, if I had begun to love you anyhow?'

He shook his head. 'Not with you. You're different. You don't drop into one's arms. You need to be wooed, and I haven't a chance.' He struggled on, faltering between his desire to express the truth he felt about her and his fear of giving offence. 'You see, your dreams and your reality have got to be made one. At present you live in a realm of disembodied ideas. You love the idea of love, but not love itself—the idea of a soldier, but not me.'

'That's rather—dreadfully—true,' she agreed.

'I only mean,' he added hastily, 'that it makes you more difficult to get hold of. But I adore you for it—for everything that makes up you; your inaccessibility, your—your sort of white glitter. To me you've always been the "Young Princess," you know, "a frost of beauty white." '

Her eyes lit up. 'Oh . . . how does it go? I've forgotten for the moment.'

He quoted half-tenderly, half-sadly:

> ' "The South sang like a nightingale
> To thaw her glittering dream,
> No wine of love her bosom gave,
> She drank no wine of love, but grave
> She held them to love's theme." '

Joan sighed in response to the beauty of the lines, ignoring their application to herself. Her friendship with Colin had, from the beginning, been fed by their common love of poetry, and it was the fact that he knew such a quantity by heart that warmed her specially towards him. From Michael Drayton's sonnet: 'Since

there's no help . . .' to Masefield's 'Daffodil Fields' they had discovered, with growing enchantment, that their favourites were
almost always the same; and an incredible amount of their time
together was spent in quoting, and in looking things up.

Colin raised his eyes. They were curious eyes, the colour of
dusty iris-petals, but saved from an almost unmasculine beauty by
the straight thick lids. The passion in them contrasted with the
clear impersonal enthusiasm in Joan's.

'It's for me to thaw your "glittering dream,"' he said. 'But there's
no time—no *time*; and I've so little skill. In your presence I'm
just a choking idiot.' He put his hand to his forehead in a sudden
hopeless gesture.

At that she leant towards him and began speaking quickly—rather
desperately.

'Oh, Colin, I *do* care for you, you know. I *am* your friend. And
it's not that I despise the sex business, but I just don't want it—
yet. To me, friendship between a man and a girl is the loveliest
thing in the world. Why can't you think so too, and leave the
rest? What I want is that your thoughts of me should bring you
joy—not misery. I should hate to be a weakening influence in
anybody's life. Let's be the greatest and happiest friends that ever
were—you and I!'

His hand had dropped from his eyes.

'Joan, tell me, have you never felt anything for any man except
this friendship?—which, mind you, I love too,—but haven't
you?'

She looked away from him out of the window.

'Yes. I've had faint stirrings—if you must know. But there
seem to be two streaks in me which are never melted together; it's
rather disheartening really. You appeal to one of them, and my
cousin Jack, for instance, appeals to the other. Jack has no brains,
but he's gay and attractive and makes me laugh. He isn't particularly attracted to me, I may say—perhaps that's part of his
charm. Anyhow there've been times at dances when I've wanted
to kiss him. I know what the feeling's like.'

She was only analysing herself of course—only answering his question—not wantonly inflicting pain; but he nearly groaned. Such a clod she made him feel—such dull earth. His in-love-ness was only a weight on both of them. She wanted gay self-confidence in a man, and how could he give her that? If only he had been able to remain heart-whole one month in her company he might have had a chance.

Her thoughts, temporarily diverted, came back to him. She saw his distress, yet felt powerless to comfort him. He was looking at the floor, his hands clasped, his face red and wretched.

'You shall love me,' he blurted out. 'With both the streaks in you—with all of you—you *shall* love me. Meanwhile I will try so hard to be a good friend to you in the way you want—if only you won't tell me that it's all hopeless for ever.' He swung round on her. 'You can't tell, Joan, you can't tell what you'll feel in a year or two's time. I used to think it was foolish and undignified to go on caring when it was no good, but now there seems nothing left to matter if I stop. Do you know? I believe you are terrified of the whole business of love and marriage. I was in a way—until I met you. But you needn't fear I shall bind you, or attempt to. It's a thing I've a horror of. You need never fear that.'

He had no definite idea of what he meant, but he was blundering towards something, and his tongue, too often tied in her company, had been for a moment unloosed.

'You're a dear, you're a dear,' she stammered, uncomfortably moved, hating to be moved at all, hating not to be moved a great deal more. 'And if it were anyone, Colin, I think it would be you. But now isn't the time to think of these things. There's just the war. For good or ill we've got to give ourselves up to it.' Her eyes were bright. She spoke to convince both herself and him. 'It's the justest war there has ever been, and the finest cause since the Crusades. You are a modern knight, Colin; think of it like that!'

He gazed at her, wistful but enchanted. 'Your knight! Yes. I'll think of it like that. And perhaps deeds will move you more than stumbling words can do. Suppose we were to meet in France—in "la douce France" that we both love . . .'

'Oh, wouldn't that be queer and romantic,' she broke in. 'You'll get there first of course—but I shall get there some time.'

Queer and romantic? Yes, if that was how she chose to look at it. He would accept that aspect of things. It was easy to do so at this particular moment of the world's history. Romance was reality— reality romance. And nothing in mediæval legend could be queerer than the life they were plunged in now.

'Oh, look!' She had turned to the window, and burst out laughing. For there, at the bottom of the garden, under the sycamore tree, was her young brother Jimmy holding the Airedale terrier between his knees, and trying to force something into its mouth.

'I must go and help him!' cried Joan. 'Tam simply loathes that medicine.' And she dashed from the room, followed at a slower pace by Colin.

.   .   .   .   .   .

Out in the garden she bent with her brother over the struggling dog.

'Give me the stuff, Jim. You hold him.' Taking the bottle and spoon she poured the liquid, sideways, between the reluctant canine jaws, and held them firmly pressed together for a moment or two afterwards.

'There, I think he's got it all,' she said, sitting back on her heels. And Tam, released, bounded and sniffed, clumsily jabbing his great paw against his nose in an endeavour to be rid of something horrible.

Jimmy straightened himself, and said in his slow way: 'I'm always sorry for the poor old chap when he has to be made undignified like that.'

'So am I,' said Joan, 'but he is so frightfully funny—I can't help laughing at him.' And they both watched in amusement the capering great hairy creature whom they loved as though he were one of the family—as indeed he practically was.

Colin, standing a little apart, watched them all three.

'I think perhaps he ought to have more vegetables with ,his biscuit,' Jimmy said thoughtfully.

'All right, see that he has them,' said his sister from her kneeling position on the grass. 'You're responsible for him during the holidays.'

Jimmy was sixteen, loosely-made but graceful, and still growing fast. People said that he and Joan were alike, but the likeness was superficial, and consisted merely in their having the same sort of light thick hair, the same creamy freckled skin. Jimmy's face had none of the well-cut neatness of his sister's—it was broad and babyish, the features unformed, the expression dreamy. The size of his mouth—a caricature of Joan's—was a constant subject of jest in the family. Like hers it could break into a smile of morning brilliance, but it did so far more rarely, and more gradually.

He stood there in his flannels, his weight balanced on one foot, his young arms bare to the elbow hanging loosely down, when suddenly Joan, who in spite of Jim's height still thought of him as her 'little brother,' sprang to her feet and, in a fit of affectionate mischief, seized him by the hair which stuck out behind, and which she called his 'scalp-knot.'

'Oh, let *go*!' he yowled, cringing. 'Not *fair*! You haven't got a pigtail any more!'

'If you dare clutch my bun . . .!' she warned him, and sprang away from him round the sycamore tree. He was after her—Tam leaping and barking at his heels—up the path, and through the hedge into the kitchen-garden. There were sounds of laughter and a scuffle. After a few moments they returned, with sober steps but faces still flickering, across the sunlit lawn to where Colin waited.

The chase between brother and sister, of which outwardly Colin had been the mere amused spectator, had roused deep hunting instincts in him. He saw with an ache of longing Joan's boyish shoulders, small round breasts, all the movements of her compact little body, and vowed that this modern Atalanta, though she might run free for years, should succumb at last to her Milanion.

He was brought back from his dream to everyday life by hearing her ordering off Jimmy to bathe and change; and then, when the boy had gone, saying: 'You'll keep the ball rolling to-night, won't you, Colin? There'll be some people to supper, and I don't want Auntie to see there's anything up between us.'

'I'll do my best,' he said, looking down at the untroubled eyes lifted to his. It sounded a small thing that she asked of him compared with what he was ready to go through for her sake, yet it struck him that the leading of a charge would present fewer difficulties.

All afternoon she had been ragging about with those twin kids her cousins. It was no wonder that children adored her, he thought, and of course it was delightful to see her with them; but there were occasions when children could be disconcertingly in the way. He had only had her to himself since after tea.

Stammeringly he tried to express his admiration of her, his anxiety lest she should be tired; but she only shook her head, gave him a little smile, and vanished into the house.

. . . . . .

As Joan sat in her petticoat, hair-brush in hand, there was a perfunctory knock at the door, and Jimmy clattered down the two steps into her bedroom. The room which opened out of it, and through which he had just come, was the old nursery, converted now into their special sitting-room. Jimmy used both apartments as though they were equally his own, and strayed from one to the other regardless of his sister's state of toilet. That this was right and wholesome for the boy Joan knew, but her chief reason for allowing it was quite simply that she never found him in the way. In spite of the differences between them, of age and of character, these two found deep contentment in each other's company.

Sitting on the edge of the bed, his flannels exchanged for a dark suit, his hair sleeked to comparative smoothness, Jimmy watched Joan's proceedings in silence.

'Fed Tam?' she asked, without looking round.

'M'm; he's a bit off his food to-night. Who's coming to supper?'

'Uncle Robert, and Aunt Rose, and Philip Nichol, and—I think that's all. You like Philip, don't you?'

'M'm.'

'Pity he's so unattractive-looking, because he's extremely clever,' she sighed. Then after a brief pause: 'Do you like Colin?'

'Yes. I think he's an awfully decent chap.'

Jimmy could seldom be drawn into giving an opinion on his sister's various young men. He took them for granted. They were always drifting in and out of the house. About the exact emotional relation in which they stood to Joan he didn't worry. He felt, however, that on this occasion something more was required of him, so he said reluctantly:

'I could have taken on the kids myself this afternoon you know, if you'd wanted to be alone with him.'

'I know you could, Jim-pot darling—but I didn't particularly.'

'*He* did!' Jimmy's voice got slower and growlier the more a subject embarrassed him.

'Oh, well,' she declared airily, 'you effaced yourself after tea all right.'

He grunted. Effacing himself was never any difficulty. It was only when Joan required him to be brightly there that he felt such a hopeless ass.

She was climbing into her frock now, a taffeta garment the colour of a spring leaf, bunched at the hips, tight at the feet, in the fashion of last summer. It had been worn with a *bergère* hat in May-week and at Lord's. Now it was reduced to gracing 'home evenings.'

'Fasten me up,' she commanded, turning her back to him.

That, at any rate, he could manage efficiently.

'You'll make a good husband,' she told him. 'I've trained you well. Will I do?'

He stood back to survey her. His admiration for her personal appearance, as well as for her intelligence, was none the less real for being very seldom expressed.

'Ye-es. Isn't that velvet band in your hair a little too wide?'
'No, not a bit.' Then swiftly looking at herself in the glass: 'Yes,
it is—damn! You're right as usual.' And she tore it out,
smoothing down with impatience the ruffled hair. 'Now come
on, I expect we're late.'

    .   .   .   .   .   .

Round the dining-room table faces danced and swam in the
candle-light. Time had dealt gently with Florence; her cheeks were
still rosy, her hair hardly touched with grey. Beaming affectionately about her she ladled out the soup. She liked things to continue as they had always done, and Sunday supper at Beechwood
—her girlhood's home, where she still lived—had been an institution for years. As in her parents' time, relations and friends still
gathered for it. But nothing was stable nowadays. People were
getting scattered, especially the younger ones. Even Joan would
be off soon, and really in her case it was quite unnecessary. She
was looking a little pale to-night, the dear child, though she was
talking animatedly enough. How like her father she was at
times!
Florence had been devoted to her younger brother John, and
ever since his tragic death in India, and that of his girl-wife
fifteen years ago, she had brought up his two children, and lavished
on them all the affection and care which once had gone out to him.
Her elder brother Robert, so like her in appearance, though
more rotund, sat beside her, sipping his sherry, and delivering
opinions on the war. Fortunately the family tea-business, of
which he was senior partner, had not been badly affected. Robert's
wife Rose, among all these grey-eyed Seddons, seemed like a bird
of another flock. She was small and brown and surprised-looking,
always apt to think other people more wonderful than herself, yet
faintly resentful that they should be. She delighted in coming to
her friends' houses, particularly to her sister-in-law's, where
the servants seemed to remain for ever, and where there was a sort
of easy casual peacefulness which she could never achieve in her
own home, a little way off, in Willoughby Road.

'Oh, Joan,' she chirped, 'you did give the twins a good time this afternoon! They came back in roaring spirits—a bit grubby, but after all one expects that.' She laughed, as though to excuse the implied criticism.

'Of course, my dear Florrie, what you ought to do,' boomed Robert, as he leant back wiping the soup from his grey moustache, 'is simply to refuse to keep the fellow on.'

'But, Bob, I can't dismiss my gardener just because he doesn't want to join up. After all it's his own affair.'

'That's where you're wrong. It's *your* affair. It's the affair of all of us who are patriotic employers to see that . . .'

'But he's so splendid with the antirrhinums.'

'*Antirrhinums*, Florrie? Are you crazy? What do *antirrhinums* matter in times like these? As a matter of fact I shouldn't wonder if we had to convert all our flower-beds into vegetable-plots before we're through.'

'In that case all the more reason for keeping on Wilson,' said Florence placidly.

Robert snorted with irritation. His sister seemed sometimes congenitally incapable of following an argument.

'All I want to point out,' he pursued, 'is that there's a war on, and that all young chaps who don't join up . . .'

Florence saw her brother's steel-grey glance wander across the table to where Philip—so hopelessly civilian-looking in his dark suit and his spectacles—was talking to Joan.

'Mr. Nichol has been ill,' whispered Florence. 'Appendicitis or something. He's on sick-leave. Rejoins his regiment next week, I believe.'

'H'm, ah!' said Robert, in what he believed to be a subdued voice. 'Very bad luck on him in the middle of his training.' He turned to Colin. 'My boy Jack,' he resumed in his usual hearty tones, 'says he has never felt fitter in his life. Of course he's a bit tired of being kept hanging about at Aldershot—they all are. You're off to-night I understand?'

'Er—yes, back to Shorncliffe,' said Colin, suddenly realising that he was being addressed. 'I'm only on week-end leave. There's an early morning train gets me down just in time.'

'Ah! Your people will have been glad of a sight of you. They're all well, I hope?'

'Oh yes, rather, thanks.'

Colin had a feeling that he ought to regale Mr. Seddon with boisterous military anecdotes, but he could think of none. He answered questions at random. His eyes moved constantly to Joan.

She was quite indispensable to him. He had realised this ever since last summer, soon after leaving Oxford. Queer that until then he had scarcely known her, although his family and hers lived such a little way apart in Hampstead, and she was such a friend of Betty's. College life, college friends, and holidays abroad had filled the last few years. But those years had not been wasted. They had been used, unconsciously, in preparing his whole being for that tremendous moment of recognition. All the pride he had taken in the fitness of his body, all the delighted labour he had spent on literature, had found in Joan their shining justification. And then the army had taken him. Meetings during the autumn and winter had not been frequent, but they had confirmed what he already knew. No other girl could be such a fit companion for him—so intelligent and understanding, as well as bright and beautiful. She fulfilled all his requirements. But he, alas, did not—as yet—fulfil all hers. Her feelings were still dispersed over so many people. Why, even that funny hatchet-faced chap beside her seemed able to interest her more than he could. What *were* they talking about?

'But it was only in his prophecies that Norman Angell was wrong,' Philip was saying, 'not in his ideas. He said that the present generation of Germans would never live to see a battle, and the facts have unhappily refuted him. But his main thesis that war is economically unsound still holds good.'

Philip Nichol, history master at St. Paul's, was a fairly frequent visitor at Beechwood. Joan liked him for his eager mind, his varied knowledge, and the idealism concealed under his dry, sceptical way of talking.

'Do you still believe, then,' she asked him, 'that if we were victorious we should be no better off than if we were conquered?'

'Individually we shouldn't be,' he replied. 'It was different in Roman times—indeed throughout all the ancient world—when conquerors could directly enrich themselves by carrying off slaves and treasure, but we're not dealing with those conditions. We might conquer Germany to-morrow, and no single Englishman would be a penny the richer in consequence—notwithstanding the war indemnity.'

'Well, perhaps that's true,' said Joan. 'But it's hardly the point at the moment. We've just got to beat them, haven't we? They can't be allowed to swarm over Europe, like the old Goths, messing everything up.'

'They certainly can't,' he conceded grimly. 'Our job is to push them back behind their frontiers, and then leave them. Thank God we can say we didn't begin it, though all Europe's responsible more or less. It's an iniquitous business.'

They went on to pour scorn on that phrase, beloved of the warmongers, 'human nature does not change'; and then passed to ribald laughter as they vied with each other in conjuring up more and more extreme examples to prove its idiocy. Joan cited Aunt Florence going merrily to Olympia to see a band of girl-guides devoured by lions. And Philip, his thin mouth askew, his eyes behind their glasses moistly apologetic, finally instanced Sidney Webb creeping stealthily up behind a clergyman, braining him, and carrying him home to devour in silent relish with his wife. It was ridiculous! Of *course* human nature changed!

To the whole conversation Jimmy had listened absorbed, heedlessly swallowing large portions of cold beef and baked potato while he leant round his sister's shoulder so as not to miss a word. Not for anything would he have interrupted—they were so much cleverer than he was; but when they reached the 'human nature' subject his deep, slow-moving mind questioned their view of it.

Surely what they meant was that human institutions changed—
not human nature? However, he must think it over.

Suddenly, across the gold of the daffodils and of the candle-
flames, Colin caught Joan's eye fixed on him reproachfully. He
reddened. How long had she noticed him piggling with that bit
of beetroot on his plate, sick at heart, and distant? This supper-
party was hell. He pulled himself together and turned with some
remark to Aunt Rose. To his great relief she responded at once,
and was soon embarked on a twittering account of her husband's
duties as special constable.

'It's all very well, though,' she concluded; 'I'm proud that he
should be doing his bit and all that, but it's a great strain on a man
of his age. Those long night hours after an ordinary day's work
at the office . . . and the streets so dark . . . I sometimes tell him . . .'

'Rose worries quite unnecessarily,' said Robert, who had overheard his wife, and, though not displeased to be praised, felt
bound to pooh-pooh her womanly fears. ' There are plenty of
men older than myself who are Specials. And the work's got to
be done. More and more of the regular constables are being
drawn upon for foreign service.'

'Extraordinary, don't you think, the technique of *Chance*,' Philip
remarked courteously to his hostess.

'The technique of chance?' Florence repeated, a little baffled.
'Well, I don't know. Personally, I believe in a wise Providence . . .'

'I meant the book,' interposed Philip. 'Conrad's *Chance*.'

'Oh, yes, yes!' Florence blinked. 'Wonderful, wonderful, of
course.'

Joan came to the rescue and diverted the topic, stifling her feeling
of exasperation. Why *would* Auntie always pretend to have read
books of which sometimes she hadn't even heard the titles?

The meal went on. Plates were removed. Fruit-salad, junket
and trifle circulated. The talk wandered from Florence's Belgian
refugees, and their perplexing problems, to the various forms of
women's war-work.

'Yes, the women are showing up well,' boomed Robert. 'And to think that only last summer they were causing us so much anxiety!' His eyes twinkled as he looked across at his niece. 'No more talk of the Vote now, eh, Joan?'

'No more *talk* of it, Uncle Robert,' she threw back, 'but our energies are only temporarily diverted. You wait!' She hated flippant allusions to the cause she had been so much wrapped up in before the war, but it wasn't worth getting angry with Uncle Robert at this time of day.

.   .   .   .   .   .

'Do sing for us, Joan dear,' said Rose in the drawing-room later.

'What would you like?' asked the girl, wandering to the piano. The question was perfunctory. She was well aware that Aunt Rose hardly knew one song from another.

'Oh, that pretty little thing . . . *you* know . . .'

'Yes, I know,' said Joan, containing a smile. 'Come on, Jim-pot.'

For an English school-boy—even at one of the newer and more enlightened public schools—Jimmy played surprisingly well. He made up for technical deficiencies by a sensitive and genuine love of music. As an accompanist Joan preferred him to many more accomplished performers.

She bent over his shoulder and whispered something in his ear, then stood a little away from the piano, the lamplight falling on her hair and pale green dress, and began to sing. Her voice was not powerful, but it was accurate and sweet. There was no breathiness, no slurring of the notes. Within its limitations it was a voice that gave real pleasure to its hearers.

She sang, to begin with, three French Bergerettes: 'Jeunes Fillettes,' 'Maman dites-moi,' and 'Bergère Légère.' Their daintified pastoral melodies hung about the room like the roses and blue knots of a Louis XV *fête-champêtre*.

> 'Bergère légère, je crains tes appas,
> Ton âme s'enflamme,
> Mais tu n'aime pas.'

The lines were lightly, deliciously tossed off. Joan seemed to be identifying herself with that sophisticated shepherdess whose soul took fire but who could not love. Her swain Colin, sitting in the audience, sighed as he heard her. But almost immediately, as though to efface that impression, she passed to another mood in the singing of some Shakespeare lyrics set by Roger Quilter. Into her voice there crept, now, something of the tender loveliness of all lost English Aprils. The lute-player wandered through budding beechwoods in pursuit of his roaming mistress.

> 'Trip no further, pretty sweeting,
> Journeys end in lovers meeting.
> .   .   .   .   .
> Youth's a stuff will not endure,
> No-t endu-re.'

She stood, while the last chords were played, as though listening to a woodland echo. Then, in the midst of the little murmur of applause, her eyes dropped to Colin's, and found them fixed on her burningly beneath their straight and heavy lids. A moment more and the trance broke. He slightly unfolded his arms and glanced down at his wrist-watch.

'Ought you to be going, Colin?' Joan asked.

'Well, I think perhaps . . . if I'm to say good-bye to them at home . . .'

'Yes, yes, we mustn't keep you,' Florence interposed.

'Won't take you more than fifteen minutes by the Heath, will it?' said Robert genially. 'It's a fine night. Shall we be seeing you again?'

'Oh, I expect so. We're under orders for France, but . . . well, you never know.'

He forced a smile, and Robert shook his hand.

'I'll see you out,' said Joan, in a casual voice, when he had said good-bye to everyone. And with Colin's muttered 'Please don't bother' they left the room together.

'Oh, you darling! I hoped you would,' he said when they were outside. His heart was beating heavily. 'I needn't go just this minute. Come into the garden—if it's not too cold for you.'

'Of course I will.' Joan took an old cloak from a peg in the hall, and they wandered down towards the sycamore. The pale young leaf-buds gleamed above them; the daffodils in the grass were small pale lamps; Joan's face above the darkness of her cloak looked pale as a spring moon.

Of her singing Colin couldn't speak, although he longed to. His whole being had been wrought by the cruel delight of it to a pitch of emotion, to a poignancy of awareness of *her*, which could find no relief in words. All he could do was to blurt out some apology for having been so inadequate at supper.

'What must your relations have thought of me?' he asked in a contrite voice.

'Nothing, only that you were a dear,' she assured him. 'I was awfully grateful to you for pulling your weight as you did.' This was not altogether true, but she was ashamed now of the passing irritation she had felt with him at the supper-table.

'*You* were simply *wonderful*,' he told her, 'and looked wonderful, and . . . and I've never adored you more.' His voice sank to a whisper.

She shivered, drawing slightly away from him, then said with all the compensating warmth she could put into her words:

'I can't bear to think of you travelling down by that beastly train . . . no sleep . . .'

'Give me something before I go,' he pleaded, 'something of yours.'

A little startled she felt vaguely about her person. 'I don't seem to have anything—no beads—not even a handkerchief to-night. How stupid,' she laughed. Her eyes drifted here and there as though the trees or the grass could help her. All at once she stooped and picked a daffodil.

'Take this for the moment,' she said, holding it out to him with a shy abrupt gesture. 'I'll send you a real keepsake later on.' He stooped over it, trembling. And then in an attempt to lift the scene on to the level of their romantic game she added tenderly, half-laughing:

'And don't let your "Joyous Gard" become "Dolorous Gard," my knight. I'm not worth it, you know.'

But he could bear no more. In a flurry of feeling he threw his arms round her and kissed her. It was a clumsy kiss, for he was not sure of himself; and Joan at the same time had turned quickly sideways so that it lighted half on her cold cheek, half on her mouth. His arms dropped as she stepped back. She had shown no resistance, but she had shown no response either—not the least confusion even. In the short silence which followed they mastered their separate disappointments.

'I must go,' he said quietly. 'Good-bye, you completest thing in my world.' There was a humbleness and dignity about him now. She was glad that he made no attempt to apologise.

'I'll come with you to the gate,' she said.

And there they parted, and she waved him down the road until he had disappeared from sight.

. . . . . .

There was something in his hand. Abstractedly he opened it and looked. It was the crushed daffodil. His steps slowed, and he put it to his lips. Small, breezy, cool, and single like herself, he thought. She couldn't have chanced on a more perfect symbol. His heartless shepherdess, his pretty sweeting. And yet, and yet (the truth of her song came echoing), did not 'journeys end in ...'? He choked, and went forward across the dark Heath to his home.

Chapter Two

BETTY PALEY sat wrapped in a blue cotton kimono, her uniform of the Women's Volunteer Reserve in un untidy heap on the floor. Joan sprawled on the bed; empty tea-cups stood on a table, a packet of Gold-Flakes beside them. As none of her family had been in to tea when she came back from the office, Betty had taken a tray upstairs for herself and Joan.

The two girls were linked in a friendship which dated from their school-days; and although Betty had gone on from school to college, and Joan, to her disgust, had been kept at home, the friendship had deepened through the years of grown-up girlhood.

During the year before the war they had been thrown more closely together than ever before, for Betty, now down from Cambridge, had joined forces with Joan in working for the Suffrage.

Together they had done secretarial jobs at the head offices of the W.S.P.U. in Kingsway. Together they had carried sandwich-boards; walked in processions; stood in Leicester Square and Piccadilly Circus selling copies of *The Vote*; and submitted to scathing remarks from passing men. Together they had done picket-duty at the House of Commons; been stewardesses at meetings in Caxton Hall, or at Monday afternoon matinées at the London Pavilion; together gone to Holloway in the early mornings to meet friends coming out from prison and escort them triumphantly to restaurants for breakfast. What they had not done (to Joan's everlasting regret and to Betty's secret thankfulness) was to go to prison themselves. Joan had begged to be allowed to get involved in a riot which would end in her arrest, but her adored leader had smilingly denied her the privilege, told her she was too young, and must be content with the jobs assigned to her.

Once only did Joan feel she had actually suffered for the Cause. At a political meeting at Middlesbrough town-hall she had stood

up and shouted 'What about Votes for Women?' Immediately
she had been seized, not by an official, but by an infuriated member
of the audience, dragged to the door, and flung down a flight of
eight stone steps. By a miracle she had escaped injury, and been
only badly bruised. But she was prouder of those bruises than of
anything in her life, and the storm of anger and fright which the
episode aroused in her family only increased her pride.

It was not in Betty's nature, as it was in Joan's, to become exalted over 'causes.' She had worked for the Suffrage less because
she believed in the overpowering importance of the vote than because it was the civilised, the inevitable thing to do for a young
woman of her generation. Her attitude to the war—that nuisance
on so infernal a scale—was fundamentally the same. She did not
require, to sustain her, a passionate conviction of its rightness.
She had never had a *passionate* conviction of the rightness of anything. There was always so much to be said on every side, and
for every point of view.

She surveyed life through her lovely sleepy eyes with gentle
amusement, delicately enjoying its variety, and conscientiously
pursuing any occupation she found herself involved in. She had
not enough initiative, nor did she consider it worth the effort,
ever to take definite steps to exchange one form of occupation for
another. She had been pushed into Newnham by book-loving
parents; swept into the Suffrage movement by an enthusiastic
friend; and, during that first dreary uncertain winter of the war,
into the offices of the W.V.R. by an energetic aunt.

'But you've been at it long enough now,' declared Joan. 'I feel
that the time has passed for pottering at those various jobs—
office-work, Belgians, bandage-rolling, etc.—which can quite well
be done by older women; just as the time has passed for cursing
the war for interrupting our peace-time pursuits. Already it has
boshed the careers of most of the girls we know. Soon it will
begin to take the lives of the men. Either we must stand aside
and do nothing about it at all—which doesn't seem possible—or
else we must be used right up by it. So you see, darling, you must

follow me out to Boulogne as soon as ever you can. Remember
that Barbara Frewen, who's been out there two months already,
says that workers of the right sort are badly needed in those
Y.M.C.A. huts. And who, I ask you, could be a 'righter' sort
than you, my Betty?'

'Who indeed?' replied the other with a twinkle. 'But if the
Ladies' Committee over here don't think so, what can I do?'

'The Ladies' Committee are a parcel of idiots!' retorted Joan.
'You go along and see Lady Blenkinsop. She'll scan you dis-
approvingly just as she did me. She'll tell you you're too young,
too pretty, too inexperienced, that your collars are too low, that
your heels are too high, that in any case no more lady-workers
are required in France, and a whole lot of rubbish that's completely beside the point. Stick to it, though! Don't be over-ridden!
Tell her it's character, and not years, that count; give her your
most respectable friends as references, and then see if you don't
get sent. She's not a bad old buffer if you take her the right way.
Oh, Betty, you *must* come! Think of all the sporting things we've
done together in our time!'

'We-ell,' drawled Betty in her soft curling voice, 'I'll see about
it.'

'You *are* a nice thing!' cried Joan, in a sudden access of affection.

'Nice . . .' conceded her friend, 'but rutty.'

Joan giggled. 'You mean you're apt to get stuck in a rut until
somebody with more energy than yourself comes and pulls you
out of it?'

'Exactly!' Betty yawned. 'All I ever want to do *really* is to sit
about in the sun, and paint a little from time to time.'

She recalled with regret those holidays in France during which
she and her mother had spent heavenly hours in sketching, while
Colin and her father had tramped the country and looked at
cathedrals.

'My goodness, I wish somebody would paint *you*!' exclaimed
Joan.

Betty, in appearance, was a feminine edition of her brother—

though better-looking as a woman than he as a man. She too was large of build, slow and gentle of movement. She too had iris-petal eyes. But hers were fringed with lashes of such length and thickness that friends were wont to ask her teasingly whether she plaited them at night. And her hair, which, unlike his, had scarcely darkened from its childhood's gold, rippled round a face that had the deep bloom of a peach.

'No, I'm under no illusion about my looks,' responded Betty. 'They're of the obvious, blowsy and barmaidish order—totally devoid of interest, and apt to give a wrong impression of what I am.'

'Oh, *that*—possibly,' agreed Joan. 'Men are fools—the kind that are attracted by you, anyhow. They only see skin-deep.'

For it was an absurd but undoubted fact that intellectual friendships of the kind that Joan went in for were made almost impossible for Betty by reason of her appearance. The meltingly feminine exterior with which she was endowed indicated so little the fastidiousness, and the shrewd and sensible mind which lay beneath it, that oncoming males were often bewildered by the rebuffs which they received—rebuffs none the less definite because of the unfailing kindness which accompanied them. The contrast was marked between Betty's philosophic acceptance of the world as it was—of men as they were—and Joan's exasperations and idealisms.

'Talking of men,' said Betty, 'were you nice to my poor brother last night? I gather he more or less proposed to you.'

'Oh, ye-es.' Joan's eyebrows went dolorously up in the centre. 'Yes. He—"more or less"—proposed to me. But, you know,' she continued, 'I'm afraid that this fortress of my heart requires Krupp's guns for its reduction, and he uses only shrapnel!'

They looked at each other a moment, their eyes flickering. Then Betty shook her head as she might do over a wayward child.

'If you really loved him you wouldn't need to be "reduced." You'd find all his inadequacies and bunglings charming. Although, perhaps, if you were just wavering on the edge, a greater assurance on his part would topple you over. But there you are! he hasn't got it, poor duck. And he's far too much afraid of hurting and annoying you. Oh, it's rotten luck on people in love! They are at such a frightful disadvantage. And the more sincere and decent they are, the worse it is for them.'

Joan nodded humbly. 'I know. And Colin is so terribly nice. I honestly mean it when I say I'm not worth his devotion. Do you know, he asked me once to tell him what his faults were so that he might try and correct them; and I couldn't think of a single one. He seems to me almost perfect. He's got a lovely mind, and an athletic body. He's keen on walking, and on architecture, and on pictures, and poetry—really keen, not just superficially. His views on women and love are ideal. And he's tender and he's true, and yet . . .' Joan made a movement of comic despair.

'He leaves you untouched,' finished Betty. 'Oh, Joan, you are a funny child! As though there were ever any *reasons* for falling in love. One either does or one doesn't. And apparently you're not ready for it yet. Colin used to wonder whether your passionate devotion to the cause of women had anything to do with your coldness towards men—meaning, of course, towards himself. But I think I convinced him that your general anti-man opinions didn't influence your personal feelings to individuals. Meanwhile, my dear, I shouldn't worry too much about what Colin's going through. It's quite good for him. He was apt at one time to be a little conceited about the effect he had on girls. This experience has knocked it clean out of him. Oh, you're his fate, and the love of his life all right. I know Colin. Of course it *would* be nice if . . . But you won't do anything out of pity, will you?'

Joan shook her head. 'Not I. I'm far too selfish and hard. Besides, it wouldn't be fair on him. I say, is your mother awfully sick with me?'

'Mother? Good lord, no. I don't think she suspects how serious it is on Colin's part, and even if she did she'd never think of condemning *you*. I will say for Mother she's awfully good at not prying into her children's affairs. Molly's the only one she ever shows any maternal agitation over. Molly's her ewe-lamb.'

At this point voices were heard in the back-garden.

'That'll be the kids,' said Betty. And with a cigarette still in her mouth she wrapped her kimono round her, and moved lazily to the window, where she leant with folded arms upon the sill. Joan tumbled off the bed and joined her.

From the lawn below three twelve-year-old faces looked up into theirs—Molly's, Billy's, and Babs'.

During the holidays Molly Paley and the Seddon twins were constantly in and out of each other's houses; they were equally at home at Heathfield (the Paleys'), at 30 Willoughby Road (the Robert Seddons'), or for that matter at Beechwood. Their families never quite knew where they would be found.

'Hallo!' called Betty. 'Had a good time?'

Her golden-plaited, long-legged little sister threw aloft a bubbling account of her afternoon, while the twins leant on their bicycle saddles and grinned. She had been over to tea with them; afterwards they had worked the magic-lantern, and then she had been brought home on the step of Billy's bicycle.

'I say, Miss Paley,' cried Bill eagerly, his little freckled face framed in a grey pudding-like Prep. School hat, '*do* tell me if you know when your brother'll be sent to the Front?'

'I don't know,' said Betty. 'Soon, I should think. Why?'

'Oh, because, you see, Babs and I have got a bet on with Molly that our brother will be out before hers.'

'You heartless infants, what a thing to bet about!'

'Ah, but we've got another bet . . . haven't we?' said Babs, her eyes dancing. 'Shall I tell you what it is?'

'No. You're not to,' said Molly, turning on her friend. 'That's entirely a secret thing! I told you . . .'

'It's about you, Joan,' continued the irrepressible Babs, 'about you and——'

'Shu-*tup*,' growled Bill, red in the face, and putting a grimy hand over her mouth.

Joan laughed down on her small cousins, scrimmaging. 'Well, whatever it is, I should think you two ought to be off home

now. And I advise you not to bet about the affairs of your
elders!'

'But we can't think of *you* as an "elder," Joan,' pursued Babs, one
foot on her pedal. 'Except that I suppose you're old enough to
marry. Or—or *aren't* you?'

She was driven off, cowering, under the shouts and hustles
of the other two; and the faces at the window above were withdrawn.

As Joan was being seen off a few minutes later she encountered
Mr. and Mrs. Paley in the hall.

Large and loose in figure, emotional in temperament, scholarly
in mind, Roger Paley would like to have devoted his whole time
to research on the subject of place-names. As it was he supported
his family by running a small bookshop in the city, through which
he had worked up a considerable foreign and colonial trade.
Utterly devoted to his son Colin, whose tastes and temperament
resembled his own, his great hope was to bring him into the business as soon as the war was over.

He greeted Joan expansively. It was always with difficulty that
he concealed his feelings, and Joan was frequently embarrassed,
sensing how much he would have liked her confidence.

Mrs. Paley was of an entirely different stamp—reserved, unde-
monstrative, a little sarcastic. But it was from her, and not from
their father, that the children had inherited their stateliness and
good looks.

She didn't allude at all to her son's departure, nor to the fact that
he had spent nearly the whole of his last day at Beechwood. She
merely inquired after Miss Seddon, and hoped that her Belgians
were not causing her too much anxiety.

'No, there haven't been any upsets among them lately,' replied
Joan. 'Old Tante Léonie is completely bed-ridden now—she'll
probably die on us before the war ends. And there's the usual
difficulty about pork—they never seem able to get enough, and
no other meat will do—but apart from that all goes well.'

'By the way, I always meant to ask you, did you ever take back your Botticelli prints?' Mrs. Paley smiled from under her heavy-lidded eyes.

She was referring to the previous autumn when Joan had helped her aunt to prepare a house for a refugee Belgian family. Some-how Joan had got it into her head that the family would be of professional rank, and had therefore done all she could to make their rooms attractive according to her own standards. She had denuded her bedroom walls so that theirs might have Italian mas-ters, and her floor that theirs might have rugs. She had spent a considerable sum on bath-towels, and on pretty quilts and eider-downs; had placed note-paper, pens, and blotting-pads on the tables, and volumes of English poets in the shelves. She was therefore a little dismayed when the family, on arrival, turned out to be heavy peasants on whom all these arrangements were com-pletely wasted, and who, after the first few bewildered days, settled firmly down to a comfortable unhygienic life in the kitchen, and in one only—it was feared—of the bedrooms.

'She's not to be ragged about it, Mother,' interposed Betty. 'It was a perfectly sweet idea on her part!'

Joan, laughing reminiscently, confessed that the Botticellis, etc. had long since been removed.

She said good-bye, and Mr. Paley, who had been hovering in a sort of uneasy geniality, wiping his spectacles and clearing his throat, gave her a hand-shake which seemed to convey all that circumstances and discretion prevented him from putting into words.

. . . . . .

In the long Morris-cretonned drawing-room at Beechwood Joan found Jimmy seated at the piano, inaccurately but absorbedly play-ing Beethoven sonatas. He did this often for hours on end, rapt away from the world, playing simply for his own delight, far too shy and conscious of his deficiencies ever to play for other people.

He had been out all day, and Joan hadn't seen him since break-fast. She dropped on to the sofa and watched his engrossed pro-file—the funny round nose, and the sucked-in under-lip. It was only when he was at the piano that Jimmy wore this particular expression. From the back of his head the characteristic 'scalp-knot' stuck out as usual.

He played on, as though unaware of her presence, until he got to the end of the first movement of the D minor—that sweetest and most dramatic of the less often-performed sonatas. The urgent reiterations of the mounting quaver-groups were taken up first in the treble and then in the bass; till finally, in the dark brown waters of the bass, they muttered themselves into silence through six bars, and came to repose on a long-sustained D minor chord. Then abruptly he dropped his hands, sprang to his feet, and stood with his back to the piano, smiling at her.

Beautiful eyes. Luminous. A saint's eyes, or a seer's. No, those were morbid comparisons—Joan dismissed them. But what a lamb he was standing there with the thick mat of his hair swept back from his bumpy forehead, and with that shy and shining smile, in which pleasure at the beauty of the music, and at his having not too badly got through it, mingled with pleasure at seeing her again, and with readiness for the next thing—big or small—which this jolly life might bring along.

And in that smiling look which passed between them—in that charged second of eternity—there was a more tender recognition of each other as human beings, a clearer awareness of the beauty and uncertainty of things in general, than could have been made plain in months of words.

It faded—though not into forgetfulness—and Joan frowningly reverted to what she had had in mind when she came into the room.

'Auntie really is exasperating at times!' she burst out. 'She met me just now on my way back from the Paleys and started on the subject of Colin. Such a charming young man, she said he was. Asked me what I had against him. Said she did *hope*—and so on, and so on. When I told her that we were just friends she sighed— you know the way she does—and "oh-deared" about this curious generation. It's not *her* business. Why doesn't she leave my affairs alone? And then about France. Why did I want to go? What good did I think I'd do? A lot of vague cackle. Is it that she wants me to stay at home with her, or is it that she fears for my safety, or what? Reminds me of the sort of fuss she made last summer when I disturbed the meeting at Middlesbrough.'

Joan was striding up and down the room by now. Jimmy was sitting silent, his legs crossed, in a large armchair.

'Yes, old thing, I know,' he said slowly. 'But remember how proud she was of you afterwards over that business. She's just as likely to be proud again over your war-work—once you've gone. It is annoying when she fusses like that, but it's no good getting upset.' He paused, and then brought out half-apologetically: 'It's all part of the way she cares for us. She *means* so awfully well, you know.'

Joan, soothed, gave a little laugh. 'Yes, I know she does, and I'm rather a beast. You're ever so much sweeter than I am, Jumbles, and wiser too. What I should do without you I'm sure I don't know!'

She came over to him, uncrossed his leg, and sat herself on his knee. There was a silence between them—her cheek against his hair. Then she began reminiscently:

'Do you remember, Jumbles, when you dressed up a bolster and put it in my bed? I don't know why I think of it now except that it was the only time Auntie has been really angry with you.' They both chuckled. 'Lord, I was terrified! I can see it now—that awful apparition in a Jaeger dressing-gown, with its sleeve over the sheet, and a moustache of false hair on its ghastly painted face! It was cleverly done.'

'I *was* rather pleased with it,' said Jimmy, 'but I didn't know it would have such an effect. Auntie said I'd nearly given you a fit of hysterics. She made me feel thoroughly ashamed of myself.'

'I thought it was very funny once I'd got over the fright. And do you remember our Red Indian days, when Jack used to come over, and we painted our faces and rushed about the garden scalping the gardeners and carrying off their caps?'

'Yes, I can feel that funny stiff feeling in my skin now, that the paint made when it dried.'

'Oh, Jumbles, you were a funny little fat boy then!' said Joan, squeezing her arms round him. 'It used to be awfully difficult to make you up like a Redskin because your face was so round, and you used to keep looking anxiously up at me, and saying, "Do I look fierce? Do I look fierce?" I sometimes think that Jack and I were too quick for you, and expected you to do too much. It must have been rather a strain pattering along in our wake.'

'I couldn't bear not to be with you both. And you always helped me, Joan, even when Jack was impatient.'

There was a pause.

'How are you getting on with *Diana*?' asked Joan, in a sudden flight from the past.

'Oh ... pretty well. But Meredith's prose isn't easy, is it? Got a bit stuck in the "Dame Credit" and "Dame Debit" part.'

'Yes—you might well,' she laughed. 'But you must struggle on. And you *must* love Diana. If you don't I can't bear it. For you see in spite of all her faults, and the messes she gets into, she's a glorious creature. She was struggling in her own way for all that we're struggling for now.'

'M'm,' said Jimmy, rather subdued.

Joan ruffled his hair. 'Poor Jim-pot! The things I force you to read—and to listen to! It's a shame—when really you're only interested in mathematics.'

'"Tisn't. I like you too,' he brought out.

There was a quick sigh. 'Oh, Jumbles, I really only want you— only you—ever!

'No young men,' she went on to herself, 'no marriage, no "horrid blood emotions" as Diana calls them, no one at all but you.'

She was perfectly sincere at the moment, but she couldn't have felt that special rush of feeling for her brother—half-virginal, half lover-like—if the atmosphere over the week-end had not been charged with romance, and she herself both attracted and repelled by it. She was more wrought up than she was aware of.

'Just you, Jumbles—and Tam,' she sighed.

Tam, lying on a distant rug, hearing his name, gave a series of rapid drum-like thuds with his short tail.

'It's a quarter to eight, children,' came Florence's voice from the upper landing. 'Aren't you coming to change?'

'Co-ming!' called Joan, as she slid off her brother's knee.

And with their arms round each other's waists, stumbling and laughing at every step, they climbed the stairs together.

. . . . . .

Next morning came a letter from Colin.

'ADORED JOAN,

'Sunday was quite wonderful. You gave me golden hours. But I am bound to tell you that the morning after it was terribly hard not to be unhappy. In one thing, however, Providence was kind. I had a crowd of uncongenial work to do, and I think I did it well. Every now and then you came into my mind like a vivid dream, making me gasp. I thought I should have fallen out during route-marching. Not that unhappiness really matters now that I have perfectly loved a soul like yours, exquisite as the little sheath through which it shines.

. . . . . .

'Daffodils are very dear to me now. But Herrick says they "haste away so soon." Will the "Time of Roses" follow?

'Joan, if ever you change your mind about me, send me a "damask bud" in place of the daffodil. (Do you remember that Hood poem?)

'Your poor crazed friend,
'COLIN'

And two days later, in answer to a letter of hers into which she had poured all she could of encouragement, came another. He told her first that his battalion (Lancashire Fusiliers) was being moved to Bedford for a fortnight's intensive training with the Territorial Highland Division before going out to France. He ended:

'Oh, Joan, you say lovely things to me! You've lifted me out of my selfish bog, and turned my thoughts to the High Adventure. Did you ever doubt me about France? No, for several months now I have been convinced that whatever England might have done *I* should have been fighting for that dear country. It has become a fantastic wish of mine that we may both be together there—whether or not we meet.

                        'Good-bye, my lady,

                              'He who wears your flower.

'I am taking the O.B. of E.V. with me in my haversack!'

Chapter Three

IT was seven o'clock in the evening, and the Connaught Hut at Boulogne was swarming with soldiers. At the far end, on the platform, one of them was thumping the piano—a group gathered behind him hoarsely singing. The floor-space was dotted with tables round which they crowded, eating, smoking, writing letters home. The air was thickly blue. Against the food-counter they pressed in patient, persistent groups, waiting to be served. Behind the counter, backwards and forwards from the little kitchen, darted the girls. Ceaselessly came the demands.

'Two cocoas.'

'Packet o' Woodbines.'

'Three teas, please, Miss, three packets o' Woodbines, and three eggs.'

'Miss! Miss! Two hot Horlicks', please, Miss.'

'Choke, please, Miss.'

'What did you say?' asked Joan, leaning forward.

'Choke,' repeated the stocky soldier with the ragged moustache. Joan smiled at him vaguely. 'Er . . . *Choke?*'

Barbara Frewen, passing behind her at that moment, a plate in each hand, murmured 'British Oak . . . packets of tobacco . . . on shelf.'

'Oh!' Joan turned, relieved, to where, on the shelves at the back, were stacked cigarettes, tobacco, soap, tooth-paste, mouth-organs, vaseline, etc.

'British Oak! Here you are. Tuppence a packet, isn't it?'

'Threepence,' grunted the man, put down his money, and moved off.

Joan blushed. It was her first evening. She was grappling valiantly with the problems of prices and of change, but without the helpful honesty of the men she would often have cheated the till. It was a marvel to her, too, that during these rush hours they

31

didn't simply help themselves off the counter to the rolls and cakes and sandwiches—as they could so easily have done—and make off to some table with them unobserved. What patient darlings they were!

Seated on a high stool at one end of the counter was little red-haired Mrs. Jessop, the Senior Lady of the hut. From two huge bowls in front of her she ladled out stewed fruit and custard for the waiting crowds of men. Splashing juicy pools all round, unable to remember what change belonged to what man, she was never upset, but continued to hand over plates with a perfectly contented smile, occasionally shrieking to the orderly in the kitchen for more spoons. It was an amusing sight, though the mess she made on the counter distressed the order-loving Barbara.

There were no queues, and there was no particular system. The note of the hut was good-tempered friendliness. Joan usually found herself attending to the man who called the loudest or who had the nicest face. She was getting into it. You seized a couple of mugs, filled them at the great tin urn, grabbed some cigarettes from the shelves as you passed, shoved the lot across the counter, dived to the cash-box for change, nodded to a man who was reiterating a demand for Horlicks' milk, lifted an inquiring eyebrow at another, and finally flew off to get tea for a third who had been waiting longer than any. It was hectic, and a bit bewildering, but she enjoyed it. She liked the soldiers' faces and friendly smiles, the way their caps were pushed back from their bushy front locks, their slow heavy treads. She liked all the din and warmth and smokiness of the hut.

'This is something better than the trenches,' said a voice. And she looked up into the brown eyes of a very young soldier who was leaning over his tea-cup on the counter. The rush had slightly abated for the moment, so she entered into conversation with him. He told her he was in the Devons, and that he was only sixteen. He had enlisted as eighteen, had been to the Front, seen hot fighting, and had then owned to his real age and been sent down, two days ago, to be kept on fatigue duty at the Base. In his soft burr-

ing, monotonous voice he told her something of what it was like
'up there.' Sentry duty was a nervy job, he said. You were all on
your own, and liable at any moment to get sniped. 'I was in a
bayonet charge once—awful it was—but the funny thing is I
don't remember much about it. Just the piles and the masses of
dead afterwards—the piles and the masses of dead. Seemed as if I
couldn't stand it somehow.' His eyes stared in front of him.

'Look here, you must write to your mother,' said Joan quickly,
'you must write and tell her you're safe. Or shall I do it for
you?'

But no, he had done that already, he assured her. He had written
four letters last night.

'I like getting letters, you see, that's why I write them.' And he
went on, a little gleam in his poor vacant eyes, to tell her of his
family. She listened sympathetically, though she found it difficult,
because of his accent, to understand much of what he said. He
would probably have talked for hours if she hadn't been forced to
draw away and attend to other men. 'All right to be talking to an
English lady again,' she heard him murmur, as he moved off with
his cup.

At about nine o'clock they began clearing the counter and putting things away for the night. Joan noticed that it was she and
Barbara who did most of the work. Mrs. Jessop sat on smilingly
on her high stool, and the other girl, Mavis Dempster, a tall, fair,
pretty creature, very soon drifted away down the hut, and sat at
the piano dreamily playing through some songs.

Mr. Baxter, the 'hut-leader,' who had not hitherto been much in
evidence, counted the day's takings. He was referred to by the
others, among themselves, as 'Buster.' His dark puffy face and
casual manners had displeased Joan from the first. She couldn't
quite 'place' him, or make out what he was supposed to do, and
resolved to ask Barbara about him later.

At last the soldiers had all gone, and a Ford car arrived to take
the ladies home. Mrs. Jessop and Mavis were dropped at their
billet a little way down the road, and Barbara and Joan were

driven on to Temple's Hotel, in the Boulevard Prince Albert,
where they lodged.

.   .   .   .   .   .

'Well, this all seems too good to be true!' sighed Joan as they sat
at supper. 'I can't believe I only arrived last night. I feel as
though I had been here at least a month.'

'You're picking things up at a tremendous rate,' said Barbara.
'I'm awfully glad to have you out here, Joany.'

Barbara Frewen, who had been at school with Joan and was a
few years older, was an aquiline-featured, fragile-looking girl, but
with far more strength, both of physique and of character, than
her appearance seemed to warrant. She came of a Sussex family
who had lived on the same spot since before the Conquest.
Modern life and thought had scarcely touched her, but she had a
tolerant mind, and was at ease, in her dignified little way, among
any surroundings however alien.

'But tell me more about it all,' pursued Joan. 'I thirst for information.'

And Barbara launched into a description of the Y.M.C.A. in
Boulogne. There were three other huts, each with its staff of lady-
workers, and its one—or more—hut-leaders. The hut-leaders, or
'Young Christians,' as they were irreverently called, were a
strange breed of men, mostly in the Nonconformist ministry,
whose duties consisted in managing the money, conducting services, and seeing in a general way to the spiritual atmosphere of
the huts. For practical work they could rarely be counted on.
Lack of manners and lack of energy were their chief character-
istics. Mr. Baxter was a fair example of the genus 'Christian.'

'You must just take him as he is, and rub along as pleasantly as
possible,' said Barbara. 'Oh, and, Joany, do be most awfully careful in your letters home. Say nothing about the troops. If we
were found to be indiscreet, the army authorities could turn the
whole Y.M.C.A., neck and crop, out of Boulogne.'

Temple's was an old-fashioned little hotel, with rather a charming character of its own. There was a lot of marble and red plush

about it, and it was run by a fierce diminutive couple whose name it bore. Mr. Temple was French, and did the cooking; Mrs. Temple was English, and saw to the business; and Dorcas, Mrs. Temple's sister, did the waiting, and most of the housework.

Anything less like a hotel servant than Dorcas it would be hard to imagine. She was more of the family retainer type—devoted, hard-working, intimate and grumpy. She was not more than four-foot-eight, and her figure resembled a cottage loaf. Her little eyes twinkled out from a face that was like an amiable pink pig's. She made no secret of her likes and dislikes among the hotel inhabitants—at present mostly English war-workers. Luckily Barbara was one of her favourites; and luckily, too, she had taken instantly to Joan. It was her custom to linger about until everybody had gone upstairs, in order to put the lights out; so that late bed-goers always had a feeling of guilt.

High up in her little room on the third floor, Joan, tired and excited, fell asleep like a child. Colin's face and Jimmy's were mingled in her dreams with the thronged faces of the soldiers.

.   .   .   .   .   .

It was a bright May morning, and after breakfast Barbara took Joan down to the market-place. All around sat fat old peasant-women in black shawls and blue aprons—large baskets by their sides containing eggs, butter, fruit, live rabbits, and glowing masses of flowers. Standing in the sunshine the girls bought, for a few sous each, bunches of kingcups, bluebells and wallflowers. The high-pitched French voices dinned pleasantly in their ears; the warm foreign smell of bread and garlic was in their nostrils.

Afterwards they wandered down the narrow streets to the quay. Here all was dust and traffic. It was difficult to avoid being run over. Squealing trains bumped along railway-lines that were flat with the surface of the road. Lorries and Red Cross cars dashed in all directions. Everywhere British uniforms mingled with the French crowd in this extraordinary Boulogne of war-time.

Down on the edge of the quay they watched some wounded being conveyed from ambulances to a hospital ship. Some were on stretchers, some hobbling along supported by comrades. Already the ship seemed crammed; men leant over the rails, and here and there on their slings and bandages were stains of blood. All of them, as the ship steamed slowly past, waved their hands and smiled; and the two girls, standing a little apart from the crowd, waved back, and watched until the ship was a grey spot upon the sea.

It was Joan's first glimpse of the havoc of war, and she walked back subdued and silent beside her friend. Her only comment was: 'Anyhow they're going *home*, they'll be safe for the time being.'

At two o'clock they turned up at the Connaught, and took over from Mrs. Jessop and Mavis, who had been doing the morning 'shift.'

Barbara dumped her flowers on the counter, put on her apron, and looked round severely.

'Heavens, what a mess!' she exclaimed. 'Those two are supposed to prepare all the food during the morning, but nearly always I find things in this state—only half done. They've gone and burnt the custard too!' she added, as she inspected the pans in the kitchen. 'Come on, we must set to work.'

For the next hour Joan helped her friend to make up the required quantities. She buttered rolls, cut ham and sardine sandwiches, squeezed lemons for lemonade, put on figs and prunes to stew, and learnt the rather tricky art of boiling custard.

'That's better!' said Barbara at last. 'What I think I shall do is to get Mrs. J. and Mavis to take the afternoons, and leave the mornings to you and me. Of course from six o'clock onwards we're all on.'

Joan surveyed the hut with satisfaction. Empty, except for a few soldiers writing at distant tables like good little school-boys, it was seen to better advantage than on the evening before. It was a long wooden barn, airy and clean. Through the cretonne-curtained windows and the half-open door streamed the sunlight. At intervals along the counter, between the plates of food, were arranged the flowers they had bought in the market that morning. From the kitchen came the sizzling sound of the boiler. There was a delicious peacefulness about the place.

'Are all the huts as fresh and pretty as this one?' she asked.

Barbara shook her head. 'I should think they aren't! The soldiers call this one the "drawing-room of Boulogne," and we take special care that it shall live up to its name.'

All through the afternoon men dropped in, and Joan, at her own request, was allowed to serve them alone—for practice.

She found them pathetically willing to talk.

One of them, with a weary expression, told her that the Germans were not really as savage as the papers made out; that he thought they behaved pretty badly where they couldn't be seen, but that certainly they were not all brutes—just as our own men were not all saints and heroes. He had himself seen a 'Jock' finish off a wounded German by a kick on the head. It all depended on a man's mood. In this case the Jock had just seen his special friend killed, and was in a state of revengeful fury.

Then came another whose attitude was very different. He was a dispatch-rider in the Cyclist Corps, and had been at Cambridge before the war. He had a small strained face, and very bright blue eyes. No moderation here. His loathing and disgust of the Germans knew no bounds.

'Nothing can be too bad for them,' he said bitterly. 'It's all very well for Mr. Asquith to sit at home and say we mustn't make reprisals, but he hasn't been out here. He hasn't seen fellows writhing and gasping for breath in the fumes of that abominable gas. There should be no quarter given to the Germans—none!'

It was clear that every separate soldier's view of the state of things 'out there' was coloured by his individual experience. No general conclusion could be reached. But through contact with these men direct from the line an ever clearer picture of horror was forming in Joan's mind, such as the reading of accounts in the papers at home had been unable to produce.

'You're powerless when the gas comes along,' a certain mild-eyed man in the S.L.I. remarked. 'You have to give ground. You see it comes like a great cloud. Nobody can stand against it. I shouldn't mind going back to the Front—only for the gas.' He looked round the hut with wondering grateful eyes. 'This is a pretty place,' he said. 'I've seen nothing but ruin and ugliness ever since October. Been in the Salient, you know. Ypres . . . well, it's enough to make you cry. Ruins . . . We'll hold it, though. The Canadians are wonderful. We couldn't have done without them —for all they're supposed to be undisciplined.'

All these men, who came in and out of the Connaught, were, in various degrees, unfit, and were on light temporary duty at the Base.

As the evening wore on there was less time for conversation with the men; they crowded more and more thickly to the counter to be served. The little Devon boy with whom Joan had talked the night before came up to her shyly, and looking already less strained, but she could only spare him a minute. He told her that he had had three letters from home that day—one of them from his sweetheart.

'Your *sweetheart?*' she asked, amused, as she was hurrying to get some cups filled. 'And how old is *she?*'

'Sixteen, same as me,' replied the boy.

'Little pet!' she thought, and turned the scalding brass tap of the tea-urn. She had by now mastered the trick of holding three mugs in one hand; the only snag about this speed-saving method being the difficulty of extracting one's finger afterwards from the thick handles without spilling the contents of the mugs on the counter.

At seven o'clock an impromptu concert was given, got up by Mavis. The food-counter was, for the time being, closed, and the men turned all the chairs towards the platform, and sat on them in serried khaki rows. Joan, who had been begged to help, clutched her songs nervously as she pushed her way with the other girls to the front row, and sat waiting for her turn. Mr. Baxter, looking slightly less puffy and bored than usual, presided, and read out from Mavis's programme the names of the performers. As each was called he rose from his seat and went up on to the platform. Mrs. Jessop played most of the accompaniments; she had an immense facility, and sat smilingly ready to read any music put in front of her, or, if there were none, to vamp.

It was the first concert of its kind that Joan had attended, and she was to learn that a soldier audience during war-time was the most delightful and easily-pleased in the world.

The songs ranged from 'Glorious Devon,' and 'Trumpeter, what are you Sounding now?' to ballads of an interminable number of verses, one of which was about 'a bit of cold meat on Sunday night, and a little bit of cucum, cucum, cucum, a little bit of cucum*ber*.'

When Joan's turn came she sang two folk-songs, 'Dabbling in the Dew' and 'Oh no, John,' which went down quite well, and after the first minute or so she found that she was enjoying herself enormously. The hut was good for sound, and the rows of brown appreciative faces in front of her gave a glow to her spirits.

The only officer who performed—a friend of Mavis's—was a distinct success, both because of his pleasant personality and his amusing songs. He sang about 'My Little Damp Dug-out in France' to the tune of 'My Little Grey Home in the West,' and the topical allusions all through called forth boisterous laughter.

But the success of the evening was Mavis, who, coming at the end of the programme, sang in a pretty sugary soprano 'The Sunshine of your Smile' and 'Somewhere a Voice is Calling.'

Joan's slight sting of jealousy was swamped by her sympathy with the general elation, and with Mavis's satisfaction at the way the concert had gone. It seemed a pity that Mr. Baxter should feel it necessary to end it on a religious note, with a short prayer and a hymn, but this apparently was the custom.

As soon as it was all over the girls went back to the counter, and in a few minutes the men were thronging in front of it like water released from a dam. By nine o'clock they had cleared every fragment of food and every drop of drink.

As the last of them were leaving Joan found herself—she scarcely knew how—plunged in a conversation on Woman's Suffrage with a tall good-looking sergeant-major of the K.O.S.B.'s whom she had noticed in the crowd the night before, and had, for a moment, taken for an officer. To her delighted surprise he expressed the opinion that after the war, women would certainly get the vote. 'I've been verra much impressed by the conduct of the ladies of England during the warr,' said this magnificent creature, 'and I canna see the sense of keeping them fra pawlitics.'

Joan leant forward on eager elbows, and encouraged him to go on. A little later, at a call from Barbara, she bade him good-night, and went into the little room where the others were already putting on their coats and hats.

'What an adorable creature!' she exclaimed.

'If you're going to annex *our* Sergeant-Major,' Mavis warned her, 'I shan't be answerable for the consequences!'

'But do you know what he said . . .?'

'Come on now, Joan, come on!' said Barbara, laughingly pushing her out. 'We don't want to keep Weary Willie waiting all night.'

'Weary Willie,' otherwise the Rev. Mr. Wilkinson, was the man who had driven them home the night before. He was a depressed Church of England clergyman of about forty who had given up his living to come out to France to 'do something' for the war. His bad eyesight and his varicose veins had precluded any work of a strenuous nature, and in the end he had found himself ingloriously driving the ladies of the Y.M.C.A. to and from their different huts in a dilapidated Ford. He said little, but from behind his large spectacles he observed much, and he was a storehouse of all the gossip and rumour that floated about among the British community at Boulogne. In his present capacity he wore riding-gaiters and a soft felt hat, and nobody could have told that he had once been a parson.

As he stood waiting for them just inside the hut, he presented such a patient and dejected appearance that Joan felt a little rush of contrition.

'I *am* sorry you've been kept waiting,' she said. 'I'm afraid it was my fault.'

'Oh, it doesn't matter—it doesn't matter a bit,' he muttered, as though rather surprised that anyone should trouble to notice him —much less to apologise.

But the next moment he was forgotten, and on the drive home Joan was gabbling away about the concert, and the incredible intelligence of the sergeant-major.

Dorcas greeted the two girls with a scowl.

'Later and later,' she grumbled. 'Time was when you all 'ad supper together at a quarter-past nine. A body knew where she was. Now you come back at all hours.'

Miss McNare, who sat at the same table, twinkled at them over her coffee. She was an elderly Lowland Scots woman, with a kind face and a mass of grey hair piled untidily on her head. She worked at one of the other huts, and had been established at Temple's even longer than Barbara.

'You gerrls are catching it to-night!' she said. And to Joan: 'Do you think you'll like the wurrk now that you've had a whole day at it?'

'I shall adore it!'

They told her about the concert as they ate their belated meal.

When Joan went up to bed that night she felt that for her the war had now begun in earnest.

Chapter Four

OSTROHOVE CAMP was the name given to the collection of tents on the bare high ground above the town. Whenever new troops came through from England it was here that they stayed the night, marching away the following day to entrain for the Front from the little station of Pont-de-Briques, a few miles off. On these occasions some of the lady-workers from the various huts were called upon to go and help at the camp canteen.

'But so far,' explained Barbara to Joan, 'this camp job has devolved chiefly on the Connaught workers. To-morrow, for instance, Mrs. J. and Mavis are taking the early shift from six to ten, and you and I will go on from ten to two.'

This was only a week after Joan's arrival, and news had been received that part of a new division would be landing that night.

The following morning, therefore, which happened to be misty and drizzling, the two friends set off by a little steep field-path, and arrived at ten o'clock at the camp. In among the army tents that spread over the ground like a flock of alighting gulls, swarmed men in kilts and Glengarries—men with pink-brown faces and bony knees. On the fringe of the tents was the huge Y.M.C.A. marquee. The floor was of mud, there were no tables and chairs, no atmosphere of permanence or comfort. Stores were only got in when troops were known to be coming through.

In the odour of damp canvas and damp uniforms, the girls stood, one at each end of the counter, with an immense urn of tea and of cocoa beside them, and a large wooden box full of slabs of cake.

With scarcely a pause they filled and put down cups, and handed out cake to rows of soldiers who came and passed, and came and passed, slamming down their pennies on the sloppy counter, and moving off into the crowd beyond. The amount they consumed was amazing. Joan's only fear was that the food and drink would

42

run out; but the two little Christians behind her—one of them especially, Mr. King—worked hard at keeping her supplied. Great boilers with fires beneath them were kept going just outside the tent, and a small, intelligent, brown-eyed French boy called Marcel, who seemed to have attached himself to the camp, washed up dirty cups with unflagging ardour. Gradually the spot of ground upon which each girl stood became a slippery bog by reason of the constant drip from the tea and cocoa taps, but on they went, with aching arms and scalded fingers, handing over cups and scooping up wet pennies.

Joan learnt that these men formed part of the Territorial Highland Division, and that they had come straight from Bedford, their last training-place.

'Do you know whether the Lancashire Fusiliers have come over?' she asked casually of a gigantic 'Seaforth.'

The man said no—that he thought they would be coming tomorrow, or the day after.

More men came crowding in. 'Encore des tasses, Marcel!' she called. 'Tout de suite, Mamzelle!' cried her valiant little henchman.

The broad-shouldered hungry Highlanders pressed against the counter. 'Two pieces o' kehke, and a cup o' cocoa.' 'Two pieces o' kehke, and a cup o' cocoa.'

'Mr. Ki-ing! Cocoa's run out.'

'All right, Miss Seddon. Just coming.'

Mr. King staggered in with the new urn, and, assisted by a soldier, heaved it into place on the counter. Thud. Splash. 'Thank you.' The tap was turned. The boiling liquid hissed into the mugs. 'Piece o' kehke, and a cup o' cocoa.'

At about twelve o'clock the sound of bagpipes was heard. Immediately everyone left the tent. Marching down the road, in full war-kit, was the 7th Battalion of the Black Watch headed by its pipers. The men tramped past, kilts swinging, rifles on shoulders. Joan's throat ached with the sobs that rose in it; her mouth was stiff with forcing smiles—for every soldier smiled at the girls as

he went by. The last few, bolder, kissed their hands. And then
the whole battalion had swung round the bend, and out of sight.
Only the faint notes of the bagpipes, stirring and melancholy,
were brought on the wind.

It was the first time Joan had seen a battalion marching to war,
and it was one of the most emotional sights she had ever witnessed.

'Que voulez-vous?' said the small boy Marcel, who had been
standing close by. 'Que voulez-vous? C'est la guerre.'

Silently she took Barbara's hand, and they went back into the
tent.

Soon after two they left. Their overalls—clean that morning—
were soaked and filthy. Their hands, and even arms, were brown
with mingled dirt and cocoa. Back at the Connaught they were
welcomed with relief by Mavis and Mrs. Jessop, who had been
working since six—first at the camp, and then at the hut—and
who went quickly off to their lunch.

Barbara made an omelette for herself and Joan, and they settled
down to the afternoon shift.

'It's always awful to see them go,' she said, referring to the
soldiers. 'But one has to remember that they're not always sent
straight up to the line. They're often kept behind for a spell of
training first.'

But Joan wondered: 'What will it be like to see men one *knows*
marching off?'

At nine o'clock it was quite a comfort, for once, to see Mr.
Wilkinson's melancholy countenance in the doorway, and to be
driven home.

.   .   .   .   .   .

Again the camp was full of Highlanders, and the rush was even
greater than yesterday. But on the third morning, which was
brilliant and very hot, the tent was less crowded, and this time the
men were English. Sunlight penetrated to the shadowy spaces of
the interior, and there was a smell of sun-baked canvas and sun-
baked trodden grass.

Each behind her urn, Barbara and Joan, rather languidly, served the drifting groups of Tommies. They had been at it little over half an hour when Joan, who had been stooping to get out some cups from the rack beneath the counter, raised her head to find herself looking straight into the eyes of Colin. There he stood, only four feet away from her, looking as fit and as bronzed as though he had already been on a campaign.

For a moment she saw him in a totally new light: not as her embarrassed boy-lover, but as a man among men, as an officer of England's new armies, taut, self-sufficient, prepared.

For a moment he, too, saw her differently: not as an adored argumentative girl in pretty clothes and pretty home surroundings, but as a companion-worker, a sort of 'ancilla domini' among those crowds of soldiers. A sunbeam shone through the opening in the tent, on to the gleaming urn beside her, on to her hair, and into her boy-angel's eyes. He felt as though he had never seen her before, and yet that he had known her always.

'Colin!'

'Joan!'

Red mounted in his cheeks; a faint pink in hers. They smiled.

'Come round here to the back,' Joan commanded him.

And round he came; and there, in the space behind the counter, all among Christians, orderlies, dirty cups, and buckets of water, they laughingly shook hands.

She turned from him for a moment, went and said something to Mr. King, and came back.

'He'll take my place if necessary,' she said. 'Thank goodness things are pretty quiet this morning. We can talk for a bit.'

They sat down on some remote packing-cases, and looked at each other again. Colin couldn't get over their meeting.

'It's what I've been praying for,' he told her, 'but I hardly hoped it would happen like this, or so soon. I didn't notice the Y.M.C.A. tent at first—I was busy in another part of the camp—and when I did come in it was only to inquire for your whereabouts. Then to see you—you yourself—in that white overall—actually before me——!'

'I was awfully surprised to see you too. Not *really* surprised of course, because I knew your battalion was in, but I hadn't expected you to materialise at that particular minute. When did you come over?'

'We crossed last night—the whole brigade—and marched silently through the town and up to this place in a drizzling dawn. It wasn't particularly pleasant, but then later on when the sun came out—I can't tell you how thrilled I am to be over!'

He certainly appeared to be. Joan had never seen him so happy, and on top of things; and never had she liked him so well.

He told her about the last fortnight's training at Bedford.

'Simply gruelling it was! On one of the last days we had a route-march in full marching order under the broiling sun. The men felt the heat and the dust terribly. Some of them simply collapsed. I finished up with two rifles, and if we had gone a mile further I should have had to carry half the platoon's!'

'Oh, Colin, weren't you glad you had been such a great walker all your life? It stood you in good stead, didn't it?'

'Yes, I suppose so,' he mused. 'Curious to think of those happy walking tours in France. I wonder if I shall go over any of the same roads again now. It seems centuries since I was last here, and yet it isn't a year.'

They were both silent. The noise of the camp hummed outside, but they were unaware of it. Colin's voice came dreamily.

'". . . Farewell happy fields,
        Where joy for ever dwells! Hail, horrors! Hail,
    Infernal World! . . ." '

'Colin!' she protested.

'It's all right!' he laughed. 'I don't feel a bit like that really, but the words came into my mind—they seemed to have a general appropriateness. Didn't you know, by the way, that I had once, in my earnest youth, learnt two books of *Paradise Lost* by heart? But what's more to the point,' he went on, 'is the fact that I was rather successful at revolver-firing the other day. Second out of a total of thirty officers. Not bad! Although probably when I have to use a revolver in reality my temperament will prevent me from hitting anything!'

Joan took her cue, and laughed with him. He was making things very easy.

Soon after eleven he had to go off to a parade.

'It ought to be over in about half an hour,' he said. 'Shall you still be here?'

'Heavens, yes, until two o'clock.'

When he came back she took him up to Barbara, standing by her urn, and introduced him.

'Look here, Joan, why don't you and Mr. Paley go for a walk somewhere, instead of sitting uncomfortably on those packing-cases?'

'But I can't leave you,' said Joan. 'Suppose there were a sudden rush?'

'There won't be now. Besides, I can manage perfectly well with Mr. King.'

'Well, if you really think . . .'

There was that in Colin's face which made Barbara insist.

'Now take yourselves off at once. And don't bother to come back again, Joan,' she added. 'Join me down at the hut later.'

'What a ripping person!' said Colin as they left the tent together.

'Oh, she's a darling! Absolutely one of the best. I'm lucky to be working with her.'

In a sunny field, a little way beyond the camp, they sat and talked.

'Then you honestly don't mind going?' she asked. 'You needn't keep things up with me, you know, Colin.'

'I know I needn't, Joan dear. But believe me, I don't mind. I'm keyed up now, and I want to be at it. It may be lack of imagination, but I don't think so. It's more that I have a feeling of complete readiness, of complete serenity. All that tedious and terrific training is behind me. Now comes the job itself. There are no more doubts as to its value, no more harkings back. It's as though one had given oneself; and I suppose a complete surrender always brings peace.'

'I know what you mean,' said Joan. 'I feel that, too, since I've been out here. But then . . .' her voice sank, 'the difference between what you and what I have got to face . . .'

All Boulogne lay at their feet, and beyond it sparkled the sea. High over their heads, like a silver bird, an aeroplane hovered, while on the still air could be felt, rather than heard, the thunder of the guns round Ypres.

'*Did* you bring out the "Oxford Book"?' she asked after a pause.

He assured her that it was in his pack at that moment. 'I feel it'll be as useful to me in its way as my revolver!'

Her heart went out to that. It was as though a desolation had been touched by beauty. For Colin had spoken—though neither knew it—in the very spirit of 1915—that year of the 'enchanteds,' to whom poetry and the war were one, and the war still worth the winning.

They were still talking—happily, hopefully—when Joan found it was time for her to go. His battalion was not marching off till the afternoon. She wouldn't be able to come back. They rose and walked to the top of the little lane which led from the fields into the town. The sun was very bright, and the hedges were a pale bright green. She gave him her hand, and a smile that was almost gay.

'Well . . . the very best of luck, darling. You'll take care of yourself, won't you . . . and . . . *and* write?' Banal, inadequate words! One could hardly say less to someone going on an ordinary railway journey.

Holding her hand he looked deep into her eyes.

'Is it still "no"?' he asked.

This was awful. At the beginning she had feared it, but as the morning had gone on his manner had been so reassuring that her fear had vanished in the pleasure of being in his company, and in sorrow at his departure.

He had her at a terrible disadvantage. He was marching to the

Front that very day. A hundred little voices dinned into her ears: 'Say yes, say yes, say yes. Even if it isn't true, be kind to him— say yes.' But to engage herself to marry him (which was what he meant)—wouldn't that be unkinder still? Because when he came back . . . if he came back . . .

'Oh, I don't know, I don't know!' she moaned.

Curiously he seemed less upset than she was. At the back of those dark blue eyes she was just aware that there lurked a confident tiny smile. It was as though their rôles had become reversed, and that he were the stronger now.

'It wasn't fair of me to ask that,' he said. 'I give you my word I never meant to. It wasn't necessary either.' At her look of incomprehension he went on: 'Not *really* necessary—as on other occasions. You see, I believe in portents, and it's a portent of joy that I should have met you out here in this particular place, on this particular day. Our meeting has been better than I could have dreamed. Good-bye, dear one. Don't distress yourself about me.' He raised her hand to his lips.

If it hadn't been for a group of French children a little further on at the bend of the lane, who, for the last few minutes, had been watching the scene with interest, Joan would have thrown her arms round his neck and kissed him. As it was, the grinning ragamuffins were just enough to put her off.

'Good-bye, Colin. I shall think of you a lot. Good-bye.' And she turned and went quickly down the lane, the children and the bright green hedges a blurr upon her eyeballs.

Barbara had already arrived at the hut, and was making lemonade.

'Go and have some lunch, my dear,' she said. 'I've put it ready for you.'

But food was impossible. Joan washed her hands, swallowed a glass of milk, and came and sat on the other stool, and squeezed lemons with her friend.

'What an awfully nice boy,' said Barbara. 'He's in love with you, isn't he, Joanikins?' It had been Barbara's pet name for her at school, and was only used in moments of special tenderness.

Joan nodded.

'But perhaps not you with him, altogether? Oh, well, it's beastly saying good-bye to them, however little or however much one cares. And one seems to realise it all so much more out here— what they're going to, I mean.'

'That's just it.'

Although by the time she got back to Temple's that evening Joan was physically and emotionally worn out she felt unable to go to bed without writing to Colin. She kept thinking how much nicer she might have been to him. A dozen things occurred to her that she might have said at that last minute, short of the little binding 'yes' he asked for. And she had only murmured idiocies, and broken away from him in tears. She couldn't rid her mind of vague horrible pictures of what he was going up to face; and 'poor darling!' she kept saying to herself, 'poor darling!'

   .   .   .   .   .

In three days and nights the Territorial Highland Division had passed through Boulogne, and gone. No more workers would be wanted up at the camp until the next batch of new troops came from England.

Chapter Five

THE days fell into a comparatively peaceful routine. Barbara and Joan, who were now on the morning shift, arrived at the hut at ten, and Mr. Baxter greeted them with unshaved cheek and bleary eye. Like most Christians he slept on the premises, but that didn't seem to make it any easier for him to be ready in time. He would loll through half the morning, paring his nails or reading little bits of newspaper. Sometimes, as a concession to duty, he would stroll among the soldiers, and sit and talk at one of their tables; but manual work of any kind he eschewed. Even the opening of large packing-cases he left the girls to wrestle with by themselves—or with the help of Hinkley, the soldier-orderly.

Hinkley was an endearing little man, with the qualities—and somewhat the appearance—of a Skye terrier. He was cheerful, faithful, and pathetic, and could almost be seen to wag a tail when he received the smallest attention. He was rather ill from the effects of gas, and was devoted to Barbara and Joan, whom he called 'ladies in deeds as well as in looks.'

Joan, while boiling pans of custard in the bright little kitchen, would listen tirelessly to his accounts of life in the trenches; while Barbara, at the counter, would be cutting sandwiches and attending to any men who came along.

One morning, when Barbara had left her post for a few minutes to distribute writing-paper at the far end of the hut, Joan heard the sound of a penny being gently tapped on the counter, and emerged from the kitchen.

The waiting soldier was a merry-faced lad, and in no hurry to move away when he had got his cup of tea. Instead he stood talking to her about the miraculous escapes he had had at the Front.

'See this, Miss?' he said, pointing to a hole in his tunic just below the breast-pocket; 'that was made by a bullet. Went bang through me chest, it did, and out at me back without doing any vital inj'ry. Wonderful, ain't it!'

'Yes, indeed!' said Joan, and leant forward the better to contemplate the hole. 'How extraordinary!'

'Like to see the wound?' he asked, encouraged by her evident interest.

And before she could reply he had ripped open his tunic and shirt, and she found herself gazing at a bare white chest on which was a pad of dressing held by plaster.

'Close thing, that!' said the boy, smiling proudly. 'By all the laws I oughter be pushing up daisies now.'

She caught the infection of his amazed delight at being still alive, and laughingly congratulated him.

'Yer milk's boiling over!' called little Hinkley from the kitchen, and she sprang away to see to it.

.   .   .   .

Under the new arrangement all the cooking and preparing was got through easily by lunch-time, so that when Mrs. Jessop and Mavis came on they had nothing to do during the afternoons but serve the men, and entertain their officer friends to tea in the annex. All four women were perfectly contented, and all worked harmoniously together. It was not from the inside, but from the outside that the peace of the Connaught seemed at this juncture to be threatened.

At the head of the Y.M.C.A. in Boulogne was a certain Mr. Goodge. He was attached to no particular hut, but was responsible for all, and when he was not going his rounds, or holding services, he was to be found in the office which was Y.M. Headquarters. He was a pale, fish-eyed young man with a great sense of his own importance, but with nothing like the character required to fill his rather difficult position. From time to time he had murmured complaints to Mrs. Jessop, which, because they seemed to have no bearing on anything, she had smilingly ignored.

One day she came into the hut looking extremely amused.

'What *do* you think Mr. Goodge has been telling me this morning?' she exclaimed. 'That he feels we're not nice enough to him! He says there isn't a welcoming atmosphere in our hut.'

'But surely that's just what there is!' cried Joan.

'For the soldiers, yes; but not, apparently, for him.'

'I hope we're not definitely rude to him,' said Barbara.

'No—only indefinitely,' twinkled Mrs. Jessop. 'Anyhow he thinks we're too independent here, and don't consult him enough, and run things altogether too much on our own.'

'You'd think he'd be only too glad to have one hut, at least, where the workers gave him no trouble!'

'He'd like us better really if we gave him more. Anyhow, what we've got to do, my dears, is to be more respectful to him. We oughtn't to find it hard.'

'*I* shall find it *extremely* hard,' said Barbara. 'I dislike the man. He's not hard-working, and he's not straight.'

A day or two after this conversation Mr. Goodge appeared at the Connaught just before lunch. Barbara and Joan were busy at the counter, and at first took no notice of him beyond a nod of greeting.

When the crush had thinned down, Joan turned to where he was standing awkwardly against the cigarette shelves, and, with a smile, apologised for having kept him waiting.

'Don't mention it,' he said, blinking his pale eyes. 'Glad to see you working so hard.'

'Oh, we do, you know, sometimes,' said Joan sweetly, 'although I gather that this hut has the reputation of being chiefly a rendez-vous for officers.'

A glance at Barbara's firm little profile told her that no help could be expected from *that* quarter in the task of placating Mr. Goodge, so she shouldered the burden herself—not altogether without amusement—and conducted him into the staff-room.

'Do have some lemonade, Mr. Goodge. We make it rather well here. I expect you're thirsty.'

'Well—er—I've been on my feet more or less all morning. It would be nice. Thank you.'

Mr. Goodge began to feel at home. This was more the tone he had been accustomed to in other huts. He began telling Joan something of the woes of his position. Joan hated his oily voice and his mushroom-coloured mouth.

'It requires such a lot of tact, Miss Seddon. You, who have only recently joined us, would hardly believe—— Why, some of our men-workers actually resent the intrusion of ladies in their midst.'

'So I've gathered; and I can understand it in a way,' said Joan, with wide-open eyes. 'But as it's war-time, and the Y.M.C.A. has spread to such huge dimensions, they could hardly have managed without us, could they?'

'That's just what I tell them. It's my most earnest wish that we should all work happily together. But even among the ladies there's a good deal of jealousy. Many of them consider, for instance, that the Connaught is altogether too *young* a hut—that it needs a steadier, a more elderly element.'

'But *you* don't think so?' Joan's gaze became ever more candid and angelic.

'I? Oh—er—no,' he replied, unable to meet her look. 'I had perhaps, at one time, thought of effecting certain changes in order —er—to placate—er——'

'But you wouldn't really do that, Mr. Goodge?' she interposed quickly. 'I can't imagine you kow-towing to any mere gossip and unpleasantness. Of course if you want to move me from here I shall have to go, but people work best where they're happiest, don't you think?'

However much Mr. Goodge might inwardly have doubted the truth of this doctrine he hastened to agree with it, and added that he had no intention of moving Miss Seddon, or anybody else— *now.*

He finished his lemonade, and while smoking a cigarette listened with a smug smile to Joan's enthusiastically expressed admiration of the Y.M.C.A. and all its works. He took his departure feeling soothed and benignant.

'Well, I think that's done the trick,' sighed Joan. 'He'll stop making himself obnoxious about our hut now. I hope Mrs. J. will be pleased.'

'You are a little devil, Joany!' Barbara's eyes were lit with half-shocked amusement. 'I didn't think you had it in you!'

'Oh, if one uses the methods of the harem one can get most things done,' said the younger girl, with a note of the old Suffrage scorn in her voice. 'But, Lord, doesn't one despise the man on whom one has to use them!'

.   .   .   .   .   .

Sometimes, during their afternoons off, the girls were taken for joy-rides by two cheerful young officers called 'Barnum' and 'Bailey' (their real names nobody could remember), whose ordinary duties consisted in driving King's Messengers between Abbeville, Paris, and the coast.

The orchards just now were pink with apple-blossom, and the feathery French poplars stood like nymphs on either side of the straight white roads. The girls returned refreshed from these outings, and Mr. Wilkinson, observing it, ventured in his melancholy way to ask them to go out with *him* sometimes. 'Although, of course,' he added, 'a Ford is a sad substitute for a Rolls Royce.' This they politely denied, but always they declined his offers on some pretext or another.

Weary Willie, hitherto only noticed as the depressed and gentle-manly driver of a Y.M.C.A. car, had begun lately to loom a little larger in the lives of the Connaught workers. He would drop into the hut about twelve o'clock, and stand mournfully watching Joan and Barbara while they were making sandwiches. Then he would place a bag of sweets on the counter, murmuring 'For all of you,' and depart. The contents of the bag would be more than half-consumed by lunch-time, and the other two, coming on for the afternoon shift, would demolish the rest.

'Which of you is the chosen, I wonder?' twinkled little Mrs. Jessop one day.

'Oh, safety in numbers!' giggled Mavis, her rosy cheek bulging with a *marron glacé*.

'I don't know. I feel that as chaperon of the party I ought to ask him his intentions, and tell him that he may be blighting many young lives!'

One evening when he came to fetch them at the hut he solemnly presented Mavis with a rosebud. 'Very marked!' the others declared.

The following morning, on their way to work, Barbara and Joan asked him to come into a tobacconist's and help them choose pipes and pouches for some men who were going back to the Front. When the things had been chosen the French shopman, evidently thinking they were for Mr. Wilkinson, tied up the parcel and handed it to him with a 'Voilà, Monsieur!' The girls were much amused; and Mr. Wilkinson, looking embarrassed, murmured: 'No such luck!'

As they climbed into the back of the car he said to them over his shoulder:

'Do you know what's the matter with Miss McNare?'

'With Miss McNare? No. What?'

'She's suffering from the same complaint as myself.'

'And what's that?'

'She thinks you are the two most charming girls in Boulogne.'

The car rattled forward. The girls shrugged.

'Man must be potty!' declared Joan.

Later on they told Mavis what he had said.

'So you see,' exclaimed Mavis, laughing, 'I'm no longer in the running. It's one of you two!'

That evening a more than usually immense bag of sweets was placed non-committally on the counter. Mrs. Jessop remarked that Weary Willie kept his harem well supplied.

.   .   .   .   .

A few miles outside the town stood the ruined castle of Hardelot in its dreaming grounds. Barbara and Joan had lately discovered it. A little yellow tram ran out part way, and the rest of the way one had to walk, or trust to lifts in passing cars. It was a place of peace and beauty, and where, incidentally, tea could be obtained.

On the broad ramparts, covered with ivy and pink roses, and overhung with the milk blooms of tall acacia trees, they sat one May afternoon. Away beneath them spread shining buttercup fields and a lily-covered mere.

'Can't you just see the knights and ladies trooping across the meadows on steeds caparisoned in crimson!' sighed Joan.

'Yes, you funny kid!' said Barbara.

Joan murmured on.

> ' "Lo! I must tell a tale of chivalry;
> For while I muse, the lance points slantingly
> Athwart the morning air: some lady sweet . . ."

I forget the rest. Something about a "stout defender," and the "worn top of an old battlement." '

She turned on her front, propping her chin in her hands. The shadow of the acacia leaves dappled her light frock. She looked at Barbara, who sat clasping her knees and staring out across the meadows. She knew that, for the moment, her friend saw nothing of their sunny greenness, but instead was trying to visualise a far-off barren peninsula, infected with disease and dust, from which there was no retreat and no home-leave, and where the early hope of swift victory was fading.

'When did you last have a letter?' she asked.

'A week ago. Oh, I'm not worrying, you know. I've an absolute conviction that he'll come through. It's just that he's such miles away, and conditions out there are worse than in France.'

'Different,' said Joan. 'Perhaps not worse. Tell me, Barbara, is it your religion makes you so quietly sure?'

'That, and . . . Well, when you've known a person so long and so well as I've known Sam you just can't imagine life without him. We've been engaged on and off for five years.'

'I wonder you didn't marry him before he went out.'

Barbara shook her head.

'It wouldn't have done. We agreed that nothing mattered now but the war, that we must be absolutely free to give ourselves to it.'

'Queer,' murmured Joan, 'that's exactly what I said to Colin. But then I didn't mean it as you meant it—unequivocally. I gave it as an excuse because I wasn't in love with him. If I *had* been...'

She brooded silently. If she *had* been, the war would have made no difference—nothing would have made any difference.

Barbara's feeling for Sam Wyndham was of the same nature as her feeling for her Church: steady, woven into the very woof of her being, and impossible to discuss. And Joan marvelled at, while she half envied, the quality both of her love and of her faith.

After all what did poetry matter? What did dreams matter? What did worrying about 'questions' matter? Here was Barbara quietly living poetry and dreams, deeply rooted in the soil of life, not clamouring for the stars; a complete, an unselfconscious and loyal human being.

After a time they came down from the walls and had tea at one of the little tables on the grassy lawn, or 'pleasaunce,' as Joan called it, which the walls encircled.

As they left they saw a solitary British officer riding on his horse along the edge of the mere, and in that landscape, under the slanting sunbeams, he looked a figure of romance. Romance! What a perfect place for it! thought Joan. And turning saw Mr. Wilkinson, with his gooseberry eyes and his groggy knees, waiting silently to drive them home.

The fact that he was so well aware of their movements rather irritated Joan, but she gave him a more or less friendly smile. After all it was kind of him to have come to fetch them.

Barbara had wandered off towards the car, but Mr. Wilkinson remained rooted to the spot.

To Joan's 'Are you coming?' he turned a deaf ear; and, after a silence, asked her ponderously whether she had ever noticed that this lawn they were standing on was shaped like a heart.

'No, is it?' she said, looking vaguely round. 'I hadn't particularly noticed.'

He went on to inform her that Hardelot was the place where Henry the Eighth had wooed Katherine Parr.

'Do you like the word "wooed"?' he asked, drawing out the vowels and lifting his mournful eyes upon her.

'Oh—oh, yes,' said the bewildered Joan. 'It's a nice mediæval sort of word, isn't it?' By this time she had decided that he was a little touched.

Mr. Wilkinson looked at his boots.

'I think it must have been in the month of June he wooed her,' was his cryptic utterance.

'I shouldn't wonder,' she cheerfully agreed. 'But we must come now, Barbara's waiting.'

He dropped them at the hut, and they were caught into an evening of hectic work. Mavis and Mrs. Jessop were plunging about, vainly trying to cope with the rush of men. Already food was running short, and to make things worse, 'that ass of a Buster' had got no change in the cash-box. Being Sunday, the day on which the men were paid, the problem was serious. There they stood, pressed against the counter, clutching their franc and half-franc notes, and unable to obtain anything for their money.

'This situation is ridiculous, Mr. Baxter,' said Barbara. 'It's you who are responsible for the cash. You must do something about it.'

'But what *am* I to do, Miss Frewen?' asked the wretched Christian.

'Go out and get some change at once, of course—from anywhere,' she told him.

'But I can't do that, I've got to take the evening service in a few minutes.'

'Very well, *take* it!' said Barbara, 'and we'll serve the men free. There's no other way,' she continued, cutting short his shocked protestations. 'We can't let them down.'

He crept off, shattered, towards the other end of the hut. It was seldom that the gentle Miss Frewen took the bit between her teeth in this way, but when she did, nothing could stand against her. Luckily the K.O.S.B. sergeant-major came to the rescue and offered to go out for change.

Joan, with little Hinkley to help her, cut sandwiches at frantic speed in the kitchen and boiled up new brews of custard.

When the service had begun, and the counter was temporarily closed, Barbara came in and shut the kitchen door.

'Not going to join in the hymns?' asked Joan mischievously.

'No, I'm not! When religion takes that sort of form I've no use for it. A mere camouflage for laziness.'

Back at Temple's the day's events—Weary Willie and all—were poured into the sympathetic ear of Miss McNare. The girls confided in her as they might have done in a dear old family nurse, whom they could trust, and who loved to be kept *au courant* of everything concerning her charges.

Just before they went upstairs a breathless Christian arrived with a message from the head office. New troops were coming through. Would Miss Frewen and Miss Seddon take the early shift at Ostrohove to-morrow? A car would call for them at about five.

'Off you go! Get what sleep you can,' said Miss McNare, dismissing them like children.

But it was after midnight when Joan fell asleep. She had caught the faint sound of bagpipes far down in the town, and had leant out of her window to listen. More Highlanders, then! The ship must have just come in.

Chapter Six

WRAPPED in a kimono, her hair a dark cloud round her small face, Barbara crept into Joan's room and gently shook her shoulder. The younger girl sat up, wide awake at once.

'Oh—oh yes, I remember. What time is it?'

'Half-past four. Come into my room when you're dressed, and we'll have some tea.'

Joan's mirror reflected flushed cheeks and brilliant eyes, and, though she was too young to realise just *how* young she must be in order to look like that after a tiring day and only four hours' sleep, the sight gave her a swift moment of surprise and pleasure.

Over Barbara's little spirit-lamp they had tea and biscuits, then stole downstairs, and out on to the boulevard where Mr. King was waiting for them in a car. It was an exquisite morning. The sky was pearly-pink, the air sweet and cool. Past the shuttered houses they drove, under trees that stood motionless as courtiers waiting for the day, up the bumping lane to the camp.

Here all was life and stir. Kilted men moved among the clusters of tents, and the girls had just time to ascertain that this was part of the 9th Division—the first division of Kitchener's new armies to come through—before they dived into the gloom of the Y.M. marquee, and gave themselves over to buttering rolls as though the lives of the British Army depended on it. To judge by the way the rolls were disposed of this almost seemed to be the case. The two girls, a Christian, a Highland orderly, and little Marcel, working till the knives dropped from their hands, were scarcely able to keep pace with the demand. The tent was not supposed to be open until six, but the men had poured in before anything was ready. Eight hundred long French rolls to be slit and buttered in no time at all, the cocoa to be mixed, the tea-urns to be filled; and hordes of Highlanders, wedged against the counter, waiting like wolves to devour what was thrown to them. After a time Joan became weak with laughter. It was so frightfully funny, when you looked up, to see all those piercing blue eyes fixed ravenously on the rolls—a concentrated fire of gaze, solemn and insistent. Without their rolls the men refused to budge.

At last the store was exhausted, and the immediate stress relieved. The girls were able to stand fixed by their urns and deliver the usual hot drinks and slabs of cake. For two more hours the tent seethed, and then there was a lull while first the 8th Gordons and then the 5th Camerons paraded outside, and swung off into the road.

The men were of magnificent physique, and of a ruddiness and gaiety that matched the morning. The sun, the sea, the sweep of the bare hills all combined to give them a glittering send-off; and the pipers at the head of each battalion drew from their preposterous and inflated instruments that music which tore the heart and defied death. Waving, smiling, rhythmic, exuberant, the men crashed past. Wildly the girls waved back until they were out of sight and hearing.

The vanguard of 'K.I.' was through.

.   .   .   .   .   .

For two more mornings Barbara and Joan worked at the camp before beginning their normal day, and then the 9th Division had passed, and there was breathing space again.

.   .   .   .   .   .

The flowers on the counter had changed from bluebells and cowslips to irises and cornflowers and pinks. Mrs. Jessop had taken it into her head to have the inside of the hut distempered, and was now to be seen at all hours, assisted by a fatigue party of Tommies, splashing about among buckets of yellow paint, the red tendrils of her pretty hair shining in the sunlight. Mavis, who had seemed strangely *distraite* of late, spent most of her time languidly at the piano. Barbara, whenever she could get off from the hut, was pursuing investigations in every quarter with regard to a brother-in-law 'wounded and missing.' The strain and the constant disappointments were telling on her. Her face seemed to get smaller and whiter, her eyes larger every day. But the more she worried the less did it appear in her manner, and Joan recognised to the full the value of that queer thing called 'breed.'

.   .   .   .   .   .

A week or two later part of the 14th Division was in camp. The thick human khaki stream flowed steadily before the counter.

When, during the first lull, at about eight o'clock, Joan dropped her aching arms and turned to the tent-opening for a breath of air, whom should she see standing there, with a grin on his merry face, but her cousin Jack.

'Hullo, barmaid!' he greeted her. 'How's life?'

'Jack, you idiot, how lovely to see you! Why didn't you let me know you were coming over?'

'Didn't know myself till yesterday. They never tell us anything in the jolly old army. My word, you do look a sight!'

'So would you if you'd been slooshing cocoa about for a couple of hours in the atmosphere of this tent. Sit down and talk to me.'

'Half a mo'. I've got some chaps out here—friends of mine. Could you raise a drink of any sort for us?'

'Yes, I think so—of a *sort*. Bring them in.'

She got Marcel, who ever leapt to do her bidding, to open some tins of camp coffee; and a few minutes later Jack Seddon and his friends were seated among the litter of margarine boxes and empty milk-tins behind the counter, sipping happily from thick mugs.

Two of them Joan had met before: Maurice Fleming and 'Brab' Malcolm. Maurice had brains, Brab was a Rugby 'blue'; but both were of the same lean, brown-cheeked type, gentle of manner, and with firmly-cut lips that broke into slow smiles over white teeth. They had been up at Cambridge with Jack, and she had danced with them last summer at the Trinity Ball.

The third was a little red-haired man whom Jack introduced as 'Ginger,' and whose eyes were of the vivid green-blue of a hedge-sparrow's egg.

'He's not much to look at,' said Jack, cheerfully explaining him, 'but he's an absolute terror on parade. Got the voice of six sergeant-majors rolled into one.'

'Oh, stow it, Seddon,' said Ginger, blushing brick-red over his mug of coffee.

Jack gave him a hearty clap on the back which sent him forward spluttering. 'Cheer up, Ginger! You're our mascot, remember. If you get pipped the company's done for. Not that I think you will, you're far too small. You'll dodge about among the bullets like a fire-fly.'

The egg-blue eyes blinked comically at Joan, as though to ask what was to be done with this eternally-ragging cousin of hers. Joan decided that she liked Ginger. He was different from the rest, but he was a genuine dear.

Conversation with the other two consisted chiefly of May-week.

'Do you remember,' Brab was asking her, in his pleasant voice, 'how we danced every single encore of "When the Birds Began to Sing"?'

' "*Wasn't that a funny thing,*" ' hummed Joan. 'Oh, do I not! And there must have been about fourteen encores! I nearly dropped.'

'What was it of yours that actually *did* drop when you were dancing with me, Joan?' Jack fixed her with mischievous grey eyes. 'Something very strange . . .'

'*Really*, Jack!' she retorted, as she remembered the unfortunate occurrence to her petticoat that evening.

'And then being photographed at 6 a.m.?' pursued Brab. 'That ghastly group in the quad!'

'And how we ate quails and hard-boiled eggs on the Backs in the morning sunshine, all in our evening clothes!'

'And then we changed,' said Joan, 'and had a huge breakfast at the hotel, and I had to leave you all and go back to London the same day for a Suffrage meeting. Heavens, how sleepy I was!'

'I remember old Maurice was fairly played out after that night,' put in Jack. 'It was his third ball running, and before that he'd been swatting like hell for his Tripos. I'll say that for you, Maurice, you did work that last term we were up. You deserved to get through. Though what good it's done you so far, old bean, I'm dashed if I know. As far as the B.E.F. is concerned my "ordinary" is quite as useful.'

'Oh, quite, I admit,' smiled Maurice.

Joan looked at them—at Jack with his laughing eyes and pink girl's cheeks; at Brab and Maurice with their admirable soundness of body and of character; at funny little Ginger. She couldn't express to them what she felt, or she would probably have hugged the whole darling English group. Either that or prayed over them.

All she said was: 'What good times those were! Will they ever come again? Shall we ever dance again?'

Light as she tried to keep her tone Jack's reply reproved her.

'Good Lord, Joan, don't be morbid! Of course we shall.'

But in Brab's eye she caught a look—only for a second, and she couldn't be sure of it—which seemed to say: 'We shan't.'

She asked Jack news of the family. He had seen his people a week ago.

'I saw Aunt Florence too. She seems to have a confused idea, Joan, that you are liable to be captured by Germans at any moment. I tried to calm her. Oh, and Betty Paley was there. Sent you her love. She's simply panting to come out and join you.'

'I wish she would,' said Joan.

'Well . . .' Jack got up and adjusted his Sam Browne, 'I suppose we ought to be moving. We push off at ten-thirty.'

'Oh, then I must stay and see you go.'

She shook hands with all of them and wished them luck.

'Good-bye, Jacko; you'll take care of yourself, won't you?'

'You bet! Topping to have seen you, Joan. Carry on with the good work.'

Dear careless Jack. He seemed hardly older than when he used to play Indians in the garden with her, and now he was going off to the war in the same sort of spirit. An hour later the 7th Battalion of the King's Royal Rifles marched away. It was bugles this time instead of pipes; breeches and puttees instead of kilts and bare knees. The Tommies waved, but more restrainedly than the Jocks had done. Jack gave a cousinly wink as he passed. The other officers gravely saluted.

'Ce sont vos amis, cette fois, Mamzelle?' piped a voice at her side.

'Oui, Marcel.'

'A-ah, c'est dommage. Ce sont de beaux officiers—Faut pas pleurer, Mamzelle. Ils reviendront peut-être!'

Ils reviendront—peut-être. . . .

Chapter Seven

THE hut was invaded one morning by Mrs. Mendip, the stout secretary of the Ladies' Committee of the Y.M.C.A. She was over from London on a tour of inspection. She seemed pleased with the Connaught, talked to Barbara and Joan for a time, and then produced blank consternation by telling them that Mrs. Jessop would now have to return to England. It appeared that under the new rules no woman who had a husband in France was allowed to go on working there; and Mrs. Jessop's husband had just come out to take up a Staff appointment at Abbeville.

Later the girls longed to question Mrs. Jessop herself on the subject, but as she made no reference to it they thought that they had perhaps been unduly scared, and kept a discreet silence.

It was at the end of a performance by a Lena Ashwell concert party, an evening or two later, that the bombshell burst. Mrs. Jessop hopped on to the platform and announced to everyone the news that she and Miss Dempster were leaving for good. Miss Dempster because she was going to be married, and she herself because of the arrival of her husband in France. She made a charming little farewell speech, in which she told the men that she was deeply sorry to leave them and would often think of them.

Colonel Weston, who was taking the chair, then rose. He was O.C. Base Details, and incidentally a staunch supporter of the Connaught. With a certain amount of pompous sentimentality he thanked the two ladies for the splendid work they had done, and for bringing to the hut so much grace and charm. He said how much the soldiers loved to hear the voice of an English lady again after months of trench-life ('Oh, don't!' whispered Joan), and added that the spirit of refinement which prevailed at the Connaught was so much appreciated that every man of them would rather be dead on the battle-field than allow that spirit—er—to be

67

—er—sullied and extinguished as it had been in Belgium. Terrific cheering. Whatever the girls felt, the soldiers, at any rate, didn't appear to find the speech embarrassing.

Then a vote of thanks was moved, and at the request of one of the men Mavis got up to sing for the last time. She sang better than Joan had ever heard her, and with more feeling. She gave 'Parting' and 'Somewhere a Voice . . .' which the men always associated with her, and were especially fond of. 'Somewhere a voice is calling, ca-alli-ing for me-e.' The last sweet notes died away; and the song, together with the singer's pretty face, and the general emotion of the occasion, roused a tempest of applause.

Before going home that evening Mrs. Jessop told Barbara and Joan that her departure was not quite so unexpected as it seemed. The London Committee had already written requesting her to leave—implying that there had been too much gossip about her, and that she was not a suitable person to be head of a hut.

'I'm pretty sure Mr. Goodge has something to do with it,' said poor little Mrs. Jessop. 'The "husband in France" reason is merely a blind.'

The girls were indignant, and, when they were back at Temple's together, Barbara let herself go.

'Of course it's true,' she said, 'that Mrs. J. has often been indiscreet and thoughtless, and it's true she has no head for management, but she has never done anyone any harm. I think it's disgusting of the other lady-workers, and of the Christians, to have circulated stories against her just because she happens to be popular with officers.'

Joan couldn't help being amused at Barbara's violent partisanship of a woman whose slackness and vagueness she had so often deplored, but she understood it well enough. And they both became more and more depressed as they envisaged the changed character of their young and happy hut—for they were convinced that the Committee would send out a couple of perishing blights in place of the other two.

Next day they stood on the quay and watched the leave-boat

steam away bearing Mavis and Mrs. J. to England. They waved till they could see them no longer, then turned sadly back into the town.

.   .   .   .   .   .

The Connaught was now reduced to two workers—for Buster hardly counted—and these two had to remain on all day, and were doing early shifts at the camp as well. There was no movement on the part of the Y.M. office to supplement the staff. With the departure of the others the Connaught seemed to have been forgotten.

The atmosphere was queer, and rather desolate at first; and to add to its strangeness their dear little Hinkley had left them to rejoin his regiment. In his place was a new orderly, a pale, depressed youth who seemed bewildered by his surroundings, and whose first question to Joan was to ask her what sort of a 'place' she had been in before, as she seemed so 'well versed in cooking.' When she told him that she had never before done work of this kind he seemed more bewildered than ever, and murmured that he had supposed her to be 'something in the pastry line,' adding that people who led idle lives ought to be ashamed of themselves.

.   .   .   .   .   .

David Frewen, Barbara's younger brother, came through one morning, and, as his battalion didn't march off till the evening, he obtained leave from his colonel, and spent most of the day down at the hut.

At tea-time, in a moment of unexpected expansion, Buster sent them all off for a drive with little Bailey, saying that it would do them good to 'have a blow,' and that he would manage on his own for an hour or two.

They drove to Montreuil (for this was before G.H.Q. had moved there from St. Omer) and wandered about the little mellow town with its narrow streets and great red ramparts, and then drove back through the slanting sunlight of a perfect June evening.

'It's somehow worse parting with David than with the others,' said Barbara to Joan that night, having seen her brother off. 'I suppose it's because he's younger, and delicate, and I've always had specially to look after him.' But thinking of her luck in having had him to herself all day, her eyes were starry in their darkened sockets.

. . . . . .

'Funny life,' said Barbara, when they had come down from the camp next day, and had perspiringly attacked the morning's cooking. 'I wonder if they're ever going to send us any more help!'

'I don't much care if they don't,' Joan replied. 'It's rather nice like this—just you and me. Though I suppose we can't go on indefinitely working fifteen hours a day.'

At that moment in came Weary Willie with a gigantic bag of peppermints, and asked whether there was anything he could do for them. 'You two really deserve the V.C.,' he remarked funereally. And then, as though it were the brightest diversion he could suggest for them at the moment, he told them he had overtaken some guns coming up the road, and that they would probably be passing now.

Out went the girls and stood on the pavement. Two traction-engines were lumbering along, each dragging a grisly-looking gun, with skyward tilted nose. Great guns, squat and blind. Nine-point-twos. Barbara, the dark wings of her hair blown back from her forehead, had the look of an avenging angel. 'Why aren't there more of them?' she muttered. 'Splendid guns! I hope they kill mi-illions of Germans!'

Joan looked at her gentle friend surprised. Did Barbara really feel like that about it? Or was it lack of imagination? If so, what a blessed gift! Better just blindly to hate your enemy, better just blindly to love your country, better just blindly to believe in the return of your loved ones. And if the loved ones did not return, then blindly, uncomplainingly acquiesce in their loss—as Barbara would do. Barbara had two brothers and a fiancé fighting, a brother-in-law wounded and missing; was it any wonder she felt as she did? Perhaps it was in herself—not in Barbara—that imagination was lacking. She recalled the sinking of the *Lusitania* a few weeks ago; the barbarous poison-gas, the use of which by the Germans had turned the good-tempered Tommies into horrified vindictive foes. She saw with her friend's eyes. She was lifted on a wave of undiluted patriotism. 'Yes,' she said, 'I hope so too. I hope they kill millions of Germans!'

.   .   .   .   .   .

Two days later a new Senior Lady came to the Connaught. She was large and sweet and tranquil; and the two jaded girls, who had been expecting somebody of quite a different calibre, took to her at once. She was sympathetic over the Mrs. Jessop business, and evidently anxious to get on well with the remaining members of Mrs. Jessop's hut. With her came a young cousin. So the Connaught was once again numerically complete. That night Barbara and Joan slept the clock round.

.   .   .   .   .   .

At breakfast Joan was bewildered to find by her plate a large and dew-besprinkled bunch of pink roses. Suddenly she remembered that it was her birthday and that she was twenty-one. 'Oh, Barbara, you darling . . .' she began. But Barbara shook her head. 'Not from me,' she said; 'I'll give you something later.' Joan looked at Miss McNare. That lady also shook her head, and advised Joan to look at the label. Joan did so. The roses were from Mr. Wilkinson
'Good Lord!' she exclaimed. 'But how on earth did he know? Oh, I think you're all cats to have given me away!'
The breakfast-table shook with laughter.
The note contained an invitation to Joan, and to Barbara too if she liked, to go out to Hardelot that afternoon. Now that the new workers had arrived, it was suggested, they could surely spare the time.
'Do you a lot of good,' said Barbara. 'You go!'
'But not alone?' cried the dismayed Joan. 'You'll come too?' But it seemed that Barbara had arrears of correspondence to make up, and would rather be left behind. Miss McNare's eye held a significant twinkle.

Joan saw that she was 'for it,' and resigned herself. 'Though I shall be so dead with boredom by the time I come back,' she smiled, 'that you'll have to have black coffee ready to revive me.'

So she and her silent escort drove off in the Ford through the sunshiny afternoon. When they got to Hardelot they wandered for a time about the grounds, and Mr. Wilkinson became quite communicative, and told Joan about the little village in Lincolnshire where he had been vicar.

'I lived a quiet cabbage-like existence there,' he said, 'it suited me. I think it's best to be a cabbage, don't you?'

To Joan's emphatic denial he replied sadly: 'No, I suppose you wouldn't.'

He told her that he liked sweeping up leaves in the garden on autumn afternoons until his imaginary wife called him in to tea. He added, though, that he didn't find the imaginary wife very satisfactory. He talked of flowers and old houses. In fact he made distinct efforts to be entertaining. Joan lent him a surface-sweet attention.

They walked slowly back to the château and sat on the ruined ramparts. He sprawled beside her in an attitude which in some men might have been graceful, but which was hardly suitable to him. His hat was tilted over his spectacles, and he chewed a bit of grass. Joan unfolded *The Times* she was carrying, and began talking rather rapidly about the Russian retreat. Mr. Wilkinson agreed that it was serious. And then, in the same lifeless, monotonous voice that he always used, he said:

'I have been wanting for some time to get you out alone to Hardelot, because I thought that as this was the place where Henry the Eighth wooed Katherine Parr it might be a good place for me to woo you. Also it *is* the month of June.'

Heedless of Joan's little gasp, and of the mirth which flickered suddenly over her grey eyes and freckled nose, he proceeded to tell her that he loved her, and had done so almost from the first moment of seeing her.

'But—but——' she stammered, 'I had no idea—no inkling. You treated us all exactly alike. This is extraordinary . . .'

'It was always you,' he went on heavily. 'I tried not to show it, not to make any difference, but it was always you. I was glad when it was you who sat in the front of the car.'

It was serious then! For, in spite of the constant chaff which had gone on about Weary Willie, Joan hadn't really believed that he was attached to one of them more than to another; hadn't really believed that he felt anything towards them except in a sort of avuncular way. And here he was actually proposing.

'I'm awfully sorry, Mr. Wilkinson,' she answered, 'but it's quite impossible, you know.'

Upon that followed the inevitable question: 'Is there anybody else?'

'No—not at the moment,' she told him. 'But that makes no difference.'

He gave her a glance whose mournfulness was tinged with a pale hope.

'Of course I'm not the sort of fellow people fall in love with. But I shan't give up. I shall keep on. I always try to get what I want, and this time what I want is you.'

It was pathetic, this rôle of dogged and relentless pursuer which he sketched for himself. Joan could think of nothing adequate to say, and kept feebly repeating:

'I'm very sorry, Mr. Wilkinson, but I'm afraid it's no use. I'm very sorry.'

Then, seeing his gloom, she added brightly: 'I shouldn't be in the least the right sort of wife for you, you know.'

But Mr. Wilkinson was certain that she would be. If there was one thing he was perfectly certain of it was that.

Joan tried to picture herself calling him in to tea, having his slippers ready, sharing his cabbage-like existence. Imagination failed. It was with difficulty that she controlled an hysterical desire to laugh.

After a time she got up and said she wanted tea. He held out a dry hand, pressed hers silently, and followed her down to the tables on the lawn.

After tea, as they were walking towards the car, Mr. Wilkinson said that he hoped he hadn't spoilt her birthday. She assured him that he hadn't, but asked him never to refer to the subject again.

'Oh, but I can't promise that!' he exclaimed lugubriously. 'If you don't actually dislike me, and if there is nobody else, I don't see why I shouldn't have another try.'

'But it's no *use*,' said Joan, stopping dead, and looking at him full in the face. 'If you go on it will only mean that I shall never be able to speak to you any more, or to come in the car any more either. I mean it.'

That frightened him. 'Very well then, I promise to let it drop,' he said. 'Only don't avoid me, and don't—please don't—be cruel to me.'

As he drove her away she looked back at dear lovely Hardelot. Perfect place for romance! Perfect place to be 'wooed' in by . . . by . . . Her glance fell to Weary Willie sitting beside her, clutching the steering-wheel, his goggle eyes fixed on the road ahead. Well . . . not by *him*.

No more was said on the drive home. He dropped her at the hut, raised his hat, and went on. Immediately she was caught into a swirl of work, and to Barbara's lifted eyebrow gave back a comically woeful nod.

Later, at Temple's, she told them about it.

Miss McNare chuckled and said she had known all along what would happen.

'That he could have thought, for a moment, he had a hope!' cried Barbara. 'Poor old thing though, I'm sorry for him.'

'Well, I feel I ought to be,' said Joan, 'but as a matter of fact I'm not. He's somehow too absurd to be sorry for. My theory is that he's been rather dazzled and unhinged by the lot of us, and thinks it would be pleasant to have a young wife. I expect he'll try for someone else before the summer's out.'

And later on rumour certainly had it that he was making efforts in other directions; and Joan, though relieved to be rid of him, was amused to find herself just an atom piqued.

. . . . . .

At the end of June Barbara went home on leave, and Betty Paley was sent out.

Joan, enchanted to have her friend with her at last, established her at Temple's, and arranged for her to work at the Connaught during Barbara's absence.

Chapter Eight

BETTY'S face glowed behind the delphinium and peony-decked counter like a larger and a moving flower. All that Joan could tell her of the working of the huts, and of the Boulogne community in general, she absorbed eagerly. From the very first she 'fitted in.'

It was a comparatively slack fortnight. The weather was hot. Raspberries and strawberries were added to the attractions of the counter. Red currants were laboriously strung and stewed.

When Barbara came back from leave, Betty was sent to work at the Alexandra, the big hut down near the quay.

.   .   .   .   .   .

From half-way through July until the end of August Kitchener's 2nd Army poured through Boulogne. Sometimes there was not even a day's pause between the divisions. Through the short night the sound of drums and fifes was heard as the troops marched up from the quay; and often the sound of singing.

After the recent quiet spell the Y.M.C.A. was working at full stretch. An extra Christian was turned on to Ostrohove, and Betty shared the early morning shifts with Barbara and Joan. Betty was the most difficult person in the world to rouse from sleep, and time and again the other two waited on Temple's doorstep fearing they would have to start without her; but always she joined them just at the last moment, flushed, dewy and serene.

The three of them could hardly cope with the work. Outside the Y.M. tent, at a table in the sunshine, the brown-faced officers gathered for breakfast—relays of them—twenty at a time—and were served with boiled eggs as well as with coffee and rolls. This arrangement had developed from the haphazard gatherings behind the counter, and 'officers' breakfasts' were one girl's whole-time job. Inside, the other two served ceaselessly at the Tommy-thronged counter, while the Christians hopped about renewing supplies. ' "Christian, seek not yet repose," ' murmured Joan, suddenly finding in the old hymn a new and most appropriate meaning. And urns were filled, and filled again, and rolls were handed up, bought and devoured, and the eye saw nothing but tightly-moving masses of khaki.

All day, now, and far into the evening the tent was kept open, for the troops marched off at all hours. Different lady-workers came up from their huts to take the different shifts. Somewhat to her surprise, Joan was asked to go up one evening in place of someone who had fallen through. She had never been in the camp at that hour before, and rather enjoyed it. At the other end of the tent there was an impromptu concert going on, conducted by Mr. Pringle, one of the extra Christians. Suddenly this strange beast, who had hair like a golliwog, and no conception of hard work, hove up by Joan's elbow and asked her to come and sing. Horror-struck, Joan protested that she had got no songs with her. That didn't seem to perturb him; he had a few of his own which he insisted she should try. 'Go on,' said Mr. King, twinkling at her. 'I'll take the urn.'

There was nothing for it. Joan forged her way down through the crowd in the dim evening-lit tent, and climbed on to the platform. The only two of Mr. Pringle's songs that she found she knew at all were 'Because,' and 'I know a Lovely Garden.' These she warbled to the best of her ability, standing in her dirty apron and rolled-up sleeves. It was greater fun than she had expected, and the men were delighted. 'Where grow the *swe-e-etest* flowers,' they cooed after her as she went back to her urn.

It was queer and glamorous watching them march away an hour later—Royal Fusiliers—through the soft still evening. They were not, like so many, a jovial crowd, but looked sternly ahead, and marched with an almost tragic discipline. A band of great drums went before them. Low over the fields the moon was rising.

But the evenings up there were an exception. It was by its early mornings that Ostrohove would be for ever remembered. Shining mornings when the sun rose over the hills. Friendly mornings, chattering of this and that among the rolls before the tent was open—splitting, buttering; splitting, buttering. 'Have you heard . . .?' 'No, not really?' 'Our new Christian is perfectly *hopeless*!' 'What do you think our orderly said to me yesterday?' Mornings of gaiety, mornings of heart-ache, as the very stuff of England poured into the tent, ate, drank, poured out again, and was drained away—battalion after magnificent battalion—into France and silence. Cousins, brothers, friends appeared suddenly, talked for a moment—an hour—and were gone. And everything and everyone was young, young, young.

.   .   .   .   .   .

There was a day when Philip Nichol came through. Joan had heard nothing of him since that Sunday supper at Beechwood, just before she left for France. Although she liked Philip, and found him interesting to talk to, she had never been really intimate with him.

He came towards her in the tent now with an eager look on his face. He had grown a moustache. It was curious seeing him as a soldier. His high shoulders stooped a little, but he seemed more at ease than she would have expected in these clothes, and among these surroundings.

He told her that he was not going away until the evening, so they arranged to meet that afternoon when Joan was 'off.'

They went for a walk in some fields outside the town, and Joan was surprised to find how much he had changed—or rather to what an extent he had slipped that dry and clever shell which she remembered, and allowed something more human to glow through. He was evidently very pleased to see her.

Over going to the war he attempted no gay 'insouciance.' He was a teacher, a man already rooted in his career, with purposes to achieve—not a boy just down from the university. He knew what he was sacrificing. He knew what he was going out to.

At first Joan did the talking. She told him of her work, of her conversations with the men, of her admiration for them. He listened, his sensitive mouth twitching a little, his eyes blinking behind their glasses. After all he *wasn't* so unattractive-looking, she thought. Perhaps it was because of the uniform, because of his moustache, perhaps because of her own growing sympathy for him.

He seemed surprised to hear of the hours she worked.

'Every morning so early?' he asked. 'How do you do it? You look extraordinarily fresh.'

He had always been so impersonal before that Joan almost blushed—although he spoke in a detached way.

'Of course one's pretty tired at night,' she said. 'Not with a tiredness that matters at all, except that it prevents one reading, and that's annoying. When I have a holiday, I shall plunge into an orgy of reading. I feel I have so much to catch up.'

And then they were off on to pre-war days, and Joan encouraged Philip to talk of them.

'They had a special atmosphere, those few years just before the war,' he said wistfully, 'which only now we are beginning to appreciate. I'm glad to have been steeped in it, because nothing will ever be like it again.'

Joan was too young to be able to savour the period with quite the regretful relish that Philip did, also she had not so definitely bidden it farewell, but she agreed with him that it already seemed faint and far away—already to a large extent be-glamoured.

'There were such a lot of different things that we were keen about,' he went on. 'There was every sort of promise in the air, every sort of hope. It makes me tired when I hear the older generation saying that we were far too comfortable—even decadent—that we needed the war as a moral shake-up. Depends what sort of society they're referring to, I suppose. There's always a set that's too frivolous—always will be. They don't count. They're only the froth on the top. It's the stream beneath that matters; and our stream ran strong. Look at all the good-will, and intelligence, and idealism that was going about among *our* sort of people; all the thrilling movements that have now come to a standstill. Norman Angell's for peace; Mrs. Despard's and Mrs. Pethick Lawrence's for the freedom of women; Hobson's and Cole's for National Guilds—to take only a few. Then look at the writers: Shaw, and Wells, and Barker; Masefield, and Flecker, and Abercrombie—what a crowd! All of them *at* something, in their different ways. What'll happen to them I don't know—whether they'll wither or run to fat, whether a newer generation will think them faintly absurd—but they're *ours*; we've had them at their most vital and significant.'

'Those hectic Suffrage days!' murmured Joan. 'Barker's Shakespeare season at the Savoy, three years ago . . .'

'The Frohman Repertory season five years ago!' chimed Philip. 'All our hopes for the National Theatre . . .'

' "Pygmalion" at His Majesty's, only last summer. Mrs. Campbell saying "Walk! not bloody likely." Shall you ever forget her voice?'

'And of course, last and most glorious, the Russian Ballet.'

'Karsavina! Karsavina in "Carnaval," in "Spectre de la Rose," in "Thamar," in "Scheherazade"! Where is she now do you suppose? Will there ever again be such an intoxication as that first Ballet season brought us?'

'I can't imagine it.'

There was a pause while they looked back at the two London summers of '13 and '14, which had been coloured by those amazing bursts of vivid foreign flowering.

And then they rambled on, recalling this and that book, this and that play, people they had known and admired, until the inexorable present broke in on their golden recollections, and Philip had to go back to the camp.

'I'm more glad than I can tell you to have seen you,' he said in his rather concise voice. And from that day onwards—that curious day hanging between France and England, between one life and another—their friendship took roots, and grew.

. . . . . .

Betty had been introduced to Hardelot and fallen under its spell.

But no longer could tea be obtained at the château, for an English duchess had recently taken it over for a hospital, and workmen were encamped there. It seemed an extraordinarily unsuitable place for the purpose—apart from its beauty—for there were no conveniences of any sort.

The three were all 'off' together one afternoon, and came and sat upon the rose-embowered ramparts, and rested and talked, and read.

Joan brought out some letters which she had only had time rapidly to skim that morning. One was from Jimmy, home now for the summer holidays, and missing her.

'Tam is very well,' he wrote, 'but he wishes *you* were here, and sends you a "brotherllmrl." That is supposed to be an imitation of the noise he makes with his tongue when trying to lick your face. I have stopped cook giving him bits, and have ordered that he is to be driven from the kitchen-yard whenever found therein. Also I let him out myself in the morning when I get up to do Greek, and Auntie and I keep him with us most of the day. The consequence of all this is that he is much hungrier for his meals. I have also actually taught him to die for his country, which he does quite well, and only jumps up' when I say "Germans are coming"!

'I expect I shall go and stay with Sanderson part of these hols. Are you ever going to get leave?

'Good-bye, ὦ φιλτάτη ὅμαιμ' ἐμή . . . which being interpreted is: "O dearest sister mine." '

Another was from a soldier who had washed up for her one morning at Ostrohove. She read it out to the others. It began, surprisingly, with her Christian name.

'DEAR JOAN,

Just a few lines in answer to your most thankful parcel, well I give the boys some and they thank you very much, well I should like to be washing up cups now as that was the best time I have had since I have been in France. I hope you are all write as

I am. I shall be glad when I can have a bang at the Germans it seems a long time out here a week seems like a year here I would rather be back in England as you cannot understand what they say out here. Dear Joan if you write I will answere it as I have not got anythink else to do only write to Mother every day and I will let you know how I am getting on and how many Germans I kill.

'I remains your sincerely friend,
'Pte. TUPPER, Buffs.'

Yet another was from little Hinkley. He wrote frequently, and always in the same affectionate and reminiscent strain.

'Please remember me to all at the hut. I often wish I was there to see you all jolly and happy amongst the flowers. It's a pity I'm not permanent custard-maker and tin-opener for you, I could do with that till the end of the war. There is fellows watching me write this letter and they say if my sweetheart or Mother get $\frac{1}{2}$ a page she will be lucky. We have got some queer fellows in our dug-out, I think one of them is a bit balmy, he shouts to the Germans and says all kinds of things to them. Hoping to hear from you soon.

'I remain your affectionate HINKLEY.'

The last was from Colin. He had been in action for the first time.

'At last I am able to write to you again. We are behind the lines now after nine days in the trenches. It was supposed to be a fairly safe trench, but as a matter of fact we had many casualties. I was well broken in as my first casualty occurred during morning "stand-to," just at dawn on a miserable pouring-wet day. I was ploughing my way along to find one of my section when I heard a crack and saw the upper part of a man's head lifted almost off. Of all people it was that of my favourite sergeant who had been struck by a stray bullet—one of those wicked reversed ones which the Bosche uses against us all the time. The first letter I wrote on coming out was to his father—the second is to you, Joan. I don't know why I should harrow you with these details, but his rank, my affection for him, the ugliness of the wound and the awful conditions under which it occurred made it somehow different from any of the other casualties I have experienced.

'It is extraordinary how fiendish one becomes when one sees the mess made of material, and—far, far worse—of men by bombardment. One feels one *must* run across to the German trenches. I thought once I could never kill anyone, but that day I could have hewn with an axe.

'The second night we were in I crawled half-way to the German trenches after getting nearly torn to bits on our own barbed wire. Coming back I was marked down by a sniper and thought I should never see you again. Three flares were sent up at once—it was a near thing.'

Then followed a description of a bombing episode, and the letter ended:

'It was a weary trudge back to billets after nine nights of little or no sleep. The officers are in the remains of a large farm or château, and the country is lovely and soothing.

'I wonder how you are getting on, and if you are thinking of going home yet? When shall we meet next? I have thought of you constantly—constantly. You are a wonderful ally. Goodbye. I kiss your hand in thought.

'Your friend,

'COLIN'

Her eyes lifted and fixed themselves on the mere. It was with difficulty that she imagined those trenches, and the gentle, poetry-loving boy who was her friend hurling bombs like some strange giant against a ghastly dawn. Pride in him rose like a wave. He was dauntless. He cared for his men. He told her things, and called her ' a wonderful ally.' If he could truly feel her as that . . . But oh, this war!

She picked up the little green cloth volume of Shelley's *Defence of Poetry*—a present from Colin, which she had brought out with her—and turned the pages. She had dropped asleep last night while half-way through it. 'At length the ancient system of religion and manners . . .' 'utter anarchy and darkness . . .' No, where was she? She turned another page. 'But mark how beautiful an order has sprung from the dust and blood of this fierce chaos! how the world, as from a resurrection, balancing itself on the golden wings of knowledge and of hope, has re-assumed its yet unwearied flight into the heaven of time.'

It was as though someone had given her a rose.

.   .   .   .   .   .

Towards the end of August Joan went home for a fortnight's leave. She planned to spend most of it in London, but some of it down at Wallingford at the house of a childhood's friend.

Chapter Nine

BELOW the meadow which lay along the bottom of the Butlers' garden, near Wallingford, ran the Thames.

Pamela and her cousin Dick Butler had put the punt away in the boat-house, and were strolling back along the willow-girt path. The man carried cushions and a picnic-basket, and walked like an amiable gnome; the girl carried a folded red cotton parasol, and walked like a wood-nymph. The only resemblance between them lay in their dark eyes, which sloped upwards, at the outer corners, mirthfully.

'That was a lovely afternoon, Dickie! Quite like old times.'

He turned his honest grinning face to her.

'Do you remember when I was staying here the summer before last, and you and Leo and I went bathing far up the river?'

'Oh, *that* day? Yes.'

'I shall never forget you standing among the bulrushes with your hair screwed up. You did look a comic! You screamed because your feet were squelching in the mud, although we'd warned you not to go in at that place.'

'And you and Leo sat in the punt and laughed at me—brutes!'

'Couldn't help it, you looked so distressed, and so absurdly small and young.'

'Well, I was only eighteen. I'm immensely older now.'

The sunbeams slanted over the meadow. There wasn't a soul about. The boy of twenty-three who had known the girl all her life, but whom nine months in France had skinned to a greater awareness of familiar beauties, looked at the vivid little face with its expression of mock-primness, and its redly-tantalising mouth. Well, of course, if Pam *would* look like that . . . He dropped the cushions he was clasping and came towards her.

'Keep away, little boy, keep away!'

She rocked in front of him mischievously, the parasol pointed in an attitude of playful defence. He seized its end, still laughing, and with a twist of his wrist sent it flying. Then he took her in his arms and lightly kissed her mouth.

'Now, if you'll kindly pick up all those things,' she commanded, 'and keep three feet away from me, we'll proceed home in an orderly manner.'

'Pity a pore bloke wot's going back to the trenches soon,' he pleaded, as, laden once again, he trudged beside her. And his look of assumed mournfulness sent her into ripples of laughter.

'Oh, I do, Dickie—I do. And so doubtless will many another girl—in just the same way!' (For she had returned his kiss.)

Dickie had every reason to suppose that they might. Girls were such darlings—bless their little hearts. But this time he countered his cousin's ancient jibe about the catholicity of his love-affairs.

'I seem to remember,' he remarked, 'that in your distant and giddy youth you announced to a mixed company in Eights Week that you would like a circulating library of husbands. An odd statement, I thought it, for a carefully-brought-up young girl!'

'Possibly,' said Pamela demurely; 'but you must remember, dear, that however careful my upbringing has been, the same blood runs in our veins.'

They had passed through the gate now, and were walking up through the garden where the heat-wilted petals of the roses lay scattered on the beds. The herbaceous border was a weedy tangle. It was more than old Perkins by himself could do—with the fitful assistance of Miss Pamela—to keep the whole place looking trim and cared-for, these days.

'Pammy dear, why don't you come and stay in town for a bit?' asked Dick.

'And amuse you during your leave?'

'Yes, why not? Mother would be delighted to put you up.'

'No, Dickie. War-work in Wallingford calls me! It is a far, far better thing that I do here—rolling bandages, making swabs, and wrapping up parcels of abominably sewn shirts for our brave lads who will probably only curse when they get them. Besides, I've got a friend coming to-morrow for a few days; she's been in France, and I haven't seen her for ages. *You*'ll manage to amuse yourself all right!'

They were in the hall now, and he was putting on his coat, and wrapping his scarf round his neck. He was ridiculously broad, thought Pamela, watching him—and very, very nice.

Mrs. Butler drifted through from one of the doors with some letters in her hand.

'Oh, good-bye, dear boy; are you off?' She put her frail, once lovely arms on his shoulders. 'Be sure to give my love to your mother.'

'I will. Good-bye, Aunt Milly. It's been a topping day. Jolly to see you all again. I've just been saying I wish you and Pamela would come up to town for a bit.'

'My *dear* Dick!' said his aunt with a little indulgent laugh (it was difficult to resist Dickie), 'we're up to the eyes down here. Pamela and I can't *move*. There'd be nothing done at the sewing depôt without us.'

'So I rather gathered.'

Pamela wrinkled her nose at him from behind her mother's back —implying that he might take *that* statement with a grain of salt.

As his little car crashed away over the gravel, bearing him back to London, she turned dejectedly indoors. Her mother, in a languid way, was picking over some bowls of sweet peas.

'Pamela dear, when *did* you last do the flowers? Half of these are dead.'

'Oh, all right, Mother,' said the girl impatiently; 'I'll do them to-morrow,' and she went streaking up the dark oak staircase to her room.

. . . . . .

Twenty-four hours later Joan Seddon was sitting in Pamela's bedroom. She had arrived a little before tea, and had ever since been feeding her friend's avid ears with stories of Boulogne. Pamela was now talking about herself, and with all the unrestraint of months of repression.

'I tell you it's sometimes more than I can bear,' she exclaimed, 'to go on being my polite outside self, doing the flowers, pouring out tea, and smiling prettily. I have moments when I'd give anything to get away from everyone, and just cry and scream like a maniac. And the fuss Mother makes about her war-work! To hear her you'd think she was the sole support of that sewing depôt, whereas the truth is I do most of her share as well as my own. Of course I have to remember that she's on the rack the whole time about Leo. Leo's a dear, of course, but he's a waster, whom Mother persistently regards as a Galahad. As a matter of fact I shouldn't be a bit surprised if he got the V.C. and then idled and drank for the rest of his life.'

'Pam!' cried Joan, rather shocked, 'he *is* your brother, and he is at the war!'

'Oh, I know, I know. I'm being awful, you must forgive me. But if you knew how sick I was of everything—of pretence and ineffectiveness! Any talents I possessed have dried up like wash-leather gloves in the sun; I can neither read, write, act, nor talk amusingly; my capacities are limited to swab-making. I tell you I'm not going to stay messing here much longer. I shall go and nurse, or do something drastic, soon.'

'I certainly should,' said Joan, 'if that's how you're feeling. It's no good staying where you're exasperated and unsatisfied.'

'And the desolation among the families round here!' continued Pamela, hardly heeding her. 'Only cackling women left! When I think how little I valued my men-friends, and my cousins, when they were alive—or rather the way I just took them for granted. Dickie Butler, who was here yesterday for instance: he's about the only one left, and he'll probably be killed.' She paused. 'And if he is . . . if he is I know that he'll leave a gap nobody else can fill. Under that rather light-come light-go manner of his he's always been devoted to me, and it's awful to think I may never see his dear ugly face any more, and his squeezed-up smile. I think I'll *have* to dash up to town, if only for a few hours,' she added.

There was a longish silence between them, and then Joan said:
'I wonder whether you'd have gone on with your acting if it
hadn't been for the war?'

'Why ever not? Don't you think I have "the gift"?'

'I certainly do. The thing is, would you have been able to stick
the life? You're a bit of a flibbertigibbet, and apt to get bored
with things; and apart from that you'd probably have hated most
of the stage folk you had to mix with. The army-county side of
you is stronger than you realise.'

Pamela considered this with a lifted eyebrow. 'Maybe,' she
admitted. Then bubbled on fountain-like: 'Oh, but I should
have been all right if I'd had lots of parts. The excitement would
have carried me through. And I'd have had my real friends to
play about with as well. I'd have kept both lives going. Of course
I know you've always thought of me as a snob.'

'Not that so much,' protested Joan. 'More as "the last exquisite
flower of a dying stock," incapable—however eager—of competing in this rough democratic world.'

'Yes, that's your romantic idea,' grinned Pamela. 'But let me tell
you that dying stocks, whatever their charm, seem depressingly
incapable of producing the necessary lucre. Without Leo's help
I shouldn't have been able to be at Tree's School at all.'

'Sickening for your career to have been cut off like that,'
brooded Joan. 'I know so many . . .'

'Oh, as to careers,' said Pamela airily, 'I don't believe in them
with the seriousness you do. "Careers for Women" sort of touch.
I just wanted to act. I admit, too, that I wanted to get away from
home. I'm different from you; I hold no ideas or theories about
anything.'

'That doesn't matter. The point is you wanted to do something,
and you've been prevented by the war. We're all more or less in
the same boat. By the way, Pam, you're not in love with anyone
at the moment are you?'

'No, worse luck! It's an unusual situation. Perhaps that's
partly what's wrong.'

'Cruel little butterfly with men, aren't you?' said Joan, smiling at her.

'Not nearly so cruel as you are, with your preposterous, so-called "platonic" friendships! You don't even let the poor dears have the satisfaction of a kiss, do you?'

'I don't "lead them on," anyhow.'

'Earnest pet! But you're much nicer really than I am, Joan.' She sighed. 'You're sort of steadfast . . .'

'Oh, shut up! You'll be telling me I'm a "good sort" next.'

'What I *will* tell you,' said Pamela, suddenly serious, 'is that when I really love a man—if ever I do—I'll be his slave. He'll be able to do anything he likes with me.'

Joan looked at her astonished.

'What a queer primitive thing you are underneath! A squaw! You want to be mastered!'

'Don't you?'

'No, I certainly don't. Companionship, yes. In-love-ness, yes. But not slavery.'

Pamela jumped up as though to shake off the subject.

'Look, my dear,' she said, pointing to a pile of clothes, and other objects, on the sofa. 'I've been having a clearance.' She held up various pairs of battered dancing-slippers. 'Poor little things, don't they look jaded! But they've had a good life—carried me through lots of Hunt balls.'

'I always thought your home-made frocks were prettier than anyone else's bought ones,' Joan said.

'They're not too bad. But don't imagine I'd *touch* a needle if I had any money.' She paused with a frock over her arm, and regarded her friend critically. 'You know, you don't make the best of yourself, my dear.'

'Oh, don't bother me, it's war-time,' said Joan, laughing.

'No excuse! Besides, you never did take enough trouble—too spiritual, I suppose. Now just let me do your hair for you, I've got an idea.'

They spent the next half-hour in hair-dressing, and in discussing the different merits of Pomeroy and Icilma face-creams. (Elizabeth Arden had not arisen in those days.)

Pamela sat in front of the glass, attired in a petticoat and camisole, putting on, at various angles, old hats which had been trimmed and re-trimmed many times. Finally she crammed on a cherry-coloured crinoline straw, pinned its floppy edges, with two fingers, to her cheeks, and turned provocatively to Joan. ' "Tell me, Constance, how do I look this evening? Is there anything whimsical about me? Is it one of my well-looking days, child? Am I in face to-day?" '

But Joan, not having learnt *She Stoops to Conquer*, was unable to answer in the words of the play.

Pamela sprang to her feet. 'As a matter of fact, what I think I really am made for is Musical Comedy—not the "legit" at all. I haven't much voice, but I *can* dance.'

Humming a tune from *The Girl in the Taxi*, she lifted her lovely slim legs and pranced across the room. She still wore the pink hat, and she smiled up at an imaginary gallery.

'Yes, you're an attractive thing,' said Joan, contemplating her. 'Queer how you always make me feel so *solid*. My other friends don't. Lord, that isn't the gong is it? You should have told me the time, Pam. How awful of you to keep me dawdling here!'

She jumped up, and dived down the passage to her room.

'Pamela, I do *wish* you would contrive not *invariably* to be late,' said Mrs. Butler, in an injured voice, as the two girls appeared in the drawing-room, changed and breathless, ten minutes later.

'My fault, I'm afraid,' said Joan, taking the blame with school-girl honourableness.

'Oh, Joan, I'm sure it wasn't, dear.' Mrs. Butler turned on her a semi-sweet smile. 'And it doesn't matter a bit as far as I'm concerned, but Pamela knows quite well that her father hates to be kept waiting.'

Colonel Butler, a spare, parchment-coloured man of mild temper and few words, didn't hate anything much—or love anything much either. A link in a large network of well-connected families, the life in him seemed almost to have petered out. His children had caused him a good deal of worry, especially his son Leo, who was now, however, redeeming himself in Gallipoli. In silent bitterness at having been kept by ill-health from foreign service, Colonel Butler was 'doing his bit' by serving on Red Cross and recruiting committees. He drove himself in and out from Reading every day.

He was courteous to Joan at dinner, as indeed he was to every-one—young or old—who came to the house; but it was up-hill work talking to him. Mrs. Butler gossiped away about the neigh-bours, 'this frightful war,' and what So-and-So had said, who knew So-and-So at the War Office. It was all superficial and life-less, and Joan was relieved when dinner was over. She was relieved when all meals in that house were over, and she could talk and wander about with Pamela.

Their friendship was of long standing, dating back to the time when Pamela, a leggy, turbulent child of ten, had boarded for a year at Joan's Hampstead day-school while her parents were abroad. In spite of the difference in their environments, outlooks and temperaments, the attraction between them was strong. For in youth the character is still liquid in the mould, and differences which later on may harden, and cause separation between friends, are, in the happy 'teens' and 'twenties,' as delicious and har-monious as the varied colours in a bed of flowers.

Joan had always enjoyed coming down to Wallingford, especially in the summer when the garden was full of roses, and the whole Thames valley a sleepy enchantment; but she would have hated to live the sort of life that Pamela did all the year round. Her own relations, of whose intellects she was rather scornful, were lamps of enlightenment beside these dry and faded Butlers and their empty-souled neighbours. She had always encouraged that side of Pamela that wanted to break away, that was enterprising and creative, for she was aware of the seeds of weak will in her mercurial friend.

Pamela had managed to get out of a certain amount of work at

the depôt in order to be with Joan, but on the last morning of
Joan's short stay she felt she had scarcely seen her at all.

'*Don't* go!' she pleaded, childlike. 'Stay a little longer. Ah, *do!*'

Pamela could be very alluring when she pleaded like that, especially when she used the little phrase 'Ah, do!' which Joan remembered of old. She knew how much Pamela enjoyed trying to
make people change their minds—alter their plans—and how
frequently she succeeded, so she had to steel herself.

When she left the house to go back to London she saw for a
moment Pamela's merry slanting eyes look large with loneliness.

.   .   .   .   .   .

Florence Seddon, rather to her surprise, had found Joan looking
so well on her return from France that she concluded the work
must be suiting her. As well as health there was a sort of light in
the girl's face which had not been there since her ardent Suffrage
days.

It was during this leave that Joan got to know the poems of
Rupert Brooke. Colin had told her of them, and now she bought
for herself the little dark '1914' volume, and learnt the war-
sonnets by heart. For a time that shining son of England, who
had died just off Gallipoli a few months ago, became her hero.
He made her feel justified in what she was doing, and set a seal of
nobility upon the war to which a whole side of her hungrily,
gratefully, responded. She realised that these poems would probably be part of the language for ever, but did not realise—could
not at that date—that they might also be beautiful bells ringing
nations to slaughter.

Jimmy, who had spent part of his holidays with a school-friend,
was now at home, and he and Joan had some happy times together.
They practised songs, among them some new ones from 'To-
night's the Night' and 'Push and Go,' of which Jimmy was pro-
foundly contemptuous, but which Joan thought would appeal to
the soldiers. They played energetic singles. They went expeditions into the country.

Joan went over once or twice to the Paleys', and talked to them about Betty and Colin. Mr. Paley listened with bursting eagerness to all she had to say; his wife with an interest more restrained. They were both immensely proud of the letters they were receiving from their son, and Joan allowed them to suppose that her own were not so frequent or so lengthy. She did not enlarge on her meeting with Colin at Ostrohove; merely said that she had thought him looking well and happy. But of Betty, and the way Betty had settled down to the work in Boulogne, she talked with freedom.

August was hot; dear old Hampstead dusty and dead-alive; but Joan enjoyed her leave, and—excited no doubt by the prospect of so soon returning to France—felt an unusually sentimental affection for Beechwood, Aunt Florence, and everything connected with her home.

Chapter Ten

JOAN'S journey back to Boulogne was not the simple affair which she had expected it to be. She discovered at Victoria that the ordinary Channel service was suspended for that week, and that she would have to go by Dieppe. Rather damped, but far from imagining that this would mean more inconvenience than a slightly delayed arrival, she returned home for another night, and set forth again next day, leaving Folkestone at eleven o'clock.

The sea was calm as a silver pond—which was fortunate, as the crossing took six hours, and the ship was packed to suffocation. As soon as she landed at Dieppe she inquired about trains to Boulogne. There were no more that day—the first went at nine the following morning. So there she was, stranded in a foreign town in war-time, and with not an idea where to go. After the first moment's discomfiture she recovered her spirits, and, accompanied by an antique porter trundling her luggage on a barrow, left the wharf and plunged into the town. A narrow little hotel with green shutters, and a fat motherly-looking 'Madame' on its doorstep, attracted her, and she stopped there and inquired about rooms. She was told that there was only one that was empty, 'une toute petite chambre au quatrième.' Having inspected it she settled on it at once. It was indeed 'toute petite'—its available space being almost entirely taken up by the feather bed—but it was clean and had a delicious view over red roofs.

She had dinner downstairs at a long communal table among chattering French people, after which, considerably fortified (for she had had nothing to eat since breakfast), she wandered out into the streets. She looked at the little shops full of carved ivory objects—elephants, pigs, bracelets, boxes—decided that she had not got enough money to spend on souvenirs, and strolled down to the sea-front.

The moon was full, and made a silver pathway on the water. Leaning on the parapet a little way off was a British officer. He looked at the solitary girl gazing seawards, so obviously English in her light dress and jersey, with a book under her arm; wondered whether he would be snubbed if he spoke to her; decided to risk it, and did.

'Lovely night!'

A pair of steady grey eyes were turned on him.

'Lovely.'

Pause. What the hell was she *doing* here then, all by herself at ten o'clock at night, and looking so innocent as that?

'Don't mind my pipe, do you?'

'Not at all.'

But all the same she moved quietly away from him, and sat down on a lamp-lit seat behind, and opened her book. He followed her after a moment, and sat down at the other end.

'Don't mind if I sit here, do you?'

She raised her eyes. 'Why should I mind? These seats are public, I suppose?'

Snub direct, but manner lady-like. He swung his crossed leg, and puffed at his pipe. Never mind—one more shot.

'Interesting book?'

'Very. *Poems of To-day*. Do you know it?'

'Can't say I do. Poems aren't much in my line.'

'This is quite a new anthology. You ought to read it. Modern things. Rather a jolly little one by Rose Macaulay about a sister whose brother has gone to the war, and who is bored at home.'

'Oh? Well, p'raps I'll get it.' Rum girl! He moved a little nearer along the seat.

'I say . . . You're awfully pretty you know. Do you often come out here at this time?'

'No. I'm only passing through. Good-night.'

She was gone.

Up in her little 'quatrième' Joan cursed herself for a fool.

'Of all the feeble efforts!' she snorted. Either you didn't answer at all when spoken to by a strange man on a pier, or else you carried the adventure through. After all what could have happened? It would have been amusing perhaps to see . . . but perhaps, on the other hand, not . . .

Sleep descended on her. The question would never be solved.

At seven o'clock next morning a damsel poked her head in at the door, shouted something, and withdrew on a slam. Not even the tiniest jug of hot water was brought. Joan struggled up and grimly washed in cold. Downstairs she drank a bowl of *café au lait* at a marble-topped table in the bar, in company with two fat Frenchmen who had just returned from bathing. She paid her bill—amounting in all to five francs twenty-five—and then made her way to the station. As there were no available men to take her trunk she carried it herself, assisted by a rosy and powerful female domestic from the hotel, who gabbled the whole way about 'mon mari au front,' and 'cette sacrée guerre.'

After a good deal of fuss over her passport Joan was booked to Eu, where she was told she must change for Boulogne. For two hours she travelled on the hard wooden seats of a third-class carriage crammed with French 'poilus,' and from behind the pages of *Poems of To-day* listened to their conversation. This was carried on without pause, at the tops of their voices, and threw instructive sidelights on the spirit of the 'Entente.' She gathered that the French resented the superior attitude of the British soldiers at the Base towns. 'Ils sont insupportables avec leur petites cannes,' was one of the phrases. They were jealous of their better uniforms, better equipment, better pay, and were firmly convinced that England was going to hang on to all the French coast towns after the war was over. Upon this point Joan was able to reassure them; but although they listened to her with courtesy, their talk became less interesting after she had intervened, and she was rather sorry she had done so.

There was one other woman in the carriage, a sad-looking little Frenchwoman in black. She was going to Boulogne to meet her husband, a sergeant, who had eight days 'permission' from the

Front, and she was already looking forward in despair to the moment of parting from him at the end of that time. She confided to Joan that she was a waitress in a hotel at Trouville, and had been travelling ever since the day before, and was 'terriblement fatiguée.' Train journeys in France were no joke in those days.

At eleven o'clock they arrived at Eu, and were told that the next train to Boulogne didn't start till three-thirty. Joan would have preferred to potter about the town alone, but the little woman suggested so pathetically that they should cling together that it would have been heartless to try and shake her off.

The cool morning had now turned into a noon of blazing heat, and the English girl and her companion wandered about the little dusty streets of Eu, and filled in time as best they could.

It was an unexpected delight to Joan to come upon the old and very beautiful cathedral. She explored it thoroughly, lingering in the quiet gloom among crusaders' tombs, while the Frenchwoman, quite uninterested, waited for her outside.

Left to herself Joan would probably have bought some chocolate and greengages for lunch and taken them to the woods beyond the town; but discovering, remorsefully, that her companion had had nothing to eat since the day before, hurried her to a café, and gave her a *déjeuner* of omelette, veal and red wine. To see the famished creature's appreciation was almost too great a reward for so easy an act of kindness; and the tearful thanks with which Joan was loaded filled her with embarrassment.

Waiting at the little station was like waiting in an oven, but it was pleasant compared with their four-hour journey to Boulogne. This time there were only two soldiers in their compartment; the rest were civilians—all perspiring, spitting freely, and with stomachs of immense proportions. No sooner had the train started than Joan's little friend was telling them all the whole story of her life. The food and wine had loosened her tongue, put colour in her cheeks, and she was hardly recognisable.

The pottering stuffy journey came to an end at last. Joan piled herself, and her luggage, on to a fiacre, wrung the hand of the Frenchwoman—who hovered near her to the last, murmuring: 'Ce repas, Mademoiselle, jamais, jamais je ne l'oublierai,' and rattled off to Temple's.

Oh, it was good to be back again, to be greeted by the beaming Dorcas, and later by the excited girls. The meal that night was a babble of news exchanged, of questions, and of laughter. Everything here was exactly the same, but Joan felt as though she had been away for months.

'I've got precisely half a franc in my purse,' she declared. 'I think on the whole I managed my finances rather cleverly considering I had no idea, when I set out, that I should have to spend a night *en route*! Were you anxious about me, any of you?'

'Not when we got your telegram,' said Barbara, 'though even then we couldn't imagine what you were doing at Dieppe!'

'Oh, Joan, that telegram!' gurgled Betty. 'How we shrieked over it! 'Je me trouve à Dieppe. Revendrai quand pourrai.' So characteristic somehow, and telling us really nothing!'

'It told you all I knew myself,' said Joan, infected by the general amusement.

'Oh, they may laugh now,' put in Miss McNare, nodding from her corner, 'but believe me, Joan, they were worrying over you quite a lot at the time!'

It seemed that things had been very slack during Joan's absence, but that new troops were expected through any day now, and all hands would be wanted. So her return was welcome from every point of view.

Chapter Eleven

BETTY was now firmly established at the Alexandra, and growing to have something of that fondness for it which the others had for the Connaught. Mr. Roscoe, the new and energetic Y.M. secretary who had replaced Mr. Goodge, was enthusiastic in praise of her, and had been heard to say—though the others declared he could only have been joking—that he would trust her with any responsibility.

'I feel as though I had been here years, and that Temple's was my eternal home,' Betty sighed contentedly to Joan. 'I can never be grateful enough to you for making me come out. Without you I should still have been stodgily working for the old W.V.R.'

On Ostrohove mornings Mr. Roscoe would often look in and lend a hand with the rolls (a thing his flabby predecessor had never dreamt of doing), and engage the girls in eager discussion on the conduct of the huts, and on religion and morals in general.

Joan had often wondered whether the little notices hung on the walls of some of the huts with the words: 'Life's Problems. We are always happy to help with these. Please make an appointment for a twenty-minutes talk,' ever had the effect of inducing soldiers to seek spiritual comfort of the Christian in charge. She questioned Mr. Roscoe about it, one morning over roll-buttering, and he was delighted to have the topic raised.

'Of course they do,' he said, fixing his dark gimlet eyes upon her, 'and that side of the Y.M.C.A. work is extraordinarily interesting. If the men meet an understanding mind they derive great benefit from these talks.'

'Yes, if!' said Joan doubtfully. 'But in any case do you think it's possible to discuss a problem of the soul by appointment, for twenty minutes—like booking a game of billiards?'

'Certainly. Why ever not?' Mr. Roscoe looked surprised that it should be considered at all odd. 'I cordially invite *you*, Miss

Seddon, to make an appointment with *me*, at any hour you like, and we'll discuss any subject you like.'

Joan laughed, and said she would certainly do so one of these days—not in order to discuss her own soul's problems, but to hear more of that other side of the men's lives which they didn't show to 'the ladies.'

'Though I should have thought,' she pursued, 'what with the descriptions of trench life which they give us, and the confidences about their families at home, that we knew a good deal about them.'

'You do,' he assured her earnestly. 'Don't for a moment imagine that I underrate your value to the men—it's probably greater than you have any idea of. But they have certain difficulties—religious and otherwise—which you can't be expected to deal with.'

A little later some soldiers at the other end of the tent began singing 'Get Out and Get Under,' one of them thumping the tune on the piano. Joan hummed it under her breath, and slightly swayed her shoulders without pausing in her work.

'Fond of dancing?' Mr. Roscoe shot at her.

'Yes, awfully.'

'Immoral pastime!'

He was usually so broad-minded, and, for a Christian, so un-christian in outlook that she gasped.

'Immoral? What on earth do you mean?'

'Young couples tightly clasped, and gyrating round a ballroom to titillating tunes . . . nothing could be more dangerous, more deplorably enervating.'

Joan took up the cudgels hotly. She declared that dancing was nothing of the kind, but that of course if anyone chose to read disgusting significances into what was merely an innocent exercise . . .

'It's only because you're so innocent yourself that you don't see what I mean,' he interrupted.

'But, good heavens . . . !' She turned to Betty, who was

methodically buttering rolls, and had so far not joined in the argument. 'Isn't it an astonishing point of view?'

Betty raised her lashes. 'We-ell—no-o,' she drawled in her thick attractive voice. 'Dancing *is* immoral, of course, but . . .'

'What?' Joan dropped her knife.

'But it's so delightful,' Betty pursued, 'that one deliberately puts aside any other aspect of it.'

'*Well!*'

'There—you see?' said Mr. Roscoe, in triumph, to the temporarily knocked-out Joan. 'Your friend, Miss Paley, has a much better-trained mind than you have, and she has exactly stated the case.'

Betty was teased a good deal, after that, about her 'better-trained mind.'

'Perfectly true, of course,' said Joan. 'But at the same time you're so sleepily and dewily lovely in the early mornings, darling, that better men than Roscoe might tend to confuse your mental with your physical endowments!'

.   .   .   .   .   .

Through the dim gold autumn days Kitchener's 3rd Army streamed into France. Joan and Betty declared—and Colin in his letters agreed with them—that their dear France looked lovelier and more characteristic at this time than at any other, with her waving yellow poplars, and the mists that lay along her flat fields and slow canals.

'Of course France was never decadent,' wrote Colin, 'but there is something in the autumn air which seems to suit her—a gentle and courtly decay. Claude Lorraine knew it, though he never painted France. Far behind the lines, where I now am, in the silence of ruined châteaux and villages, I love her more than ever.'

But he gave other pictures. In the trenches the rats were becoming a pest. They ran over the faces of the men at night. He had furiously shot, with his revolver, at the silhouettes of six fat monsters trotting in file along the parapet. They had been having a lot of shelling. Joan got the impression that Colin was entirely fearless. He always seemed to be crawling out on his stomach in the moonlight—undertaking difficult and tiresome jobs. His descriptions were vivid. Betty, who to a large extent shared her brother's letters to Joan, got all the news she wanted of him that way. 'More than I should ever get if I were alone!' she said.

He was enthusiastic over his men. 'Some of them will, if we survive, be friends of mine for life. I shall never quite lose touch with them.'

Then the tone changed.

'We have had some horrible casualties lately. A sergeant and a corporal of mine died in a dressing-station, a few hours after they were hit. I was with them at the time. I will spare you a description of what I saw of the ghastly condition of these men. The sergeant, an invaluable fellow, is a married man with five children. One cannot really get used to these things. I wish sometimes one had the particular grim brand of humour that the Tommy has. This is what I overheard my servant saying to his friend after a good dose of trench-mortars: "D'ye know what them letters means they puts on Tommy's grave? You know—R.I.P.?" "Well?" rejoined his pal suspiciously. "Ripped in pieces, of course," came the ready reply. (All that could be found of one of our men not long ago was buried in a mess-tin.)

'Please don't bother to answer these letters. They are not written to be answered. I just feel I *must* write and tell you things.'

.   .   .   .   .   .

With the shortening days expeditions into the country were gradually abandoned. The girls went one dripping walk into the woods and meadows of Hardelot, but they were rather sorry they had come. It was essentially a place of summer, and best left to summer memories.

It was dark now, getting up in the early mornings to go to Ostro-hove; in fact quite often the moon was still shining. The men marched off in the mist—huge eerie figures. The sudden thought struck Joan that for many of these men she and Betty and Barbara were the last Englishwomen they would ever see.

The huts in the town became more and more crowded. Indoor games were organised. Concert succeeded concert.

Joan, at this period, took charge of the small library at the Connaught, and tried to start a 'higher literature' campaign. She pressed Kipling and Dickens, instead of their favourites Garvice and Zane Grey, upon the unprotesting soldiers—with occasionally quite satisfactory results.

She scattered about the hut, and enclosed with letters to her Tommy friends at the Front, specimens of *The Times* Broadsheets. These were selected passages from the English classics, suitable for soldiers, and arranged in a portable form. They were done by Sir Walter Raleigh, and issued by *The Times* in envelopes of six. Philip Nichol, who had told her of them, had warned her that their level was more for officers, though here and there among the ranks they might be of interest.

The two outstanding comments Joan received on them were hardly encouraging.

In a letter from one of her favourite soldiers, in which he thanked her profusely for a parcel of food she had sent him, was the following:

'Thanks very much too for *The Times* Broadsheets. I took them into the field with me. I wonder if any of you can half realise what it is like on a battle-field; to put it mildly it is Blue Hell, and I am sorry to say the Broadsheets did not help a bit. You cannot very well think of these matters when you have your bayonet halfway through a German, we only see Red and smell it too and even do not have time to think, we just go forward till we meet and then the fun begins.'

He enclosed, as a souvenir, some tiny yellow flowers he had picked a few yards behind the firing-line.

Little Hinkley disposed of the Broadsheets in a less crushing manner, but he was more bewildered by them.

'I would have done a war-dance,' he wrote, 'when I received your letter, if it had not meant my head above the parapet to be shot at. I see tobacco has gone up now. I think it is a great pity as every Tommy likes his smoke, but no one more than I, and my poor old Mother cannot afford to send me any now. The next time you write please explain what those papers are for—you know, *The Times* Broadsheets—as I cannot make out what they mean. It is not because I am dull of apprehension but I will let you know what I thought they were when I write again which will not be long hoping God spares me to do so.'

Joan couldn't imagine what the poor man supposed them to be for, until Betty, choking with laughter, suggested an explanation. 'Either for *that*, or for shaving papers!' she said.

'Betty! And you a college-bred woman!' gasped Joan, joining in the laughter. 'Aren't you appalled at such a use for the Higher Literature?'

'Not at all. I don't see to what better use literature could possibly be put in the trenches.'

After that the Broadsheets campaign was pursued with a lighter touch.

At concerts too it was much the same. Joan had made a definite bid to gain response to 'good' songs, and even to recitations from Shakespeare, but the courteously unenthusiastic way in which they were received soon caused her to drop them completely in favour of musical-comedy and revue stuff, which always went with a roar.

The treacly 'Blue Eyes' from 'Push and Go,' which she and Jimmy had laughed over in the holidays, was the most popular of all.

> 'Blue eyes, true eyes,
> Ever I'm thinking of you;
> Blue eyes, true eyes,
> *With*out you *what* should I do-oo?'

She threw into its dragging intervals all the fervour of which she was capable, and its success was so terrific that almost always there were two or three soldiers round her at the end of the concert asking her when she would be singing it again. A certain sentimental Canadian, who was particularly devoted, implored her, with tears in his eyes, to write out the words so that he might have them with him in the trenches as a remembrance of the song, and of her.

.   .   .   .   .   .

One evening, as they were standing together behind the counter during a temporary lull, Barbara asked Joan in a casual way whether the Y.M.C.A. life completely satisfied her.

'How curious you should ask that!' said Joan, withdrawing her eyes from the groups of sitting soldiers in the smoke-filled hut, and fixing them on her friend. 'Do I appear restless or discontented, then?'

'You don't *appear* so in the least, but I've a feeling that you are, underneath—because, you see . . . I am a little myself.'

They then confessed to each other that they had both been worried lately by the idea that they ought to take up nursing. This work was all very well—useful, and delightful, and in no sense 'cushy,' but they knew that the need for workers was greater in the hospitals than in the huts.

'Damn! that settles it then,' said Joan. 'I hadn't quite made up my mind before, but now I shall send in my resignation, and leave before Christmas.'

Barbara said that she wasn't going to do anything quite so drastic as that.

'I've got one of my funny intuitions, which you always laugh at, Joany, that I must stay on here a bit longer—I couldn't tell you why. But sooner or later I shall have to go and nurse.'

.   .   .   .   .   .

Early in December Colin wrote that he had been given leave, and was going to spend the first two nights of it in Boulogne. Betty booked a room for him at the Folkestone Hotel.

When the night came for his arrival, both girls went down to meet the leave-train, and on the dark and windy quay they waited for him in varying degrees of emotion.

'I'm glad you're with me,' said Joan, squeezing her friend's arm. 'It makes it somehow more everyday-ish. Oh, I do hope he won't . . .'

Betty encouraged her. 'You've only got to remember what he's been through, poor boy, and be nice to him. No need to wind yourself up and get bothered.'

Caked with mud, and looking gigantic in his British Warm, and haversack, Colin came towards them through the surge of leave-men.

Voice, smile—everything about him—was quiet and controlled. 'Betty!'

'Hallo, old boy!' They kissed.

'Joan!' A handshake and a long look.

They made their way to the Folkestone together, and the girls sat at his table while he had a small late meal; but his tiredness and the strange delight of seeing them prevented his either eating or talking very much. Joan felt an unusual shyness, and because of the circumstances was inclined to be in awe of him. True he was his dear gentle self, but as well as that he represented to her, just then, all the gallant, overworked and trench-weary subalterns of the B.E.F. He was a piece of that dark background of mud and khaki, in front of which she and her like spun their days in safety, and from which he had been flung forth for a little while— curiously, romantically, miraculously *here*.

But Betty's presence helped to link them together, and to keep the atmosphere normal. She questioned him about his journey, and pattered gently on about her own daily life at the hut. When they left she told him with sisterly firmness to go straight to bed, and to have his sleep out in the morning.

'Perhaps I shan't be able to sleep at all in a *bed*,' he smiled, as he saw them out on their way back to Temple's.

Joan tried to analyse the subtle change in his appearance. He looked fit; but the particular soft glowing look, which was almost as much a characteristic of his face as it was of Betty's, had be-come dimmed and hardened. A film of dust, either actual or imagined, seemed to lie across the features. The war was obliterating boyhood.

They divided Colin's day in Boulogne between them—unequally, but, with regard to the circumstances, fairly. Betty arranged to take the morning off from the Alexandra, and Joan had no difficulty in getting the whole afternoon and evening off from the Connaught.

This second meeting of Colin's and Joan's in France contrasted oddly with their first. Then it had been under the morning sun of May, when the world was a lyric of white and green, and he was just going out. Now the trees stretched naked arms against a leaden sky, and he had *been* out, and knew.

They went for a wintry walk round the ramparts of the Hauteville. Joan found her shyness vanishing, and during their ramble told him everything she could think of to amuse him—anecdotes about the Christians, about the Tommies, about her concerts, and details of her leave in England, of her people and of his. They discussed modern poetry, and soon it was almost as though he had never been away.

Then she took him back to tea at Temple's. They had the little red sitting-room to themselves, and Dorcas, with a twinkle in her eye, assured them that they wouldn't be disturbed. Dorcas was always delighted if any of her young ladies showed signs of having a romance. She was all for matrimony—in spite of her own single state, and the quarrelsome example she had continuously before her of her sister and brother-in-law below.

Colin talked disjointedly, but quite tranquilly, about the war. He said that in a way he was enjoying it—it was such a test of hitherto unused powers.

'Except now and then,' he added, 'when the mask seems suddenly to be removed, and one sees it in its reality. The trouble is that once one is safe in billets, one's real feelings are almost entirely forgotten. That's the trouble—and I'm as bad as the rest. I think people with shell-shock see things in a truer light than is commonly supposed.'

'But what a mercy that the sane men *do* forget!' said Joan. 'I suppose it's something like that saying in the Bible about a woman having a baby, "but as soon as she is delivered of the child she remembereth no more the anguish." '

'Yes . . . something like that.'

'Curious how differently people take the war,' she mused. 'There's my cousin Jack, for instance. He writes quite gaily. Doesn't seem really to mind it—not in the deeper sense. Whereas another man I know, Philip Nichol, although he writes bravely enough, genuinely loathes the whole business. It sickens him, soul and body. He's always harking back to life before the war.'

'Was that the man you wrote to me about who suddenly turned up with a moustache, and whom you went a walk with?' asked Colin.

'Yes. You met him at home, didn't you? But I'd forgotten I'd mentioned him in a letter.'

'*I'd* not forgotten,' said Colin with a hovering smile. 'I was a bit jealous of him, you see. In fact I wondered terribly for a few days whether he was *the* man! Of course,' he hurried on, 'it's none of my business to wonder anything . . . "Save where you are how happy you make those." '

She gazed at him, melted.

"Oh, Colin,' she broke out, 'you are a beautiful person! You're so unpossessive and generous. But, my dear, you've no need at all to be jealous. I don't love Philip—or anyone else.'

But mixed with her genuine gratitude to him, and her appreciation of his delicacy, was a slender thread of disappointment that he did not show more possessiveness, that he did not—in all senses—grab hold of her and shake her into feeling she was his.

As he was silent she went on: 'Do you really think about me so much then, Colin? I had somehow imagined that . . . with everything out there . . . you wouldn't have time.'

He looked at her with the old look in his eyes—that look of adoring tenderness.

'I think of you more and more,' he said. 'In fact I think of little else in my quite lone moments. But you are always *there*, you know—sometimes fainter, sometimes vivider, according to happenings.'

'Colin dear . . .' Her voice was husky. She cleared it, and began again, speaking in jerks. 'Colin . . . I will be engaged to you . . . if you'd really like me to be . . . but I'm not a bit worthy of you.'

There was a silence, while the preposterous ormolu clock on the marble mantelpiece ticked away the seconds.

When she looked at him again she saw that his face wore the smile of one who repudiates a long-hoped-for prize, or who gives a new lease of life to a too-easily surrendered foe.

'No, you darling, I can't take you like that—it would be too unfair—I've too many advantages at the moment. I'm war-be-glamoured. You're sorry for me. You even feel more tenderly towards me than you ever have before, but . . . you're not in love with me.'

If there was the smallest fleeting hope that he might be miraculously contradicted it was quenched by her silence, and by the sad honesty of her eyes.

He came over and sat beside her on the little sofa, and put an arm round her.

'Could you—do you think—give me a kiss?' he asked

She raised her lips and gravely pressed them to his brown cheek. It was like kissing a very dear brother. In fact she experienced less feeling over it than when she gave Jimmy one of her impulsive embraces.

It told Colin all he wanted to know. The time was not yet. Doubtless he was unwise not to make better use of the present, but that would have required more skill than he possessed, and a different character. It was only when he was out of her presence that he felt himself really enterprising.

He sat now in quiet uncraving happiness just to feel her head

upon his shoulder, like a little sister's. He deserved no more—
had hardly hoped for as much.

The clock ticked on. They talked. She told him of her nursing
plan, of which he approved in theory, while expressing a hope
that she wouldn't be sent on foreign service. But foreign service,
she told him, was just what she wanted, as it meant greater
opportunities—harder work.

'Insatiable little war-worker, aren't you!' he smiled at her.

They agreed that it was sickening that their leaves hadn't coin-
cided, that they weren't both going home together now. Colin
was very rueful about it. The usual war-luck!

They had dinner at the Folkestone; and later Betty joined them,
and Colin ordered more wine, and on the whole it was quite
a merry meal. The girls saw him off on the night-boat to
England.

'I suppose I ought to be enjoying my leave,' he wrote a few days
later, 'but a blankness has fallen around me. I would rather be
fighting in France where you are, than be comfortable in England
where you are not. I find it difficult to keep my feet from straying
over the Heath to Beechwood. But I don't intend—and you
wouldn't wish me—to give in to the blankness, to let a numbed
feeling develop into that spiritual paralysis which is chiefly the
product of self-pity. I need no pity—least of all my own. No
one who has received what I have received from you, during the
past year, needs pity.'

He barely saw her on his return to France ten days later. His
mother had not been well, or he would have tried, he said, to get
away sooner. Yes, he had seen a few 'shows,' a few friends, but
England was not a cheering place just now.

.   .   .   .   .   .

Exactly forty-eight hours after Colin was back in the line Joan
was spending her last evening at the Connaught.

Betty and Barbara, Mr. Roscoe, Miss MacNare, Dorcas, and all
her friends—but Betty of course especially—were acutely depressed at her going. Joan herself hated it. She knew how much

she would miss the life here, the men tramping into the hut and talking to her over the counter, the concerts, the freedom, the friendly family atmosphere at Temple's. But it was no use thinking of all that. She had made her decision, and was anxious now to start that other life.

The men had known for a week that she was leaving, and on this last night they were particularly endearing. One of them, a Scotch corporal, got up and made a speech in the name of them all—quite unexpectedly to Joan—saying how sorry they all were that she was going, and how different the hut would be without her. Joan was overwhelmed; and, feeling that she must make some sort of a reply, struggled on to the platform. It was awful. There she was, quite alone at the end of the hut, addressing the attentive khaki crowd in a voice which she hardly recognised as her own, and with knees that trembled under her. She scarcely knew what she said—something to the effect that only the great and growing need for nurses at home would have made her leave them, and that she would keep them constantly in her thoughts. A warm roar greeted her as she finished; and Barbara at the counter assured her—which she found it hard to believe—that her every word had been distinct and clear.

With a heavy heart she fried eggs, and sold cigarettes for the last time; and at nine o'clock all her favourite Tommies came along to say good-bye, and gripped her hand so that she felt she had hardly a bone left in it.

The girls sat beside her as she packed. At the bottom of her trunk were two boot-bags full of souvenirs, given her at different times by friendly soldiers; bullets, bits of shell, and tunic-buttons; cap badges, and shoulder-badges from every regiment in the British Army. Strange tokens of regard which Joan treasured for the spirit of their givers.

1915, that year of radiant hopes, was almost over; and in France the position was still unchanged, and Gallipoli had just been evacuated. There was personal comfort, however, in the knowledge that both Pamela's brother and Barbara's fiancé had escaped from the peninsula alive, and that the immortal '29th' to which they both belonged was being sent, for a time, to Egypt.

Joan crossed on the following day, in a grey gale of wind, in a shipful of home-going soldiers. The little group of friends who were seeing her off from the quay were soon obliterated from sight by the spray of the heaving waves.

PART TWO

1916

'*We were not all unkind, nor all deserve*
The common stroke of war.'

Chapter One

THE Christmas pudding had been removed, and the dining-room table at Beechwood was a glinting litter of crimson and yellow and blue. Chairs were no longer facing foodwards, but were drawn back at various angles, and their occupants were crowned with preposterous paper caps. The warm air quivered with shouts of laughter, and with the sharp little bangs of crackers.

Robert Seddon, a tall purple mitre on his head, continued to peel walnuts in unassailable dignity. Florence, completely given over to the spirit of the occasion, looked rosily out from a vast sunbonnet which became her extraordinarily well. Rose darted her bird-like eyes and twittered her amiabilities from under a flaming cap of French Revolution fashion. And all the younger Seddons —Joan, Jimmy, Jack, Babs and Bill—were in various ways transformed.

In addition to the family there were three other people at the party: the Podberrys, a benign and elderly couple of straitened means, who lived close to, and had known Florence since her girlhood; and a speechless school-friend of Jimmy's called Wirebush—younger than Jimmy by a year and a half, and humbly and doggedly devoted to him. Nobody could quite understand why Jimmy brought him home when he had so many more attractive friends, for Wirebush's shyness and *gaucherie* were so overwhelming that it was almost a penance to have him in the house. Compared with him Jimmy was a dashing man of the world; and it was rather amusing to see the way he looked after the gaunt little boy—firmly arranging the ties that *would* climb up above the collars, seeing that he brushed his hair, and that he appeared more or less punctually for meals. The point of Wirebush, as far as Jimmy was concerned, was his terrific mathematical brain. Jimmy was a mathematician himself, but apparently not in the same street with Wirebush. 'Of course he's a hopeless fellow in company,' Jimmy would say, 'but when he's alone with me you can think how interesting he is.' That, of course, had to be taken on trust, but it was clear that the two boys had much to give one another. And if Joan thought that the giving was mostly on her brother's side, it was with secret joy at that quality in him which could be bothered with the awkward and the friendless creatures of this world—a quality which she often wished were more developed in herself.

There was a tremendous noise going on at the moment, for Bill had just unrolled a paper suit of pink pyjamas from his cracker, and was putting them on. With one leg out and one leg in he hopped round the table, shouting that he was going to sleep in them to-night, that they would be quite as warm as his own cellular pyjamas, which in any case were hateful and let the fleas in.

'Oh, stow that row, young 'un!' cried Jack. 'Joan, listen to this!' And leaning forward with a grin on his engaging face he read aloud a cracker motto.

> ' "Cupid shoots his little arrows from your soft grey eyes;
>   If I long to kiss you, darling, can you be surprised?" '

Gosh, what a rhyme! Very suitable sentiment though. Small wedding-ring enclosed.'

'Oh, Jack, let *me* have the wedding ring,' called Babs, 'do let me!'

'What do you want with a wedding-ring?' asked her brother. 'You're far too young.'

'But I want to be married! I should adore to be married!'

'Why, Babs?' came an amused chorus.

'Because then I could have stacks of babies.'

'Do you *want* stacks of babies?'

'Yes, I do. Molly doesn't, though. She wants to be a king's mistress. She says king's mistresses don't have babies.'

In the midst of the varying exclamations which greeted this

announcement, Uncle Robert cleared his throat and rose to his feet with a port glass.

'Oh, Lord!' breathed Jimmy with a despairing glance at his sister.

'I want to propose a toast,' began Robert. 'Happily our own family is all assembled and safe this Christmas-time. But there are others who are not so fortunate—whose Christmas is bound to be a mournful one. Many of us had hoped that by now, the end of 1915, the war would be over. As it is, we can only continue to keep up our spirits and to hope—er—to hope . . .'

Jack, with a hand over his eyes, murmured: 'Draw it mild, Pater.'

'To hope that by next Christmas it actually *will* be,' finished Robert on a rush, and raised his port glass.

'To our brave lads in the trenches—of all ranks!'

The toast was silently, and rather uncomfortably drunk. Then Jack sprang to his feet, and cried: 'And now for an old one! Come on everybody!

> "Here's a health to all those that we love,
> Here's a health to all those that love us,
> Here's a health to all those
> Who love them that love those
> Who love *them* that love *those* that love us!" '

The last line was joined in by the entire party—the children's voices rising to a shout at the final 'us.' After which, on a wave of good spirits, they all poured out and into the drawing-room.

A charade was suggested.

'Oh, *do,* dear!' said the Podberrys, blinking affectionately at Joan. 'You're so good at them. Your charades are always among our most entertaining memories.'

'Oh, yes, Joan—a charade!' clamoured the children.

Jack declared that on this occasion he was going to sit with the 'grown-ups' and watch.

'But you're only let off because you're on leave from France,'

said Joan, 'and are supposed to be an officer and a gentleman!
Even then I think it's rather mouldy of you.'

Out in the hall the acting group was joined by Molly Paley, who,
released from a rather dull Christmas at her own home, had come
over to Beechwood to join in whatever fun might be going on
there.

After a good deal of discussion the word 'Wipers' was decided
on. It was acted in dumb-show, each letter being taken as the
initial of some famous person's name.

'W' was, inevitably, Kaiser Wilhelm.

'I' was Iphigenia.

In this scene, Agamemnon (Jimmy) paced the shores of Aulis,
and scanned the horizon with knitted brow. Realising at last that
there was only one course to be pursued, he sent for Iphigenia
(Joan) and informed her in a series of dramatic gestures that the
gods demanded her in sacrifice. She knelt, she implored, but he
remained inexorable. The priest Calchas was sent for, and entered
in the form of Wirebush clad in one of Florence's voluminous
nightgowns, and holding a carving-knife. Iphigenia was then led
to the altar, round which stood a weeping chorus, laid herself
upon it, and stretched her throat to the knife. There was a pause,
during which a fierce whisper was heard from Agamemnon, 'Go
on, go on, you ass!' and the wretched Calchas, thus adjured, lifted
his arm and brought down the carving-knife. 'Now you can
clear off,' he was told, *sotto voce*; and stumbling on his long robe
he made for the door. The next moment Agamemnon had
stooped over his dead daughter, lifted her high in his arms and
carried her away.

'My goodness, Jim-pot, I didn't know you were going to do
that!' gasped Joan, as she was put on to her feet again in the
hall.

'Sudden inspiration,' said Jimmy, laconically. 'How else was
corpse to be removed from stage?'

'Oh, it was very effective!' she laughed.

But what had really struck her—with a sort of alarmed delight—

was the strength of her brother's arms; those arms which only yesterday had been the thin little arms of a Preparatory Schoolboy. He had picked her up as though she had been a feather. Never had he had occasion to carry her before, and up till that moment—so conservative are early impressions—she would more easily have imagined herself carrying *him*. It was a significant realisation—this of his physical manhood—and one which long afterwards she was vividly to recall.

The next scene, 'P,' represented the judgment of Paris.

'E' was the Princess Eleanor sucking the poison from her husband's wound in Palestine. Molly, this time, had the leading rôle, and she played it with an intensity that was almost disturbing in so young a girl, and indicated either an incipient actress or an incipient lover. Her performance was all the more creditable that she had to play with the unresponsive and embarrassed Wirebush.

'You might have given me Jimmy!' she whispered tearfully to Joan in the hall afterwards. 'Or at least Bill. That boy's *hopeless!*'

The last two scenes were Richard III murdering the little princes in the Tower; and the dying Sir Philip Sidney.

The whole word 'Wipers' was played by a single character— Bill's terrier-pup, who happened to bear that name. He was brought out of the vestibule, where he had been lying all evening, angelically, on his master's coat, and was pushed in at the drawing-room door. The cries of 'Wipers!' which greeted his appearance were sufficient to enlighten those who had not yet guessed the word.

After the company had been congratulated the gramophone was turned on in the hall, and there was dancing.

Joan did her best with Wirebush, but finding that he genuinely hated dancing she abandoned him to a comfortable chair where he sat—far happier—with Wipers in his arms.

While dancing, or rather galloping, with Bill, Joan noticed Molly with Jimmy, and thought how nice they looked. Molly's glowing little face and tawny head were about on the level of her partner's chest, but she danced with a grown-up dignity. The

four years' difference in their ages—a difference now immense—
would later on dwindle to nothing. 'Funny if it were to be me
and Colin, and Jimmy and Molly,' she thought. 'The families
would be doubly-linked.' But it was the merest feather of a
thought, and it floated away as Jack came up to claim her. Jack
was the best dancer she knew, and even at a small impromptu hop
in the hall he had to be concentrated on.

Sitting half-way up the stairs, a little later, they chattered away
companionably.

'The bore about the Pater,' confided Jack, 'is that he insists on
my talking to him about the war. Thinks I'm a sort of authority
on it. Well, I don't mind the bally old war, but what I do bar is
having to give my views on it. As if I *had* any views, good Lord!
I say he'd much better take those of *The Times*. I feel a perfect
fool being talked to as though I were Kitchener or Douglas Haig.
The actual amusing or disgusting details of trench life I couldn't
tell the Pater at all—the war's too sacred to him.'

Joan asked about Jack's friends in the regiment.

'Oh, they're still alive and kicking,' he replied. 'Maurice went
home with a wound in the arm, but it was nothing much, and he's
back again now. Dear old Brab carries stolidly on. You remember little Ginger?'

'Rather!'

'Well, he's justified his name all right. I thought he would.
Nothing can quench him. And his command of language! Simply
curses his men at times. But looks after them too like a mother,
and they'd follow him anywhere.'

'What was he before the war?' asked Joan. 'I gather he wasn't
up at Cambridge?'

'No, and he's got a perfectly unreasonable sort of admiration for
us because we were. Awful rot, of course. His father was an
auctioneer in Ealing, and he was educated at a Grammar School
and the London University. Was going to be an engineer. Awfully clever in his own line, I believe. Got an old mother who
adores him, and to whom he's devoted.'

'I like him,' said Joan. 'And I like your enthusiasm for him. Bring him here some day.'

'If we're ever both in England together I will, but he'd probably expire of shyness. He says 'ladies' always paralyse him. . . . *You* mightn't, though.'

Friends and cousins departed at last. Christmas Day was over. It had been a happy one for the Seddons.

. . . . . .

Joan had entered her name on the Red Cross lists at Devonshire House for service in a military hospital at home or abroad, and, while waiting to be called up, spent her afternoons at a small V.A.D. hospital in Hampstead. Here she peeled potatoes, cut stacks of bread-and-butter, laid the men's tea, waited on them while they had it, and washed up afterwards.

It was a gloomy winter, that second of the war. Everyone was economising in coal. At Beechwood the drawing-room and dining-room were scarcely used; the family had meals in the hall, and gathered afterwards round the anthracite stove. Guests, when they came, brought their knitting and departed early. Everywhere—in buses, trains and homes—'socks for soldiers' were being furiously knitted.

Letters from the Front were full of the frightful weather conditions. Trenches were a swampy or a freezing hell. Colin wrote that one of the men in his battalion had been drowned. Pumps were working all day, but could only just keep pace with the continual flow from above. The work of trench repairing was endless. Yet in the midst of all this physical wretchedness he could still write to her sweetly.

Towards the end of January Joan received, within a few days of each other, a letter from Philip Nichol and a letter from Jack. One man had lost a brother, the other a friend.

Philip's note was characteristic. He gave her the brief information with scarcely a comment. 'My brother was in a distant part of the line. I hadn't seen him for six months. It appears that he rallied his men three times before he was killed. I was very fond of him; I suppose I must be proud. But the whole business is a wasteful farce. Here things go on much as usual. I'm commanding my company and have only one other officer left. Excuse the filthy state of this paper, but the roof of my dug-out has ceased to be weather-proof. I wish I were coming out to call at Beechwood next Sunday. It was a good world before the war. Please write to me.'

Jack's letter, on the other hand, was so unlike him that it made Joan shiver. 'I am full of black hate,' he wrote, 'for last night old Brab was killed by a German sniper. You know how thick we were at Cambridge, and how frightfully I have admired him since. He was my best friend, and now he is dead. He never recovered consciousness, thank God, and I was with him when he died. Till now I never hated the Germans, but now it gives me a savage joy to hear our shells bursting in their lines, and to hope that they too are losing friends as I have lost mine. I shall never feel happy till I have taken at least ten lives for his, or have been killed myself. It seems monstrous that a man like Brab—brave and unselfish and clean-living—should be killed, while wasters and swine live.'

That the amiable, unimaginative Jack should have been shaken into writing like this showed what a shock he had undergone. The horror of the war had got hold of him in the only way it could have got hold of him—through personal loss. Poor Jack! He who, with all his limitations, so generously loved his friends.

'When the Birds Began to Sing!' The ridiculous tune, to which she had danced with Brab, came into her mind, 'Wasn't—that a —funny—thing.' . . . Oh, frightfully funny! Brab . . . Cambridge . . . Ostrohove . . .

But there was worse news to follow—or rather news which affected her more closely. A week later she received the following letter from Betty in Boulogne.

'I was going to write to you anyhow to-night about poor Barbara. She heard yesterday that her brother David had been killed. She went home to-day, and you can imagine I am miserable. She found the telegram when she came in from a drive in the afternoon. I wasn't there, but they came and fetched me from the hut. She was awfully brave about it—as of course she would be. Did I tell you that David came down here for a day and a night a little while ago? And we three had such a nice time together, and he didn't seem depressed about going back. Nice sweet David. One can't associate these boys with dying—it's no good. Do you really believe that it was us that went to Mayweek, and worked and played in London? Because I don't. I think it was some people that I read about in a book once.'

David dead too! David who had come that sunset drive with them last summer to Montreuil . . . David, the apple of Barbara's eye.

Joan wrote to Barbara somehow—crying over it—and a few days later had a reply. The last part ran:

'Our dear Betty was just an angel, and did everything for me. That telegram . . . Only now and then do I realise that he is gone for ever. I've just got to bear it. I believe in God. I believe this war is right. What's the good of faith if it fails one in a time like this? But oh, he was such a dear, and I was so proud of him. He turned to me for everything. Now I know why I couldn't leave Boulogne when you did, Joany. It was for this—to see David once again. Now I am going to nurse. There is nothing to keep me any more. I want to nurse hard, hard, hard—and, with the top of myself at any rate, forget.'

That evening Robert happened to drop in—as he often did on his way back from the office—to have a few words with his sister. Joan was sitting, subdued and listless, in a corner.

'Yes,' said Robert, standing with legs apart before the stove, 'as I was only saying to Burchington at lunch, we live in wonderful times! I wouldn't have missed them for anything. To see the way the old country has risen makes one proud—proud. . . .

We were only wishing we belonged to the younger generation, and could take an active part.' He cast an affectionate, half-envious glance at Joan. 'It's you young ones who are having the opportunities.'

She raised blank eyes on him and said:

'Do you think so, Uncle?'

'Well, don't you think so yourself? Aren't you glad to be of an age to do your bit—you and your friends? To bear such a splendid burden, to—to . . .'

Suddenly Joan cut in. She could bear it no longer. Her lassitude slipped from her, and she felt as though a fiery snake were uncoiling itself in her stomach and darting from her mouth.

'No, I'm *not* glad!' she cried. 'I think it's utterly damnable to be young at this particular time of history. The "splendid burden" as you call it will break us before we're through. Everybody we care for is being killed every minute, and you can stand pompously there—your own son at the Front—and talk about the luck of our generation! It makes me sick. If I had my way I'd put every man over fifty into the trenches, and every woman over fifty into the hospitals, and let them get on with it. They've had their lives. We're only beginning ours. If the beastly war has got to be gone through with, then it's got to. We're not going to shirk it. But for the Lord's sake don't pretend to *envy* us!'

Her voice suddenly became high and broken. The back of her hand went to her mouth and she ran quickly upstairs.

'Florence—dear! What's the matter with her?' asked the bewildered Robert. 'What have I said?'

'Don't worry, Bob,' said his sister soothingly. 'She's a bit overwrought. She's had a good deal of bad news lately. Nothing personal, but her friends have suffered, and she can't be expected to take a broad view of the war at the moment.'

'Well,' said Robert, 'I'm extremely sorry to have upset her. But what an outburst! You don't think, Florrie,' he continued, as he was putting on his coat in the vestibule, 'that she's turning *pacifist,* do you? But, no, no—that's absurd. "Overwrought," as you say. She's only a girl after all.'

. . . . . .

The weeks dragged on. Joan went daily to her work. In her off-times she read *War and Peace, The Idiot, Crime and Punishment, The Way of All Flesh,* and waited impatiently to be called up.

Chapter Two

AFTER a time she was moved from the kitchens into the wards. Her hours were now from seven in the morning till two in the afternoon. She was glad to be in closer contact with the men, but even here, in the wards, she was almost more of a housemaid than of a nurse. It was an unexciting and not very strenuous life—the men were mostly convalescent—but she knew she was only marking time, and meanwhile she learnt everything she could.

The other V.A.D. in her ward was a girl called Phyllis Shirley, known among her intimates as 'Thrush.' Joan was not an intimate, but as soon as she heard of the pet name she had laughingly begged to be allowed to use it—it so exactly fitted the large brown eyes and soft round form of its owner. Miss Shirley was delighted, for she had from the beginning conceived an admiration for Joan—none the less deep because it was tinged by a faint contempt. She herself, in spite of her mere nineteen years, considered that she knew far more about 'life' than Joan did. She was an artist; had trained at the Slade; racketed about in a Bohemian set; painted rather advanced still-life pictures; posed as a model; and had her wings singed in more than one love affair, while managing rather miraculously to preserve her virtue, and to live on the tiny allowance made to her by an old aunt in the country.

Thrush Shirley was rather a surprising type to find in a hospital, and the reason she first gave to Joan for being in one at all—namely, that she felt she must 'do something about the war'—was somehow not quite convincing. Later on, as intimacy grew, the real reason transpired, which was that a few months ago she had become engaged.

'The best boy in the world,' she confided to Joan in her husky little voice. 'Never met anyone to touch him. Oh, he's my "one-and-only!"' Met at a party when he was on leave. Both fell for each other. Got engaged on the third day after, but by then his leave was almost up. We're going to get married when he next comes home. Oh, he's straight, is Ginger—the kind to keep a girl straight too. And what's more he's a jolly good officer, in a jolly good regiment. So, you see, what with one thing and another, I felt I had to try and live up to him. Didn't want to go on living the same old life, in the same old way, with him in the trenches. Asked him what I could do, and he got me taken on here—where he happened to know the M.O. Personally I loathe the whole beastly war, and I'm not doing this job out of any high-falutin' patriotic motives like you people, but just for Ginger's sake—to be more worthy of him. See what I mean?'

Joan saw. But what she immediately asked, at the end of this pelting confidence, was the name of 'Ginger's' regiment.

'Oh, didn't I tell you? The 7th K.R.R.'s.'

Somehow she had known what the reply would be. But of all extraordinary coincidences! Thrush's fiancé was the same Ginger who was Jack's friend.

The discovery caused much excitement, and drew the girls at a bound closely together. Thrush couldn't get over the fact that not only was her man in the same regiment as Joan's cousin, but that Joan had actually met him. She wanted to know just what impression he had made upon her. And then all at once—as Joan was relating the meeting in France her excitement subsided, her dark eyebrows drew sullenly together, and she began to make explanations about Ginger—almost to apologise for him.

Joan listened in growing perplexity and annoyance to murmurs of: 'I suppose he's not exactly what everyone would call a gentle-man . . .' 'Bit awkward in manner perhaps . . .' 'His mother's one of the best, but a comic old frump . . .' till she recalled how, now and then, Thrush had been unnecessarily defensive about her own people and origin, and shown an uncomfortable streak of snobbishness quite out of keeping with her essentially courageous and honest little character. It was extraordinary to Joan—know-ing that she herself has never been 'up against it' as Thrush had, knowing too that Jack's life had been soft and easy compared with Ginger's—that such values could possibly be entertained. She set herself immediately to laugh them away, and by repeating—with amplifications—her cousin's praise of Ginger soon restored the glow to the girl's face.

'I was a pig to have seemed to run him down,' said Thrush in contrition, 'a perfect pig—when I *know* what my real feeling for him is! Funny thing,' she gabbled on, 'I'd quite made up my mind, you know, to marry somebody rich. I was so sick of just scraping along. And now I've gone and hitched myself to someone who hasn't got a bean—not a bean in the world—apart from his pay!' She laughed happily. Then her tone changed again. 'But oh, hell, how I do want him! You don't know what it is to want a man as I want Ginger!'

Joan acknowledged that she didn't. She could only imagine.

After that the two were friends, and Thrush found hospital work much easier to bear. Joan sometimes brought her home for meals at Beechwood; and once she went to see her in the little studio which she shared with another girl off the Fulham Road.

.   .   .   .   .   .

A letter came from Colin, written in a mood—rare for him—of thorough depression. He confessed that he longed for promotion, and was sore at certain injustices which had kept him where he was. But what worried him even more was that his requests for decorations for some of his men had been ignored. He was extremely tired, and for the moment was seeing the army, and everything, 'through a glass darkly.'

'Oh, my dear,' wrote Joan, 'I do so sympathise with your grousings. I think it not only scandalous, but simply *idiotic* that you are still a second lieutenant after the way you have slaved for the battalion, and the length of time you have been out. However, if it is the faintest comfort to you, *I* know how splendidly you have carried on, and what weary, monotonous, filthy jobs you have put through. It's not as though soldiering were your line, either. Remember:

"Fame is no plant that grows in mortal soil,
  Nor in the glistering foil set off to the world,
  Nor in broad rumour lies;"

Remember too: "And gilded honour shamefully misplaced."
The poets do understand; they do—always.'

It was not strange that the usually hopeful and even-tempered
Colin should have felt suddenly so low. A few days later he
developed a species of 'flu,' and it made things no easier that he
was kept in France to recover from it, thereby forfeiting his leave
which had just fallen due.

.   .   .   .   .   .

In April Jimmy came home for the Easter holidays. Every time
she saw him now he seemed to Joan to have grown larger, more
attractive.

Her work at the hospital prevented her from accompanying him
on whole-day expeditions into the country, but they did manage
a few walks together near London.

There was one especially enchanting afternoon at Kew. The
sun was silvery and mild, and pale buds were on the trees. They
strode along, for Jimmy was always a vigorous walker, and even
in a place which was—to him—as tame and circumscribed as
Kew, his long young strides went forward as though upon the
open hills he loved. Nobody could be so correctly clothed, when
required, as Jimmy; but nobody so much enjoyed physical ease
and freedom. Whenever he could go hatless, and attired in grey
'bags' and a sweater, he did so; and it was thus that he appeared
this afternoon. Every movement of his loose-knit body was a
delight to Joan; a delight his grace and swiftness; a delight the
slabs of gold-brown hair on the broad head. A greater delight
than all was the guilessness of his eyes—when for a moment he
turned round at some remark she made—eyes which, in spite of
the young-manliness of his body, still somehow trailed the
'clouds of glory' of a child.

To hide the tenderness which overcame her at the look of them,
she said laughingly:

'Do you know, Jim-pot, I believe God made your features with a wooden spoon! He decided for some reason that you should always look a baby.'

Jim gave her one of his rare enormous smiles, said nothing, and swung on.

A sudden fear leapt into Joan's mind. 'If any woman got hold of him and spoilt him I'd kill her!' she cried to herself. And on the almost physical faintness which followed, she went on: 'He must be loved in the right way—he *must* be loved in the right way.'

A few moments later her eye was caught by a carpet of small wild daffodils which ran up to the roots of a tree. She put out a hand to Jimmy's shoulder (he was always a yard or so ahead of her while walking—partially oblivious of her) and pulled him round, and pointed.

'Aren't they adorable!'

'M'm. Bit late aren't they?'

'I suppose they are, but anything's possible at Kew!'

A couple of swans lifted themselves lazily from the river-bank, and flapped away through the still air. The eyes of brother and sister followed their flight. Beyond the tufts of trees the incongruous Chinese pagoda reared its height, contriving, as ever, to give that odd impression of being at least ten miles away. A crescent moon, the colour of skim-milk, hung in the afternoon sky.

'I think, when I go to Cambridge, I shall probably become a Socialist,' announced Jimmy, breaking the silence.

Joan, quite accustomed to her brother's irrelevant remarks, answered without surprise:

'I expect you will. You've got an unformed mind—it's like your face—but it's a nice tolerant mind, it doesn't shut out any possibilities. It might even develop into something powerful! I say, what fun it'll be when you're at "Trin. Col. Cam." studying Higher Maths. and what not!'

Pictures floated through her mind. She saw herself married to

Colin, living in some little house in London, both of them working at their own jobs during the day, coming back to companionship and talk in the evening; and Jimmy dropping continually in and out. There would always be a bed for Jimmy. How desperately interested she would be in his college life—in his career. Colin, as a husband, was somehow shadowy in this dream-home of hers; but Jimmy, as a grown-up brother, was not at all shadowy. In fact the home seemed to consist primarily for him.

The actual Jimmy broke in upon her reverie.

'Extraordinary to think that the light from the nearest fixed star takes four years to travel here! This little earth we're on, you know, is only one of three thousand million stars belonging to *one* system, beyond which again . . .'

'Oh, that's enough, Jim-pot! Thinking about the universe makes me feel quite sick.'

'Funny! To me it's rather comforting to think how utterly unimportant we must be in the general scheme—for after all we've no right to suppose that terrestrial man is the one and final purpose of it all. Why should we *matter*? Imagine yourself looking down at a battle of ants . . .'

'I won't imagine anything so disgusting!' interrupted Joan. 'And personally I think that we do matter quite tremendously.'

She found that, of late, she felt curiously uneasy when her brother gave vent to his detached speculations about life; formerly they used only to amuse her.

Jimmy had one arm stretched above his head, and was clutching the overhanging branch of a fir tree. He rocked meditatively to and fro on his toes.

'Some people think that the fourth dimension is the spirit-world,' he said. 'I shall—have to—investigate—the fourth dimension.'

'Jimmy, don't be a fool!' Joan snapped. Then gasped, for her own tone, with its panic-stricken undercurrent, had utterly surprised her. Why had those words, quicker than any conscious thought, leapt from her mouth? Jimmy's remark had been quite harmless and vague, and not particularly foolish. She laughed to cover the effect of her words; but Jimmy, it seemed, had noticed nothing strange. He was pulling himself up by both arms now, and his chin had reached the level of the branch. His absorption in the perfectly normal muscular activity transferred itself to her, and she watched him as he lowered and raised himself six or seven times, and finally dropped to the ground with a long breath, dusting bits of bark from his hands.

'Muscles all right,' he murmured.

'That's a comfort anyhow, considering how groggy the brain-pan is! Come on now, I'm pining for some tea. Let's have it at one of those cottages at the gate.'

When they got home, soon after six o'clock, they found some-one in the outdoor uniform of a V.A.D. sitting by the stove in the hall, talking to Florence. The back, which was turned to the door, seemed vaguely familiar to Joan, but it was not until she approached that she recognised its owner. Pamela Butler sprang up to greet her.

'Pam! What a lovely surprise! How long have you been here?'

'Only a few minutes. Been having tea with some dull relations in Hampstead, and thought I'd drop in.' She turned, sparkling and gracious, to Jimmy. 'Jimmy, how enormous you are! It's simply ages since I've seen *you*! Too old to be kissed nowadays?'

The faint glow which air and exercise had brought to the boy's cheeks deepened at her words. He stooped with a 'Ra-ather not,' and a grin of shy pleasure, and they kissed.

'I must try not to think of you always as a Preparatory School-boy,' said Pamela. 'Do you remember: "Thyme and lavender, mint and rue"?'

' "But never forget your Jaeger shoe!" ' chimed Jimmy. 'Of course!'

They were referring to a distant summer holiday when Pamela had stayed with the Seddons in Devonshire, and she and Joan had had a craze for old ballads and folk-songs. During walks on the moor the two of them used to repeat as many as they could remember, while little Jimmy padded silently beside them. On one occasion, in a fit of brilliance, they had invented a folk-song— taking it verse and verse about. Its theme was a poor farmer's daughter who had gone out to meet her lover in the dew, and caught cold and died. The refrain was 'Thyme and lavender, mint and rue,' and the last line of all—a moral warning—'But never forget your Jaeger shoe!' The girls had been very pleased with it at the time—especially when they realised that Jimmy had quite solemnly swallowed it as genuine. It was not until much later that Joan had disillusioned him; and, although he had pretended to join in her laughter, his crestfallen expression had made her determine never again—even in the mildest way—to 'have him on.'

Jimmy had always liked and admired Joan's friends; and they, on their part, had liked him. He was the kind of small brother who was somehow never in the way. Seeing him now, talking to Pamela, Joan realised—her perceptions sharpened by her thoughts of the afternoon—that it was probably because of his contact with older and delightful girls that he showed no tendency to be attracted by 'minxes.' Perhaps he was safe after all . . . perhaps she needn't worry . . . And aloud she said:

'Do you know, Pam, I think your uniform rather suits you.'

'Nonsense, it's frightful! Helen of Troy couldn't look "becomed" in this rig-out. I've only got it on now because I was kept late at the hospital. Usually I rush home as soon as I'm off, and shed it instantly.'

'That's what I do, too,' said Joan. 'Well, how are you getting on? You are a rotter not to have looked us up before.'

Pamela, having taken a short rigorous training in Reading, had now, for a couple of months, been working at an officers' hospital in Bruton Street. She was staying with her aunt, Lady Butler, and was enchanted to be in London again, to be meeting people, and to have a real job. She talked of her patients.

'Some of them are utter lambs!' she declared. 'Of course, in the wards, I'm extremely strict and business-like—a thorough starched nurse. But in off hours I'm myself again, and it's rather pleasant to be taken out to tea and dinner, and so forth, by such of the "lambs" as are getting better.'

Her elf-like eyes danced.

'There'll be heart-break in that hospital before you're through!' Joan warned her.

'Not at all! It's only that life's rather fun just now!'

On the doorstep she turned, and said seriously.

'Nice person, your Jimmy.'

Joan nodded.

'How old is he, just? I forget.'

'Seventeen next month.'

'Ah, well . . . Good that he's still so young.'

With which Pamela kissed her friend and tripped down the darkening drive to the gate.

.   .   .   .   .   .

Ginger was coming on leave. The exact date was uncertain, but he had told Thrush that he would wire when he knew. Thrush moved quietly about her work with the look of a listening bird, and Joan had the impression that if she were to put a hand on the girl's breast she would feel it feathery and throbbing.

One morning she arrived on duty a few minutes late. Thrush was bending over the sink in the housemaid's pantry, polishing the taps.

'Where have you put——?' began Joan, then stopped, for Thrush had raised her face, and was looking at her with eyes that were like warm black pools.

'He's coming to-day!' was what she said.

'Oh, my *dear*! Shall you ask for leave off while he's at home?'

'No . . . I don't think so. It would be rather letting the others down. *You*'d go on coming in the same case, wouldn't you?'

Joan wished that Thrush wouldn't look up to her as an arbiter on all questions of duty and decency—it was such an embarrassing rôle to have to fulfil. She left the question unanswered except for a doubtful 'Well . . .'

'Of *course* you would,' said Thrush. 'One can't just chuck one's work when it becomes inconvenient.' This was the sort of thing that she felt Joan would say if she were to speak truthfully. 'Besides, it's not as though I shouldn't have all the afternoons and evenings with him—those that I don't have to share with his mother,' she added with a rueful look.

At two o'clock she was in her coat and cap. She hesitated as she was going out of the door, came back, and flung her arms round Joan. 'You are a dear soul!' she breathed impulsively, and darted away.

For the next few mornings Thrush came on duty with a face of rose. Ginger was perfect; she adored him; and his mother was an old pet, and didn't mind their going out together every night. They were having a wonderful time. Of course it was much more of an effort getting up early now, but what did that matter? It was worth it.

The only thing that surprised Joan was that there had been no mention of the wedding. She questioned Thrush about it. The girl turned an uncomfortable crimson.

'Can't be done this time,' she muttered.

It seemed that it was to have taken place quietly in the country from the house of her aunt, but that the aunt had, most inopportunely, been laid low with bronchitis.

'I've never liked her,' explained Thrush, 'and I never go to see her if I can possibly help it; but after all she did bring me up, and was kind to me in her way, and I'd promised to do this one thing to please her. Of course Ginger's mad I should marry him at once in London with a special licence—but I'm not going to. A promise is a promise. After all it'll only mean the silly ceremony will have to be postponed. What's a wedding anyhow? Ginger 'll be back in a month or two; he's going to train for the Flying Corps, then we can be properly together for a time. Oh, it's a bore of course, but I don't so much mind—for myself.'

Ginger came to fetch Thrush at the hospital one day. 'I want you to meet him,' Thrush had said to Joan beforehand. 'He was no end bucked and interested when he heard that we were working together. He thinks a lot of your cousin, you know—and a lot of you.'

Joan shook hands with the blushing Ginger, and congratulated him. She talked of their last queer meeting in the tent at Ostrohove. She told him that she felt she knew him quite well. She hesitated a moment whether to ask them both back with her to a meal at Beechwood—they had so little time to be alone—but she risked it, and they accepted with such evident pleasure that she was glad she had done so.

Florence was at her kindest.

Thrush sat rather silent, not attempting—as on other occasions —to show off. She listened to the conversation, which ran mainly on 'war' and 'regiment' lines; made occasional abrupt little remarks; answered adequately when addressed; but kept her eyes almost all the time on Ginger.

He talked of Brab Malcolm's death.

'Just the kind of fellow we could least afford to lose,' he said to Florence. 'I thought your nephew would have gone mad, Miss Seddon. I never saw anyone so changed. He's jolly enough on the surface again now, but I know he misses Malcolm all the time.'

Florence drifted off, after a while, to attend a committee meeting.

When she had gone the atmosphere relaxed, and Ginger's greenblue eyes turned to his sweetheart's. It was clear that the two were madly in love with each other, though they did their best to keep up an outward decorum.

'Well, Funny-Face, what are you thinking about?' asked Thrush.

He grinned. 'Oh . . . nothing. You. You and me here. This jolly old world.'

'We're certain about each other now—that's what it is,' she said.

'O-o-oh! *I* was certain enough from the first!'

'No you weren't, Ginger—not altogether. When you met me at that party you thought I was just an attractive gad-about loose little studio "bit." I had to show you I was more than that. Had to find out about *you* too—whether you really were the decent sort you seemed. There'd been so many of the other kind!' she finished comically.

'You wouldn't believe the ragging I get from this kid,' Ginger smiled at Joan. 'But I shall keep her in proper order when she's mine—in more ways than one!'

Having hitherto envisaged Ginger chiefly as an admirable little soldier, Joan began to see him now in the light of lover and husband. She noticed the small red hairs on the back of the hand that slid towards Thrush's arm, and realised that it could either grip fiercely or hold with the tenderest care. Yes, he would look after her—never let her go. She was a flower in his hitherto rather beauty-starved life. But would she be the wife he wanted? Joan wondered. So long as love held . . .

When she said good-bye to them she watched them down the drive. Not once did they look back. Evidently thinking that the door was closed—or not thinking of it at all—Thrush raised her face to Ginger's and received a quick hard kiss. After that they ran towards the gate like a pair of children.

.   .   .   .   .   .

But when the first week of Ginger's leave was nearly up, Thrush began to look strained and restless. In a way, she confessed to Joan, 'leave' was an anguish. No sooner had you got over the rapturous beginning than the end, like a spectre, hove in sight, and your time was spent in pretending not to see it, and in being feverishly gay.

During the second week she moved in a dream—a stupor. Her hands accomplished their work mechanically, and if she were spoken to she answered as though she scarcely understood. And yet in the soft vagueness of her voice and of her eyes there was something which had not been there before, and which was not wholly to be accounted for by the pain of an approaching parting.

But on the last morning of all she was scarcely recognisable. Her eyes were like bits of black velvet laced with red. Her cheeks had shrunk, and her pretty mouth was swollen and shapeless. At 6 a.m., it seemed, she had seen Ginger off from Victoria, and he had spent the previous night with her at her flat.

If Thrush had not been so utterly spent she would probably not have given Joan the second part of this information; but it just dropped dryly out, as though it were of no particular importance and required no comment.

Immediate duties separated the girls, but when they were alone together again Joan gazed at her friend in a mixture of interest and awe. This little girl beside her had experienced—and just recently—that mysterious consummation of love of which she herself had only dimly dreamed—had on the whole kept resolutely from her thoughts.

'Was—was it lovely?' she stammered, her grey eyes very wide. Then immediately blushed at the intimacy of the question.

Thrush gave her a curious look, and answered slowly through curved lips:

'Lovely . . . it's life itself. But last night wasn't the first time. Five nights I've had him with me. His mother thought we were always out at parties or dancing somewhere. But its being "lovely" isn't the question. When the boy you adore is going out to those awful trenches again you give him everything he wants—and you don't know whether it's him or you who's wanting it most. Queer that *I* had to overcome *his* scruples! But they were only silly surface scruples—deep down inside him he had none, and that's all that matters.' She gave a sudden little cold sigh. 'But you can imagine that it's harder than ever to let a man go when he's belonged to you in that particular way.'

'Oh, my dear . . . yes,' said Joan, and she had a stab of shame at her own niggardliness in love. Yet could one go against one's nature? What Thrush had done was right—for her. It might not be right for another. In any case without the one thing needful—passion—it was unthinkable. Now was explained that brooding secret look which Thrush had worn all week; explained too, perhaps, her casual attitude towards her marriage. The war

—always the war! Sometimes its effect was to keep people apart; sometimes to drive them too suddenly together; but always somehow to strain and to complicate relationships.

A little shaken, a little ashamed, subdued, and yet exalted, Joan carried on for the rest of the day with the sense of having been let more deeply into life—of having almost herself experienced some new and lovely thing.

For Thrush it had been a comfort to speak out—particularly to speak out to Joan, whose good opinion she was more relieved than she would acknowledge not to have forfeited.

Chapter Three

IT was an afternoon in May, about three weeks later, and, in the garden at Beechwood, Philip Nichol was lying in a long deck-chair under the sycamore. His face was drawn, his eyes wandering and listless. Joan was at his side, an open book on her knees.

'Enough?' she asked.

With difficulty he smiled.

'For a bit perhaps. It is good of you to read to me.'

'Rot! I like it. Tea 'll be coming out soon.'

Tam, the Airedale, who had been lying inanimate upon the grass a little way off, suddenly leapt to life, and rushed, with a series of staccato barks, towards the garden wall where he had espied a cat. The effect on Philip was to make him start violently. His face twitched, and it was some minutes before the quivering of his whole body subsided.

Joan scolded the dog, and apologised to Philip.

'Too stupid of me,' he said, with an ashamed little laugh. 'Any sudden noise like that sets me off. Oh Lord, if only it were an ordinary wound one would know where one was! It would heal, and then one would be fit again, but this business . . .'

Philip had been invalided home with 'nerves' about five weeks ago, and, after spending a month in Lord Knutsford's hospital in Holland Park, he had been boarded, and given two months' sick-leave. He was going to spend it with his mother in Somerset, but Joan and her aunt had persuaded him to put in a few days at Beechwood first, so as to become a little accustomed to normal life before undertaking the journey.

Florence had been delighted to have someone whom she could mother. She kept him in bed to breakfast, and fussed over him (but never tiresomely) in a hundred little ways; she quite forgot that she had been rather awed by his 'cleverness' in the old days. In the afternoons, when she came back from her hospital, Joan sat and talked or read to him in the garden, and they had been one or two short walks on the Heath.

Philip had changed very much. He, who had always been such a talker, now sat for hours without saying a word; and his voice, when he did speak, was hoarse and dull. He didn't refer to his experiences, and Joan, who knew only the barest outline of what had led to his breakdown, carefully avoided questioning him.

But now on this particular afternoon, when Tam had so startled him, Philip departed from his usual reticence. He had had a bad night, and had begun—for the first time—to dream of shells.

'It brought it all back again,' he explained to Joan. 'I wanted to forget. Apparently one can't.' He took off his spectacles and rubbed his eyes wearily.

'Don't talk,' implored Joan. 'Just lie quietly. I'll read again.'

'No, I think I want to talk now,' he said—'that is, if you don't mind. I want to straighten out events—to see *why*, exactly, I'm like this.'

He began jerkily, but gathered momentum and composure as he went on.

'I was very tired all winter—I had had no leave at all since first coming out. In January I was half buried by a shell. Then came my brother's death—a bad shock. We had always been tremendous friends, and he was my mother's favourite; I worried about *her* a lot. I began finding it more and more difficult to force myself to patrol lengths of trench that were under shell-fire. Of course there was also the growing loathing of the mud, and the feeling that war was quite insane. Then in March I went down with bronchitis. They sent me to Nice—I wrote to you from there if you remember—but it didn't do me much good, and by that time I had a dilated and irregular heart.'

'*That* you never wrote to me about,' put in Joan.

'No . . . well . . . it didn't seem very important. From Nice they sent me to Rouen—a dismal filthy spot in that weather. Nothing to do. I got fed up after a bit, and bluffed a medical board into passing me fit—not because I had a hunger for the front line, but because I hated the Base, and felt I was shirking. When I got back to the battalion they were in trenches north of Arras—a pretty hot bit of the line. I found I was sicker than I had thought—short of breath—face burning—heart pounding. The bronchitis had come back. One evening, just as we were standing-to, the Bosche opened up. Well-directed stuff, and a lot of trench-mortars. On my way up to the fire-trench I was caught between two big trench-mortar bombs—one on each side. They were near enough for me to feel the heat of the burst, and to hear, as well as the noise of the explosion, that sharp crack of splitting metal.'

Philip paused, and drew a long breath, and stared in front of him.

'I can still see them—I saw them last night—exactly like those pictures of shell-bursts in the *Illustrated London News*. The black fountain of smoke and earth sort of mushrooming at the top, with little black specks of flying metal all round.'

Joan, at this point, had an impulse to stop him—he was looking so haggard—but, realising he would prefer to go on, kept silent.

'After that I picked myself up and went on to the fire-trench, where I appear to have been normal, and even cheerful, and taking quite intelligent precautions for the men. Then when the shelling had died down I found that my will-power had gone—I couldn't force myself to go round the line. I went back and asked to speak to my company commander. I stammered and groped for the words I wanted. Must have looked a pretty sight. He took me down into a deep dug-out while he telephoned for the Colonel. I was going from bad to worse, jumping at any sound, and drawing my breath in long sobbing gasps as if I had run a mile. Then he took me down to Battalion Headquarters. The Colonel was quite admirable. I was in a bad way by this time, and talked a lot of rot about being a coward, and as bad a failure as . . . a certain other Johnny in the battalion who had been sent home as incompetent. But the Colonel told me he knew quite well I was capable, but that my nerves had cracked up, just as my leg might have been broken. And he gave me some whisky and shoved me into a bunk, where I slept like a log.'

Of what happened after that Philip said that he remembered scarcely anything. There had been an interminable journey from the Casualty Clearing Station to Havre, and there he had been put upon a hospital-ship, and had sailed for home.

Philip had spoken as though scarcely aware of an audience. He came to himself after a long silence, and turned his head to Joan.

'What a debauch of egotism!'

'It's an absorbing account,' she said quietly, 'and I expect it's been a good deal edited for my sake, too. I think the way you stuck things is wonderful.'

'Oh, don't, don't!' he muttered, with a painful flush. 'I didn't speak for *that*. And when I think of other men . . . But it's good of you to have listened. It's—it's awfully good of you and your aunt to have me here at all . . . This normal happy home . . . where I loved coming before the war . . . you can't know . . .' He bit his lip, and blinked to keep back the threatening tears.

Joan was amazed and disturbed. That the dry, brainy, unde-monstrative Philip should be almost crying showed her more than anything else the measure of his present weakness.

She rose quickly, and with a little comforting laugh put a hand on his shoulder. 'Goose, we love having you,' she said. 'For heaven's sake don't begin being grateful! Look, here's tea!'

Florence appeared in the French windows at the other end of the lawn, and wafted smilingly towards them, followed by the maid with a tray.

'Philip, you've been tiring yourself,' she said, shaking a finger at him as though he were a small boy. 'I shan't trust you with Joan any more.'

'Oh no, Miss Seddon, really I haven't!' he urged. 'I've had a splendid afternoon—Joan's been perfect. You're all far too kind to me—I'm a wretched specimen to have about.'

'Now drink up your tea, and don't talk nonsense.'

Philip did so, gratefully, greedily, cup after cup.

Joan couldn't help thinking of their old cook's panacea for every emotional upset: 'A good cry, and a cup of tea all round.'

Philip's stay at Beechwood prolonged itself to ten days, after which he went home to Somerset.

His two months' sick-leave was twice renewed. During his time at home he tried to do some reviewing for a paper, and to read history and economics, but found, to his annoyance, that he was mentally unable to tackle books. He was not actually ill, but suffered more from an immense lassitude and indifference. After that one outburst to Joan he never referred to his war experiences. In March 1917, ten months after he had been invalided home, he returned to take up the hated burden in France.

.   .   .   .   .   .

One morning, a few days after Philip had left Beechwood, Joan arrived at the hospital to find that Thrush had not yet turned up. There was nothing extraordinary in that—Thrush was quite often ten or fifteen minutes late; but when an hour had gone by and there was no sign of her Joan began to get anxious. Sister was extremely annoyed. If Miss Shirley had been unwell, she grunted, she might at least have telephoned. Joan did double work that morning, and determined to find out later what had happened.

When she got home, soon after two o'clock, she was startled to see Thrush hanging about in the drive, evidently waiting for her. One glance at her face told Joan of tragedy.

'My dear—*wounded?*' she breathed, coming up to her.

Out of a mask of marble dropped the monosyllable 'Killed.'

Joan put a hand under the girl's arm, and led her straight into the house and up into her bedroom.

'Telegram came last night,' said Thrush. 'I was with his mother. Couldn't face hospital this morning. Felt I had to tell you, though—you've been so decent to both of us.'

Suddenly the immobility of her face and the flat, toneless quality of her voice were invaded by panic. She leapt forward and seized Joan by the wrist.

'Joan, Joan, it isn't true, is it? He isn't dead? Ginger isn't dead?'

Joan looked at her with miserable compassionate eyes and forced her to sit down.

'I didn't believe it till now,' stammered Thrush, 'not till this minute. I even slept last night. All morning I just sat about, not believing it. Then I came here. I thought perhaps you'd tell me there'd been a mistake, that it wasn't true after all—you always know such a lot about the war. But now I know it is true.'

Then fury gripped and shook her. Her voice came tearing through her throat, hoarse, primitive, unrecognisable. Her fists beat the bed where she was sitting.

'Hell take the whole bloody army! What did they want Ginger for? Why Ginger? There were lots of others. I ought never to have let him go back. He was mine, we were going to be married, we loved each other, and they've murdered him. Curse them to hell!'

Her face was utterly distorted. Then, 'Ginger! Ginger! Ginger!' she moaned, and fell face downwards on the bed.

Her storm of weeping might have lasted a quarter of an hour, or an hour, for all Joan knew. She knelt on the floor beside her, stroking her, murmuring little silly things, herself so sick and shaken she could hardly speak.

The bed was turned down, for Florence always hoped that Joan would rest a little in the afternoons, so as it happened there was no quilt between Thrush's face and the cool linen of the pillow. By the time she had dragged herself up again to a sitting position the frills of the pillow-case were torn, and the case itself was soaked.

Joan brought her a glass of water, which she drank in gulps. Quietly, like a child now, she allowed her eyes to be bathed and dried. She was the white spent husk of a once living girl.

They sat on through the afternoon, the May breeze gently

billowing the curtains inwards. Thrush talked spasmodically, not looking at Joan, but feeling in a dim way the comfort of her presence.

'He was so very sweet, Ginger was. Nobody could know how sweet. I'd never been loved like that before . . . I never shall be again. He had such funny hair . . . people used to tease him about it. But the way it grew—in a little tweak at the back of his neck! It was one of my favourite places for kissing him . . .'

Her lips began to quiver again and droop at the corners. Joan felt as though a small piteous animal, that couldn't understand, were being tortured.

'Will he really not come back again? Not ever any more?'

'Oh, Thrush . . .'

'I'm glad about—all that happened between us. And I think I'm glad we weren't married after all. I shouldn't have liked to be a widow.'

There were occasional renewed fits of crying, but none so long or so abandoned as the first.

Joan brought tea to the bedroom, after which, rather to her relief, Thrush began to harden again. Questioned as to when she would be coming back to hospital, she answered briefly:

'I'm not coming back.'

'Do you mean not at all?' asked Joan.

'No. Tell Matron for me, will you?'

'Of course. But don't you think'—Joan was very tentative—'don't you think that work would help you? That after a few days perhaps . . .'

'Oh, I don't know! Perhaps—perhaps not. Anyhow I couldn't work again in *that* hospital—it would be too . . . No, I don't think in *any*. You see, I don't really want to do war-work. I only did it because Ginger was a soldier. Now that he's dead I've no interest in the war at all. It can go hang for all I care—so can everyone connected with it.'

Joan felt wretchedly baffled. In the face of such an attitude it was impossible to put forward general pleas of duty and patriotism.

Grief took different forms, and the form which it took with Thrush was not a comfortable one to come in contact with. Those people who felt as deeply, but whose code it was to 'keep a stiff upper lip,' and to 'carry on,' made sympathy a much easier thing for their friends.

'What shall you do, then?' she asked.

'I haven't the least idea. Get along somehow.'

'We won't lose touch with each other?'

'I shouldn't like to. You've been frightfully decent to me. But I don't know. I don't know anything.'

When Thrush had gone, Joan wrote to Jack asking him to send a letter as soon as possible to Ginger's little fiancée, and to give any details which would help to comfort her and keep her pride alive.

As far as imagination could carry her, Joan put herself in the place of the bereaved girl. But just as there were intimate joys that were outside the pale of her experience, so there were intimate sufferings, and neither could be pictured. Thrush had had the joys; she was to pay for them now, in the months to come, with night upon night of gnawing fleshly misery.

Chapter Four

BESIDE the last of the six beds in one of the flower-filled wards of the officers' hospital in Bruton Street, Pamela was clearing away dishes and instruments. Sister Stewart addressed her from the doorway.

'Will you get dinners in as soon as possible, Nurse? We're behindhand this morning. And you might count the clean laundry before you go off duty—and see this time that it's *correct*.' With which parting injunction she sailed out of the ward, her high floating cap and Wellingtonian nose somehow giving the impression that she was at least six-foot-two.

'The "Iron Duke" seems to be on the war-path this morning!' remarked Bobbie Winthrop, a small-moustached subaltern whose foot had just been 'dressed.' 'Amuses me the smiling way you receive those sarcastic shots of hers.' He lazily turned the pages of a *Tatler*.

'Well, you wouldn't have me put out my tongue at her, would you?' said Pamela. 'Sure you feel all right, now? Bed comfortable?' She tucked in a drooping blanket and turned one of the pillows.

'O.K., thank you—*Nurse*!' He laid mocking emphasis on the last word, looking up at her starched slimness and white-bound head. For yesterday afternoon they had been to 'The Bing Boys' together, the new revue at the Alhambra, and Pamela had been so completely the charming girl-companion, in her 'civvy' clothes, that the contrast tickled him.

'You never asked me how *my* pillows were!' came a plaintive drawling voice from the next bed. 'And, as it happens, they're simply beastly!'

'Kitten, you're a nuisance!' laughed Pamela, going up to where Lieutenant Kitcat, aged nineteen, lay with his arm in a sling. 'I fixed you up only half an hour ago.'

'All I can say is they're simply beastly,' reiterated 'Kitten'.

Pamela plumped the pillows into shape. 'You know you simply trade on being the baby of the ward,' she told him, as though she herself were a woman of fifty, and Lieutenant Kitcat, who had won the M.C. for holding a forlorn post in 'the Salient' against overwhelming odds, were a small tiresome boy. 'There now. Anything else before I go?'

'Well . . . you might give a cigarette to a fellow—might even go so far as to light it for him!'

His impudent eyes were not to be resisted.

Pamela did as he asked, and then whisked off, on slender ankles, with the dressing-trolley.

' "If I were the only girl in the world," ' sang young Winthrop as she passed, without raising his eyes from the *Tatler*, ' "And you were the only boy" . . .'

'Ah . . . *if*! But you're jolly well not!' Kitcat informed him triumphantly. '*I* exist too, if I may be pardoned for mentioning it. Really, Winnie, I marvel at you,' he continued. 'As though you hadn't girls enough, as it was, coming in to visit you. Look at all those pink tulips on your locker—disgusting I call it! *And* I bet you make the most of the old crutches when you go out to theatres. It's not as though that foot of yours weren't practically well!'

The fact that Kitten's temperature still kept waltzing playfully up and down contributed a flush to his already babyish countenance.

Pamela returned with dinner-trays. While courses were being consumed she was outside on the landing counting laundry.

'Good old boiled fish!' exclaimed Kitten, eyeing his food with melancholy distaste. ' "Plus ça change, plus c'est la même chose!" '

'P'raps you'd prefer bully-beef and biscuits?' inquired Pamela. 'You've only to say so.'

'When I'm in the trenches,' Kitten grumbled on, 'I don't care if I eat rats. When I'm in England I like delicate variety.'

'Delicate fiddlesticks! You're too spoilt for words.' And Pamela left him.

When she came in again with the sweet course she heard Winnie, whose appetite, unlike Kitten's, was now in the ravenous stage, and who had just polished off a large plateful of meat and vegetables, say to his neighbour:

'You're wrong about my foot, Kitten. It's very far from being "practically well." Personally I shan't consider it's of any use to me until I can dance again. That'll be the test. Jove—*dancing*! I say, Miss Butler—"Nurse" I mean—it's a queer thought, isn't it, that you and I were both at the Sandhurst ball two summers ago and didn't know each other! What a waste! Never mind, we'll make up for it—we'll dance together some day.'

At the window end of the room Peter Boyd—who would never dance again—was up and dressed, ready to go out motoring with relations. He was leaning against a table, and the stump of his right thigh, over which the tartan trouser-leg (for he was in the K.O.S.B.'s) was neatly folded, was exactly on a level with the table's top. Propping himself on his arm, and taking a stride on his good leg, he swept his stump nonchalantly along the polished surface, leaving a pathway in the dust. He was a lean young man with an ugly amusing face.

'Really, Nurse, I shall have to speak to you severely about your dusting!' he called out. 'Look at this table—disgraceful! Better leave the job to me in future, and you'll be saved from the wrath of the " Iron Duke." And he took another stride or two round the table, still using his stump as a polisher.

His executions were extremely funny, and the ward gave him appreciative laughter; Winnie's was especially loud, for, in his talk about dancing, he had, for the moment, forgotten Peter, and felt remorseful.

'You're an absurd creature!' cried Pamela, gaiety and tenderness fighting in her voice. For the note of the ward was gaiety—always and always. Nobody must appear, for a moment, to be seeing beneath the surface, to be envisaging the tragedy, and not the comedy, of wounds. She was on her way to the door again when little Kitcat arrested her.

'I'm rather afraid, Nurse,' he drawled, 'that a fellow won't be able to cope with this stewed fruit without assistance.'

Pamela drew up by his bed. 'Kitten,' she said severely, 'allow me to remind you that you have a perfectly good left hand.'

'Yes. It can manage to prod things like bits of fish,' he admitted, looking up at her with woeful blue eyes, 'but when it comes to sloppy juice the problem is really insoluble.'

She shook her head at him, took up the spoon and began to feed him.

'One for Daddy . . . two for Mummie,' jeered Winthrop, watching the spoonfuls as they went in.

'All right, Winnie, all right! You're very funny, aren't you?' called Kitten, flushed and happy, 'but you can't conceal the green in your eye!'

Pamela went round collecting empty plates. The tall New Zealand officer with bandaged head, who lay in the bed in the far corner, stopped her as she was taking his.

'Do you think, Nurse, that I might have another pillow?' he asked in a deep courteous voice which had the faintest tinge of a Scotch accent.

'Certainly, if you need one,' she answered rather stiffly. 'Why didn't you ask before?'

'I didn't want to bother you, and besides it wasn't strictly necessary.' His steady gaze never left her face, and it seemed as though the request for the pillow were merely something which floated on the surface of an attention occupied with other and less simple matters.

'I'm here to be bothered,' she informed him, 'and if an extra pillow will make you more comfortable it *is* necessary.'

She walked quickly away, carrying the tray of plates, her face wearing the 'duty' look of the perfect nurse—every glimmer of friendliness gone.

The other men continued to read their papers, and to smoke their cigarettes with extravagant unconcern. The difference between Nurse's manner to Captain McLane (or 'Skipper' as they called him) and her manner to the rest of them was too marked to pass unnoticed, and must therefore, at all costs, appear to *be* unnoticed. It was nothing to do with them, of course, if she happened to dislike the poor blighter, but it was at times—well, just a shade embarrassing.

'Is that all right?' asked Pamela, returning with the pillow, and arranging it behind McLane's head.

'Perfectly. Thank you very much.' For an instant her eyes met his—eyes dark and sunken in a lean face—and a little gust of irritation shook her. Her irritation was not justified, for there was nothing offensive in his look, but she was vaguely aware that he was making some demand on her—was almost accusing her of something—and she resented it.

'You'd better get some sleep now,' she told him; 'I hear you had a bad night.'

Slowly he smiled at her. Only once before had she seen him smile in all the fortnight that he had been in hospital, and she felt all at once that she simply couldn't stand him.

'Yes—that's a good idea; I think I will,' he agreed. And she turned from him to say very brightly to Peter:

'Off now? Have a good time. Don't tire yourself.'

Peter Boyd, hopping down the room on his crutches, very lean and smart, his Glengarry on one side, gave her a grin and a semi-salute from the elbow.

It was two o'clock. Pamela bestowed a few last tidying touches on the ward, and went off.

'Good-bye, my lambs!' she called back at the door.

'Good-bye, Peg o' my heart! Peg of all our hearts! Be good. See you at seven to-morrow. What a life! What a war!'

But as Pamela had declared to Joan, that day in April, life was rather fun just now.

.   .   .   .   .   .

'Yes, that's healing up very nicely, Captain McLane,' said Sister, bending from her hawk-like eminence over the head-wound which she had just finished swabbing. 'I'll leave you to bandage it, Nurse Butler.' And she sailed off into the next room where there were more urgent cases to attend to.

Although it was the first time Pamela had been left to finish this particular dressing by herself, she knew its every move from having assisted at it from the beginning. With firm fingers she placed the pad of gauze over the gash which ran from forehead to crown, then drew the bandage backwards and forwards across the top of the head, with an occasional turn round the circumference to clip in the looped ends, until at last a neat linen cap resulted which she fastened with a safety-pin.

The job, as a job, was easy enough, but there was more involved in it than mere bandaging. From the first few days of McLane's arrival Pamela had experienced a reluctance to have anything to do with him or with his dressing. It was a sensation so novel, so ridiculous in connection with a wounded soldier that she forced herself to overcome it; but the sensation persisted, and she was always thankful when the dressing was over and she could move off to other beds.

Her reason could bring nothing against McLane. He treated her with extreme deference—in fact very rarely addressed her at all—and made far less fuss than any of the others. But something which was not reason was kindled to discomfort by the way in which he followed her about the ward with his eyes, so that even when she was not looking at him, even when she was giving all her laughing attention to one of the 'lambs,' she was aware of those eyes in the corner—enveloping, compelling, pathetic. Yesterday, over the pillow business, her discomfort had turned to active exasperation. But to-day it had travelled yet another stage, and had become something which it took a great deal of will-power to control—but which she was further than ever from being able to understand or to define. To-day, to her amazed disgust, the fingers which so swiftly wound the bandage would, she found, if left to themselves, have slipped down to the man's brown cheeks and caressed them.

To McLane, leaning forward a little with bowed broad shoulders, the girl was merely skilfully accomplishing her work; and if, every time that her bare arm passed in front of his face, he had an aching desire to press his lips against it, that was something which she must have no inkling of—now—or, perhaps, ever.

And all the time the gramophone by Winnie's bed was playing 'And when I *tell* them how *beau*tiful you are! They'll never believe me.'

As Pamela fixed the safety-pin McLane raised his hand—quite mechanically, and with no ulterior intention—to feel if the bandage was firm, and by accident encountered hers, not yet withdrawn. At the thrill up her arm which the contact, slight as it had been, produced she whitened; and the next instant was busying herself with the things on the trolley.

'Thank you—Perdita,' she heard him say in a low voice; and whipping round saw that he was leaning back once more against the pillows, his face flushed, but looking at her with unwavering eyes.

'I don't like being addressed by joking names,' she fired at him.

'Don't you? You stand it very well from the others.'

Her eyes glittered. 'The others are the others, and what I stand from them is entirely my own affair, and has *nothing whatever to do with you*. Besides, they're my friends as well as my patients.'

'Yes . . . and I'm only your patient. Very well then, we'll keep it at that. Nurse and patient, not friend and friend. Well, it's not my fault.'

Only then did his eyes leave hers, and turning his head on the pillow he murmured barely audibly: 'But I wasn't joking . . . To me you *are* Perdita—a princess in disguise.'

'That from this great big world you've cho-sen me-e,' bawled the gramophone. And the dishes rattled angrily on the trundling trolley.

.　　.　　.　　.　　.　　.

For the next few days they kept it 'at that.' McLane never missed an opportunity of reminding Pamela that she was his nurse. The constant little demands he made upon her services, though none of them (as he had remarked of the extra pillow) was strictly necessary, all bore a reasonable enough appearance. He would ask for his bandage to be loosened—or tightened; for a blanket to be tucked in; for his locker to be cleared of accumulated objects. He developed extraordinary thirsts, and sometimes asked for lemonade, and sometimes for tea. On one occasion, having made a cut in his finger while sharpening a pencil, he required her to bathe it for him, and to bind it up. Humiliated and maddened (especially by this finger business, which she was certain he had contrived on purpose) it was yet impossible for her not to comply —all the more so as it was invariably when Sister Stewart was in the room that McLane made his requests.

The morning dressing, always an ordeal, was now hardly endurable to Pamela. She did it in tight-lipped silence, and with the utmost rapidity which efficiency would allow.

Then there came a day when Sister declared that the bandage might be left off, and strips of plaster substituted to keep the gauze in place. 'A dab of iodine, Nurse. A pad of several thicknesses of gauze. And you'll have to press hard so that it doesn't come off.' With a little smile at Captain McLane, and a serene unconsciousness of what her injunctions implied, the "Iron Duke" passed on. Between nurse and patient, however, looks were crossed that were like rapiers before a duel.

Probably because the need for effort, on this occasion, was even greater than it had been before, Pamela felt a rare and steely calm descend upon her. Standing beside the bed, her weight a little on one foot, she looked the picture of graceful unconcern; and her fingers cutting the plaster into lengths were absolutely steady.

Then she bent to the dark head and applied the pad. A moment passed, and then: 'I think if you pressed the strips with your own hand it would be more satisfactory,' she said in a sudden high, hard little voice.

'I don't agree with you,' McLane replied. 'You'll manage it much better yourself.'

Both his voice and his posture had an immovable quality about them which told her that if she had hoped at the last minute for a 'let-off' she was not to obtain it.

'Keep still then,' she said between set teeth; and with first her thumb, and then the padded base of her hand, she pressed down the plaster.

But instead of continuing to offer a rock-line resistance his head swayed away from her, so that instinctively she put out an arm and caught it back, while with the other hand she finished what she was doing. It had all been the work of a moment, but during that moment he had been held tight against her, and had felt—or thought he felt—beneath his cheek the beating of her heart.

Released, he fingered the dressing.

'Splendid!' he remarked. 'That ought to stick.'

'Yes, and hurt damnably when it comes to be pulled off!' she shot back; and, gathering up the utensils, was gone

In the bath-room, where the washing-up was done, she leant trembling.

'How abominable!' she cried. 'How filthily unfair! I won't . . . I can't . . . *Damn*!' She turned on the taps viciously, and, before proceeding to wash up, held her hands and arms beneath the running water.

Dinners were served and cleared away in an atmosphere of high-pitched hilarity between Pamela and the boys; and never once did she cast a glance at McLane.

At two o'clock Peter came swinging down the ward.

'Going now?' he asked. 'So am I. Come with me a bit of the way?'

He waited for her below while she put on her coat and hat, and together they sauntered out into the May-warmed London streets.

'I say, Peg, forgive me for butting in and all that,' began Peter

with charming well-bred awkwardness. 'But couldn't you manage
to be a bit more decent to the poor old Skipper?'

'To Captain McLane?' asked Pamela. 'But don't you consider
that I am?'

'We-ell—*hardly*. Mind you, the others don't notice things to
the extent that I do, and just lately you've been covering your
feelings very carefully, but . . . dash it all, Peg, what's wrong
with the fellow?'

'Oh, nothing, Peter, nothing. Simply he's not a gentleman.'

Peter's eyebrows twisted comically.

'Oh, come, be fair! Of course he's not exactly one of our little
crowd, if that's what you mean. How could he be? His people
have been in New Zealand for two generations. But they're all
right—his people—damned good stock. Scotch—no hairiness at
the heel. And if it's a war record you want he's got us all beat to
a frazzle. Anzac Beach, and then France, and twice Mentioned in
Dispatches. He gets yarning to us in the ward sometimes, before
they put lights out. What he's been through . . . Gosh,
hair-raising! *I* wouldn't have been on the Peninsula for a lot.
Never a word about himself either, but of course we gather
things. Kind of beggar the men 'll follow into hell. Feels a bit
lost and lonesome, I think, over here—and you manage to make
it worse, Peg. Couldn't you stop being sore with him, and just
switch on a bit of the charm stuff—*you* know! Rope him in a bit?'

'That's all very well, Peter, but when I said he wasn't a gentleman I didn't mean from the class point of view. There are things
about him . . . You don't understand everything. What's more,
I can't explain.'

'Don't bother. I *do*—more than you think!' he grinned.
'Well, this is where I leave you.'

They had come opposite Stanhope Gate, and she watched him
as he hobbled across Park Lane to go and sit beneath the plane
trees and budding little hawthorns, and await his friends.

What a darling that boy was! How sensitive and generous
beneath his every-day mask of absurdity. One would have

thought that the loss of a leg would have embittered him, shut him off, instead of which it only seemed to have opened him more delicately to the feelings of other people. But how much, Pamela wondered, in this particular instance, *did* he understand?

She turned, softened, and in a strange way relieved, and walked back to Curzon Street.

.   .   .   .   .   .

Next day McLane was up and dressed a little before two o'clock. He had been going out for the last few afternoons, but as he had not happened to start until Pamela had gone off duty she had never, until now, seen him in uniform. She was struck by his great size, by the way he held himself, and by the far healthier appearance of his face. His eyes, too, though they retained that odd, secret, questioning look, disturbed her less beneath the Anzac hat than when they followed her about from the bed.

She was still furious with him over yesterday's dressing (this morning, owing to being put on to another job by Sister, she had escaped having to do it), and all night she had felt against her breast the odious pressure of his head. But since her talk with Peter another strand had woven itself into the mixed plait of her emotions—that of pity. It was a frail strand, but it enabled her to ask him, as he was passing the bathroom, where she was drying instruments, what he did with himself when he went out in the afternoons.

'Oh, I stroll around,' he told her from the doorway. 'Good place London. Haven't been here since I was a kid.'

'Are you . . . do you find it lonely at all?'

'Well—yes, I do. You see, I've got no people here.'

She caught her breath, and then brought out with elaborate casualness:

'Should you like me to come with you some afternoon? Show you things?'

There was a short pause.

'That's kind of you. But nurses don't go out with patients, do they? Only friends with friends.'

Their eyes met, and she reddened.

'Thank you all the same,' he said. 'I must be going now, or I shall be late for my matinée.' And, saluting, he walked away from her and down the stairs.

The snub direct! For the first time in her life she, Pamela, had been snubbed by a man. Well, that was that. Not again—not ever again! At Peter's instigation—*solely* at Peter's instigation—she had held out the olive branch, and it had been refused. Vindictive boor!

She swept back into the ward, her head held high. The gramophone was playing 'They Didn't Believe me.'

'Oh, take that record off, Winnie,' she cried.

'Take it off? Why?' asked the astonished Winthrop.

'Because I'm sick of it.' She was rapidly dusting lockers and emptying ash-trays before going off duty.

'But it's a jolly good tune.'

'I tell you I'm sick to death of it! You play nothing but that ghastly record, day in and day out, hour after hour. It's enough to drive one mad.'

'All right, Peg, keep your hair on. I'll just let it finish.'

She turned on him, dustpan in hand.

'If you don't take it off this instant I shall break the record! I mean it.'

They were all laughing now. They had never seen 'Nurse' like this before, and it was amusing, and a little exciting.

'Splendid!' cried Kitten. 'You make him do as he's told!'

> 'Your lips, your eyes, your cheeks, your hair,
> Are in a class beyond compare,
> You're the loveliest girl that one could see,'

sang the gramophone.

'Are you going to take it off?' asked Pamela warningly.

'Not till it's over. Why should I?'

Without a word she came up to Winnie's bedside, jerked up the needle, removed the record, and with a sharp movement broke it into two pieces. Still without a word she put the pieces into the dustpan and left the ward. A burst of astonished and slightly embarrassed laughter followed the closing of the door.

.   .   .   .   .   .

Pamela came into hospital next day hard and bright as ice. She had to endure a certain amount of chaff, but she met it gaily, and admitted that she had lost her temper.

'You should have seen her, Skipper!' crowed Kitten from his bed. 'She simply took and did in that record as though she had had a personal spite against it! Nervous outbreak due to prolonged war-strain,' he continued with mock sententiousness. 'This patient should be carefully watched.'

Pamela avoided McLane's eyes, which she felt were fixed upon her with more than a suspicion as to the cause of her 'nervous outbreak.' But that morning he did nothing to which she could take exception. He was humbleness itself, worried her with no demands, and even quietly insisted on fixing his dressing himself.

At the same hour as yesterday, while she was finishing washing up in the bathroom, he again passed the door, and hovered for a moment uncertainly. Wisdom and dignity enjoined her to keep silence, but an unreasonable desire to speak to him caused her to kid herself into thinking that *this*, after all, would be the most dignified course, for it would show him that she disdained bearing resentments, and that she was entirely unaffected by anything which he could do.

'Enjoy your matinée?' she threw out.

Instantly, as though in gratitude, he halted; but his voice was colourless as he replied:

'No-o, I can't say I did. Not much fun, really, going to the theatre alone. Shan't do it another time. I'm going into the Park this afternoon—just to sit and watch the people. The air's too good not to be out.' He was turning to go, then paused, and, looking at his boots, remarked: 'I expect that between half-past three and four I shall be sitting near that statue of Achilles.'

She gave him a little stare conveying that such a piece of information could not be of the remotest interest to her, and resumed her work.

. . . . . .

By half-past three she had had lunch, had changed from her uniform into a flower-embroidered summer frock and shady hat, and was standing in the small dim hall in Curzon Street. Her eyes turned slowly this way and that—to the grandfather-clock ticking away the minutes of the warm afternoon—to the pictures gazing blankly back at her—to the visiting cards upon the table. It was as though she were seeing all these objects for the first time—and for the last. There was a hush in the air—a suspense.

Then she moved forward and opened the door, and the London sunshine struck at her.

Down white streets, through humming traffic, her feet carried her like birds. In her mind was no thought; she had no identity, no will. Even her body seemed not to belong to her; it had lost its compactness, and had become a fountain of some liquid, warm and wine-like, which curled and jetted and mingled with the air.

Streets slid behind her, and she passed into the green and gold of trees. People were dotted about—people, and bright flowers. She saw them all. Her feet sped on. She was vividly aware of everything around her. Then suddenly she was aware of nothing —save of her heart thumping to sickness, and of McLane before her on a chair.

She was close to him now. He had risen. And from his humble and transfigured face there came the one word: 'Perdita!'

Catching at a remnant of convention she managed to stammer: 'I was just on my way . . .' when, before his authoritative 'Sit down,' she sank into the chair beside him. There was a mist against her eyes, and her knees were trembling.

'Look at me,' he commanded.

She raised her face as though from drowning.

'Why have you come?'

'I love you!'

People still strolled aimlessly up and down—up and down. Motors still swept honking under the arch at the corner. But they might not have existed. She heard only the astonished echo of her own low-breathed words; saw only his eyes—awe-struck —looking into hers. The waves of relief, of bliss, which followed her avowal broke over her with the sweetness of a summer sea. She wanted only to float on them. She wanted no next step.

And then time, which had been suspended in a golden ball— how long?—resumed its course. The world around came into focus. And McLane, with upward-tilted profile, murmured to himself, 'It's true then!'

They broke into a rush of words.

'You lovely thing! How brave of you to come—how brave!'

'I don't think it was specially brave. I didn't in the least mean to come. As I was changing, this afternoon, my mind quite honestly supposed that I was going out to see some friends. And then I found myself here. I don't a bit understand it.' And then, after a pause, and with a glimmer of old mischief in the tremulous happiness of her tones: 'You didn't *think* I'd come?'

'No—I didn't think so, but I had a sort of wild irrational hope. It was almost like a bet with Heaven. I put forth all my will-power. And then when I saw you coming towards me under the trees . . .!' He broke off and said shyly: 'I've never seen you in anything but your nurse's uniform until to-day.'

She blushed. 'Do you like me like this?'

'Well . . . "like" is mild! I've always thought of you as a princess in disguise, and here you are—without your disguise. I can't believe it—I just can't believe it—this, I mean—you and me.' He repeated her name, dwelling on it in delight: 'Pamela . . . Pamela.' And leaning towards her: 'You do know *my* name, don't you?'

'Ian,' she smiled.

He drew a deep breath as though the happiness of hearing it from her was almost too great. After a moment he looked round restlessly. 'Is there no place we can be alone in? Come to tea with me somewhere.'

'There'll be people everywhere,' she replied. 'Better come home with me—lonely Colonial! After all, that *was* what you were cadging for when you told me you'd be here, wasn't it?'

She rose, and he smiled down at her from under his wide hat. She could rag him as much as she liked, the sweet! It made him feel hers, and happy.

In a dream they paced back through the Park and across into Mayfair, keeping, half-deliberately, a foot or so of space between them, aware of each other with an acuteness that was delicious and fearful. They shed, as from the top of a shining tower, their happiness on passers-by—prodigal to them, and indifferent.

In the library that opened off the hall—a room that was practically given over to Pamela during her uncle's absence in France—they stood about shyly. Here they were alone and free. Yet not so free as in the Park. An inner restriction bound them now. Pamela took off her hat, ran her fingers through her hair, then went to the door, murmuring something about tea. At the door she stopped, head drooping, hand on knob.

From somewhere behind her in the middle of the room she heard his voice, deep and strangled:

'Pamela! Don't go—come here!'

She turned at that, but instead of going towards him leant with her back against the door. The soaring strength which had carried her right up to him through the Park, which had lifted her confession from her lips, and brought him back with her here, had suddenly deserted her and left her limp.

'Ian—my dear, I can't—come any further.' She laughed a little, but her face was drawn. 'Don't you realise that by your ruses you've already forced me to be—the most oncoming minx! I've dared so frightfully—yet all the time *you've* never said . . . never said . . .'

In a stride he was up to her, and had taken her in his arms, and she was sobbing against his shoulder.

'Sweetheart, I love you. Don't you *know* I love you?'

A moment later, sitting side by side, close, on the leather sofa, she asked him:

'Since when? . . . *Tell* me!'

He looked into her face—rosy now—almost dry-eyed.

'Since the first day. I'd never seen anyone like you. You were a flower, a breeze, a bubbling brook, you were all the girlhood of the world. Oh, you'll laugh at me for a heavy romantic—which of course I am!' (But Pamela was not at all inclined to laugh.) 'Well, I knew I was "for it." No good fighting these things. And then I was jealous—miserable and jealous. Did you know that? You were such friends with all those lads; you sort of belonged together, had the same background, the same jokes. I hadn't been to Sandhurst, or to Oxford, or to anything—my life had been so different. Of course I understood you couldn't be as friendly with me as with them, but all the same I didn't see why you should be quite so cold. It seemed, even, as though you hated me.'

'I did. Or rather I thought I did. But my hardness to you was my attempt at self-preservation. Underneath I was terrified of loving you. I didn't want to love you. I see now how it worked.' She smiled at him. 'You were very clever with me, Ian!'

'Oh, not clever,' he assured her with remorse. 'But I had to do something to make you notice me, and by a sort of blundering instinct I managed it. Don't think I didn't feel a brute—a boor. At the same time when you began resisting me and being angry I was glad, for I knew there was a hope. You were the kind who'd always had a lot of easy adoration—men came to *you*. You *had* to come to *me*. You must forgive me, sweetheart.'

She stretched her arms. 'Oh, Ian, Ian, you queer man! What have you done to me? I've been in love before—often—in a way. Never this. It's too quick—it's madness. What do I know of you, or you of me? And yet we know all that matters. We must begin to discover each other from the inside out, instead from the outside in—in the usual way.'

He took both her hands, and held them against his face.

'But we've found each other.'

'We've found each other.'

'I think that somewhere deep inside me I knew it would come true—just because I wanted it so desperately.'

She drew his face down to hers, and their mouths met and clung.

Somehow, at some period, they were having tea. Somehow, at some later period, 'Aunt Maud' was talking to them—gracious, and small, and chiselled-featured. 'Another of Pammie's young men,' was all she thought. And she looked with amusement at this different type, at this huge Anzac with the severe mouth and the honest eyes. It didn't occur to her that her niece's radiant face meant anything out of the ordinary.

.   .   .   .   .   .

After that there were afternoons of happy exploration—of London, and of each other. Wandering in parks, sitting in the house in Curzon Street, or in 'The Shamrock Tea-Rooms' in Bond Street (most comfortable and best adapted to private conversations of all London's tea-rooms), they talked their hearts out.

She told him of her life in the country, with its occasional 'spots' of town; of her bringing up, of her boredom, of her tastes and ambitions. She described her effete and class-ridden family, her scapegrace brother. She talked of the two sides in her—the frivolous and poverty-hating side, and the side that had pluck and decision.

He told her of his father and mother, now dead; of their steady courage in the face of hardships; of their deep undemonstrative affection for their children. He told her of the sheep-farm on which he had been brought up, and which was now run by his brother and himself—his young sister keeping house; of his pride in the farm, of his solitary reading—chiefly Shakespeare. He told her of his brother's wretchedness at being unfit for service; of his own sailing for Gallipoli in a ship full of friends; of his romantic love of England and the Empire. To all of which Pamela listened enthralled.

'One thing you're certain to like about New Zealand, sweetheart,' he said, 'and that's the riding. Horses are the chief means, there, of getting about—not expensive luxuries as in England. You'll be able to ride to your heart's content.'

'But, Ian!' she exclaimed, assuming an astonished stare. 'You don't imagine that I'm coming out to live with you in New Zealand, do you?'

Over his face, after the first swift dismay, there settled what Pamela called his 'rat-trap' expression. Without raising his voice he pronounced:

'There's no question about it. Do *you* imagine that I'm just going to frivol about with you in England—much as I love England? Run some tin-pot show? Or worse, be given a job—possibly as estate agent—by one of your relations? No, my dear. You're coming out with me.'

'But I'm *fond* of my country,' she protested. 'And I could earn money too. I was going on the stage anyhow. I've talent. Oh, Ian, let *go*!' For his fingers had closed like iron on her wrist.

'I don't happen to see myself as Pamela Butler's husband,' he told her. 'You're going to be my wife, in my home. You're coming with me.'

'Yes, my cave-man, yes!' she laughed. 'I'll follow you anywhere. Only do let go!'

He released her, and she looked ruefully at her red-marked wrist, and then up at his face. 'I was only pretending,' she said. 'Don't look like that!'

'Well, don't pretend again. That was too like reality.'

Realising that she had, for a few moments, rather barbarously, 'put him through it,' she fell on her knees before the chair where he was sitting, and threw her arms round his shoulders.

'As if I could possibly live anywhere you didn't choose, my own—my funny dear! But do you think you'll still like me when

I'm out there with you? Do you think your brother and sister will like me? I couldn't bear it if they didn't."

' "And when I tell them—how wonderful you are!" ' he murmured teasingly, and holding her close. ' "They'll never believe me . . ." '

'Ian—don't! How dare you remind me of that awful record!'

' "That from this great big world you've chosen me," ' he continued in spite of her. 'It *is* rather extraordinary, you know!'

She slid from his arms and sat back on her heels, gazing at him in an odd detached way.

'It isn't really. You just happen to be exactly right for me.'

'Your people won't think so. They'll think me most unsuitable.'

She shrugged. 'I'll settle them.'

'Do you think you'll be able to stand the life?' Suddenly, after his display of cave-mannishness, he had become anxious and boylike. 'Because, you know, I'm not fundamentally a selfish beggar, and I care far too much for you to make you unhappy. It *is* a lonely life—compared with what you've been accustomed to— though it has its points.'

'I realise that!' she twinkled at him. 'You're one of them! Besides, as a girl friend of mine told me once, at heart I'm a squaw. You'll see! I shall settle most wonderfully down.'

'You love me—with all of you?'

'I love you—with all of me.'

. . . . . .

Pamela had standards of the fitness of things, and to introduce an 'engaged' element into hospital work did not accord with them. So in the mornings she was still merely his nurse (though with what different feelings!), and in the afternoons she was his sweetheart.

But although the ward knew nothing of what had taken place between them it felt the result in an immensely increased smoothness of atmosphere, and in the apparent total disappearance of

what it had termed 'Peggy's dislike for the poor feller.' Peter
Boyd may have guessed at the truth, but if so he was far too
discreet to show it, and was content to hope that the shoving in
of his own oar at a particular moment may have been effective.

For a week Pamela and Ian kept their changed relationship
private. It was something so precious and so new, something
that seemed at first so entirely to concern themselves, that
they couldn't bear the thought of the breath of the world
upon it.

But there came a time when it no longer seemed fair or desirable
to hide it; and as Pamela was living in her aunt's house, and was
constantly bringing Ian home, Lady Butler was the first to be
told. It cannot be said that she was exactly enchanted, and she
submitted the girl to a good deal of worldly advice. To Captain
McLane she had no personal objection—liked him in fact; and
the discovery that certain Highland ancestors of his had been
connected with some of hers went far to raise him in her esteem.
But married life in New Zealand . . .! It was a queer look-out
for a niece of hers. Also Pammie had had so many affairs before.
When she realised, however, that this time it was serious, she
only stipulated that the marriage should not be rushed.

'You owe something to your family after all,' she said, 'and
something to yourself. Wait until his next leave, and then if you
are still both of the same mind . . .'

Rather to Pamela's surprise Ian agreed with her aunt over this.
He wanted to be perfectly certain that his girl came willingly.
She was young, and she must have a chance of backing out.
Pamela was piqued at his attitude, and protested against it a good
deal, but in her heart she respected it. When it came to a question
of what he considered right she knew him to be inflexible.

It was well into June now. Ian's wound was healed, and in a
few days he was going to a Convalescent Camp. There was no
time for Pamela to take him down to Wallingford, even if she
could have left her hospital work. She would write to her parents
later.

'Don't be afraid, dear one,' Pamela said to him. 'I'm not going to waste our last precious days together in "showing you round" unnecessarily. Only to my very specials. Joan Seddon, for instance, you must meet. She's a darling, and the salt of the earth. Part of her will think me insane for marrying you and going off to the "colonies"; part of her will adore our romance.'

They made the most of every hour; they lived in an enchantment which they allowed no shadow to dim; and their love, which had burst into such a swift blaze of blossom, took root and deepened.

'But I shall get leave, and come up and see you, sweetheart; it's not so far away. In any case I shall come up before . . .'

It was the evening before his departure for the 'Con' Camp, and he was holding her, slim and soft, in his great arms.

'Yes, yes,' she moaned, clinging to him, 'but we've been together every day till now. How am I to bear even a week of separation?'

Love of her and the wrench of parting made his voice husky.

'We belong to each other,' he muttered.

'We belong to each other.'

.   .   .   .   .   .

But Ian was unable to get leave; and less than a fortnight later he was pushed off with a draft to France. Huge preparations were going on out there, and every available man was needed. He was not even able to come up and say good-bye.

At the end of the letter which he wrote to her on leaving England he said:

'In case anything should happen to me I've arranged with the W. O. to send a telegram to you as well as to my family—otherwise you wouldn't hear. Also a friend of mine in our crowd will write any details you may want to know. But all this is mere formality. Don't worry, little sweet, the war is going famously, and I've always had the devil's own luck. I shall be back again soon. Before ever Kitten's arm is properly healed, or Winnie can dance again, I shall be back, and then . . .! Take care of your precious self. I go happily. England would be worth fighting for if she only contained you.'

Through the summer days Pamela nursed on at Bruton Street.

Chapter Five

MEANWHILE, during the last few months, in the vast Alexandra Hut among the wharves of Boulogne, Betty had been working steadily—the stablest member of a large fluctuating staff of ladies and of Christians. The Senior Lady, Mrs. Burbage, known as 'Mother B.,' was a kind creature, but afflicted with spasmodic ailments; and among the other workers the only one whom Betty really liked was a Miss Bingham, a girl a little older than herself, who came of a hunting family, and was breezy, brotherly and good-natured.

It was at Temple's, in the evenings, that Betty specially missed her friends. No Joan, and now, since David Frewen's death, no Barbara with whom to laugh and gossip. But the days were full enough, for, in her off-times from the hut, she helped Roscoe with typing and odd jobs at the Y.M. office. With Roscoe—who had become ever more friendly, and at the same time more proselytising, since last summer—she had recurrent rows. The rows were always about perfectly ridiculous things, and Betty was always humbly apologetic, but to no purpose. He couldn't let well alone.

'If only he'd occasionally deliver his harangues to other women,' she said to herself, 'who deserve them more than I do!' But it was only Betty who seemed to have the power to rouse Roscoe to moral indignation, and whom he admired sufficiently to try and convert to his views.

Relief from the daily round of canteening, typing and rows with Christians was provided by the passing through of officer friends on leave. They would drop into the hut, spend an hour or so there, smoke, exchange news, and go off again. Tired, but happy if they were on their way to England; spruce, but depressed if they were on their way back. They felt at home in the little staff-room behind the counter. It was a half-way house to 'the line,' and a last link with all they cared for. And to Betty, whatever their age or the splendour of their deeds, they were all just 'boys on leave' to be pitied, to be cheered, and to be given affection.

She reflected how little of the actual 'war' was seen down here at the Base—especially in the part where the Alexandra was situated. It was rather like being behind the scenes at a play, and seeing only scene-shifters and call-boys, while occasionally getting a glimpse of the actors themselves on their way to the stage.

. . . . . .

At six o'clock one cold March evening, when she was having a late cup of tea in the staff-room, the door was pushed open, and she looked up into the smiling light blue eyes of Captain Lovatt, D.S.O., of the Royal Field Artillery.

'Hullo, Betty! So I've tracked you down!'

'Guy!'

She was so surprised that she felt herself blushing. She hadn't seen Guy Lovatt since before the war, when she used to meet him at the house of a married cousin of hers near Aldershot. She had liked him, but had only thought of him in connection with Cicely, to whom in those days he had been devoted. Then the war had come; he had gone out; and since August 1914 she had heard nothing of him.

'Just been on leave,' he explained. 'Saw 'em at Aldershot, heard you were working here, found out your hut, and rolled along. What fun meeting you after all this time! You're not a bit changed—even in that comic overall. Do they work you awfully hard? Cicely wants to know why you never write.'

He rattled away, perfectly at home, sitting on a little hard chair. One leg, in its chestnut-coloured field-boot, was crossed at right angles over the other. His breeches stood away in stiff half-moons, and his slim body was clipped at the waist by the perfectly-polished Sam Browne. To look at him one would have thought he was the perfect type of petted peace-time regular soldier, caring only for the spit-and-polish side of his profession; as a matter of fact he was one of the hardest-working officers in his division, and, although he had had several opportunities of joining the Staff, he preferred to remain with the guns.

'Well, I've got to begin wending my way back to the battery to-night,' he told Betty. 'Heaven knows when, or where, I shall find it. You'll come and dine with me, won't you?'

That was Guy all over. He took it for granted that people would just fall in with his plans, and do anything he wanted on the spur of the moment.

Betty told him that she couldn't come until late—that as a matter of fact she ought to be at the counter now.

'Oh, blow the old counter! However, I'll clear out if I really must.' He rose to his feet. 'What time then? Nine o'clock? All right, meet you at Mony's. Don't be late."

He saluted, pushed his way smilingly, and without the slightest embarrassment, behind the busy lady-workers at the counter, and left the hut.

. . . . . .

Dinner was a success. It was characteristic of Guy that he should have chosen Mony's—a small restaurant of doubtful repute and excellent cuisine, favoured by Base officers, and by those who wanted an hour of something like 'life' before going back up the line.

The tables were divided off from each other by wooden partitions about seven feet high, and at one of them Betty and Guy sat, and consumed an admirably-cooked meal and a bottle of champagne. It would be champagne, of course! It didn't seem to occur to Guy that anything else could be ordered when dining out with a woman. He came of people whose standards of living were far above their means, and though he 'never had a bean' he managed always, somehow, to give the impression of affluence.

The talk was chiefly of England and 'before the war.' Guy asked numerous questions about Betty's work, but of his own life at the Front spoke little, and never seriously. He told her an episode about a new subaltern who had recently joined them, a cheery individual with a game leg. 'At least I thought it was a game leg,' said Guy, 'till the first night we shared a billet, when he diffidently inquired whether I minded him removing it, as it was more comfortable sleeping without it! He had lost his original leg as a result of a wound earlier on, but the substitute appeared to be quite efficient, and he seemed very little inconvenienced.'

He made Betty laugh over this, and over other stories. He had a particularly pleasant quality of voice which made whatever he said, however absurd, appear worth listening to, and an odd engaging mouth, set a little on one side, over very white teeth.

As the meal came to an end he stretched a hand across the table and laid it on one of hers. She remembered that she had admired the shape of his hands, and now she found that the feel of them as well as the shape was pleasing to her. No uncomfortable dampness here, no blundering beefiness of touch which compelled withdrawal, or else a pitying endurance.

'Glad I found you, Betty. Nice of you to come. You're a darling!'

Betty looked up at him, her hand lying contentedly beneath his, the merest line of amused violet showing between the dark arcs of her eyelashes.

'Nice of you to look me up!'

There was something about Guy which put her completely at her ease—a feeling which she experienced so rarely with men that she was grateful to him. She knew so well, and was so tired of the position of being on guard with them, of having delicately to keep them at a distance, of having to manipulate their burden of emotion *for* them. The basic pity which she felt towards all male things didn't prevent her from experiencing relief when that pity was not called actively into play. Sometimes she felt that to be *amused* by a man was the sum of what she asked of him. She didn't want a furious onslaught of caresses, for that only drove her deeper into herself; she didn't want intellectual earnestness, for that was associated with people who were neither lively nor pleasant; she didn't want 'love,' for that seemed only to reduce people to idiocy. She wanted—at present anyhow—just this unstrained and ever-so-slightly love-tinged companionship that she was having with Guy.

He was an entertaining gossip. He sketched people with vivid touches, but with no malice. In his own world he was 'a man of the world,' but in Betty's he was a boy—deferring most simply and charmingly to *her*. He knew perfectly well that, in a bookish sense, he was uncultivated, but he was not hide-bound enough to be proud of the fact.

'Cicely was awfully good for me,' he remarked. 'Really did brighten up my poor brain-pan a bit. And with it all so decent, and so gay. There *are* married women who want to clutch at a fellow—sort of suck 'em into themselves. Flattering and all that at first, but . . .'

Betty inferred that he had been a good deal 'clutched at,' and wondered whether Guy, the philanderer, had not perhaps been more sinned against than sinning. At the moment he seemed to be heart-free.

After dinner he saw her home. It was a still moonlit night, and there was a thin layer of snow upon the ground. As they walked along the boulevard towards Temple's the ramparts of the Hauteville, with their ghostly trees, rose on the left—romantic and unreal like the setting of some Wagner opera.

They were about to say good-bye to each other—or Betty thought they were about to—when Guy suggested that they should go for a walk round those old ramparts. It was such a lovely night, he said, and there was no hurry about his train, and surely Betty needn't go in just yet?

Betty stifled a tiny voice of prudence and consented. It was a jolly idea. Why not? He was being so nice, and she was sorry for him going back to the Front.

And so they ascended, and walked round—Betty in a softened mood, responsive to the black and silver beauty; Guy a little too jaunty and flippant, almost as though he were making fun of her. He looked down at her skyward-turned face.

'Oh, you women! Always ready to get melted up by this sort of thing—surroundings, atmosphere, the picturesque!'

His tone jarred.

'What's the matter? Don't you like it? Wasn't it you who suggested coming here?'

He threw up his chin, and said with an amused contempt which couldn't entirely defeat his essential good-nature:

'Oh, yes—yes. But it wasn't altogether for love of old walls and the moon. Don't mind me,' he added. 'Men are different I suppose—always wanting something tangible. And you seemed suddenly as remote as the moonlight.'

'I wasn't *feeling* remote,' she explained. 'I was feeling very friendly and pleased, as a matter of fact. And I think your generalisations about men and women are out of place. Please be nice again.'

'All right, all right.' He laughed, and touched her elbow.

The slight acrimony had passed, but he continued to talk about women—their faults, their queernesses, their charms. His attitude towards them was fundamentally conventional, but tempered by a certain amount of individual thinking. Although the women with whom he mostly mixed did little but hunt and amuse themselves, he saw no reason why they should inevitably do nothing else. When he came across others, who had ideas of their own, or even work of their own, he was quite interested and sympathetic. He didn't mind cleverness—rather liked it in fact—so long as it didn't exclude charm. His idea of women as adorable creatures, as delicate flowers, was tinged by no kindly superior male contempt, but he did think that they should be protected and cherished, and given always, as a matter of course, 'a good time.'

When finally they said good-bye outside the door of Temple's, he bent over Betty's hand and kissed it. It was gracefully and spontaneously done, and fitted in with the romance of the evening and her mood. She thought, 'He's an attractive creature!' Instantly responsive to the temperature of another human being —especially to that of a woman—Guy didn't let the opportunity slip, but drew her to him, and kissed her face, her eyes, her neck. This was what he had refrained from doing on the ramparts, and now, because of its being rightly timed, it was doubly sweet.

She laughed a little, and 'That's enough,' she said, but she was willing, at that moment, to let him have what he wanted.

Soon after midnight Guy was rumbling in a dark and draughty train towards the Front.

.　　.　　.　　.　　.　　.

Thinking it over later, Betty reflected that it was hardly fair the way that the Guy Lovatts of this world just walked away with things. She couldn't help comparing Guy with a certain silent adorer of hers, now at the Front, called Pritchard. Pritchard was in every way an admirable little man. He was unselfish and brainy; had hung about her in pre-war days with a dog-like devotion; had done innumerable boring jobs for her in connection with the Suffrage; had sent her flowers and presents, and was longing, she knew, to marry her. Yet in spite of all this he had scarcely ever touched her hand. What would he not have given, she asked herself, for an evening of exactly the kind that she had just spent with Guy?

Betty had discounted the moonlight episode as anything *but* an episode, and so she was astonished when she found herself engaged in a correspondence with Guy. She came more and more to value it. It was exactly of the kind she most liked—gay, friendly and entertaining. There was no strain about keeping it up, and—for once—she felt no sort of responsibility about the man she was writing to. Thank heaven Guy could take care of himself. But she wondered from time to time whether, if chance were to throw them more together, that other side of him would develop—the side which was thoughtful and sensitive, and was not the mere charmer, and kisser of pretty women by moonlight.

.　　.　　.　　.　　.　　.

News came to the hut one afternoon that the Dieppe boat, the *Sussex*, had been torpedoed. Betty and Miss Bingham, eager to see it, climbed to the cliff behind, went through the Labour Corps Camp, and penetrated to the edge of the French anti-aircraft battery. From here they could just see the funnels of the ship where it had been towed into the big breakwater. It was clear and blowy where they stood, and all Boulogne was sparkling in the spring sunshine. Not a sign of war—except the rows of camouflaged ammunition-sheds down below.

That same evening about forty gunners trooped into the hut—all very hungry and thirsty. They were just out from England, and were going up the line for the first time, but had been detained in order to help unload the torpedoed *Sussex*. One of them cheerfully told Betty that he had found several dead bodies in it. It transpired afterwards that thirty people had been killed, and that a number of injured women had been taken to hospital.

A day or two later Miss Bingham dragged Betty to inspect the *Sussex* where she lay. The tide being out they could walk right up to her. It was an extraordinary and gruesome sight. The whole of the front part, from the bridge, was cut clean off, so that it was like looking at the section of a ship in some boys' magazine—except that everything was messy and untidy, with cabin-doors hanging open, and a lot of dirty sheets flapping about. Betty got up as near as she could, and peered through an enormous hole right into the ship's 'innards.' It seemed incredible that anything could have been strong enough to make a hole like that. Up alongside the shattered *Sussex* was the *Breslau*, formerly German, and later used by the British for transport of horses. On the edge of the muddy sand lay the skeleton of a horse or cow—the bones not yet washed quite clean.

.   .   .   .   .   .

For some time now she had heard nothing from Guy, and it surprised her to find how much more she thought about him in consequence. Perfectly stupid, she told herself. If he had forgotten her he had forgotten her. It had been delightful while it lasted. And she laughed at the vanity in a woman that was so easily hurt.

Then it flashed across her that his battery might have been in action . . . worse . . . She realised, too, that not knowing Guy's people it might be long before she heard of it 'if anything happened' to him. Her only link with him—and that an uncertain one—was her cousin Cicely.

Hard work at the hut, and occasional jaunts with chaplains or Base officers, filled her daily life, but there was an underlying flatness about it now, and more than ever she missed her real friends.

.   .   .   .   .   .

And then, at last, came a letter from Guy, and her heart rose. He had not forgotten her, he said, but for the last fortnight his battery had been very heavily engaged. At the end of his letter he told her that the previous night he had dreamt of her so violently that if it had been humanly possible he would have dashed down to Boulogne for a glimpse of her in the flesh. 'Though why I should suddenly have dreamt of you like that,' he added, 'when my mind was full of quite different, and less pleasant things, I can't imagine!!!'

Through the three exclamation marks she could see Guy's engaging, mocking, man-of-the-world, yet boy-like smile.

Chapter Six

ONE evening, about the middle of June, Betty was sitting in her bedroom writing to Joan.

'It's all so quaint and different this summer,' she wrote. 'We don't go expeditions to Hardelot in our off-times, but instead we play tennis or bathe. Bathing is rather an ordeal for *me*! But with the aid of a voluminous peignoir my modesty, at which you always jeer, is preserved.

'It's so comic the way men one knows, even slightly, ask one to bathe with them, bless their hearts! And almost always they are the ones that I, personally, am most anxious to avoid. *So* difficult to explain.

'One of the things which the Y.M.C.A. insists we shall all do now is to wear our brassards—*always* (by order of the I.G.C.). I forget if they had come in while you were still here—hideous things like the labels on Bass bottles. You can imagine what a fool one looks! Problem of the day: are we to wear them with "costume de bain," and if so WHERE? Round the knee looks quite chic. We have not yet consulted Roscoe about it!

'Guy Lovatt will probably be stopping here a night on his way back from leave—I haven't seen him since March, or whenever it was, though we've been writing to each other spasmodically. I can't think it will be a success—his stopping here. He will be certain to discover this time how lumpish and "unsmart" I really am, and be disappointed. Whereas if we never met again he might retain quite a pleasant impression of me! People like Guy should keep a sort of mental gallery of fair women, add to it from time to time, but attempt no renewals in the flesh. . . .'

She was letting her pen run on in this frivolous and non-committal vein about Guy because she was unwilling to examine her own sensations regarding him. As a matter of fact, at the moment she seemed to have none; and that dinner at Mony's and the moonlight walk appeared very distant, and quite unlinked with reality. She paused for a time, the tip of her pen against her teeth, sunk partly in thought, partly in physical lethargy. Then she pulled herself together, filled a couple of pages with Y.M.C.A. gossip, and ended:

'Dorcas inquires about you frequently. She is amazed that you aren't married. "So bright and all, Miss Seddon was," she sighs. Can't you come back? As usual all the huts are short-handed, and you do sound so bored at your little Hampstead hospital.

'Love ever, BETTY'

.   .   .   .   .   .

But when Guy came into the Alexandra, buoyant and friendly as ever, it seemed as though no time at all had elapsed since their last meeting. After five minutes' talk in the staff-room Betty felt that delightful sense of ease, that gently simmering amusement, which his company always provoked.

'I've got a room at "The Dervaux," ' he informed her, 'and I needn't go until the day after to-morrow. You'll spend all the time with me, won't you?'

'Guy!' she expostulated. 'The things you ask! Haven't you yet taken in that I'm here on war-work?'

'Certainly I have. And I'm your war-work for these two days —it's your duty to look after *me*! I suppose I'm a soldier as well as the rest?'

'You argue very prettily,' she told him. 'But I don't see Mother Burbage—my Senior Lady, I mean—letting me off my shifts at the hut because of a passing officer.'

'Don't you? Well, if that's all, *I'll* settle old Mother B. Where is she?'

'Guy, don't be ridiculous. I don't want to get into bad odour.'

'You shan't. Leave it to me.'

How it was managed Betty never knew exactly, for at that

minute she had to go to the counter; but, while serving the men, she observed, through the corner of her eye, Guy and Mrs. Burbage in close consultation.

'Nine o'clock at Mony's as before,' Guy said to her as he left the hut. And a moment later Mrs. Burbage sailed up to Betty, and, with a smile that was almost coy, said:

'I see no reason why you shouldn't have the day off to-morrow, dear. You're my best worker, and a holiday will do you good.'

'That's most awfully kind of you, Mrs. Burbage, but are you quite sure . . . ?'

'Quite, dear, quite. I'm feeling so much better now, and can do so much more that you'll hardly be missed.'

'What *did* you say to her?' asked Betty, when, two hours later, she was seated with Guy in one of the 'cubicles' at Mony's.

He gave a slight shrug, and busied himself with the *hors d'œuvres*.

'She's not a bad old geyser,' he remarked. 'I happen to have met her sister once—at some house. She was awfully excited over that. Then we just yarned on, you know.'

And that was all Betty could get out of him. 'I suppose,' she said, 'it was because of your social qualities, your uncanny knack of somehow knowing everyone's relations, and of being able to get round people, that made them want you on the Staff.'

'Oh, give me credit for some brilliance in my profession!' he grinned at her.

Guy was in high spirits, and began rattling away about this and that person he had met on leave, the shows he had been to in town, the loveliness of the English country in June.

'By Jove, Betty,' he cried, 'it makes me come over all sentimental, you know! Green lawns, and roses, and the smiling landscape, and so on. Tea under trees, and lovely women in white. Quite makes one want to settle down. Why are we never at home at the same time, you and I? You don't know what a lot I thought about you in England. If you'd only been there, what a time we should have had! Barging about London together, staying down at Cicely's perhaps. It would have been quite like old days. As it is we just meet in khaki, and in overalls, at this God-forsaken Base—the old war hammering away around us. Doesn't give us a chance. Never mind, we'll make the best of it. Nothing like making the best of every old occasion.'

What touched Betty, in all the bubble of his talk, was the fact that he had thought about her in England. It touched her extraordinarily. It was fairly natural to be thought about 'up the line.' Most men who knew one at all might be supposed to brood wistfully, now and then, on one's image while far from their womankind in dirt and danger; but that they should do so in England— that the popular Guy should do so—was hardly to be expected.

Softened by the obvious pleasure which he took in her company, and which enhanced her own in his, she opened out in a way which she rarely did with a man, and found herself telling him of the queer contacts of Boulogne life, and especially of the relationships which it involved with the 'Christians.'

'Sometimes they begin with religion,' she said, 'and drift into love; sometimes with love, and lead upwards to religion. Mostly, I'm bound to say, it's the first. They seem to have an ardent desire to convert me—why, I can't think, because I'm quite prepared to live and let live, myself.'

Guy was all sympathy. For his own part, he declared, he couldn't stand 'that gang'—they were all so 'messy' somehow.

'But you know, Betty my dear,' he added with his sideways smile, 'you can't expect the poor blighters not to fall in love with you, and wanting to convert you is part of it all.'

'I dislike Christianity, and I dislike Christian affection as exhibited down here,' she said firmly.

There was still a light in the sky as he saw her back to Temple's, and into their minds came the remembrance of that other night, three months ago, when they had stood on the same spot, and there had been snow upon the ground.

This time he made no attempt to kiss her, and for that she gave him full marks. A repetition would have been bad technique.

But any kiss, wherever it had taken place, would have been out of the spirit of this particular evening. Each felt it; each knew that the other felt it. And if the man realised with more precision than the girl just what the omission of a kiss on his part signified, she at any rate felt, as she went upstairs to-night, that she was *fonder* of him than ever before.

. . . . . .

Next day, without quite knowing how she had got there, Betty found herself with Guy in a rowing boat—a French sailor at the oars—lapping up and down on a gentle sea somewhere off Wimereux. He had not consulted her about the arrangements for the day—for which she was grateful, for nothing bored her more than to have to make decisions. He had simply said, 'I've chartered a boat—thought it would be rather fun,' and carried her off.

She was extremely content. She enjoyed sitting quietly in a sunny blue world; and her eyes, under the drooping brim of her hat, were fixed in that remote and narrowed gaze peculiar to women in boats, and which erroneously gives the impression that some profound problem is being pondered.

'I say—about religion,' began Guy, breaking a longish spell of silence. 'Did you really mean what you said last night—that you hated Christianity?'

She brought her eyes round to his.

'Only in the form it takes in the Y.M.C.A.,' she said, a little surprised at his question. 'Oh, and in the Church of England too, if you like. What all these people ought to do, instead of trying to stuff Christianity down the men's throats, is to go into the army themselves; and then, after the war, those who want to be clergymen can be—with far more knowledge of humanity, and a greater likelihood of inspiring trust.'

'There I'm with you,' said Guy.

'And it's all so narrow and uncivilised here,' she continued; 'that's, I think, what chiefly annoys me. Christianity to me is either an inward life to be lived, or else it's an institution like the Roman Catholic Church—vast and old and civilised and powerful. In any case it's never been really tried, and to talk about it now, with the war going on, is farcical.'

Guy looked at her with growing interest.

'Besides . . . Christianity . . .' she went on dreamily. 'Think how obscure it once was. Just one of the many religions competing for supremacy in the old Roman world. And then, when it did triumph, having to adopt all sorts of old Pagan festivals to keep itself popular. Christmas—nativity of the Sun. Easter—death and resurrection of Osiris—Adonis—Athis. Forms remain the same, though the god changes. Diana dies; the Virgin Mary takes her place.'

'I never knew any of that,' remarked Guy after a silence. 'You've read a lot, haven't you?'

'Not really. But at Newnham I got rather bored with the ordinary stuff, and strayed about in the by-ways of mythology and anthropology.'

'I like you to be learned!' exclaimed Guy. 'But as a matter of fact I never feel you *are*! I mean you don't give the impression of a learned women—that's what's so nice about you.'

'Well, I'm not,' she assured him, laughing. 'I detest "learned women." And I only got a third in classics—to the grief of my parents. I never could quite manage to take college with becoming seriousness.'

'So you'd say you were a Pagan?' asked Guy, changing on to the seat opposite so as to observe her better.

'Well, I wouldn't even tie myself to that! Just gently interested in all religions. I like all the gods and all the saints. I burn a candle to the Virgin; I'd lay an offering on an altar to Pan if there were one; and I always mutter a prayer to St. Anthony when I've lost anything. But if I worship anyone,' she added, turning her face skywards, 'it's Phœbus Apollo!'

'We're *both* Pagans,' Guy asserted. 'But you're a more culti-vated one than I am. I've never really thought about anything. I just carry on somehow with a set of decent instincts. I think,' he continued, in a lower and slightly apologetic voice, 'that I do appreciate beauty. You're an artist, of course—at least you told me once that you painted a bit—so it must mean a lot to you. And probably that's why you're so keen on the outward forms of things, and why you hate things being badly done.'

Betty's eyes rested on him tenderly. There was a grace about Guy—that was it. A grace not only of physique, but of mind and personality. A complete lack of that uncouthness which so jarred on her, and which was all too frequently an attribute of those more earnest, or more gifted, or more good. And how perceptive he was suddenly showing himself! She did 'hate things being badly done'—a job of work, a bit of love-making, a ceremony—though she hoped she didn't make this too obvious.

He seemed to feel her softening mood, for although his face— his thin, irregular, amusing face, from which at the moment the stark sunlight had drawn the colour—was turned a little away from her, he turned to her fully now, and between them a smile passed that said: 'You're there! I'm glad.'

.   .   .   .   .   .

A few hours later, in a wood beyond Boulogne, they were having a picnic tea. Guy, with no apparent difficulty, had procured a car, and Betty had brought the food. He was lying full length on his elbow; she was sitting with her back against a fallen tree trunk. They had just ended a discussion on morals— an offshoot of the morning's talk—and had discovered that the one thing they both held in real abhorrence was the hurting of other people's feelings.

'Up to a point I suppose it's a virtue,' said Betty, 'but it can so easily become a weakness. Think of the awkward situations it lands one in!',

'Lord, yes!' said Guy. 'You've told me a bit about yours, but they're simply nothing to my predicaments!' He pulled at blades of grass, and his face clouded. 'I—I've been an awful rotter, Betty. Didn't think so at the time perhaps, but looking back *now . . .*'

'Oh, my dear, I don't suppose you have. Besides, after all, it isn't to do with me.'

'It *is* to do with you!' he burst out. 'That is if I mean anything to you at all. *Do* I?'

'Of—of course you do,' she replied, avoiding his eyes, 'but . . .'

'Oh, Betty, I do love you so! I don't know what to do about you, or what to say. At first I was just attracted because of your loveliness, and then the feeling I had for you grew and grew, though I didn't let it appear in letters, partly because I didn't want to bother you, and partly because I wasn't sure. I know myself so well, you see. I'd often been practically engaged before—to say nothing of "affairs"—and I did want, this time, to be sure. Well, now I am. And yet,' he broke off miserably, 'and yet I can't—I daren't ask you to marry me.'

'Well, *don't*,' she implored him. 'Really and truly, Guy, I'd much rather you didn't. You're not to worry yourself over this. If you did ask me I couldn't possibly answer. Or rather I could —I should say "no" straight off.'

'Because you don't care for me?' He was sitting up now, his hands clasped round his knees.

'Not because of that. I do a lot. But . . . Well, shall we say for one thing,' she brought out with a little smile, 'that I don't quite see myself fitting in with your set.'

'Oh, that's absurd! As if any "fitting in" would be required! You darling, that's not the point at all. The point is, I've got to be able to keep you properly. I've always been an extravagant fool . . . there are debts . . . and quite honestly, if I've found it so difficult to manage for myself, how am I going to manage for two? I will not have my wife just scrubbing along. Anyone as exquisite as you ought to . . .'

'Oh, you funny pet!' cried Betty. 'Don't you bother about such things as that! Don't you bother about anything—either your money affairs, or your feelings for me, or my feelings for you. Just leave it all alone. Something may happen, or nothing may. Anyhow we're friends.'

'Betty! You're—too—*adorable!*' He tried for a moment to keep back the tears, then suddenly moving forward, buried his face in her lap.

Astonished and melted, she kept very still—from time to time just touching his hair. If this had happened with any other of the men who had cared for her she couldn't have endured it. And yet with Guy it unloosed all that maternal tenderness which, much as she might deny it, much even as she might resent it, lay at the foundation of her make-up. The man of the world, the smart artillery officer, the D.S.O. had vanished, leaving her with a small boy—not a clumsy and self-conscious small boy either, but one of a moving simplicity and charm. She had no particular wish for him to go.

After a bit Guy sat up, and blinked at her, and smiled. 'Sorry, Betty. Didn't mean to give way like that. But there was something about you that simply did me in.'

'*Il n'y a pas de quoi!* Honoured, I am sure!'

The lightness of her tone put him at ease, while the gentleness of her eyes assured him he was not being laughed at.

'No, there's no woman like you—none,' he declared, shaking his head. 'Always they want to know—almost from the first— just where they stand. As if, nine times out of ten, one could possibly tell them!'

'Well, you've met an exception at last,' she informed him, teasingly. 'Because if there's one thing that I never know, and never want to know, it's where I stand!'

When Betty laughed it was with no sudden flash of whiteness. Her mouth scarcely lengthened, but the oval cheek-lines rounded upwards till the eyes were curved violet slits that brimmed amusement.

Guy looked at her in delight; then stretching out, with the back of his forefinger very delicately stroked her cheek.

On the way home in the back of the car, her hand in his, he talked more interestingly than she had ever heard him about subjects dear to him. She was amazed at the knowledge he possessed of old houses and gardens. Of his knowledge and love of horses she was already aware; and although he had always talked of them in an intelligent, and not in what she called 'a tiresomely horsey' way, on this occasion he conveyed his enthusiasm in speech that was almost lyrical. He made her feel not only the blood-kindling joy of hunting, but the delight that lay in daily contact with, and care of, the horses themselves—those queer beautiful creatures, so varying in temperament, so nervous, so delicately responsive to right handling. (Like women! she thought.) One of the things, Guy confessed, which most 'got' him about the war was the sight and the sound of wounded horses.

The sensitiveness which he brought to certain forms of beauty made it absurd to suppose, Betty reflected, that he might not, with a little guidance, bring it to other forms as well—to books and plays and pictures. And his mind would be fresh for them—uncluttered by the stale rubbish of literary opinions.

. . . . . .

After dinner that night they sat on a seat under the trees of the Hauteville.

They were quiet, but there was no feeling of strain between them.

'I've got to start early to-morrow,' Guy said. 'I shan't try to see you—it would only be a rush and muddle—so this'll be good-bye. I want to give you something before I go. I got it in England for you. Just the tiniest remembrance.'

He drew from his pocket a small parcel and put it into her hand.

'Don't open it now,' he asked her. 'Really I'd rather you didn't. But when you take it off at nights just think of me, will you?'

On the way down to Temple's he stopped beneath the shadow of one of the chestnuts.

'You've been an angel to me, Betty—an angel. I don't deserve that you should have been so sweet. But remember that I love you—whatever happens I do love you.'

He took her hands and held them against his shoulders, then lifting them placed them together behind his neck, and folded her in his arms.

'Darling, darling!' He kissed her. 'Say something to me.'

'Guy dear—I can't—I'm so stupid at . . .'

'Just *something*—a little word.'

'Precious! Keep safe.'

He kissed her again, sprang away from her, and cried joyously: 'You bet I will! And now I'll leave you. You'll understand, won't you? Good-night! Good-bye!'

'I understand. Good-night! Good-bye! Good luck!'

He had disappeared among the shadows.

Up in her bedroom Betty opened the parcel. It contained a gold wrist-watch. On the back of it were engraven Guy's initials and hers. It was exquisitely chosen, but 'Oh, how absurdly extravagant!' she sighed. It was the sort of thing one gave one's fiancée, and only then if one were fairly well-off. And did he suppose that she would wear it daily in the canteen? Watches, in any case, were quite useless to her—she could never make them go. But how sweet of him! She wrapped it carefully up in its tissue-paper and put it away in a drawer.

For a time she felt Guy's departure as a relief. She had been stirred quite enough for the present, and needed to collect herself. Her reserve was very real, and part of her disliked to have been made to break through it. But the curious thing was—or perhaps not so curious considering the slowness of her reactions —that for days after he had gone she felt Guy's kisses upon her face with far more intensity than she had felt them at the time.

.   .   .   .

During the last few days of June the rumble of a terrific bombardment had filled the air, and now in early July the 'big push' had started with a vengeance. Ambulances were rolling day and night through Boulogne. Wounded were being transferred straight from the trains to the hospital ships. Reinforcements were pouring through Ostrohove.

In the hut the crowds were phenomenal. Soldiers' reports floated about of this or that battalion having been cut up. Betty heard of the deaths of boys she knew, felt a momentary pang, then a stupefaction which lingered for a bit and was drowned in the hundred jumbling details of every day. There was no time to realise—no time to dwell on anything.

'Mother hasn't heard from Colin for over a week,' she wrote to Joan, 'but I tell her it's no use worrying—they *can't* have time to write.

'And you? Your silence is not so easily accounted for—bad one! Are you suddenly very busy? Have you been moved somewhere else? Send a line to poor Betty, who loves you, and let her know.'

Of Guy's visit she said nothing, except that it had been 'quite a success.' Details, she felt, if given at all, must be reserved for a talk.

Chapter Seven

JULY in England. From the Somme battle-fields the convoys of wounded poured into the hospitals. Every bed was full, new wards were being erected, nurses were rushed off their feet, and Joan had enough work at last. She had been sent, at four days' notice, to the 1st London General, Camberwell, and although she had hoped it might be abroad—Egypt or France—she was thankful to be in any military hospital at all.

V.A.D.'s all over the country, whether they had had much, or little, or no training were being called up. From their homes, from their local hospitals, they were flung suddenly into gigantic wards where they had to rise as best they could to the varied and strenuous demands made on them. Whereas hitherto they had been taken in dozens, they were now being taken in hundreds— it seemed almost impossible to obtain a sufficient number; and when there actually appeared an article in *The Times* on the subject, the middle-class, home-sheltered girls of England felt, at last, that their existence was not wholly futile. How different from being merely 'allowed to do things' was the fact of being definitely asked to come and do them. They were in the same position as their brothers now: needed by the country.

In Joan's ward there were forty beds, and almost every patient was seriously wounded. She had never seen anything like the wounds. Many had to be dressed three times a day. It had been one thing to amble in and out of the cosy little wards at the Hampstead hospital, carrying meals, doing housework, and even assisting at the mild dressings; it was quite another here, in Ward 33 of the 1st London General, to see limbs which shrapnel had torn about and swollen into abnormal shapes, from which yellow pus poured when the bandages were removed, which were caked with brown blood, and in whose gangrenous flesh loose bits of bone had to be sought for painfully with probes.

Every night during the first week Joan dreamt about the wounds, saw them floating before her eyes, almost had the stench of them in her nostrils. It was inevitable this should be so, for, during the day, sensibilities had to be hardened, quivering disgust controlled, and head and hand kept steady for the sake of the sufferers themselves. With unconscious wisdom she let down a sort of safety-curtain between her mind and the sights before her, keeping them at bay, preventing their full significance from penetrating. If she had not done so she would have been useless. The nights were reactions from this discipline, and the safety-curtain no longer functioning the horror rushed in on her in the shape of dreams.

But after the first week she no longer even dreamed. She had adjusted herself inwardly and outwardly to the conditions in which her life must now be lived—conditions which, if they could not be accepted as normal, would mean her defeat. And in the face of the gay endurance, the positively worshipful spirit of the wounded, how was it possible not to give of one's very best?

A fervent emotion—whether towards a person, a country, or a cause—may be able to express itself in a poem, or at any rate some form of words. Happy if it can. But it may also have to be expressed in ways more indirect, and less glowingly satisfactory. Joan's feeling of almost weeping admiration for the men had to show itself in the severest practical form—and this was not easy for her. Mentally she was on her knees to them; actually she was on her feet twelve hours a day, sweeping, washing, bed-making, moving down one long line of iron bedsteads and up another with the wheeled table on which were the appliances for the dressings. It was her pride, while getting ready this table in the morning, not to forget one single necessary article. She learnt them by heart, as she might a poem, and with a corresponding fervour. And though for the first few repetitions she occasionally forgot a line she was soon word-perfect.

Before the table (with its innumerable jars, pots, dishes, rolls of lint, etc.) was completely ready there was the boiling of instruments to be done. You boiled them for twenty minutes (theoretically) in the 'steriliser,' which stood against the wall in the middle of the ward. It was of extreme importance that everything connected with the dressing of wounds should be absolutely sterile; and this involved, as well as the boiling of objects, continual hand-washing.

During the first part of July the pressure of work in the wards was so great that details and niceties of method, which at other times would have been insisted upon, went by the board; it was enough if the main feck could be scrambled through.

The sister in charge of '33,' Sister Ewart, a gaunt, rather acid woman of few words but great efficiency, said to the three V.A.D.'s under her: 'Look here, you girls, we haven't time to teach you just now; you must pick up what you can as you go along.' And in a way it was perhaps better not to have been let down too gradually. Plunged into the thick of it as they were, they had to sink or swim.

Joan, having had a certain amount of previous experience, was chosen to go round with Sister Ewart; the second V.A.D. went round with the Staff Nurse (or second sister) in the lower part of the ward where the wounds were not so bad; and the third girl was either 'off' or doing odd jobs.

One of the worst cases was McNeil, who lay in the first bed on the left as you entered the ward. His right leg was fractured at the thigh, and was swung just clear of the bed in a long cradle-like splint. He might have been any age between twenty and thirty-five—when a man was as ill as this it was difficult to tell. He was running a high temperature. His dressing took at least half an hour to do.

The splint itself was not removed, but the bands supporting the leg, and pinned to the iron side-pieces of the splint, were loosened, and the leg gently lowered. Then the large piece of linen which served instead of a bandage round the wound was unpinned, and the packs of cotton-wool removed and laid on the bed to be used again. Beneath these was a piece of green oil-skin, and beneath that the thick fomentation, now cold, and soaked in blood and pus. This was lifted off—a sodden pancake from which rose a warm and sickly odour—and dropped into the pail. A large area of raw flesh lay revealed, with two pieces of rubber tubing embedded in it for drainage purposes. Each tube was drawn out with a little glooping noise and dropped into a dish. The mackintosh sheet was now slipped beneath the leg, and Sister lifted the irrigator high in her left hand, and, holding the nozzle with her right, directed a stream of saline on to the wound. Joan held the kidney-dish, and every time it came near to overflowing emptied its contents of brown water into the pail. There was a fascination in watching the way the wound grew less dirty-yellow and more bright-red beneath the cleansing stream.

None of this part of the process was painful. McNeil even watched it with faint amused interest. It was when it came to the probing that he had to shut his eyes and clutch Joan's arm. Sickening even to watch that simple little bodkin-shaped instrument working about among the lacerated muscles, and to *feel* it almost unendurable. But the bits of loose bone had to be found, otherwise they set up inflammation. It was only gradually, and day by day, that they worked up towards the surface, and as each was removed with the forceps it was satisfactory to know that there was one poison-trap the less.

'Oh, Sister! Oh, Sister!' The face on the pillow was twisted and thrown backwards.

'Steady, Jock, it'll soon be over. There now, that wasn't too bad, was it? Now, Nurse, will you wash the tubes, please, and we'll have the fomentation as soon as you can get it.' Sister Ewart's voice was of the same even, colourless quality whether she addressed a patient or a nurse.

Joan darted down the ward, the dish of tubes in one hand, a piece of clean lint wrapped in a 'wringer' in the other. It was against etiquette to run, and yet everything had to be done at such a pace, and the ward was so long, that walking seemed to get you nowhere.

Placing the wringer in the steriliser to boil, she dashed across into the annex opposite, washed the pus-filled tubes in lysol and water, rinsed them under the cold tap, dropped them into a dish of saline, and hurried with them back to Sister.

While Sister was mopping up the surface of the wound with wrung-out swabs, and re-inserting the tubes (another painful process, and a tricky one), Joan went back to the steriliser. The water was bubbling merrily over the fat, rat-like body of the fomentation lying at the bottom. She seized the two dry ends hanging over the edge (thank heaven they had not caught fire! They were apt to if you were careless), gave them a twist or two, and returned. Over the pail by the bed she twisted them again. This business needed muscle, and it needed determination. However hot and hard the linen against your hands, you had to go on wringing till not a drop more water could be squeezed out; for if the fomentation were not quite dry it burnt the patient.

Your first few fomentations were nothing; but when there were several to be done four-hourly, and day after day, the palms of your hands became so sore that they shrank from the process, and had to be forced to it like unwilling horses at a fence.

Unrolling the wringer Joan held it out, and Sister lifted the thick white steaming piece of lint, gave it one sharp flip in the air, and laid it gently on the wound. Then the oil-skin was put over it, and the wool, and the whole thing enveloped again in the piece of linen, and pinned with large safety-pins. The splint-bands were fixed again, a cage put over the splint, the bed-clothes draped over the cage, and the pillows made comfortable. It was finished at last. McNeil looked at them with tired and grateful eyes.

'Poor old man!' said Sister Ewart, her tight features relaxing so far as to give him the gleam of a smile. 'Nurse, get him some milk in a feeding-cup, will you? And then get all these things washed up as soon as you can.'

The flat little sentences fell from her mouth as lifeless as bits of lint, and she moved off in her flowing cap to the little room at the top of the ward, known as 'Sister's bunk,' to swallow a cup of tea.

Joan slid her arm under McNeil's pillow, raised his head and shoulders, and held the feeding-cup to his lips. . . . There was a little brandy in the milk.

'Better?' she asked, as he subsided.

'Grand, Nurse!'

She smiled at him, not wanting to leave him; then away she went, trundling the trolley down the ward; left it just outside the annex, carried the dishes within, and plunged them into the sink. The sink was full of warm water and lysol—a pale, mud-coloured, slightly sticky liquid, which had a pungent odour and was raw to the hands.

The pail of dirty dressings was emptied into a great rubbish bin which stood in the corner, and which, in the course of the morning, became so full that you had to ram the stuff down with a stick to make room for more—keeping the nose averted—and then quickly clap on the lid again. There was often great congestion in the annex—other V.A.D.'s dashing in to wash their dishes, sisters to wash their hands, orderlies on various errands. It was a centre, a meeting-ground, almost a 'club,' where swift comments and snatches of gossip were exchanged in the midst of a flurry of work.

While the dishes were draining on the board by the sink, the blood-smeared mackintosh was plunged in, slooshed about, lifted out, and dried. Instruments and dishes were put into the steriliser and boiled up; the trolley was swabbed over, and stood fitted out again and ready by the next bed.

Richardson, a cheery, round-faced lad, was wounded in the right foot. Joan began 'getting him ready' for Sister. She removed the bandages and dressing, and there was revealed a swollen, shrapnel-blasted lump that had lost all resemblance to a human foot.

'Going on beautiful, ain't it?' remarked Richardson.

'Does it hurt much?' asked Joan, as she laid a piece of clean gauze across the wound.

'Nuffin to speak of—yes and no. Keeps me awake nights a bit, throbbing like. Proper Blighty one, ain't it? Lord, I wasn't 'alf glad when I copped that one! Comin' out of the trench it was; we was goin' over. Just fell straight backward before I knew nuffiin. Say, Sister, you should 'ave seen 'ow they welcomed us at Victoria! Crowds an' crowds! Threw rowses on to our stretchers. Proper wounded 'eroes they made us feel. Didn't know where to look. Comic, wasn't it, Bill?' He addressed his friend in the next bed.

Bill, reading the *Daily Sketch*, grunted contemptuously.

"'Ave you seen this 'ere?' he asked. ' "Picture of cheery Tommies after Battle of the Somme!" "The Victory Smile!" Lot o' gup.' He read out in a mincing voice: ' "To judge by their smiles you wouldn't think there was much wrong with these men!" Ho no! Not much wrong! Why should there be? They've only bin on a river-picnic!'

Sister hove up by the bed, with dripping and disinfected hands. 'That's right. Now then, Nurse . . .'

The dressing proceeded.

And the next, and the next, and the next. From bed to bed all morning. Lifting and holding mangled limbs; wringing out fomentations; carting away dirty dressings; washing, boiling; trundling the trolley up and down the ward; keeping alert to be Sister's second pair of hands, her other half, to divine what she wanted almost before she knew herself, to be, in fact, the perfect V.A.D.

There was McIvor, the jaw-case, who, when his innumerable and complicated bandages were removed, revealed flat holes plugged with gauze where a nose had been, and pendulous shapeless lips. The stench which rushed forth as the last dressings dropped off was just humanly endurable, and only just. It had an acrid, putrefying quality, unlike that from other wounds.

McIvor sat up in bed against his mass of pillows, and gave little grunts—he couldn't form his words. He was stouter and older than the other men, and was known by those on either side of him as 'Dad.' But that did not necessarily mean that he was very old, only that most of the British Army at that time was in the heyday of youth. Anyone over thirty was apt to be called 'Dad.'

With the forceps Sister slowly pulled out the two twists of pus-dripping gauze from the nose-holes, and dropped them into the dish held by Joan. One side of the jaw was a mass of little broken bones and teeth. The cheek was swollen like a bloated orange. The whole thing had to be most carefully irrigated, and very little water used at a time so that it could be coughed out again. Finally, he was plugged up with clean gauze and bandaged. The bandaging was a miracle of competence on Sister Ewart's part. Joan watched it admiringly. Openings were left for the eyes, and a larger opening for the mouth; otherwise the head was a white ball.

Joan often thought about McIvor, that whatever expression had been obliterated around his mouth leapt into his eyes—eyes that were questioning and fearful at the same time. And she was always aware, too late, of having registered horror for those pathetic eyes to devour—no doubt wounding his spirit afresh.

Then there was Turner with a smashed right arm, and Tubbs with a smashed left arm—each arm bound to a padded rectangular splint. They lay in neighbouring beds, and ragged each other the whole time.

There was Sergeant King with his left leg amputated within an inch or two of the hip, who kept his lips in a thin line and never uttered a word. He was six feet tall, and belonged to the famous '29th'—last year in Gallipoli, this year in France.

And lastly there was little O'Leary, not wounded, but badly burnt by liquid fire.

Little O'Leary, aged nineteen, made no attempt at heroics—either of the grim or of the joking sort—while he was being dressed. His whole body was a mass of burns; and piece by piece the lint had to be peeled off him while he whimpered like a rabbit, and slow tears ran down his cheeks. It took endless time and patience, and the smell here was of yet another order—the stomach-heaving smell of charred flesh. As each bit of lint was removed a new bit, coated thick with boracic ointment, was instantly applied; for under these conditions it was dangerous to leave more than the smallest area of the body exposed.

Sister left Joan to 'finish off' this patient alone. She knew that the girl was careful, and that there was nothing to go actually wrong.

'All right, Pat. Never you mind. We're getting along beautifully. Now listen while I tell you a funny thing that happened this morning.' And Joan chattered on while she did her nauseous job, trying to keep the boy's attention off the pain.

When it was all over, and he had been covered up and made comfortable, he smiled at her weakly—his eyes still wet with tears.

'Thank you, Nurse. You're a foine nurse. Oi'll be all right now.'

'_You_'ll be all right!' she said, smiling down at him, and longed to give him a kiss. That being impossible, she rattled off with the trolley down to the annex.

The mental atmosphere of the ward might have been described as one of cheery pessimism. On the whole the men seemed fairly hopeful about the success of the offensive, and their spirits were good; but always it was the same tale. 'When we came out there were only twenty of us left.' 'Fifty alive out of a battalion of eleven hundred.' 'Only one man turned up at roll-call,' and so on. The same monotonous repetition of losses. It looked as though three-quarters of Kitchener's army—that incredible young civilian army which England had raised in under two years, and flung against the German military machine—were out of action. No previous casualty-lists had even approached in length those now appearing in _The Times_. Every day one or more of the girls at the 1st London would hear of the death of a brother or a fiancé, be granted two days' leave, and then return and carry on. Oh, a fine time to be young in, that summer of the Somme!

As Joan went off duty at about 8.15—the last man having been washed, the last dressing done—she looked down the ward. Almost every other bed was raised into a tunnel-like shape by a protective cage under the bed-clothes, or else looked gallows-like with some strange arrangement of wood and cord supporting the shattered arm of its occupant. And here and there a German spiked helmet hung on the wall above; and here and there on the bedside lockers lay German watches, buttons, coins—trophies of war taken only a few days ago at La Boisselle, Fricourt or Mametz; at Longueval, Thiepval or the ghastly Delville Wood.

.   .   .   .   .   .

Into the passage outside came pouring from their various wards the 'day' V.A.D.s, mingled for a moment with the oncoming 'night' staff, and wended along to the cloakroom where hung their hats and coats. Joan joined in the throng, and, after five minutes' walk from the outer gates of the hospital, found herself standing wearily on the kerb in the Camberwell New Road, waiting with a group of others for a tram. This waiting seemed always the last straw after a hard day; the necessity for effort being over, exhilaration having dropped, the strength seemed to ooze from your knees, and you would gladly have squatted down on the pavement.

At last you climbed into a comparatively empty tram which clanked along past Camberwell Green (surely the drabbest spot of public ground in London?) and up Denmark Hill. At the top of the rise you got out, turned to the right under a little avenue of pleasant trees, and arrived at a row of tall villa-ish houses, two of which, semi-detached, formed the V.A.D. hostel.

Supper was presided over by Sister Ansdell, a wilted-looking woman in a white uniform, who seemed bored to extinction by her job of 'Home' Sister. Cold meat, pickles, biscuits and cheese.

And then a swift escape, as soon as was decently possible, to your bedroom, or the bedroom of your friends.

'Coming in for a cigarette, Seddon?' asked Phipps on the landing.

All the V.A.D.s called each other by their surnames, but whether this was the usual practice of hospitals or whether merely a war-time habit they didn't know. Anyhow it was convenient, and they did it.

Joan turned into Phipps's bedroom which the latter shared with a girl called Fry. These two were known among the others as 'Epps and Fry,' or 'the two Cocoas.' Phipps was small and swift and dark; Fry large and slow and fair. They were great friends, and considered themselves lucky to have a room alone together.

'Fry's evidently in the bath,' said Phipps, producing cigarettes and a vast box of chocolates. 'She's been leaving supper earlier and earlier for nights now so as to get first bath. Soon she'll . . .'

'Soon she'll skip it altogether,' said Fry, appearing at that moment in the doorway, pink and damp-haired from her bath.

'Sister Ansdell will be sure to kick up a fuss if you do,' Phipps warned her, biting into a peppermint cream. 'As it is she casts grim glances at you when you go sloping off after the first course.'

'I don't care! If one waits to come up with the crowd one can't get into the bathroom for ages, and when one does all the hot water's gone. I shall tell Sister that it's a question either of being fed or of being clean; and that personally I prefer to be clean! Chuck us a choc.'

'Fry, you're a marvel!' said Joan. 'You're completely uncowed by the hospital Olympians. Wish I could take them as lightly, but they terrify me. Matron, for instance . . .'

'Matron has the worst manners of any woman I've ever come across!' declared Fry. 'But I *have* succeeded, now, in making her say good-morning to me when I pass her in the corridors.'

'Good heavens, but how? Whenever *I* meet her she turns her eyes the other way, and scurries on as though I were an unpleasant piece of dust.'

'Yes—but I wasn't going to stand that, so I've persistently said "Good-*morning*, Matron!" as sweetly as I could, and now she grunts out a grudging "Good-morning, Nurse," but still looking the other way.'

'There's something about common women when they get into power,' said Joan meditatively, 'that makes them far more tyrannical and beastly than men. I regret to have to admit it because I've always been a feminist, but it appears to be the case.'

'Oh, you try working under Sister Grundle,' cried Phipps, 'then you'll know what the Army sister can really be like! You've none of you lived!'

Phipps worked in Ward 34, next to Joan's, a ward which was notorious as having the surliest, most callous sister in the hospital. Nightly Phipps would wail to her two friends of the indignities and rudenesses which she suffered in that ward—and which the patients also suffered.

'This afternoon, for instance, do you know what she did?' she exclaimed. 'We've got a little dying Tommy called Woods. His relations had been sitting round him since dinner-time, and old Grundle was bored with them—she always hates the men's visitors. Well, just as she was going off she said to me, "Woods won't last more than a few hours. See that his people are turned out by four o'clock, Nurse." Of course I didn't. That wretched family had a right to stay till the boy died. Grundle was furious when she came back and saw them still there, and she went up and turned them out herself. Can you believe it? The old beast! I *was* sorry for them. It was too awful. Little Woods was still alive when I came off duty.'

During this tirade Phipps had been gradually undressing, and Joan, who was sitting on the floor, head on knees, remarked irrelevantly (not because she was unmoved by what she had heard, but because she couldn't bear to dwell on it):

'A neat ankle, Phipps, an extremely neat ankle you've got!'

'Followed by a leg,' continued Phipps, peeling off her stocking, 'of which no monkey would need to be ashamed!'

Joan laughed sleepily. 'Oh, Ph-phipps, how funny! It's
c-covered with curly black hairs!'

'What I shall do on my wedding-night is rather a problem,' said
Phipps. 'It might be best to wear pyjamas, but I do so dislike
them, apart from my figure not being suited to them. However,
it won't much matter, I shall be married by then, and a hairy
leg isn't sufficient grounds for divorce—or *is* it? Good-bye,
girls!' She seized her sponge and towels and went off to the
bathroom.

'He's a nice-looking young man,' remarked Joan, contemplating
the khaki photograph of Phipps's fiancé on the dressing-table.
'She's going to marry him on his next leave, isn't she?'

'Yes,' said Fry. 'She's been waiting months, poor darling, and
now just when he *was* coming home, all leave's been stopped
because of the Somme business."

Joan nodded.

'Hard luck on her. She's marvellously cheerful, isn't she?'

'Oh, she always rots away like that,' replied Fry. 'But at night
. . . Well, she's not sleeping much just now. Worrying, you
know.'

'I don't wonder. Well, I must depart.' Joan gathered herself
up and went towards the door. 'You know, Fry, I think this soul-
and-body-sapping hospital work is the best possible thing for us
just now. I'm glad to be in it, aren't you—joking apart?'

'M'm, I suppose so.' Fry finished a tight and methodical plait-
ing of her fair hair, threw the plait back over her shoulder, and
snuggled down into bed.

'Good-night,' said Joan at the door.

'Goo'-ni-ight.'

Joan went across to her own room, which was a large one
divided by curtains into cubicles, and which she shared with
three other V.A.D.s. As soon as her head touched the pillow she
was fathoms deep in sleep.

.   .   .   .   .   .

It seemed as though she had only been asleep a few moments

when a banging, like a dozen furious wooden mallets, brought her reluctantly to the surface of consciousness. It was 6 a.m., and Mary the maid was knocking on the door. To linger for an instant was fatal, for that meant dropping off again, and there was no second call.

She fell out of bed, splashed some cold water into the basin; washed, dried and dressed. All the little business of fixing studs into starched linen took time. Grey cotton dress, buttoned up to the throat and down to the wrists; clean apron with strings crossed behind and fastened with safety-pins at the waist; white Peter Pan collar; glazed linen belt fastened by two studs; glazed linen cuffs fastened by one stud each. Hat, coat, dispatch-case with clean cap in it, and she was ready.

Downstairs to breakfast. Little Phipps late as usual, and rather bung-eyed. Tea, kippers, bread and marmalade. Out into the summer morning air. Waiting for the tram at the top of Denmark Hill. The ride down. The hospital. As you walked through the gates the main building was on the right. This contained the officers' wards, a few medical wards, Matron's office, the kitchens, and the vast dining-room where the nurses had their meals. On the left, across a strip of garden, were all the 'huts'—the long wooden surgical wards erected since the war. They covered nearly two acres of ground. In among them was the V.A.D. cloak-room and rest-room.

Off came outdoor shoes; on went slippers. Off came hats and coats; on went white head-handkerchiefs. Methods of wearing these varied with different girls. Some let the end bits hang loose behind; some pulled them out and pinned them so that they were like the stiff wings of a pigeon framing the face.

Ready now—seven-thirty. A surge of V.A.D.s up and down the long corridor to their various wards.

Ward 33. At its entrance on the left 'Sister's bunk.' Exactly opposite the ward-kitchen. Joan slipped off her cuffs, stuck them on a shelf, rolled up her sleeves, and sped down the ward. Swift good-mornings, right and left. 'Morning! Morning! Feeling better, Pat? Sleep all right, Turner?' In the annex, half-way down, she seized a broom, as did also the second V.A.D., and back they went again in order to start sweeping from the top. Tubbs and Turner shouted at them as they passed.

'Slope arms! Quick march! Left! . . . Left! . . . Left!'

The girls involuntarily fell into step and marched. All the men who were not too ill joined in the chorus: 'Left! . . . Left! Pick it up there! Pick it *up!*'

'Babies!' cried Joan, and with a quick little *chassé* she changed her feet so that when they cried 'Left!' she was stepping on her right. This caused great mirth. Joan feared she was no disciplinarian. Luckily Sister Ewart was in her bunk, going through the report with the night sister.

Right down the ward they swept—from top to bottom and under the beds. Extraordinary the amount of grey woolly dust that accumulated on those bare boards. Into the dustpans it went, and was emptied into the bins. Easy stupid work—orderlies' work really, not usually done by V.A.D.s. But there was a shortage of hospital orderlies just now; they were being cleared out as fast as possible to fill the ranks of the depleted infantry.

Dusting the lockers and emptying ash-trays was the next job—slightly more amusing, as it afforded opportunity for a little conversation with the men. The lockers were full of the assorted possessions of their temporary owners: oranges, pots of jam, books, pipes, photographs, and bits of shrapnel.

'What *have* you got here, Richardson?' said Joan to the cheery boy with the wounded foot, as she squatted before his locker. 'A bag of half-eaten buns—how disgusting!'

''Ow, you can cart 'em away, Nurse, they're no good. Me sister brought 'em along yesterday, but they're that dry I don't seem able to get me teeth through 'em. Fact is me teeth ain't too good just now. I reckon it 'ud be better if I'd 'em out, and got false ones. Say, Bill,' he called to his comrade in the next bed, 'it was a pity you didn't keep that set you got off the dead Bosche!'

They'd have just done me nicely. Beautiful teeth they was,' he resumed to Joan, 'gold in 'em and all. But Bill sent 'em to his family as a souvenir. Waste I calls it!'

Joan, containing her amusement, passed on to the other lockers.

This first hour of the day was almost the pleasantest in ward life, certainly the most peaceful both for nurses and for patients. Dressings had not yet begun. Tempers were as yet unfretted, and bodies unfatigued. The sun had not yet begun to grill through the thin wooden walls of the hut—walls as ill-adapted to keep out summer's heat as, later, they would be to keep out winter's cold.

The only job that might be looked upon as unpleasant at this hour was the going to and fro with bed-pans. And yet, Joan reflected, you were doing almost as much for a man if you brought him a bed-pan, settled him comfortably upon it, wiped him—if he were unable to manage himself—with cotton wool, and laid him down again, as if you were dressing and bandaging his wound. It was only in imagination that it was more unpleasant; actually it was less so. And the delicacy and sweetness of the men made any embarrassment impossible. The only real bore of the whole business, when you looked at it frankly, was the dragging of the heavy screens round the beds. It was an adamantine hospital rule that a man should be shut off during these moments—a sound and right rule too; only you did wish that lighter screens, more adapted to the strength of feminine arms, could have been provided.

From nine o'clock, or shortly before, dressings proceeded without a pause—unless it happened to be the Medical Officer's morning, in which case, while he was going his rounds with Sister, work was more or less suspended. Joan did what she could; got on with some of the smaller dressings; 'took down' the bigger ones ready for inspection; and for the rest of the time hung about by the steriliser, or else disappeared completely into the annex —the one unpardonable thing in hospital life being to look as though you had nothing to do. With the exit of the M.O. the holy hush which had fallen upon the ward was lifted. The men began to chatter again, and work was resumed with redoubled vigour.

It was a source of amusement to Joan and her friends to observe the extraordinary reverence with which the sisters treated the doctors. It was as though they found themselves in the presence of a god; and if the god, when he had issued his instructions, happened to condescend to a joke, it was received with suitably subdued but ecstatic response.

This intense hierarchical consciousness manifested itself, of course, downwards as well as upwards. Inasmuch as the sisters cringed to their superiors they treated their subordinates with severity. They had always done so in the civil hospitals where they had been trained, and now, in the military hospitals, they continued in the same way. But there was this difference: the nurses whom now they bossed being temporary, non-professional, and well-educated, an element of resentment crept into the hitherto simple and not unfriendly tyranny. The genus 'V.A.D.' was suspect; and though unfortunately at present it had to be endured (there was a war on), it was none the less uncomfortable to have about. And the fact that it worked hard was not so entirely in its favour as might have been supposed, for it did so in an unorthodox spirit, and for unorthodox reasons. It was courteous (Oh, very!), it was sympathetic with the patients (too much so), it was willing, and it was intelligent, but it was not *serious*. It had blown in from the outside, and the sooner the war was over and it blew back again the better.

At twelve o'clock the men's dinners were served, and, as this couldn't be allowed to hold up the business of dressings, the bustle in the ward was greater than ever.

A couple of orderlies came along, one distributing knives and forks and tin plates, the other pushing the food trolley. Many of the men were unable to cut up their own food, and one or other of the V.A.D.s had to do it for them. Men lying on their backs had to be spoon-fed; men like McIvor given liquids from a feeding-cup. In spite of this it was extraordinary how quickly 'dinners' were over, beds straightened, and all signs of a meal removed. Food was looked upon as an interruption in the serious business of the day, and the men themselves had neither the health nor the leisure to enjoy it properly.

At twelve-thirty part of the staff went off to dinner; at one-thirty the rest. The morning's dressings had barely been got through, and some of the things had to be left in the annex to be washed up later.

Trooping down the corridor and across the garden to the main building, their closely-bound handkerchiefs outlining their heads, went the V.A.D.s to dinner like a flock of doves to corn. Looking at them all Joan realised the value of uniform. If people were in a crowd they looked better dressed alike, and particularly if they were bound together on the same work. They kept their own personalities, but were also dignified by a sort of super-personality. At moments like these, either coming on duty or going off, Joan felt herself a cog in a huge machine, and it was a satisfactory feeling. You were part of something over which you had no control, which used you as it would, paid you, bound you, and divested you of all responsibility for your own actions, your own life. The bunch of sisters walking on ahead, in their large floating caps and little grey red-bordered tippets, were just so many more cogs—larger and more important, but parts of the same machine.

At the dozen or more long tables in the semi-underground dining-room everyone sat down: sisters at the upper end, V.A.D.s at the lower.

Many girls brought books. Joan and the two Cocoas, who always, if possible, sat together, were reading respectively Wells's *God the Invisible King*, Walpole's *Dark Forest*, and Conrad's *Victory*—books fairly recently published, and which were causing, in their different ways, a lot of discussion. Phipps, usually a chatterer, sat silent and bulgy-eyed over the description of the Russian retreat in the dim forests of Galicia; Fry, the English and orthodox, screwed her blue eyes superciliously over excited diatribes on the Infinite; while Joan was away on an island of romance, absorbedly following the fortunes of Lena and Heyst, and wondering what their relationship actually was—whether they *did* or did *not*! But literature didn't prevent the girls from consuming a healthy meal; no life is so hungry as hospital life, and if the food had been even plainer and duller than it actually was they would have swallowed it unheeding.

Five minutes in the rest-room attending to the toilet, then back on the wards. The sisters were having cups of tea in their bunks. 'Tea after lunch!' Joan had thought at first amazedly. But she had soon realised that sisters without their tea were as troops without their rum—they couldn't function; and at all hours of the day and night it was equally welcome to them.

The afternoon was a trying time. The ward had heated up, and the men lay perspiring and uncomfortable, either falling into fitful dozes or grimly bearing the pain of their wounds. It was now that special attention could be given to the very bad cases; an unsatisfactory splint changed for another kind; an extra mattress put on a bed; a water-bed filled, and a patient carefully transferred on to it. Also there was the making of swabs, the padding of splints, the putting away of clean laundry.

At four o'clock the men's tea came round. Then you went off to your own tea, and directly afterwards the business of the evening began.

Joan collected tin bowls from the annex, placed one on each locker at her end of the ward, and filled them with warm water. Those who could manage to wash themselves were left to it, but most men at this stage had to be washed. Joan at first had been surprised at the whiteness, from neck downwards, of the soldiers' skins—though what else she had expected she couldn't have said. It gave her a peculiar soothing joy to take hold of a long white arm, to soap it, sponge it, and dry it; to wash a muscular young back, listening meanwhile to its owner talking desultorily about his sweetheart, his kids, or his 'mates' in the regiment. She was a nurse in uniform, and he was a wounded soldier; the gulf between them was fixed and rigid. And yet across that gulf, unrecognised and certainly unheeded by either, stretched the faint sweet fingers of sex. In such a form, so impersonal, so sublimated that its name seemed ridiculous, its presence was only proclaimed by the fact that if the patients had been women, or the nurses had been orderlies, the atmosphere would not have been the same.

In all her long months of intimate contact with wounded soldiers Joan never saw one indelicate gesture, one suggestive look. At the time this didn't strike her as remarkable—she never gave it a thought; but in after years she sometimes wondered how much to attribute it to the hospital atmosphere, how much to the decency of the men, and how much to a certain English directness and innocence in her young self. Possibly her own experience had not been quite so common as she then assumed it was. However that might be, to her—and, she imagined, to most of her friends —the memory of 'the men' was sweet for ever.

Having carried away the basins Joan set to work with the second V.A.D. to make the beds. She took with her a box of boracic powder and a bottle of 'meth' with which to rub buttocks and shoulder-blades—for bed-sores must at all costs be prevented. Those who were able heaved themselves into an arch while they were being rubbed, and those too badly wounded were held up or turned.

Beneath each man was a strip of mackintosh sheeting covered by a cotton 'draw-sheet,' and this obviated the necessity for wholly remaking the bed. You untucked the draw-sheet from the sides, drew it along until a clean cool portion came beneath the patient, and tucked it in again. Then crumbs were brushed away, pillows turned and arranged comfortably, and the bed-clothes tidied.

Meanwhile Sister was taking temperatures and marking them down on the charts which hung at the bottom of the beds. (V.A.D.s were not supposed to be sufficiently 'trained' for this job.) The number of a patient's bowel-motions during the twenty-four hours was also marked down. To Sister's lifted eyebrow he would answer curtly, 'One,' or 'Two,' or 'Three,' as the case might be; or else in silence hold up the same number of fingers. If the answer was 'None,' or a shake of the head, a pill would be administered, known jocularly as a 'Number 9.' Why a 'Number 9' Joan never made out to the end of her hospital career—unless it had some reference to a kind of shell.

And then, until the end of the evening, dressings were done—in almost, but not quite, such large numbers as in the morning. And home, dog-tired, to the hostel.

But although being on day-duty was wearing enough, being on night-duty, during this particular summer, was a great deal worse. It was at night that the convoys came in (a convoy of fifty had had to be turned away last week because there were not enough beds), and it was at night, usually, that men died. Scraps of talk, dreadful details, floated through to Joan from the night V.A.D.s, and something cowardly inside her hoped that she would be allowed to remain 'on day' for a long time yet.

Chapter Eight

FLORENCE SEDDON wrote to Joan asking whether it would be possible to see her—even for half an hour. She was upset, she said, and had something she wanted to show her. Joan managed to get two hours off, one afternoon, and met her aunt at Stewart's at the bottom of Bond Street, a convenient half-way house.

'Look at this,' said Florence, when tea had been brought; and fumbling in her large bag produced a letter. It was from Jimmy, written from school. Joan read:

'I have been thinking things over, and have come to the conclusion that having been passed fit for military service, physically, I ought to get a commission in the army as soon as possible through either of the training colleges, Woolwich or Sandhurst, whichever I pass into. I shall take the exam. in September, and if I haven't passed high enough for Woolwich I shan't wait and do the exam. again but go straight to Sandhurst—I shall have done well enough for *that* anyhow. Meanwhile I shall leave school and cram. I know you are keen I should have another term or two at school, but I feel I should be doing my bit more thoroughly by leaving and getting a proper training straight away. Remember, I am over seventeen now, and if I wait till November, and take the exam. again, I could not possibly get into the army till the following June, and by then the war might be over. I think I am now in a position to settle my own course of action, but I ask you for your sanction. Please answer as soon as possible. I am sure you will see my point and let me do this.

'Your loving nephew, JIM'

'Did you ever know such a letter?' exclaimed Florence, her kindly face puckered in astonishment and distress. 'He's a man.

Quite suddenly he's become a man—that baby. He's deciding his own life. What am I to do, Joan? What am I to say?'

And Joan, her heart sinking down, down, replied: 'You must let him do it, Auntie. You can't forbid him. If he thinks it's right he must. Once Jim's made up his mind . . . But oh, dear . . . it seems very sudden.'

She stared unseeingly at a waitress lolling in the doorway.

It had come, then. Jimmy was being sucked in too. She had known, of course, that for some time now he had been working in the army class at school, but she had not taken that very seriously, and vaguely supposed that in a term or two he would leave and join some O.T.C. Jimmy and she rarely discussed the war, and never had they discussed it in relation to *him*. And now . . . All summer he must have been quietly thinking things over and arriving at this decision. How like him to have said nothing until he was sure.

'You needn't worry, you know, Auntie,' she said brightly. 'It's a bit of a bombshell of course. But he may easily fail for both places, and anyhow the war will be over before he's through his training, whatever the dear pet says.'

'But why must be he a *regular*?' pursued poor Florence. 'It seems so very drastic, so—binding and—and real. Of course his father . . . but Jimmy's different. Is it necessary, this step?'

'Jimmy thinks so. If he does anything he always does it thoroughly—you know that. He's the most desperately conscientious creature that ever stepped. He won't like the regular army, but if he's got to have any training at all he's got to have 'a proper training'—as he says in his letter.'

Florence sighed.

'I shan't prevent him. I don't suppose I could anyhow. But . . . oh, Joan, he's so very young!'

'In some ways,' said Joan slowly, 'he's very old.'

They parted in Bond Street: Florence going north to Hampstead, considerably comforted by their talk; Joan going south to

Camberwell, fiercely convincing herself that there really *was* no need to worry—yet.

. . . . . .

It was extraordinary how quickly the men's wounds—the less serious among them—began to heal. A leg or an arm which at the beginning of a week appeared as a hopeless suppurating mass would, by the end of it, have so far cleaned up and regained its normal shape as to be hardly recognisable as the same limb. This was due to the general healthiness of the men's condition; apart from their wounds they were not ill, and, if they did not succumb altogether, they made, on the whole, good progress.

Joan was now allowed to do a good many dressings on her own, and she had a little group—Richardson among them—whom she regarded as her special children, and with whom she was on the friendliest terms.

The work, though still hard, was nothing like the strain that it had been early in July. Many patients were 'up.' The atmosphere of the ward was amazingly cheerier, and the staff could count with tolerable certainty on its three hours off a day.

Tubbs and Turner were among Joan's favourites. They were up and about, each with an arm in a sling—Tubbs his left, Turner his right—and they did everything together as though they were one man. When they helped in the ward, Turner would hold the brush and Tubbs the dustpan; Turner the basin and Tubbs the soap; in fact they did exactly the same amount of work that one man would do with two arms. They were excessively funny over it, and Joan used to be convulsed with laughter.

There were endless small jokes between her and the men. One of them was about her safety-pins. Every nurse carried a few safety-pins in her pocket—there were never enough in the ward for the pinning of bandages—but Joan wore hers linked together in a chain hanging from her waist. Whenever she saw one lying about she annexed it, and on some days the chain was so long that it reached the hem of her apron.

'Where's your little dog, Nurse?' Richardson would call out to

her as she tripped past. And then the whole crowd would begin
to whistle.

Another joke originated in a visit of the hospital Padre. He
had been going the round of the ward one afternoon, and, just
as he was leaving, stopped to have a few words with Joan. He
asked her, blinking kindly, what her religion was, and upon her
telling him that it was C. of E., observed that he didn't remember
having seen her at his services.

'No,' she said evasively. 'But perhaps I'll come some day.'

'I hope so,' he responded. 'We mustn't let you slip, Nurse, we
mustn't let you slip!' And he bustled genially off.

After that, whenever Joan came speeding too rapidly down the
ward, her arms full of dishes, one or other of the soldiers would
sing out:

'We mustn't let you slip, Nurse! We mustn't let you slip!'

Work was sweetened by such absurdities.

It was, of course, love of the Tommies that carried you through,
otherwise hospital life would have been dreary indeed. How
anyone could choose nursing as a profession was a source of
wonder to Joan, and that in spite of the fact that she had discovered herself to be rather surprisingly good at it.

Going to the operating theatre was known among the men as
going to 'the pictures.' An orderly would wheel a trolley down
the ward, the patient who was to be operated on would be laid
upon it, and then wheeled out, followed by the encouraging cries
of his comrades. 'Have a good time at the pictures, Bill! Tell us
all about it when you come back! Got the wind up, Bill? Pore
old Bill!'

But when 'Bill,' or whoever it might be, came back from the
theatre he was in no condition to talk. Sometimes he lay a long
while unconscious, green and sweating from the chloroform,
breathing thickly; and Joan, passing backwards and forwards,
would keep an eye on him, and dash to the bedside if she saw
signs of awakening. On the pillow were an ominous towel and
kidney-dish, for it was seldom that a man 'came to' without being

sick. Sometimes he would cry like a child from sheer weakness and wretchedness, and she would stay soothing him till he had regained a grip of himself and a sense of his surroundings. But sometimes, even while still on the trolley coming from the theatre, he would be singing bits of songs, babbling nonsense, often praising or cursing the doctor or one of the staff. On one occasion Joan, trying to rouse a man, asked him, 'Are you awake yet? How do you feel?' and was answered in an ecstatic whisper: 'Oh, I'm so happy—so happy!'

And all around the poor recently-operated-upon patient the work of the ward went forward as usual. The men in the neighbouring beds were being dressed, nurses darting to and fro, 'dinners' being wheeled in.

Dinners were now served out by the 'up' patients—usually Tubbs and Turner—and it was an alarming process. Tubbs carried the pile of plates, Turner sent them spinning one by one on to the beds. 'Coming over!' he would shout as a plate flew through the air; 'Wizz-bang! Got yer!' as it landed. They were forbidden to deal out the knives and forks in this dangerous way (though doubtless they would have done so if left to themselves), and so dumped them in pairs, clatteringly, on to each locker.

A rough but genuine kindness prevailed among the men towards each other. In words they were unsympathetic to the verge of brutality—calling a friend 'lead-swinger' when he was, in fact, perhaps, waiting to have his arm amputated—but in deeds they were almost as tender as the nurses. A man would go again and again to the bedside of a suffering friend and help to ease him by altering his position; would fetch him things that he needed—from drinks of milk to bed-pans; write his letters for him.

Interminable reminiscences of battles and of regiments went on between the bed-patients. Often Joan longed to listen, but there was never time. She would catch fragments as she passed: 'And the Jocks were on our left. Gawd, you should have seen 'em go over!' 'Lay out all night in No-man's land—thought I was finished.' 'Remember Hill 70?' 'Don't I just! Proper murder it was!' 'No, the Canadians take no prisoners, can't blame 'em either. Why, at Yprays . . .'

And then a man would burst into song: 'The Roses Round the Door Make me Love Mother More' (Joan always wondered why the roses should have that particular effect), until someone further up the ward would shout at him to 'put a sock in it,' or even to 'put a locker in it,' and the singing would growl down to silence.

But that doleful ditty, 'Old Soldiers Never Die,' which seemed only to have a chorus and no verse, was almost invariably joined in by everyone. 'Old soldiers never die, never die, never die. Old soldiers never die, they simply fa-a-ade awa-a-ay.' The last notes were a bellow from the entire ward—or such portions of it as had strength to sing—and even Sister Ewart's rigid countenance would relax into a smile.

Among the few who never sang was poor McIvor. He still sat propped against a pile of pillows, his head swathed in bandages, uttering now and then his guttural little requests, rather better able, nowadays, to make himself understood—at any rate by Joan. She was able now to meet his eyes without a shadow in her own, and even to smile at him while his sickening dressing was being performed.

But on a certain visitors' afternoon something happened which plunged McIvor into a deeper gloom than he had known since his arrival. His sweetheart came to see him. She was a Belfast girl, and the hospital had arranged (as it did in cases of this kind) for her to be put up in rooms close to, that she might come frequently to cheer him during her stay. Her first visit to him was her last. Joan, who was tidying a cupboard close at hand, saw at once by her appearance that she was a silly sort of girl; but she was not prepared for what followed. For a second or two, her mouth dropping open, the girl stared at the man she had once loved; at the face now a white linen ball with two terrifying dark holes in it; at the portion of shapeless lip that fell a little beneath the bandage; and she began to emit quavering screams.

'Tom! To-o-m! It's not—you—To-o-om!'

McIvor held out his hand on the counterpane. He grunted something. His beseeching eyes never left her face.

Then the screams came through, and she made no attempt to control herself.

'Come away,' said Joan. 'Come along with me. You can come back later.' She nodded to McIvor, put her arm round the shaking girl, and led her away up the ward into Sister's bunk. With the fit of hysterics that followed she dealt as best she could.

'You'll come again?' she said, when it was over. 'I can tell him you'll come to-morrow?'

The girl nodded, sniffing. But she didn't turn up next day— or the one after. She wrote to 'Tom' from Belfast saying that she would wait for him there; that when he was quite well, and out of the army, they would be married; but that she couldn't face him in hospital again.

Joan never knew what eventually happened (though she strongly suspected that the girl chucked him), for soon after this McIvor was moved to another ward, the grisliest ward in the whole hospital, which went in specially for 'face' cases.

.   .   .   .   .   .

One morning Joan was dispatched post-haste to another ward to borrow some brandy. Sergeant King had very nearly fainted after his dressing, and the supply of brandy in '33' had run out. As she sped up the corridor she met Matron coming towards her —thin as a greyhound in her grey uniform, lynx-eyed and stony-faced. Joan was passing with undiminished speed, and a murmured 'Good-morning, Matron,' when she was brought up short.

'Where are your cuffs, Nurse?'

Joan looked at her bare arms and blushed. It was a strict rule that, except in the wards, cuffs should always be worn. In the hurry of her errand Joan had forgotten this. She stammered an apology.

'What ward do you belong to?' inquired Matron.

'Ward 33.'

'Sister Ewart's? I'm amazed that a nurse of hers—that any

nurse—should appear in such a condition. I thought for a moment, as I came along, that it was one of the housemaids.' With which withering remark Matron went on her way.

When Joan had obtained the brandy and returned to her ward she told Sister Ewart what had happened. If she had expected the slightest sympathy from that quarter—a possible concession that under the circumstances it didn't much matter—she was disappointed. Sister's frosty little reprimand showed her that breaches of hospital etiquette—however small from the point of view of a V.A.D.—could not be lightly passed over.

Joan's luck was decidedly out this week, for a few days later she had a second encounter with Matron, compared with which the episode of the cuffs paled to insignificance.

She was having a morning off, and was sitting on a bench beneath one of the plane trees in the hospital grounds writing letters. Lifting her eyes for a moment she saw Richardson hobbling along on his crutches in his blue hospital suit. (The 'up' patients were encouraged to be out-of-doors as much as possible in this weather.) When he caught sight of Joan a broad grin spread over his face, and he paused as he came up to her.

'Warm mornin', ain't it, Nurse?' he said. 'My, it don't 'alf take it out of you 'oppin' abart on these sticks!'

'Better sit down a minute,' she told him.

He lowered himself on to the bench, and sat mopping his forehead, his bandaged foot sticking out in front of him. Joan, looking at it, wondered idly whether she couldn't, perhaps, in future, reduce the amount of dressing on it, so that it shouldn't look so ungainly, when a sharp voice calling 'Nurse!' made her jerk up her head, and there, a few yards away, was Matron walking rapidly from the huts in the direction of the main building. 'Follow me, Nurse!' she commanded, without pausing in her course. And Joan, feeling rather weak at the knees, but without an idea of what was up, put down her writing-pad and followed her.

Not once did Matron look round until she had reached her

office, and then she turned on the girl and rent her. Under the stream of furious words with which she was deluged Joan gathered that she had committed an appalling offence in allowing a patient to sit beside her in the public grounds.

'Aren't you aware that nurses rank as officers?' asked Matron. 'What sort of an impression do you suppose the sight of you with that private soldier would have created on a sergeant if one had happened to be passing?'

Why a *sergeant?* thought Joan bewilderedly. She gazed at the puckered purple face before her, at the two marble eyes, and heard herself murmuring:

'I'm very sorry, Matron, I didn't know I was doing anything wrong.'

'Then you have absolutely no instincts for the nursing profession,' spluttered Matron. 'You were letting down the whole position and dignity of the hospital. I can't imagine where you can have been brought up!'

For fully ten minutes (or so it seemed to Joan) she stood there receiving abuse. When finally she was told she might go she left the office trembling.

That night she described the whole scene to the 'Cocoas.' Her friends were divided between laughter and indignation.

'It's clear I shall have to leave the 1st London,' said Joan gloomily. 'It won't be particularly pleasant, either, being given the bird for a thing like that.'

Fry counselled her to go straight to Devonshire House (the V.A.D. headquarters) and lay the case before them there.

'If you get in first with your side of it,' she pointed out, 'they'll be far more sympathetic than if they hear of it first from Matron. Not that I think Matron's likely to bring it up.'

'Oh, but she's sure to!' cried Joan. 'She won't want to keep on a girl whom she considers a disgrace to the hospital. I tell you she could hardly have been more outraged if she had found me in bed with Richardson! Never in the whole of my life have I been given such a strafing—not even at school.'

'Cheer up, Seddon, cheer up!' laughed Phipps. 'I shouldn't let a brute of a woman like Matron worry you.'

'It's the power she wields!' groaned Joan.

She acted on the advice of the 'Cocoas,' and, on her next afternoon off, went to Devonshire House, and had an interview with Miss Leather—a pleasant woman in horn-rimmed spectacles, who listened to her from behind a paper-littered desk.

'Yes, I quite see,' said Miss Leather, when Joan had poured forth her facts; 'it was simply lack of knowledge, on your part, of military hospital discipline.'

'At the little hospital where I worked before,' said Joan, 'it was all so friendly and different. We often used to sit about in the garden with the men.'

'Well,' smiled Miss Leather, 'personally I don't think you'll hear anything more about it from your Matron. But if you do, and if she refuses to keep you on, I can easily get you posted somewhere else. V.A.D.s are at a premium these days.'

Joan took her departure considerably fortified, but not wholly at peace. She had been at the 1st London now three weeks. At the end of her fourth week she would be required to sign on definitely—with all the other new girls—for six months, or else would be asked to leave. The prospect of having to begin all over again at a new hospital was not one which she envisaged with joy.

She crossed Piccadilly and went into the Green Park. It was a quarter to four. If she got into a tram at Victoria by a quarter past she could be easily back in her ward by five—when the evening shift began. She sat down on one of the little green chairs.

Behind her was the long, low, chocolate-coloured mass of Devonshire House, drawn back in its privacy from the traffic of the road, unaware that it was passing through the last phase of its dignified life, and that a few years after the war it would have become a pile of rubble. In front of her was the burnt grass dotted with grimy sheep and slumbering human couples. People passed—some hurrying, some dawdling. Now an officer swinging his stick, now a pair of wounded soldiers in their hospital 'blues,' now a nurse in uniform.

After a moment she became aware that a woman had dropped on to the chair on her right. Joan looked at the crossed and out-stretched feet, observed the prettiness of the shoes, the slimness of the ankles, and with a certain amount of curiosity allowed her gaze to wander up to the face. It was Pamela Butler who was sitting there.

Joan's cry of joyful surprise died on her lips. Pamela was staring in front of her, evidently completely unconscious of her surround-ings, and in the hand which lay in her lap was a twisted piece of paper. Joan felt a sick, uneasy apprehension, dismissed it sum-marily, and said with a smile: 'Hallo, Pam!'

Pamela turned her head. For a moment she didn't seem to recognise her friend, and then: 'Joan?' she exclaimed. It was as though she were not so much surprised at this particular chance-blown meeting as that there should be any human beings in the world besides herself. Her face was small and pinched, and her eyes had the look of a wounded deer's. Joan's apprehension rushed in on her again, and turned to definite dread. Involun-tarily she looked down at the piece of paper.

'Yes,' said Pamela, speaking very slowly. 'That came—this afternoon, not quite an hour ago. I came out here . . . I couldn't —stay in the house.'

She held out the crumpled telegram, and Joan read:

'Deeply regret Captain Ian McLane New Zealand Division killed in action on July 21st the Army Council express sympathy. Secretary War Office.'

Joan blinked her eyes to keep back the smarting tears.

'Oh, my dear . . . my dear!'

'Nothing to be said, is there?' said Pamela dryly. Her mouth was set in a tight line. She appeared to have complete control of herself. For the moment it was Joan who was the more outwardly upset.

'I think the thing is—not to allow oneself—to realise it,' continued Pamela. 'Just to—concentrate on—what's to be *done*.' She was carrying her voice carefully, as though it were a porcelain cup that might at any moment break.

'Yes—yes,' breathed Joan, 'I expect you're right. What shall you—do?'

Pamela turned and looked straight at her. 'I've decided that already. I shall *make shells*!' Heedless of Joan's stupefied stare she went on: 'I shall leave the Bruton Street hospital—as soon as possible—and go into a munition factory.'

'But that's ridiculous—it's fantastic,' broke out Joan, 'for *you*!'

'It's the only thing to be done.'

The late July sun lay heartless and yellow on the grass of the Green Park, as it was lying heartless and yellow on the battle-fields of the Somme. A group of ragged children chased each other with shouts of laughter a few yards off. Joan looked helplessly around her.

'Oh, dear, I shall have to go,' she said. 'This is awful! Pam darling, promise me you won't do anything in a hurry. We'll meet again very soon. I'll—I'll write. Oh dear! Good-bye—good-bye.'

She tore herself away, and almost ran down the path to Hyde Park Corner, leaving her friend still on the little chair staring stonily at nothing. Only the unescapable necessity for being on duty would have kept Joan from her side.

By five o'clock she was back in the ward, washing McNeil, and rejoicing with him on the remarkable progress of his wound.

Chapter Nine

THAT evening after supper Joan went straight to her room, and sat for a long time in her kimono by the open window. There wasn't a breath of air.

She had been kept so hard at it for the past few weeks that she had scarcely been beyond the hospital grounds; in her rare off hours she had felt too bone-weary to do anything but lie reading in the rest-room or on the grass outside. The last time she had seen Pamela—some time in June—the girl had been like a dancing fairy over her engagement. Joan could see her now, standing in a patch of sunlight in Lady Butler's little drawing-room, exclaiming jubilantly: 'I'm done for, Joan! I'm completely done for!' and contrasted that radiant creature with the tight-lipped figure of this afternoon—the gold in her all turned to iron, the song to silence.

What was the use of winning the war, Joan cried to herself in sudden despair, if none of the men who won it were to live? The papers were for ever quoting 'Who dies if England lives?' But after all what *was* England? The old men who sat at home, and in clubs, and gloatingly discussed the war? The bustling business men who thought they ran it? The women with aching hearts? Or the young manhood of the nation—that part of the nation that should be working, mating, begetting, but which now was being cut down? There was no question—the last. And in a year or two there'd be no 'England.'

She thought of Colin, Philip, and other friends, not seen for so long, and now in hourly danger. Colin's letters had been very scrappy of late. She thought of a second cousin of hers, killed in the fighting round La Boiselle. She thought of her cousin Jack lying badly wounded at Boulogne. The waste, the waste of it all!

Sighing, she drew her writing-pad towards her. Might as well *do* something. Better to write than to think. Write to Jack. Write to Betty to go and look up Jack in hospital. Write, too, to Barbara Frewen, who had recently gone over there to nurse. She read through again Barbara's last two letters.

The first was written from Sussex, early in July. 'We really do seem to be getting a move on at last, and the guns for the past ten days have been perfectly appalling—booming incessantly, day and night. It has been like one huge throb through all the air. The windows rattle all the time, and even the china on the washstands. One daren't think what it must be like out there.'

The second was from No. 14 Stationary, Wimereux, and had come last week. 'Most extraordinary luck getting here, for I never even asked for France. The hospital is right on the sea, as you know. We work in tents and huts which are delightfully airy and bright. Of course it's within easy reach of Betty and all of them, and I've already paid several visits to the Alexandra, and also to the dear old Connaught (which, my dear, does *not* look so nice as in our day!). Yesterday I spent a heavenly afternoon in the woods at Hardelot, and how I thought of you! I could just see you there sitting on the ramparts, surrounded with poetry-books! I am much more at peace in my mind now that I am nursing, but also I shall never like the work so much. That time with the Y.M.C.A. was a beautiful time, all so sunny and romantic somehow. But it was a very easy life, we could do practically what we liked, and we felt—didn't we?—that it was too pleasant. How is your friend, that boy whom I sent you out for a walk with from Ostrohove? My Sam is somewhere behind the lines at the moment, thank heaven—at one of those instruction schools. He hopes to come up and see me at Boulogne before long.'

Yes, it *was* all sunny and romantic! thought Joan, looking back on those days, already so long ago. She envied Barbara being in dear Boulogne again—even though it was as a V.A.D., and not as a Y.M. worker.

It was nearly midnight when she finished writing to her various friends (the letter to Pamela was the most exhausting of all); and when, dazed with fatigue, she dropped into bed, the last thing that her sleepy eyes beheld was her apron, with its red cross, hanging over the back of the chair. Symbol of servitude. For how many months, for how many years, would she, and her kind, be wearing uniform?

.   .   .   .   .   .

Miss Leather was right. Joan never heard another word from Matron about the Richardson business; and her early indignation died down as she realised that Matron had no more meant the insulting things she had said to her than a sergeant-major meant the things he roared out when he strafed a Tommy. She had employed a drastic form of utterance to express disapprobation of a small lapse, and that was all there was to it.

And so, when the time came, Joan signed her death-warrant (as the V.A.D.s called it) without let or hindrance, and thankfully bound herself to serve at the 1st London for the next six months, at a salary of £20 a year.

But that the spirit of the hospital—as far as the regular staff went —was an unimaginative and flinty one was shown a few weeks later by an event which shook the whole community.

Working with Phipps in Sister Grundle's ward was a girl called O'Reilly—a good-natured creature, a little slow and vague, but willing. Somehow or other, in spite of the warm weather, O'Reilly had managed to catch a very bad cold. She took no notice of it at first, but after a time it went on to her chest, and she had prolonged fits of coughing. As the cough kept her awake for hours at night, and was a source of intense irritation to Sister Grundle by day, O'Reilly suggested that she had perhaps better 'go sick.' Sister Grundle glared at her opprobriously, for a moment, over a gigantic bosom, then took her temperature, saw that it was a few points above normal, and, more to be rid of her than for any humanitarian reason, dispatched her to Matron.

Matron received her in the stony manner which was characteristic of her, and laid a couple of fingers on the girl's pulse.

'There's nothing the matter with you at all, Nurse,' she snapped. 'Many people have a slight cough without making a fuss of this sort. What you want is a little hard work. You V.A.D.s are far too easily sorry for yourselves. Go back to your ward.'

And back O'Reilly went, swearing to herself that nothing in heaven or earth would induce her ever to report sick again.

'And she's getting worse and worse,' declared Phipps to the others at night. 'Soon she'll scarcely be able to crawl round the ward. She refuses to take her own temperature—says it would be useless. I keep pressing aspirins and cough lozenges on her, but——'

There came a point when O'Reilly's condition could no longer be ignored. Having almost collapsed one morning, she was sent to the sick-room at the top of the main building and put instantly to bed. It was found that she had bronchial pneumonia. From then onwards she received the best attention which the hospital could provide. But by then it was too late.

Everyone went about, as it were, on tip-toe. 'How is O'Reilly?' would be asked in frightened whispers—even by those who had only known the girl by sight. Guarded reports came from the sick-room. Nothing could be definitely ascertained. At meal-times Matron's face was scanned by hundreds of young eyes, but it preserved its nut-shell impenetrability.

Then it was rumoured that O'Reilly had become unconscious; then that her people had been sent for; then that she was a little better and was being kept alive on oxygen and brandy.

By the time that her parents had been able to get over from Ireland the girl was dead.

O'Reilly had not been a particularly popular or a particularly significant member of the community of the 1st London, but thenceforward she became a symbol and a martyr. For days feeling ran high among those who knew the facts about her; but Phipps's fury of indignation against Matron was mingled with remorse that she herself had not been able to do more to help the girl.

Outwardly, of course, the higher authorities proceeded on their way as before, but their attitude to V.A.D.s as malingerers underwent a profound change. In dying poor O'Reilly had done more for her companions than ever she had done by living.

. . . . . .

The stifling August days wore through, and now that work was less of a nightmare, Joan, in her off hours, used to take a bus and go into London.

She saw Pamela twice, but was unable to dissuade her friend from the munitions scheme; and when, soon afterwards, Pamela left Bruton Street and went to work in some awful factory out at Willesden, Joan realised that henceforward meetings would be impossible.

On ordinary days it was not worth while to go as far as Hampstead, but on her 'half-day' a week (from 2 p.m. to 10 p.m.) it was very pleasant to be at home, to lie curled on the old chintz-covered sofa in the drawing-room, to chat to Aunt Florence, to hear news of relations, and of how Jimmy was getting on in the country where he was 'cramming' with three friends. Not so pleasant to trek back after dinner (a little tug at the heart) by tube and bus to dreary Camberwell—allowing just enough time to arrive at the hostel before Sister Ansdell locked up for the night.

Sometimes, instead of going home, Joan would divide her 'half-day' between different friends—tea-ing at one house, dining at another; or else go to a matinée with an officer on leave, or to dinner with him at a restaurant. Swift delightful patches of another sort of life, taking the smell of lysol and of wounds from the nostrils.

These London expeditions of Joan's earned her, from her room-mates, the reputation of living 'a double life.' One of them, especially, a kindly individual called Gower with a long nose and a pronounced cockney accent, thought her almost paralysingly energetic. Gower herself seldom went beyond the hospital grounds.

'You'll come to a bad end, Seddon,' she used to say to Joan

through the curtains of her cubicle at night. 'Can't live the double life, you know—end by wearing yourself out!' (she pronounced it 'ay-out').

'Out on the tiles again, Seddon?' she would call, as Joan came in, by the skin of her teeth, at ten o'clock from a 'half-day.' And Joan would laugh at the stock joke, and keep up the fiction of secret dissipations.

.   .   .   .   .   .

September sailed in on the calm glory of a full moon.

On the second night, at about twelve o'clock, Joan was awakened from fathom-deep sleep by the murmur of voices in the bedroom. Reluctantly she opened an eye, and saw, outlined against the window, the heads of the three other V.A.D.s. But what struck through her half-consciousness as an odd fact was that their heads were silhouetted against crimson. Was it morning, she wondered vaguely, or was there a fire?

'Get up, Seddon—air raid!' she heard Gower's voice somewhere in the darkness.

'Air raid?' grunted Joan.

'Yes—Zeppelin! You'll probably see it if you go to the window. Slip on your shoes and your coat, and you'd better put a few 'air-pins in your pocket—you never know.'

Gower spoke in matter-of-fact tones, but Joan couldn't for the life of her see the necessity for putting hair-pins into her coat pocket. She knew she was excessively sleepy, and not in a condition to reason about anything—but *hair-pins?* She saw a vision of herself with Gower, Sister Ansdell, and the rest, wandering about outside, screwing up their hair in an attempt at decency while dodging German bombs. Then she dropped off.

Voices broke in on her again. 'There it is! There it is!' This time she roused herself fully, scrambled out of bed, and went to the window. An extraordinary spectacle met her eyes. Far up in a murky pink sky gleamed a small silver cigar, and near it hovered, dancingly, a fire-fly. For a moment these two objects kept at an equal distance from one another, then merged, and there was a burst of flames. A roar, as from the whole of London, went up; and the flaming cigar sank through the sky and disappeared beyond the trees.

The whole thing had been so unexpected, so eerie, and Joan had been so far from wide awake that she could never clearly remember afterwards what she had imagined, and what she had really seen and heard.

For instance, why had the sky appeared red against the window-panes when first she woke—for that was surely before the Zeppelin caught fire? And that dull terrifying roar—had it actually come from the throats of thousands of London onlookers miles away, or only from a few folk on Denmark Hill? All was confused. But printed vividly on her brain for ever was the picture of that small silver cigar and the dancing fire-fly.

Later she learnt—as did all the world—that the German military air-ship, S.L. 11, had been attacked by Lieut. Leaf Robinson, and had fallen, a burning mass, near Cuffley, Middlesex. It was considered that London had been saved by the young man's deed, and he was awarded the V.C.

'Can't 'elp being sorry for them pore burnt Germans,' remarked one of the charwomen, who scrubbed the ward-floor, to Joan. 'Mothers' sons every one of 'em. And coming by night all that way from their 'omes too, up in the air.'

This was so concise an expression of the haunting thoughts which Joan had been trying to hold at bay that she shuddered. It could not have been better put: 'Mothers' sons every one of 'em.' An instant's imagination as to what that Zeppelin crew must have been feeling as their machine caught fire would have checked the roar which had greeted its destruction.

And apart from this, although it was true that Robinson had done a very gallant thing, was there not, Joan asked herself, something distasteful in the frantic eagerness with which he had been praised and decorated?—something that savoured of smug self-congratulation on the part of the city at its escape? Every day, in the skies of France, deeds as gallant were being performed and going unrewarded; every day the stolid soldiers in the trenches were unostentatiously 'saving London.' But for once the civilian population had really felt itself to be in danger, had actually seen itself defended, and had gone mad with gratitude.

Chapter Ten

SERGEANT KING was not getting on well. Sister Ewart was worried about that stump of his. Already, more than once, his temperature had gone up alarmingly, hæmorrhage had started, and he had had to be wheeled to the theatre for another operation. Still he lay, as he had done from the first, taking no interest in anything; refusing to talk; refusing any but the smallest amount of food.

One evening, as Joan was hurrying down the ward with a wash-basin of water, she heard a cry from his bed. She looked round, startled. The sound was so unwonted that she could hardly believe it came from Sergeant King. 'Oh, Sister, Sister, it's coming through!' he cried.

Instantly she gave the basin to a passing 'up' patient and flew to the bedside. King's hands were clasping his stump, his head was thrown back on the pillow. Joan pulled aside the dressing. The femoral artery! Thank God for what training she had had! She compressed with her two thumbs—one in the angle of the groin, the other a little below, on the thigh—the pumping artery and held on for grim life.

'Get Sister at once!' she called to the second V.A.D. Next minute Sister Ewart came rapidly down the ward from her 'bunk.' She leant over, collected and efficient.

'Hold on, Nurse. That's perfectly right. Hold on.' And sending the other girl to telephone for the doctor she busied herself with preparations for his arrival.

Joan held on. No question of using the rubber tourniquet. The leg had been amputated too close for that. Human pressure was the only hope. King was showing signs of exhaustion. There was cold sweat on his forehead. He was trembling.

'Don't go, Nurse,' he murmured with shut eyes, 'don't leave me.'

The man who had fought in Gallipoli, who had fought in France, who had lain for six weeks uncomplainingly in hospital, had suddenly become like a frightened child calling for its mother in the dark.

'Of *course* I won't leave you, Sergeant. You're being splendid. It was a nasty shock, wasn't it? Never mind. I've got you tight. You'll be fixed up in a few minutes.'

What ages that girl was telephoning for the doctor! Perhaps he couldn't be found. Oh, this delay! . . . Her back was breaking. Her left wrist, which in some unremembered way she had managed to sprain, was sending little fierce arrows up her arm. *Could* she hold on? Must. Mustn't relax pressure for an instant. Life and death. What did her silly wrist matter? That white face . . .

Sister was putting hot-water bottles into the bed . . . a soldier was lifting the foot of the bed while she placed blocks beneath to keep it raised . . . the trolley was standing ready . . . screens had been brought.

'All right, Sergeant, all right.'

How much longer? Mustn't move. Keep pressing. Keep . . . Ah! . . . at last!

The doctor was there—had taken charge. Joan fell back half-fainting. Ten minutes in actual time she had knelt there—an hour to her imagination.

Somewhere down at the other end a man was singing, 'The Roses *Round* the Door.' . . . She staggered into the annex to wash the blood from her hands. The work of the ward went on.

•   •   •   •   •   •

For some days before this Joan had been feeling (in the laconic phraseology of youth) 'rather rotten.' She had had a poisoned finger on her right hand which, by copious applications of iodine, she had managed to prevent from swelling; but what worried her far more was that left wrist of hers. It was so stiff and painful that lifting patients, adjusting mattresses, carrying weights had to be done with extreme care. She saved it as much as possible. At the hostel she used to leave supper early, and fall into bed overcome by a sick lassitude quite different from the healthy dog-tiredness of July.

On the night following Sergeant King's hæmorrhage—about a week after the Zeppelin raid—she woke in the early hours with a throbbing head and her wrist on fire. Stumbling to the wash-stand she plunged her arm elbow-deep into the jug of cold water, then wrapped a towel round it, and went back to bed and to a series of nauseous little dreams. She must have talked or cried out at one point, for she heard Gower asking sleepily: 'You all right, Seddon? Anything you want?'

In the morning she just managed to dress and get downstairs, but breakfast was impossible. Sister Ansdell detained her after-wards and took her temperature. It was 103°. For far less than this, nowadays, V.A.D.s were sent to report sick. Since the tragedy of O'Reilly no risks were being taken.

A few things were packed for her in her suit-case, a taxi was procured, and at nine o'clock (the hour for interviews) Joan was standing in Matron's office. Sister Ansdell had already rung through.

'What made you think you had merely a sprained wrist, Nurse?' asked Matron.

Joan could give no satisfactory reason. She had merely 'sup-posed' it must be a sprain.

'Well, it's septic poisoning of course,' Matron informed her. 'Very careless of you. The slightest scratch on arm or finger is dangerous when you're in contact with wounds. I should have thought you nurses had been warned enough about that. Why didn't you report earlier?'

Joan gaped. The tables were indeed turned. She stammered that, until last night, she had not felt bad enough.

'You must have felt pretty bad with an arm like that!' was Matron's muttered and incredible rejoinder. 'Go upstairs at once.'

In the bare sick-room at the top of the building Joan lay bookless and alone. But she didn't mind. The extreme comfort of lying between cool sheets, of not having to drag herself up and work, was sufficient for the present. Only now did she realise what an effort the last eight days had been. A devouring feverish beast, no longer kept at bay by will-power, seemed suddenly to rush in on her, and it was a relief, and not a terror, to surrender to him.

The hours rolled past, hot and confused. She couldn't measure time. At midday one of the hospital maids brought her some soup, and later on some tea. Between-whiles she dozed. Fantastic visions flitted before her. Whenever she raised her head it whirled and waltzed. Her arm throbbed. From the gramophone in one of the officers' wards below came the strains of the 'Broken Doll.' Over and over and over again that inane and vacuously sentimental song droned its way up through the windows.

> 'And when you go away,
> You'll be sorry some day,
> You left behind a bro-ken do-oll.'

Of all the lyrical atrocities produced by the war, this was about the worst; yet it was extremely popular in the summer of 1916. That ghastly broken doll—half-waxen, half-human—stumbled its way in and out of Joan's dreams, and for ever afterwards the tune was connected for her with the sick-room at Camberwell and a throbbing arm.

The sun fell away from the windows, and with the gathering darkness a sister came in and washed her, and settled her for the night.

The next day passed in much the same way, except that during the hours of the hot afternoon the 'Broken Doll' was varied now and then by 'The Only Girl in the World.' For this slight relief Joan was thankful, as her head was becoming worse, and her arm, now swollen to the dimensions of a nightmare German sausage, was causing her a lot of pain. She looked at it with stupid eyes as it lay crimson and tight-skinned on the counterpane. She didn't recognise it. She thought at moments that it must be her leg, which had somehow got outside the bedclothes.

It was to be 'opened' to-morrow. Joan had asked, weakly, whether she might not have a local anæsthetic, for she had a horror of gas; but the doctor had refused. The incision would have to be a deep one as the poison was already mounting above the elbow.

> 'And when you go away,
> You'll be sorry some day . . .'

Joan staggered to the wash-stand to sponge her forehead, and on the way back stopped and looked at her temperature chart where it hung at the foot of the bed. She hadn't seen it before. She observed that the ink line had gone zigzagging up since she had first come in. It stood now at 105°. 'How interesting!' she thought; 'I must be quite ill!' and relapsed on to her pillows again.

In a detached way she wondered whether she would mind dying, and found that she wouldn't very much. Half of the youth of the world was dead already; she would be in good company. She thought of the patient soldiers in the ward—of Sergeant King. In a way she too was a soldier. Not much in dying these days. At any other period it would have been a far more difficult matter.

> 'If *I* were the *only girl* in the world,
> And *you* were the *only boy*.'

Something laughed inside her. 'The only girl!' Yes—*if*! But being one of thousands—of millions—she could well be spared by the country. Quite a good thing really to pop off—equal up the sexes a bit.

Next morning the room seemed to be full of Matrons, Sisters, and M.O.s. Joan hoped that nobody heard the thumping of her heart as she smiled feebly at them all before the hated gas-bag was put over her face, and consciousness was drowned in a dark roar.

An hour or two later she felt a different being. Her temperature had dropped, her head was cool, furniture and people's faces no longer swam unsteadily before her. The day, instead of being a shapeless sprawling nightmare, was divided again into neatly-stepping hours. Phipps and Fry poked smiling faces round the door; brought her books. Aunt Florence—bundling back from a few days in the country—came to see her, trying to hide her concern, and her extreme annoyance that she had not been sent for earlier.

The arm, beneath its mass of bandages, was very sore, but this was a far more endurable pain than the previous aching throb. Joan took a professional interest in her dressings, and was amazed at the quantity of yellow pus which poured forth. No wonder she had had fever. The opening, a few inches above the wrist, was the shape of the opening in a melon when a single slice has been removed. There would always be a scar where it had healed up. Horrid it would look when she was in evening dress! Then the thought came that as it seemed improbable she ever again *would* be in evening dress that hardly mattered.

It hadn't occurred to her that she wouldn't just stay on in the sick-room until she was fit again, so it came as a shock when she was told that she must be removed to 'Bart's' hospital, where all sick sisters from the 1st London were sent, and where she could be properly looked after. She was evidently a more serious case than she had supposed; and here at Camberwell they had no time for her.

.   .   .   .   .   .

The transit on the following day was the quaintest and the most wearisome that could be imagined. In an antediluvian ambulance drawn by one slow horse, Joan, accompanied by Florence, was taken across London—from South to North, from Camberwell to Holborn. Joan called the conveyance the 'Black Maria,' and smiled at her aunt over the sheaf of roses which had been bought for her. Hour by hour, it seemed, they jogged along in the preposterous vehicle—Joan stretched out, and Florence sitting amply and reassuringly beside her.

At eight o'clock that evening Joan had become 'No. 7' in Radcliffe Ward, Bart's—a ward of women and children suffering from septic complaints—and she began to realise hospital life from the point of view of the patient. Nobody took the slightest notice of her when her aunt had gone. Nurses pattered past her up and down the ward, her arm was hurting her badly, and it was with difficulty that she could keep back the forlorn tears.

'Had any supper?' a hard little nurse rapped out.

'I've had nothing since a cup of tea at four o'clock,' said Joan, very sorry for herself. 'How could I?'

'You've *not* had any supper then.' The nurse was just going off duty after a busy day, and was feeling irritable anyhow. To have a 'lady' thrust in on the ward like this, among the ordinary patients, was a nuisance, and any tendency on her part to moaning must be nipped in the bud.

A glass of milk and a stiff square of red jelly were slapped down on Joan's locker, and she was left. The bed was very hard. She passed a restless night.

By next day she was able to laugh at her low spirits of the previous evening, and she settled down to one of the strangest three weeks she had ever spent.

Nurses were brisk and kind, but they were run off their feet, and medical students were for ever mooching round. Joan was washed every day at 6 a.m.; given breakfast at 7; heard Sister read prayers at the end of the ward at 8; and at 9 had her arm unbandaged, and put into a tin arm-bath of saline, where it soaked for a couple of hours. Meals were of the plainest, though Joan (to her secret embarrassment and joy) was allowed extras not given to the other patients; and at 9 p.m. the ward was darkened for the night. A severe existence, healthy certainly, but not made more tolerable by the cries and screams of the poor sick children in the other beds. Some of these children came from the worst slum homes, and had frightful skin diseases; most of them were between five and eight years old, but there were a few of only two.

There was one pathetic infant in the bed next to Joan's (but the bed was a crib) who couldn't have been more than eighteen months. It had the face of a gargoyle, and a mat of tow-coloured hair. The first time 'dinners' came round she watched it nervously. A plate of rice-pudding and a spoon had been dumped in front of it, and as it evidently hadn't the faintest idea what a spoon was for, and was at the same time excessively hungry, it took the primitive course of plunging both fists into its food, and thus conveying it to its mouth. This process, combined with the fact that its whole face was soon plastered with pudding, was enough to put Joan off her own meal that day.

The gargoyle (as Joan called it) used to stand in its crib from time to time, holding on to the rail at each side, and lurching perilously. Joan used to suffer considerable anxiety wondering whether it would topple out. One day it did so. It fell straight on to its head with its feet in the air; but it didn't seem to mind, and, instead of the yell which Joan had expected, remained placidly silent. She called to one of the nurses at the end of the ward, who, quite unconcerned, picked it up and planked it back again.

Feeling half-sorry for and half-disgusted by these infants, and realising that in any case she could do nothing whatever to help or comfort them, Joan entrenched herself behind books, and succeeded fairly well in shutting out the life of the ward.

Florence's visits were a comfort, but always left her a little homesick, and with a bleaker sense of her present surroundings. On two occasions the 'Cocoas' turned up with gossip from the hospital, and Joan was particularly grateful to them, for the distance was long, and their time, as she knew, limited. It appeared that there was a tremendous pressure of work on again; wounded were pouring in from the Somme, where the British were making another push.

'We've got some pretty awful new V.A.D.s,' Phipps told her. 'One of them's in my ward. What do you think she said on her second day? It was after she'd been put on to the job of washing one of the men all over. "There!" she exclaimed, "the crowning incongruity of this war has happened, since a General's daughter has washed a Tommy's feet."'

'Phipps! I *don't* believe it!' cried Joan.

'Perfectly true,' put in Fry. 'Tell her what *you* said, Phipps.'

'Well, I happened to be washing the man in the next bed, and I remarked to him in an undertone: "It might be interesting to know whether it's her father or her mother who's the 'general.'"'

Joan laughed more over this than she had done over anything for weeks.

But when they had gone she cursed her fate at being laid up; it seemed particularly bitter just as she had begun to be of real use in her ward. The more she thought of it the more depressed she grew. She had come to nurse soldiers, not to be nursed herself. And now she was threatened with three weeks' sick leave when she left Bart's. Never had she looked forward to a holiday less. Her arm was progressing, but slowly; the swelling had gone down, and it remained for the gash to heal.

Meanwhile she could, at any rate, make use of these enforced hours of idleness to catch up with her correspondence; and, between the reading of one book and another, she scribbled pencil screeds to all her friends—officers, girls, and Tommies—in England and in France.

Colin's last letter, received a few days ago, was the first proper one she had had from him for a long time. He too was writing to her from hospital. He told her that he had lost two of his greatest friends, and that he had been missing them unspeakably. His division had been in and out of the line since the middle of June, marching and fighting incessantly. 'Of that particular fortnight in July,' he wrote, 'I will spare you the revolting details—unless you like to ask me questions when we meet.' (Never before had he offered to spare her anything, but then there hadn't been a 'Somme' till now.) He went on: 'But just before the tattered ribbons of our division were withdrawn I got a sort of attack of typhoid, and here I am at Rouen. I long for home more than I have ever longed for it, but with this new push I expect they'll think they can't spare me (I'm not "wounded" you see), and I shall have to go back again. By Jove, my luck is just incredible! And to think of all the officers we've lost, and even yet my name is not among them. There must be *something* looking after me. I have lost all my kit at present, and with it your letters, so I cannot answer them. I have almost forgotten how to read a book. Your war-worn and still faithful soldier.'

Yes, his luck was 'incredible,' thought Joan, and so was his constitution. Was any subaltern in the army worked so hard? Did any stick it so well, and with fewer rewards? She wrote to him, putting at the end of her letter: 'I don't forget you.'

Nor did she forget him—really. But his actual face was misty to her. So many months of absence; such a turbulent sorrowful world; so much hard work to be done. Colin had once said to her that she had a 'greatly affectionate *mind*.' But the trouble about that was, that although it enabled you to keep your friends, it enabled you also—too contentedly—to endure their absence. In a relationship like hers with Colin, where flesh scarcely counted, but wanted—dimly—to be made to count, separation was disastrous, for it threw all the burden of feeling upon the mind— already alive enough. She understood now what Colin had meant, that day long ago at Beechwood, when he had damned the war for giving him so little time.

For the last two or three afternoons of her stay at Bart's Joan was allowed to dress, and to sit out in the garden. It was pleasant under the plane trees in the late September sunshine; and the grey old walls of the hospital looked benign. But it was with a thankful heart that she stepped for the last time from the Radcliffe Ward; and if ever she had had any waverings towards nursing as a profession—which she had not—they would have been finally stamped out by what she had seen of the life in there.

.   .   .   .   .   .

Comfortably back at Beechwood she felt, at first, weaker than she would have thought possible. The wound in her arm was still suppurating a little, but she managed to dress it herself, with

Florence to do the bandaging. For the rest she sat about feeling 'a fearful slacker,' and gradually recovering strength and appetite. Robert Seddon was frequently in and out. He had never shown himself so affectionate towards his niece as now, and Joan knew quite well why it was, and smiled to herself as she noticed the efforts he made to control the proprietary family pride which welled up in him whenever he looked at her bandaged arm.

'Hadn't you better wear your sling, my dear?' he would say to her solicitously when he came to take her to dinner in Willoughby Road. 'You can't be too careful, you know.'

But Joan, who had definitely passed the sling stage, refused to revive it in order to flatter her uncle's vanity and make a better show for his friends. Dear Uncle, he was really too transparent!

Aunt Rose opened her brown eyes and twittered: 'Wonderful it must be to nurse!' and: 'Joan, dear, did they hurt you *very* much?' while an undercurrent of slight irritation ran beneath her words that it should be Joan, and not one of her own children, who was at the moment in the limelight.

Joan took it all with a shrug, and wondered how poor Jack, when he came home for his sick-leave, would put up with the same sort of thing intensified. For Jack really was a wounded hero—the showy sort too. Crutches, yet foot not sufficiently smashed to prevent eventual return to duty. Perfect. Joan did not feel un-kindly towards the Robert Seddons, but a certain amount of cynicism was inevitable in their company during the war period.

.   .   .   .   .   .

'Good Lord, I'm not particularly keen,' said Jimmy, his long legs sprawling over the arm of a chair, one hand absently twisting Tam's ears, 'only if the job's got to be done at all it may as well be done properly. I suppose it's funny I shouldn't feel more like a soldier, considering Father was in the army, but there it is—I don't.'

Jimmy had taken his exam. on the 19th, at Aldershot, and was now awaiting results. He couldn't expect to hear for at least another fortnight, and refused to discuss his hopes and fears. He didn't mind, however, discussing his attitude to the war as a whole, now that he was going to be drawn into it.

'Does one *have* to hate the Germans, Joan?'

She laughed. It was just as though he had asked her about some minor point of conduct—such as whether one *had* to change for dinner.

'Heavens, no, Jim-pot! If you don't you don't. Some people—and all the French of course—genuinely do.'

'Well, I can't. Poor old Huns! After all *they* think they're in the right too, and they're having just as filthy a time as we are—though they did begin it. I wish I could be a bit more enthusiastic about the war, but it seems to me just a boring mess. One knows too much about it nowadays to imagine it's going to be a joyous adventure.'

He spoke in his usual slow, unemphatic way, but it was a long speech for Jimmy. And it struck Joan that what he said was not only characteristic of Jimmy as an individual, but that it represented the feeling of all the younger lot who were going into the army. The war had lasted over two years now, and the early romantic attitude towards it was no longer possible.

'It's just got to be gone through with—without too much of a fuss,' said Jimmy. 'Sorry, Tam, old man!' For the Airedale had given a deprecatory squeak as one of his ears was twisted a trifle more vigorously than he could bear.

'Without too much of a fuss,' thought Joan. Yes, that was it. That was Jim all over. He had strange deep philosophies of his own. If a thing was inevitable it was inevitable. No good fussing and kicking. He would accept his part in the war—however uncongenial—as stoically as he used to accept his childish ailments, and the fact that every now and then he had had to be knocked off games and put on to hated régimes of milk.

.   .   .   .   .   .

Pale gold the leaves of the birch trees; thin blue the October sky; brown the fading heather beneath their feet. West country wind ruffled their hair as they looked away across the moor to where a faint line of silver showed meeting of sky and sea.

Kept at home by many affairs, Florence had dispatched her nephew and niece to Devonshire for a fortnight. Both needed a change—Jimmy after his exam. work, Joan after her illness. 'Take care of each other,' she had said. 'I wish I could come with you.'

And together they had tramped and climbed, and ridden Exmoor ponies, and got stuck in bogs, and returned late to gigantic teas at the inn, and afterwards sat drowsily by the fire contemplating their steaming shoes, or trying to play chess with some antique chessmen found on the premises.

Deep feather beds enfolded them by night, healthful moorland airs by day. Their eyes were clear as running water, and the freckled ivory skins which were their inheritance had taken on as firm a pink as they could ever show.

'So you see it would be fun if we four could keep together right through,' Jimmy was saying, looking across the moor. He was talking of his friends, Sanderson, Carey and Browne, who had coached with him and sat for the exam. 'Not that it's in the least likely, because we've all got such different brain capacities.' He turned to her with an inquiring, an almost apologetic smile. 'Which of them do you like the best?'

She remembered them all. Boys in and out of Beechwood during holidays. All, in a way, alike. Shy, energetic, with strange interests of their own. Yet one of them stood out—merrier—more charming.

'Carey, I think,' she replied.

'M'm. I suppose to a girl he would be the most attractive.'

'To a *girl*! What do you know about it? And as if I thought of your little Carey as anything but a schoolboy! Pfff! Race you down the hill.'

And having—while he stood brooding—the advantage of the start she nearly beat him. The tufts of heather scudded backwards beneath her bounds. Wind whipped her cheeks. But just before the bottom of the slope his high tweed shoulder shot past her, and he was up the opposite incline on legs that left her nowhere.

'Good to have friends,' she said quietly, as they sauntered back to the inn. 'Stick to them Jim-pot. Life without friends is futile.'

In their nostrils was the tang of sea, of damp roots, and of bog-myrtle.

At Taunton, on the journey home, Jim bought a *Times*; looked through the pages casually; found what he wanted; folded it down, and concentrated.

'What *are* you . . .?' began Joan from the opposite corner.

'Results are out,' he grunted without raising his eyes.

'Oh, I *say!*'

She held her breath, watching him. He was reading through the immense list of candidates' names—from the bottom. She thought it was the most typical thing she had ever seen him do. That quiet assumption that he would be among the lowest. Slowly his eyes travelled upwards. Not yet, not yet. He reddened with anxiety. He was getting near the top, and his name had not appeared. Then with sudden relief he dropped the paper on his knee and leant back smiling.

'All right,' he pronounced. 'Thought for a moment I wasn't going to be in at all.'

'Absurd you are!'

She seized the paper, and there, among the first forty names, was her brother's.

'That means Woolwich!' she glowed at him. '*Well done*, Jim-pot!'

'Gunners,' he said, 'not Sappers. Not high enough up for them.'

'Never mind! Good *enough!*'

This was proof of his steady brains, his steady power of work. Never had he had sufficient belief in his own ability. This would help him to self-confidence. He was in with Sanderson and Browne, the brainy chaps, older than him by a year. She had to confess to her own surprise. Little Carey had only managed to scrape into Sandhurst.

'How long will you be there?' she asked later on.

'About nine months I think they keep you. P'raps a bit less.'

Nine months. . . . Then probably camp for a bit. . . . On the whole a year of safety—one could count on that. And at the end of a year . . . Oh, well, by then . . .

'How queer things are, Jim-pot. Not Cambridge for you after all, but this irrelevant Woolwich!'

'Cambridge is only postponed,' he said. 'The Shop's a side-track. You don't catch me staying on in the regular army longer than necessary.'

'*Clever* little boy!' she burst out. 'Nothing he can't do if he sets his mind to it, is there? Oh dear, I would like to give you a kiss!'

Jimmy looked nervously round at the other occupants of the carriage.

'All right, Jumbles, all right!' she assured him, and with a twinkling face subsided into her book.

The train rumbled on towards Paddington.

.   .   .   .   .   .

Joan having declared that she wanted a last 'spot of life' before going back to prison at Camberwell, she and Jimmy donned evening dress, and, with the glow of Exmoor still in their cheeks and eyes, dined together at the 'Troc' and did a show.

It was 'Chu-Chin-Chow,' now in the second month of its five years' run. Joan was to see it often again and to become sick of it, for it was almost invariably the play chosen by men on leave wanting to forget the war. To-night however, with Jimmy, she thoroughly enjoyed it.

Looking round at the khaki-dotted audience she suddenly saw Thrush Shirly sitting a row or two in front. Joan hadn't set eyes on her since that afternoon at Beechwood last May, when, in her little cotton V.A.D. dress, Thrush had sobbed herself sick on the bed over Ginger's death. More than once Joan had tried to get into touch with her, but without success; and she assumed finally that the girl would rather be left alone.

The difference in Thrush, as Joan saw her now, was startling.

She had on a crimson evening frock, and such of her cheek as could be seen was like a crimson rose. Her dark hair was shiningly brushed, and coiled low into her neck. A young officer was sitting beside her, and her shoulders were shaking with silent laughter at something he was whispering. During the intervals they went out together, and all through the performance their heads were close.

In the crush in the hall at the end of the show Joan went up to her.

'Well, of all extraordinary things!' exclaimed Thrush. 'Fancy seeing you here! What are you doing with yourself these days?'

'I must ask the same of you,' smiled Joan. 'You are a little rotter to have so completely disappeared!'

'Oh, I know, but I couldn't help it.' A trace of apology and embarrassment crept into the girl's excessive brightness. 'Things weren't easy then, and I had to find my own way. Are you still working hard?'

Joan in a word or two gave her her news, and introduced Jimmy.

'Your brother—just fancy! I sort of thought he was a school-boy.' Thrush opened a wide gaze at Jimmy towering. 'You know, Mr. Seddon, your sister does far too much,' she gabbled. 'Don't you think all this war-work's bad for women?'

Jimmy grinned noncommittally, and Thrush laid a hand on her companion's arm.

'We must push off, Bobbie, or there won't be a taxi to be got. We're going on to dance somewhere. Good-bye, Joan. Let's meet again some time, now that we've run into each other.' And she was gone, with a smile over her shoulder at Jimmy, and a twitch at her evening cloak.

In the tube going back to Hampstead Joan felt curiously depressed.

'You see she was so terribly in love with that friend of Jack's,' she said, explaining Thrush to her brother. 'And now there she is, quite happy and radiant, with another man.'

'Can't say I blame her,' said Jimmy, as though he were ninety years old. 'It's awfully hard luck on girls these days.'

'I know—I know, but . . . Well, it was only a few months ago, and she does seem so completely to have recovered. Suppose it were you now, Jim, and the girl you'd been engaged to . . .'

'Shouldn't blame her,' he repeated. And Joan could have hit him and hugged him both. He was such a tolerant darling; but ought he to be quite so easy-going?

Joan refrained—partly so as not to strain Jim's tolerance too far, partly because it was the girl's own secret—from being more explicit about Thrush's affair with Ginger. But up in the old schoolroom that night she kept the talk on the subject of girls in general, and for the first time sounded her brother, directly, about his views.

'I'm quite certain, Jim-pot, that when you eventually marry— which Heaven send may be ages off!—she'll be a darling, and a first-rater. But meanwhile there are bound to be others; don't let them be the ogling chorus-girl type, because I believe they'd only sadden and disgust you.'

'Good Lord!' laughed Jimmy. 'They don't tempt *me*! But apart from that I'm not the sort to tempt *them*! If it were Carey now . . .'

'Carey! Just because he's got neat features and a "come 'ither" eye. You don't know your own attractions.'

He didn't. But that unconsciousness was his chief charm. And nothing that Joan could say would make him believe that he was anything but 'a fearful ass,' both at work and with women.

'Don't worry, old thing,' he said, grinning at her. 'Your little brother won't run off the rails, even though he is about to become a devil of a "Gentleman Cadet"!'

She smiled back at him, then said seriously:

'Whatever you do, Jumbles, you can always tell me. I'll always stand by you.'

'I know.'

'And whatever *I* did, by the way, would you stand by me?'

'Yes.'

'And whatever a friend of mine did, would you stand by her?'

'Yes.'

She kissed the top of his head.

'Good-night, Jumbles—*darling*.'

'Good-night, old thing.'

. . . . . .

On November 25th Jimmy entered the Royal Academy, Woolwich. But on November 2nd, the day after 'Chu-Chin-Chow,' Joan was back at the 1st London. It was just seven weeks since she had driven away from it in 'Black Maria.'

Chapter Eleven

DURING the last half of September, while Joan was still at Bart's, Betty was spending most of her spare time out at the Rest Camp at Ecault, a few miles from Boulogne. It was a camp for men of the First and Third Armies. They came down, so many from each battalion, for a week's rest. All were from the Somme fighting, and many were 'old soldiers' who had been out from the start and had had no leave for a year.

In charge of the Y.M.C.A. tent at the camp was a Dr. Ferguson, a small middle-aged Scotch divine, of immense vitality. He was assisted by one Christian; and, with the occasional help of girls from the Boulogne huts, the place was very well run. What Dr. Ferguson required, however, was not so much that the girls should serve in the canteen as that they should sit about and talk to the men and 'be a good influence.' Betty and Miss Bingham, who now did everything together and were good war-time comrades, filled this rôle to the best of their ability, and could be relied on to toil out to Ecault and put in an hour or so whenever they could get away.

On one of their first days out there they were invited to tea, by arrangement with Dr. Ferguson, in the tent of the 2nd Argyll and Sutherland Highlanders.

Piled up around the tent-poles, inside, were sheaves of battered rifles; and there being nothing else to sit on, the girls sat on the men's packs, and found themselves instantly surrounded by large brown Highlanders who made a ring of knees, and filled the tent with the hum of their Scotch voices. Two corporals, McGuchan and McLaughlin, were especially talkative. Both had been out almost from the beginning, and for two years on end had been in the forefront of the worst battles. What these wild creatures *could* talk about if they chose! thought Betty, as she sat with her mouth hanging open at the queerness and glamour of it all. McLaughlin had the bluest blue eyes she had ever seen—even for a Highlander. He was a primitive type of man, shy as a bird, yet not awkward; and, with a natural grace, and entire absence of self-consciousness, sat cutting bread-and-butter for them—the loaf clamped between his bare knees.

And then McGuchan recited a poem, and McLaughlin struck up a song in a soft tenor voice—a plaintive ballad about prisoners leaving 'the shores of Caledonia.' He told them he had had it from his grandfather, who had had it from *his* grandfather, and so on away back. It was an old Jacobite song. And as they listened, the hush of the tent broken only by that melancholy voice, it seemed to Betty as though modern battles were less real to this audience than 'battles long ago'—softened by the mist of years, sweetened by song—in which their ancestors had taken part.

Later, as they moved among the tents, Betty full-figured and soft-eyed, Miss Bingham brown and boyish, the men came out and crowded round them—speechless—gazing—as though the girls had been strange creatures from another world. Betty felt she would never forget that stupefied, reverent and famished look in the soldiers' eyes. She supposed that she and her friend represented to them, at the moment, all English womanhood, and the old life of peace. Men, men, men, wherever they went, wherever they looked; men straight from the line and months of fighting following them about in a sort of dream. Some pressed souvenirs on them, German post-cards, bullets, etc.; some talked; but the majority just stared. And it was these silent worshippers who to Betty, at any rate, were the most appealing.

Afterwards Dr. Ferguson told them that the Highlanders had announced to him—quite of their own accord—that their tent was henceforth 'purified' in consequence of the 'ladies' visit,' and that they were not going to get drunk or to use swear words for the rest of their stay in camp. Somehow this piece of information made the girls feel very uncomfortable. They would much rather not have produced such a wholesale effect from an action which had cost them so little; and they compared the appreciation of these seasoned warriors with the calm and rather grumbling attitude of the 'Base Details' and Labour Corps men among whom they worked, month in, month out, at the Alexandra.

. . . . . .

Towards the middle of October the Ecault period drew to an end. Fewer and fewer men could be spared from the Somme front, and when once the weather broke, and the advance stopped, the need for rest-camps would be over.

On one of their last visits the girls were asked to tea in the Sergeants' Mess of the H.L.I. They sat on two forms, at a table, and were royally entertained. It was not such an informal and jolly meal as on other occasions, but as it proceeded the sergeants unstiffened, and by the end had become quite 'matey.' Five of the nicest accompanied the girls back across the dark windy moor to the tram.

At the end of the two-mile trudge one of them—a huge creature called Stewart—thrust a small white blinking kitten into Betty's arms. He had been carrying it buttoned inside his coat.

'Brought it for you from the camp, Miss,' he said. 'Thought you'd like to have it.'

Betty was enchanted, for she adored cats, and she took it back to Temple's, and kept it with her as a treasured companion throughout the winter. She called it 'Little,' as she could think of no suitable name.

The sequel to that afternoon was that the five sergeants were given a return invitation to tea at Temple's. The day they came was their last before going back up the line. Miss McNare joined the party, and being Scotch, as well as motherly and kind, was a great asset.

After tea they all adjourned to the little red sitting-room off the dining-room, and Miss Bingham sat at the piano and played accompaniments, and two of the men sang. There was a delightful glow and friendliness over the whole party. Betty purred inwardly as she looked and listened. Lamplight. Those five great sergeants. Bingham, with her neat brown head, playing at the piano. Miss McNare nodding benignly. Nice to think one could make men enjoy themselves with so little effort on one's own part.

Miss Bingham took a song from the top of the piano. 'Who can sing this,' she asked, ' "A Little Bit of Heaven"?'

'I think *this* is a little bit of heaven,' remarked Stewart, the big blue-eyed Scotchman who was sitting beside Betty on the sofa.

Betty, to her great reluctance, had to go to her hut before the sergeants departed. She found it hateful to say good-bye, and to think that when she came back to Temple's the row of khaki Balmorals in the hall would be gone.

Both girls were sorry when Ecault closed down, and there were no more fighting troops to be visited. They had taken a far greater interest in the camp than any of the other Y.M. women, and now they scarcely knew what to do with their spare time.

.   .   .   .   .   .

'An officer downstairs to see you, Miss Paley. Couldn't catch 'is name. I put 'im in the sitting-room.' Dorcas stood breathing heavily in the doorway.

'All right, Dorky, I'll be down in a minute. Thank you.'

What a bore! Who could it be at this hour? Oh, well, whoever he was he could wait.

Betty had been checking over her clean laundry before going to bed. She finished doing this, put on her shoes again (always kicked off at the earliest opportunity), crossed in a leisurely way to the dressing-table, powdered her nose, and sauntered downstairs.

The dining-room was empty. The little tables were ready laid for breakfast. She moved between them, and up the two steps into the sitting-room.

'Guy!'

'Betty! I thought you were never coming!'

'They didn't tell me—I didn't know it was you!'

Surprise at his sudden presence robbed her of control over her blood. She stood gazing, drowned in crimson. She had a swift impression of him, lithe, eager, his boots and tunic muddy, his face pale, before he had stepped forward and taken both her hands in his.

'Managed to get twenty-four hours,' he told her. 'Couldn't let you know. Motored and lorry-jumped all the way down. Fearful luck. I say, I hope it's not too late for you to-night? Had to come round. I'm at the Burgoyne. Only just stopped for a wash.'

They sat on the little sofa, and Betty stirred up the dying fire. He held her hand in his, lifting it now and then to his cheek. Yes, his hands were dreadfully nice! He had changed rather.

'Had a hard time lately, Guy?'

'Well, I don't know about *lately*. Not been much rest for any of us since July.' He laughed. 'But things are slacking off now. I took the first opportunity . . . I say, forgive my appearance!'

'Guy! As if . . .'

'You've been a darling about writing, Betty. I couldn't manage much myself, but you've been always in my thoughts. Oh, I must tell you a funny little incident! I was sitting in a wood one day by the edge of a road reading one of your letters—the battery was "out" for once—and a lorry full of Australians came lumbering past. They grinned at me, and one of them shouted out, "A letter from your girl?" I was so happy that I shouted back at him, "Yes!" and he cried "Lucky blighter!" and they rattled on. You don't mind, do you? It wasn't stretching the truth too much? I had a ridiculous wish that those passing Australians should really think I had a girl—a proper official one who was mine. If I could have summoned you on a magic carpet and shown you to them . . .'

'Oh, Guy, you absurd creature!'

She turned away, blinking. Something suddenly seemed to break in her heart. She knew now how during all these months she had missed him, and missed him; had pretended to herself that she was merely tired with hard work, and the camp and all; had really almost believed that the attraction he had exerted over her on that last day of theirs together had been temporary. And now he had only to come back suddenly, to hold her hand, to look at her like that, with his funny crooked smile. . . . A feeling could grow then, like a bulb in the earth, while you were not attending —could burst astonishingly into flower . . .?

She faced him again, trying to say lightly: 'Guy, are you certain that you want me to be your "proper official girl"?'

'God! *Certain?* I was certain in June! And if absence *could* have made me more so . . . Betty, don't look at me like that unless . . . Betty, you love me!'

'Do I?'

Nothing was said for a moment. The ormolu clock on the mantelpiece ticked above them, as it had ticked nearly a year ago above Colin and Joan.

'Listen, Betty,' said Guy, with a mock gravity that played over the deep gravity beneath. 'Listen, because I'm going to propose to you—and after this there'll be no question of going on as friends. Betty, will you marry me?'

'It looks as though I'd have to, Guy.'

Cheek pressed to cheek they sat on a long while looking into the fire.

'Miss Paley,' came Dorcas's voice from the dining-room—from another world. 'I can't wait up no longer. I'll 'ave to put the lights out.'

'Oh, poor Dorky!' said Betty, contrite. 'I'd quite forgotten her.'

Guy rose to his feet with a 'Wait a minute,' and plunged through the door. After a moment he came back smiling. 'I've settled her! Nice old thing, your Dorcas. I told her I'd see to the lights myself.'

Doubtless he'd 'settled her' to some tune, thought Betty. There would be no difficulty henceforth about their having the little room to themselves whenever Guy came down. She knew her Dorcas.

'Guy, my dear, I've been thinking.'

'Do you mean just while I've been out of the room?' he said, gaily, as he dropped to her side again.

'Before that too. Listen. We're engaged, I suppose?'

'I was certainly under that impression. Are you going to break it off already?'

'Be serious for a moment. No, I'm not. But, Guy, I'd rather we weren't publicly engaged yet. Do you mind?'

He searched her face. 'It depends on why. If I can be sure of you . . .'

'Oh, you can be sure of me! Once I *have* taken a step I don't go back again. But I don't like taking a great many steps at a time.'

'You sweet!'

And she explained to him that she would like, for a month or two, to savour the situation of just being his—with nobody knowing; that she feared the fuss which would follow on an 'announcement'; the continual questions as to *when* they were going to get married, and the unsettled feeling this would cause her in the Y.M.C.A.

He perfectly understood, but he confessed that for his own part he was prepared to marry her to-morrow.

'In any church you like,' he laughed. 'Before any gods—Pagan or Christian!'

'What about money?' she asked him. 'Have you forgotten your anxieties on that score? *I* shan't bring you a penny, alas!'

'What do I care?—so long as you bring me yourself. It's queer what different proportions things assume at different times. I feel I don't care now if we live in a woodman's hut together for the rest of our lives.'

'My hands getting hornier and hornier,' remarked Betty. 'And you, very morose, in a beard!'

'No, but I tell you what, you lovely laggard—if you're not going to marry me till the spring I shall spend the months between in rigidly economising. No drinks, no parties; no new horses, no new anything—except a nice new set of miserly habits!'

She stroked his cheek. 'Pet! But don't overdo it, will you, or I simply shan't know you. I'm glad you're in the Artillery.'

'Why—all of a sudden?'

'Well, it's better than the Infantry.'

'Oh, I see. Yes, from that point of view I suppose it is. Haven't "stopped one" yet. Still . . .' he held up a warning finger, 'you never know! Don't play with Fate and keep me dangling too long.'

'Guy, you must go to bed,' she said, getting to her feet. 'You're worn out—though nothing, I know, would make you admit it.'

He smiled at the first far-away hint of proprietorship in her tone. 'You darling! You love me?'

She gave him a glimmer through her lashes. 'Yes, it's awkward, but I do!'

He kissed her long and tenderly, and for the first time she kissed him back.

'Good-night, then—till to-morrow.'

.   .   .   .   .   .

They spent the afternoon together—part of it walking out of doors, part of it at Temple's. After her evening shift Betty joined Guy at the picturesque old Burgoyne in the Hauteville for a late dinner.

'The last decent dinner,' Guy laughingly said, that he was going to allow himself. But they really *had* to celebrate to-night! If ever an occasion demanded it . . . Champagne, of course, such as it was. Oh, why weren't they at the Carlton!

Their eyes brimmed with delight in each other, and again and again his hand sought hers. Once he separated the fourth finger of her left hand, glanced round to see that no one was looking, and put a swift kiss on it.

'That's a promise of favours to come!' he told her.

'Guy, you're getting too indiscreet. Your *savoir-faire* is deserting you.'

'Let it—so long as you go on blushing like that! Oh, Betty . . .'

'What?' she asked, for he had heaved an enormous sigh.

'Marry me soon!'

She tried to look severe. 'This period will be a test of constancy,' she told him.

'How *dare* you! But I suppose you have every right to rag me.'

They stayed talking till the last inescapable minute. Outside in the darkness he caught her to him once with a whispered 'Mine!' and then they walked down the hill, to all outward semblance the merest acquaintances.

'Well, Little, so that's that!' said Betty, when up in her room she held the sleepy kitten in both hands and gently shook him. 'You'll have to share me now. But we won't part, my precious, you shall stay with me, however much either of us gets married!'

Chapter Twelve

ROWS of blue-overalled girls in unbecoming jelly-bag caps sat or stood all day in the long light shed of Staple and Studd's munition works at Willesden. Two hundred and fifty girls divided into sections according to the different jobs they were doing; three hundred men in other parts of the same vast shed. From eight to five, with an hour's break for lunch, they worked unceasingly.

Many of them came long distances. Liz Fanshawe, whose people kept a small shop in Brixton, took an hour to come. Nellie Crewe, ex-kitchenmaid in a boarding-house, took about the same time from her crowded home in Battersea. Pamela Butler, who sat between them, was luckier. If she caught the right trains and trams she could do the distance from her aunt's door in Curzon Street to the door of the 'shop' in forty-five minutes.

These three, with twenty-seven others, sat at the drilling-machines. Perched on high stools, their feet on the cross-bar of the bench in front of them, their left hands held pieces of steel, six inches square, which were to become the backs of signal-lamps; their right hands worked the levers which drilled into the plates five holes on five marked places. From the machine up to the ceiling ran broad leather belts which flapped and whirred. The noise made by all the belts together was like a flock of nightmare birds. Added to it was the noise of the drilling of the plates; and from all parts of the shop came a mixed din of rasping, filing, cutting, hammering. Clang, clang, zzz, whrr. Clang, clang, zzz, whrr. Deafening, stupefying, brain-shattering.

Down came Pamela's lever: once, twice . . . five times. The plate was thrown on to a pile beside her. Another was picked up, held steady, punched, dropped. She could do thirty to the hour now, like Liz Fanshawe on her right; for the first fortnight she had only been able to do twenty-four. The present pace meant keeping hard at it. Incidentally it meant extra pay on to one's £3 a week, and that was not to be despised.

A foreman wandered past, and paused behind Liz Fanshawe's stool. He was a jovial man, with a straw-coloured walrus moustache, and was known as 'Father.' He was apt at times to bully, and at times to be familiar, but on the whole he was decent enough.

"Ello, Liz, wot's up with you this morn'n? Taking it easy, my girl? 'Ad one over the eight last night?'

'Go on, Father!' she shouted through the roar of the machinery. 'Don't 'and me out a lot of 'ole balsam! My work's orl right.'

'Now, Saucy!'

The foreman came behind Pamela, looked over her shoulder, and moved on without addressing her.

"Ear that?' Liz screamed when he had gone. 'Comin' in with a lot of ole madam! 'Oo does 'e think 'e is? Does 'e think I'm a penny-in-the-slot machine? Bin on this blasted job now six weeks. So've you. *You* know wot it's like!'

Pamela nodded sympathetically. The muscles of her fore-arm were aching. Another hour till lunch-time.

'Yer don't look too grand yerself terdye,' Liz bellowed at her. 'Worst of me is, when I'm feeling all in I don't show it same as others do.'

Nor did she. Her peony-coloured face and coarse black hair proclaimed triumphant health even at her lowest moments. She was a good-natured creature, if a bit foul-mouthed at times, and it was impossible not to like her; and Pamela, who hated making the exertion of raising her voice, had evolved a whole series of facial expressions with which to carry on conversation with her cheery neighbour.

The buzzer sounded through the shop. Twelve o'clock. The machines were turned off. The belts slowed down, flapped, stopped. Blessed silence! Pamela climbed off her stool, bent and stretched her right arm several times, and followed the blue chattering stream of other girls to the canteen. This was fifty yards away, up a bit of bad road churned into mud by the passing lorries. The late September air struck chill after the heated fuggy atmosphere of the shop, where ventilation was regarded with horror by the majority of the workers. Inside the canteen it was just pleasantly warm.

An excellent lunch could be procured here for a shilling. The catering had lately been taken over and feeding arrangements reorganised by Miss Dixon, the Supervisor, a woman of great competence, brusque hearty manners, and knowledge of all grades of humanity. The men and girls were devoted to her, and among some of them she went affectionately by the name of 'Dick.'

Pamela sat with a little quiet girl, a Miss Fenton, the daughter of a country vicar of small means and numerous progeny. Miss Fenton made no bones about the usefulness of the money she was earning. She was living at present with relations in London. She had several brothers at the Front. Pamela and she, finding much in common, had clung together from the first.

In work hours the other girls treated them in a friendly natural manner, neither with suspicion nor jealousy, neither with undue reserve nor undue familiarity; in off hours they left them tacitly alone.

'The only thing that I feel I *may* not be able to stick,' Pamela confided to her companion at lunch, 'is the awful lavatory arrangement!'

'I know,' said Miss Fenton, in her unemotional little voice. 'This morning I waited outside the doors quite ten minutes in the giggling crowd, and when at last one of the doors *did* open and let out a girl—Elsie Thompson it was—and I slipped in, I found there were two or three more inside. Elsie hadn't told me, she'd just let me pass. Extraordinary, isn't it!'

'M'm.' Pamela's expression was of controlled distaste. 'I'd never before imagined that that particularly private business could be carried on communally, had you?'

'The places are thoroughly cleaned out you know,' Miss Fenton remarked by way of consolation.

'I know . . . but even then . . .! Well, I never *sit* on the seat myself—not actually—do you?'

They smoked their cigarettes. All the workers smoked after lunch—it was the only moment when they were allowed to. Then they trooped back to the shop.

Clang, clang, zzz, whrr. Clang, clang, zzz, whrrr.

Liz Fanshawe broke into song.

' "*Gawd* send you *back* to maee, *Owv*er the *row*ling saee," ' she wailed, as she punched and levered. ' "*Dear*est, I love you so-ow." '

Several girls joined in. Some sang what they called 'second,' but what was really a growling and irrelevant bass.

'Now then, Liz, stop that!' came Miss Dixon's firm cheery tones. 'You know that song's not allowed.'

'Ow, Dick, it *does* 'elp!'

'Nonsense, it hinders. Your work slows down to its pace. Try another with a smarter rhythm, and keept time to *that*! . . . All right, Butler?' she asked, passing by Pamela's stool, and received a smiling nod.

Miss Dixon strode on in her long white coat. Seeing to the welfare of two hundred and fifty girls of all types was no easy job, but she was cut out for it. And just as no malingerer could bluff her, so no ardent martyr could carry off sickness by pretending to be well. She saw through either. It was her business to keep her varied troop hard at it and yet healthy.

'Ow, Dick,' yelled Liz, 'when are them new caps coming you promised us?'

'Next week, I hope,' was the reply.

'These 'ere things make us look like Jacks-in-the-Green! Look at Nellie Crewe there! 'Ers is so big it makes 'er seem like a rat lookin' out of a sink-'ole!'

At three o'clock tea was brought round, thick cups of strong brown liquid. You paid a penny a cup. Pamela never took it. At the best of times she disliked tea, and only drank it if it was expensive China, and extremely weak. Liz swallowed hers at a gulp.

'That's better!' she sighed. 'Now come on, girls! "*Take* me back to dear ole *Bli-ighty*, Tum te, tum te, tum te, tum te, *tum*." Lor', that tea ain't 'alf made me 'ead sweat! Funny! Think I'll take me cap orf for a minute. Where's ole Dick? Don't want '*er* after me body!'

She pulled off the detested head-gear—though it was strictly against orders—and fluffed out her wiry black hair. The breeze from the flapping belt above her blew pleasantly on her hot forehead. She seized her lever.

' "Tiddely-iddely-ighty, carry me back to *Blighty*, *Blighty*—*is* the—*place*—*for*—*me*." ' The last five notes were slightly slowed down to enable her to punch her plate in time to them.

'Put your cap on again!' shouted Pamela; but the din from the whole shop, and Liz's strident singing, drowned her cry. She waved her hand, pointed to her neighbour's head, and then to her own. Liz saw the gesture, but only laughed.

'Not much! I shan't be seen! I feel fine like this!' Her hair was blowing about. ' "Birmingham, Leeds, or Manchester, I *don't*— *much*—*care*!" '

In a second it had happened. She had leant a fraction too far forward, and the wind from the flapping belt had blown her hair into the wheel of the drilling-machine. There was a yell which pierced even the usual racket of the shop, and the big Liz was on her feet, her eyes staring from their sockets, both hands to her head. The front part of it—from the forehead back—had been ripped raw.

The belt whirred on. The wheel continued to revolve; but now it had grown a wiry black beard which at each revolution flicked up into sight.

'All right, Liz,' cried Miss Dixon, who had materialised from nowhere, and was holding the screaming girl beneath the arms. 'Steady, steady now. You're all right.'

The girls round about had leapt to their feet; Pamela being nearest was best able to give assistance. But they were all ordered off.

'Get back to your stools!' thundered Miss Dixon, in the voice of a sergeant-major. 'All right, Liz. I'm with you.'

The next minute Liz, with a long moan, had crumpled up, and two St. John Ambulance men, arriving from other parts of the shop, lifted her and carried her away.

Work was resumed. But, on Pamela's left, little Nellie Crewe, having moved her lever weakly once or twice, slid from her stool and staggered off. Pamela punched on in a frenzy, fighting her nausea. One did not faint. If one had any stamina, any pride, one —did—not—faint. Work must go on—and quicker than ever now. Anything to forget that bare raw strip of scalp—like the strip made by a reaping-machine in a field of corn; anything to forget those eyes—the eyes of a panic-stricken beast. In fifteen minutes Nellie was back on her stool. Pamela shot a glance at her. Both their faces, though they didn't know it, were white as paper.

'All right now?'

Nellie nodded. She had been quietly sick in one of the lavatory basins, where the old woman in attendance had held her head; and she was now able to go on.

At five o'clock the machines whirred down to silence. The girls trooped to the cloak-room, took off caps and overalls, put on outdoor things, and poured out into the dirty purple twilight to catch their trams.

. . . . . .

A week later the interior of the shop presented a much gayer appearance. Gone were the dingy overalls and the shapeless caps. Miss Dixon, with sound instinct about every detail that made for more efficient work from females, had introduced overalls of different colours, and gay handkerchiefs that tied tightly over the head with a knot behind. The place looked like a herbaceous border, and the difference in the spirits of the girls was surprising.

Pamela had been moved from the drills and put, at her own earnest request, on to shell-cases. This was particularly heavy work, and only two women besides herself were engaged on it— the rest were men. It would have been balm to Pamela, in her

present temper, to feel that she was dealing with actual explosives
—to be filling shells, for instance, instead of merely cleaning and
measuring cases—but in these works, in which she had been
taken on, there was no active stuff, and she had to be content with
the nearest approach to the real thing which obtained.

The fact of having to stand all day—as you had to at the lathes—
was wearing enough, but the lifting of the heavy brass shell-cases
became back-breaking after a time. Nothing but the energy lent
by revengeful despair could have kept a girl of Pamela's physique
at this job for more than a month. Pamela stuck it for nearly
two.

Six shell-cases to the hour . . . eight cases to the hour . . . ten cases
to the hour. That was her maximum—and a pretty high one.
Beyond that she was unable to go. And all the time she thought
of Ian. It was a shell like one of these that had splashed his brains
into the soil of the Somme country, shattered the arms that had
held her so tight, and blown his whole strong, beautiful body into
nothingness. She had been given details of his death in a letter—
an unimaginative but well-meaning letter from one of his friends
—and never, never would she forget. Each time that she heaved
one of the shell-cases from the floor on to the fixture in front of
her; each time that she turned the great wheel which sent the
fixture driving through the case, clearing and hollowing it to the
required dimensions; each time that she measured carefully across
the diameter of the top to see that the cap would fit exactly, she
sent wishes of death with the shell. 'Do the same, my beauty, do
the same to the enemy who killed *him*!' Sometimes she felt she
was going a little mad.

In her ears the roar of the machinery; under her feet a sodden
mat of iron filings mixed with oil and the milk-like 'Gippo' in
which the machines were soaked; on her fingers, so delicately kept
till now, filth and grit. And hour by hour the shell-cases were
removed, and taken to Woolwich to be filled for the Front.

By Christmas Pamela reluctantly and disgustedly had to give it
up. She asked for a lighter job.

It was unfortunate that just as she was getting rested after about a fortnight of less arduous work she was put on to the capstan machines. One of the girls who worked at them had gone sick; and Pamela, who had the reputation of being quick at picking up anything new, was detailed to replace her.

At the capstans you were supplied with steel rods that had to be made into 'bolts.' You slipped your rod into a hollow tube, of which a portion called the 'chuck' was thinner than the rest, and was twisted like a screw. As the rod came out at the other end it was guillotined off into bolt lengths. After this process you were supposed to clean the 'chuck' with a stick provided for the purpose, for it was important that no loose fragments should remain which might spoil the thread of the next bolt. Sometimes, instead of using the chuck-stick, a girl would use her finger as being easier and quicker; but this was a dangerous thing to do unless she stood well away from her machine.

Pamela had not been on the job a week before she was witness of the ghastly result of this carelessness.

Elsie Thompson, a stodgy girl, with a thick white face, who stood to the right of her, was continually mislaying things. Sometimes it would be her hand-bag, sometimes her handkerchief (though that didn't trouble her much), sometimes a tool. On this occasion it was her chuck-stick. Peering about, and mumbling to herself, she gave up the search in a few moments and rammed her finger into the chuck, turning it this way and that. Accidentally she pressed against the lever, the capstan moved along sideways, and her finger was slowly wrenched right out of its socket, dragging the muscles of the arm behind it.

The man next to her jumped at her machine and jerked back the lever—too late. Elsie stood staring at her bleeding stump, the white muscles hanging from it like strings. At the moment she felt no pain. All sensation had been deadened by shock. A slow idiotic smile spread over her face, and she was led off giggling. By the time she reached the dispensary the blood was pumping out. Miss Dixon applied a tourniquet, clapped on a temporary dressing, and sent her off in an ambulance to hospital.

So quickly had the accident happened, and so calmly had the girl taken it, that Pamela, standing next to her, scarcely realised its import. For a brief instant only she had seen the maimed hand, and—perhaps because she had become dulled by bodily fatigue —the impression that it made upon her was far less acute than that made by Liz Fanshawe's raw scalp. That had been something abnormal, outside her experience; this other was more like a soldier's wound, of which she had seen many. She wondered that she felt no greater pity for Elsie, but the only thought that went through her mind was: 'Wounded for her country. Almost wish it had been me. Wish I could lose a finger—an arm—my whole life.'

Then Miss Dixon appeared, and began methodically and silently to clean out Elsie's chuck. Pamela saw little crimson bits of twisted flesh being scraped out and thrown on to the ground, where they lay in the bog of filings until later they were cleared away.

The after effects on Pamela were curious. Unmoved as she had been at the time, she dreamt for several consecutive nights of those mangled pieces of finger; and during work hours she sometimes felt coming over her the morbid and terrifying desire to clean out her own chuck with her finger instead of using the stick. It was like the impulse that sometimes assails a person to jump from the platform on to the railway line before an oncoming train.

Wisely she took herself in hand in time, and asked to be moved from the capstans.

She was put on to acetylene welding. Six girls were on this job —including, to Pamela's joy, Miss Fenton—and it required more intelligence and skill than almost any other. Each girl had her cylinder of high-power gas which she turned on to plates that had to be set at angles to each other, and welded together while melting. All worked in rubber gloves; and the white light from the gas-flames was so strong that dark glasses had to be worn. Even then it was a trying business for the eyes, for although the general glare was excluded, the white spot which had to be focused on seemed, after a time, to sear through the very glasses themselves. The atmosphere in this department was oven-like.

So together Pamela and her friend talked and welded, and breathed gas, and scorched their eyeballs, and ran at lunch-time through the cold air to the canteen.

.   .   .   .   .   .

One Thursday morning in January word came from the Ministry of Munitions that a thousand signal-lamps were required immediately to replace the same number that had been lost on a certain sector of the Front. Could they be rushed through by Saturday at very latest? It was a question for the Shop Committee to decide. If a sufficient number of the 'drillers' and the 'assemblers' volunteered to work all Thursday night, all Friday, and all Friday night, the order could be delivered—not otherwise. Extra hours meant extra pay, of course, but nobody could be compelled to remain. The whole lot—except two girls who had gone sick that day—volunteered.

Miss Dixon hove on the threshold of the welding department.

'Turner,' she called to the foreman, 'I've got two empty drills. Can you lend me a couple of girls for this stunt?'

Turner looked a bit glum, but supposed he could.

'Which of yer's bin drillers before?' he asked them,

Pamela and Miss Fenton replied in a breath.

'All right, Turner, I'll take those two, then. Thank you.' And Miss Dixon vanished.

Opportunity had been given everyone to send messages home, and at five o'clock, instead of the usual exodus, rows of girls were working at full pitch. There was a thrill throughout the works, a feeling of keyed-upness, of being somehow in closer contact with 'the boys in the trenches.' Pamela and Miss Fenton, back at the old drills, worked side by side; Liz Fanshawe, now more or less recovered, and with bandaged head, was on their right.

"'Ello the Buffs!' called Liz, "ere we are again! Nice set o' blinkin' fools I call us, spoiling our beauty for the sake of the bloody country. Night life in London, wot? Not a wink o' sleep did she get till dawn! No-o, and bloody well not then either—not on this picnic!'

At eleven o'clock they all trooped out to supper. Darkness and frosty stars. Voices ringing on the sharp air. In the canteen a bee-hive murmurous warmth. Irish stew, sausage and mash, rice pudding, coffee.

And then they settled down to it for the night. Clang, clang, *whrrr*. The belts flapped and roared. The hours went past. The first night, anyhow, would be nothing, thought Pamela. How often had she not stayed up till six in the morning, dancing! That was the way to look at it. But here there was no lilting music; only the monotonous beat of the machines. And on the morning after a dance—sooner or later—you went to bed; on this occasion there would be no bed.

The lights went out, the wintry day crept in. Seven o'clock, and breakfast. The joy of it! Long hot drinks, sizzling eggs and bacon. Then afterwards a wash in the crowded lavatories and back to work.

Eight o'clock. The beginning of an ordinary day in the shop. Just a day like any other, said Pamela to herself. Miss Fenton looked a bit washed out, poor dear—probably she hadn't slept very well! Punch—punch—punch—punch—punch. Good old drills!

The buzzer proclaimed twelve o'clock, and dinner. Three cups of black coffee for Pamela instead of her usual two. A cigarette, and back to the machines.

But it was then—in the afternoon—that the drag was felt. All the usual symptoms of being up late the night before were a hundred times exaggerated: the smarting behind the eyes, the gaping at the back of the throat, the feeling that ants were crawling about on the soles of the feet, the queer empty-headedness, the ache of all the bones.

When tea came round Pamela willingly paid her penny, and

gulped down at least three-quarters of her cup. It wasn't so bad—
it was *something*. She looked at herself in her small mirror and
made a grimace.

'An ancient tennis-ball with two black currants in it!' she commented on her reflection. She powdered her nose grimly. Looking up she caught Miss Fenton smiling at her. She nodded back
and waved her puff. 'All very well, but it does help!' she conveyed. Empires might rise and fall, wars be won and lost, but the
nose must be kept powdered. She pressed her head-handkerchief
further down on her forehead and resumed.

Six o'clock . . . seven o'clock . . . eight o'clock . . . *eleven* o'clock.
Supper. The girls fell off their stools, and dragged feet that felt
huge as those of elephants across the floor. Outside it was raining.
Pamela stood for a moment, her face turned up, to let the drops
fall on her throbbing lids.

'Hallo, girls! Feeling a bit all-overish,' cried Miss Dixon.

There were groans of response, and cheerfully caustic comments
on their condition.

'Tell you what I could do with now, Dick,' called Liz, 'and that's
a nice walk to Brighton!'

'Well, tuck in now. If you mayn't sleep you must eat. Keep the
boilers stoked.'

While the girls were feeding an inspector from Woolwich
arrived, and asked to see the Supervisor. He was a stout man with
a fussy sense of his own importance. He wished to inspect the
finished signal-lamps. How many were there? He hoped nearly
the whole thousand. Miss Dixon left him to consult with Mitchell,
the foreman. It seemed that there were six hundred finished and in
their cases, and two hundred empty cases.

'He'll expect more than that,' she said.

'Well, yer see, Dick, the pace is slowing down a bit now. Can't
expect 'em to keep it up same as on the first night.'

'No, no, of course not. But they will be *done*, Mitchell?'

With slow emphasis he assured her.

'They'll be done, Dick!'

She returned to the inspector. She had a plan.

'Now then, Mr. Harris,' she said briskly, leading him to the benches where the cases, filled and empty were ranged in rows. 'We'll begin here, shall we? Eight hundred you see.'

Mr. Harris, breathing pompously, lifted the lid of each case, flashed the lamp to test the rapidity of the shutter, dropped down the lid, and put a chalk mark on it. At the end of the six hundred Miss Dixon suggested that he might care for a little refreshment.

'It's a nasty night, Inspector. A drink and a bit of food wouldn't do you any harm.'

Mr. Harris, after a brief show of hesitancy, went gratefully off to the canteen, Miss Dixon contriving to send a secret message to the cook to 'fill him well up,' and keep him there as long as possible.

When he had gone she and Mitchell between them rubbed the chalk marks from two hundred of the finished cases and changed their position with the two hundred empty ones.

Mr. Harris returned rubicund, and full of pork-pie and whisky.

'Well now, where did we get to?' he asked amiably.

'Here, Mr. Harris. You did six hundred.'

'Yes, yes—I start here then.' And he proceeded to lift the lids of the remaining cases, and having tested the lamps inside, to shut them down again and mark them—blissfully innocent of the fact that he had already done so once.

The chit for Woolwich was signed. 'Eight hundred signal-lamps inspected and found correct. Two hundred still to come.'

'One up on us, I think, Mitchell?' said Miss Dixon when they were alone.

'Cush, that's a *lad*!' ejaculated the foreman on a long admiring breath. But it wasn't Mr. Harris he meant; it was Miss Dixon.

The second night ground on. It was no use pretending any more that you were at a dance. A far stronger imaginative stimulus than that was required. The Front. The dark glutinous desolate Front. Think of *that*. The soldiers. Your eyes were red-hot coals, your spine a red-hot poker, your arms a mass of leaping, tortured nerves. But what did it matter? You were warm and safe, which the soldiers were not. You were regularly fed, which they were not. Noise crashed around you, but it was only the noise of machinery—not of shells. Stick it! Stick it!

Somebody started singing.

' "Pack up your troubles in your old kit-bag, and smile, smile, SMILE!" ' Half the shop joined in on a wailing roar, their voices hoarse with sleeplessness.

"Ow, give it a drink!' cried Liz. 'Put a sock in it! Gor' blimey, wot d'yer think y'are? Ruddy canaries?'

The well-meant effort was chucked. There was no surplus energy now. Cups of Bovril came round at 3 a.m. and restored a momentary vitality, but this soon flickered down again.

The noise of the machines began to get blurred and far-off. Ears refused to register. Objects leapt and swam before your sight. The whole of your physical being was one craving ache for a mattress and a pillow. For moments together consciousness slipped away; then came jerking back again. Thank God your hands hadn't stopped. You were part of the machines. You *were* a machine. Soulless, mindless, deaf, blind—with only far inside a tiny indomitable human will, keeping you at it—at it.

Morning. Electric lights turned off. Instead, a grey astonished daylight stare. Any faces of over thirty looked like the faces of old women.

Washing was a farce. Grime and filth and sweat were not only outward but inward. Your very feet felt black.

Breakfast. No chatter now, no jokes. A herd of reeling human animals that fell upon their food, ate it in a stupor, and reeled back again to toil.

'The last lap now, girls!' cried Miss Dixon, haggard-faced, pacing down the lines. 'Remember the stuff's promised for to-day. Don't let me down. Good girls, good girls! The last lap. Put a spurt on it now!'

Somehow they did—just alive enough to respond mechanically to the whip of words. Time had ceased to count. The next few hours were a grinding nightmare.

At noon it was over. The machines slowed down, and stopped. An eerie hush fell upon the shop. The signal-lamps were finished. The order had been put through. 'How many, Mitchell?' yawned Miss Dixon, leaning in the doorway of her office, staring stupidly at a half-smoked cigarette.

'A thousand and one, Dick,' was the reply.

Liz Fanshawe, passing at that moment, observed with a final flicker of humour:

'Bet that last was the beggar I drilled!'

Out into the fog and the ordinary noises of a London winter afternoon staggered the workers. The appearance they presented was that of dope-fiends or of corpses.

Pamela never remembered how she got back to Curzon Street. The next thing of which she had any clear recollection, after leaving the shop at Saturday midday, was waking in her bed and seeing Aunt Maud stand over her, with the maid bearing a tray of tea. It was four o'clock on Sunday afternoon.

．　　　　．　　　　．　　　　．　　　　．　　　　．

Work at the shop during the following week seemed child's play. Only seemed, however. Actually the strain of the past five months was telling on Pamela. She was far more tired than she would admit, or even than she realised. Lady Butler realised it, and she implored her niece to leave 'that dreadful munition factory' and have a rest, or at any rate to take up something less exhausting and less unsuitable.

Pamela only laughed. 'I can't possibly chuck it, Aunt Maud. I should be ashamed to. I'm quite as fit as all those other girls, and *they* carry on.'

Lady Butler raised her delicate eyebrows and sighed. She saw no point in competing with the lower orders in physical endurance; they were obviously far better able to bear things than we were. But she knew also that Pamela had this fantastic notion that if she were making shells she was somehow avenging her fiancé's death, so she said no more.

And Pamela went on with her acetylene welding, and the machines clanged and whirred and hammered around her, and epidemics of measles and of 'flu raged through the shop.

Some workers pleaded sick at once. Some hung on obstinately until they had almost to be kicked from their machines and packed off home. Quite a number died; and whenever this happened Miss Dixon was required to be chief mourner at the funeral— chiefly for her own sake, but also because her uniform of the Women's Legion imparted a military touch to the proceedings.

'Going corpsing again, Dick?' Liz would cheerily call to her. 'Gawd, wot a life!'

When she was not 'corpsing' Miss Dixon was tramping the works with cinnamon and quinine, dosing the 'well' girls twice a day.

It was a detestable winter.

.   .   .   .   .   .

In February Dick Butler came home on leave. He was a major now—the youngest in a brigade which had suffered badly—and he had the M.C. and bar.

It was jolly to have him about the house. The atmosphere was warmed and enlivened. His mother seemed to shed twenty years of her age, and Pamela emerged from her thorny, stubborn little hedge of grief in his cousinly companionship.

They went out a good deal together in the evenings, dining and dancing; but whether she went mostly for Dickie's sake, or for her own, Pamela couldn't have said. As she swayed with him on the crowded floors of Ciro's or the Savoy, it was so like old times —except for the pervading khaki—that it was hard to believe that by eight o'clock next morning she would be in her overall and her goggles at the shop.

Sometimes she was wildly gay—insisting on going from theatre to restaurant, from restaurant to night-club, and if it were dry even walking home on Dickie's arm through the dark uncanny streets of war-time London. Sometimes an opposite mood would descend on her, and she would give way to the accumulated bitterness of months, as she could not possibly have done before her aunt. Youth understood youth in those times; the old had to be protected and cheered.

'You see, Dickie,' she would say, 'I've never felt like that about anyone before. I loved him utterly. I'd have chucked everything for him—stage, family, country, everything—and now he's gone, and there's no meaning anywhere.'

On these occasions Dick would cease to be the flirtatious companion and become the protective, understanding friend. It wrung his heart to see the wretchedness that looked out from her eyes; that queer angle at which they were set made anything but mirth incongruous. They were a little bloodshot too, and she had a trick of blinking them. She must have lost a good bit of weight, he thought, though she was always a wisp. And what a shame that her poor little hands should be ingrained with dirt. In a way, although it was the least of the changes in her, that one struck him as the most pathetic of all.

She suggested that she was taking up too much of his time, and urged him to go out with some of his other friends. He did so once or twice, but without much enthusiasm. And to Pamela—coming home tired from the shop—to find him there sitting by the library fire, to drop down by him and talk, to have a bath and change, and then either to go on talking or to go out to a show, was extraordinarily comforting.

'You know, Pammy,' he remarked quietly, one evening, 'if you ever feel inclined to get engaged to me you've only to say so.'

'Dickie, you lamb!' she laughed. 'It's a sweet idea, but . . .' A fit of coughing interrupted her.

'Not altogether a *bad* idea, do you think?'

She blinked at him, still shaken by little subsiding coughs.

'Well, but—darling old thing—what would *you* get out of it? I've no heart now, you know. It's dead—finished.'

'Oh, I perfectly understand *that*,' he replied, and the firelight on his face accentuated his resemblance to a good-natured gnome. 'I just thought you might like to feel you could fall back on me, as it were—use me as a sort of arm-chair where you could flop.'

'But supposing all I wanted was just to perch on its arm for a few minutes?' she asked.

He grinned. 'Well, arm-chairs have various uses. We'll let the notion simmer, shall we? Don't have it on your mind at all, I mean.'

Pamela didn't suppose for a moment that she would; but she was touched and grateful. Also she felt, to her relief, that Dickie's proposal—if such it could be termed—had in no way altered their relationship, or changed him into anything different from the dear cousin she had always loved and teased.

When Dick had gone back to France the house seemed very empty, and she missed him a lot the first few days. After that, however, the increasing physical effort which she found her work demanded of her left no room for feelings.

Her hand began to be less steady in directing the gas-jet, and several times she asked Miss Fenton whether the room were not much hotter than it used to be. She felt clammy and weak, and her heart pounded irregularly. The sight and smell of food repelled her. She began living on coffee. On a certain Friday Miss Dixon summoned her into her office and took her temperature.

'Charming!' she said, looking with pursed lips at the thermometer. 'Off you go, my dear!'

'Not *home*?' exclaimed Pamela. 'No, but, really, Miss Dixon, I can carry on perfectly well.'

'Butler, my child, sorry, but I'm not going to keep you on sick. You've reached your limit. Don't think I've not had my eye on you. Now give in your number and bundle off. I should advise a taxi.'

The attack of bronchial 'flu to which Pamela succumbed kept her in bed a fortnight. Her low condition, spiritually and physically, had rendered her a ready prey for germs. And then Dickie's leave, coming just when it did, and entailing late exciting nights—although it was a temporary fillip—was the final factor in her breakdown.

As soon as she was considered well enough to travel her aunt sent her home to Wallingford.

PART THREE

1917: EARLY 1918

*'Thou art going to the wars; and
whether I shall ever see thee again or no .   .'*

Chapter One

WHEN Joan returned to Camberwell from sick-leave she was put into another ward. She missed her dear men in '33,' and at first felt a little disconsolate and out of things. In less than a week, however, the strangeness had worn off, and she had settled down to hospital routine as though she had never been away.

The V.A.D.s now drove to and from their work in three immense char-à-bancs. These were known as the 'Tanks,' and effected a considerable saving of fatigue in daily life.

As winter came on, and the mornings grew damper and darker, the effort of rising early became almost insurmountable. Little Phipps could hardly be got out of bed. At about five minutes to seven she used to stumble in, heavy-eyed, to breakfast; swallow a cup of tea; trail out just in time to catch the third 'Tank,' and clamber on to it, holding a bit of still unfinished bread-and-marmalade in her hand.

.   .   .   .   .   .

And then, three weeks before Christmas, Joan was put on night-duty.

Night-duty meant a transformation of your entire existence. You were one of a race apart—a race of gnomes. There was only one advantage about it: you no longer slept up at the hostel, but in a long wooden hut in the hospital grounds where you had a tiny bedroom to yourself. You had breakfast in the evening, in the dining-hall, and went on duty just as the day V.A.D.s were coming off. You remained on all night, had dinner next morning, and were then free to go out until your bed-time at noon.

Joan was in ward 31; and Fry, who, to Joan's joy, had come on night-duty at the same time, was in the ward next door. There was one sister to each ward, and only one V.A.D.

'You'll find your sister a darling,' Fry told her. 'I was with

283

her in the summer. Be nice to her—I hear she's just lost her brother.'

The idea of a V.A.D. being in a position to be 'nice' to a sister was a little surprising; but Joan found that her relationship with Sister Muir was to be of a delightfully friendly and unofficial character, and quite soon they were calling each other by their surnames as though there were no difference of rank between them.

Muir was young and tall, with a sweet face, a slightly Scotch voice, and eyes like sad forget-me-nots. She was brimming with kindliness towards the men, and she knew her job inside out.

The ward used to be already darkened when they came on. One red-shaded globe hung in the middle; and placed along the floor at intervals were a few hurricane lanterns.

At about ten o'clock such patients as were on four-hourly fomentations were dressed. At twelve you were supposed to go over to the main building for 'midnight supper.' But it was so cold crossing the dark ground at that hour, and the meal itself was so depressing (swampy mince, or tough macaroni) that Joan, as often as not, cut it out, and ate cake and chocolates in sister's 'bunk' instead. Muir, not wholly approving of this unofficial meal, sometimes stayed and shared it with her.

After midnight there were all kinds of tiresome jobs to be done. Anything that the day-staff hadn't had time for was left for the night V.A.D. Joan cut up lint and gauze for dressings, tidied cupboards, and washed bed-pans and urine-bottles in the annex. She developed a mania for cleanliness, and nightly scrubbed out the big baths with Vim, or, when that gave out, with paraffin. Paraffin she found useful in more ways than one; for instance, when she was unable to get the narrow black stove in the centre of the ward to burn properly she used to throw some inside to encourage it. She was teased a good deal about this by a certain small South African soldier called Knight, who slept in a bed close to, and who told her that the flare she occasioned by her paraffin manoeuvres woke him up and gave him fits of nerves.

The hours between two and four were the hardest to get through. Drowsiness descended on you. With a couple of screens to keep out the draught you sat by the stove nodding over your letters, or over a book. Muir was in the 'bunk.' Silence reigned. Except for the breathing, and the occasional coughing from the two long rows of beds, you might have been in a graveyard. Cold too. The walls of the hut were only of thin wood. You needed all the woollen garments you could lay hands on. That winter of 1916–17 was deadly.

Sometimes 'Wee Knight,' as Muir called him, would come creeping round the edge of the screens, a grin on his face, a red blanket hugged round him, and ask to be allowed to sit by the stove. 'Can't sleep, Nurse, and it's so nice and cosy here!' And Joan would allow him to stay for a bit—though it was against the rules—on condition that he kept very quiet.

During these dead hours she would go round at intervals to see what men were lying awake, and take them drinks. Bovril, with a little milk in it, was what they most appreciated. 'That's "bon," Nurse,' they would say. 'That's the stuff to give the troops!' Joan provided the Bovril herself.

The Australians, of whom there were many, just now, in the ward, suffered badly from the cold. Many of them had bronchial coughs; others little dry hard coughs that were the result of mustard gas. Steaming inhalations did much to relieve them.

Between four-thirty and five washing and bed-making began. Lights were turned on. Muir came sailing down the ward, sprucely white and blue, with sleeves rolled up, and the men were wakened one by one. Joan was intensely sorry for them. It was just at this hour that slumber was deepest, and it seemed a shame not to leave the poor dears in peace. But hospital routine was inexorable. If things were not done at a certain time they didn't get done at all—and apparently the morning wash was more important than sleep. Then followed dressings. And then, while Muir took temperatures, Joan went into the ward kitchen to prepare breakfasts for thirty or forty men.

Cooking bacon, cutting bread-and-butter, ladling porridge into bowls—all this seemed somehow the last straw on night-duty; and without the help of an 'up' patient—usually Wee Knight—she couldn't have got through.

. . . . . .

Of the few bad cases in the ward that winter, the worst was Hinton, who had a fractured and extremely septic arm. The dressing of it was a laborious business at night; the lantern casting eerie shadows, Muir speaking in lowered voice, Hinton tossing and muttering in his delirium. His temperature ran high. It was a question whether the arm could be saved.

One night as Joan came on duty, Muir, who had been talking to the day sister, said in a troubled voice:

'Seddon, my child, Hinton's worse. Sister Smith doubts he'll last the night.'

Hinton wasn't babbling now. He lay with eyelids not quite closed, showing a narrow gleam. He was breathing heavily. His cheeks were a purplish-crimson. They did his dressing at ten o'clock. He groaned a little, but he didn't recognise them.

And then Muir told Joan to stay by him while she carried on with the other dressings. 'If there's any change, call me at once,' she said. And as she turned away Joan heard her murmur: 'I wish they'd amputated.'

An hour passed. Hinton was very quiet. Muir was moving about at the other end of the ward. From time to time Joan moistened the dry lips with a little lemon and water.

She went to have a meal in the 'bunk' while Muir took charge. When Muir went she resumed her place. Difficult not to imagine things at this time of night under these conditions. Shadows flickered. Wasn't there an alteration in the breathing? She leant forward, every sense alert. A few long rattling gasps. . . . Silence. She didn't move—not believing. . . . Then something frightening happened to the mouth.

'Yes?' Muir looked up as Joan appeared, pale-cheeked, in the door of the 'bunk.'

'Hinton . . .'

'All right, child.'

Within a circle of screens they stood on either side of the dead man's bed. Joan had insisted on helping, although Muir would willingly have let her off and have managed with an orderly.

They straightened the limbs; pressed down the lids of the eyes; pressed together the parted lips; propped up the jaw with a roll of linen. After about twenty minutes they carefully washed the body all over, and for the last time dressed the wounded arm—but now with only a little dry gauze and one thickness of bandage. They combed the hair, tied the ankles together, and wrapped the whole body in a sheet. There was no more to do.

Throughout these proceedings Joan had felt numb. There was little difference, she told herself, between the washing of a dead soldier and the washing of a soldier who was very ill. In fact she managed to keep the thought of death at arm's length. It was only when four orderlies came with a stretcher, and Private Hinton was carried from the dark ward under a Union Jack, that realisation flooded her. Sitting in the 'bunk' she cried and cried.

Muir stood beside her, a comforting sweet presence. 'Here, drink this, my dear,' she said, and put a cup of tea into Joan's shaking hands.

'It's all right—don't bother about me. It's just—just—that I haven't seen a death before.'

'I know, child, I know.' Muir's forget-me-not eyes were distressed. 'And I don't believe it gets any better. One has to develop a sort of shell.'

'Poor Hinton . . . poor Hinton!'

.   .   .   .   .   .

And then, almost before they knew it, Christmas was upon them, and all was mirth and excitement. On Christmas Eve the men hung up socks—some of the Australians even hung up pillow-cases—and Joan, in the silent hours, filled them with leather purses, tins of toffee, pipes, shaving-soap, pocket-knives, tangerines, handkerchiefs, small writing-pads, and cigarette-cases. By the light of a lantern she and Muir decorated the ward with holly, and with pink paper garlands which had been folded and cut during the nights before.

In the morning the atmosphere was that of an uproarious night-nursery. 'Oh, Sister, look what I've got.' . . . 'Oo—toffee!' . . . 'Lor', I won't 'alf swank it with this 'ere!'

Perhaps those who enjoyed it all most were the Australians, for they were so far from home. 'Oh, Nurse, Nurse! Did you give us all these things?' one of them cried ecstatically to Joan, as he pulled present after present out of his pillow-case and laid them before him on the counterpane. 'Oh, Nurse, *will* you marry me and come back to Australia?'

Among the noise and the mess of presents and wrappings the two women moved laughingly, and somehow contrived to get their ordinary work done. Into the kitchen, while Joan was preparing breakfast, crashed two exuberant Australians with a bit of mistletoe, and tried to kiss her. 'Oh, go away, you idiots!' she cried. And repulsed, but undamped, they crashed out again. She discovered later that Muir had been subjected to the same onslaught in the annex—and not only by that particular couple—and had allowed them each to have a kiss 'because it was Christmas.'

'Well, Muir, you amaze me!' cried Joan. 'And here have I been upholding discipline, and the sanctity of the uniform, and what not. . . . No wonder the ward's demoralised! A *sister* too!'

But the men took no advantage of the temporary laxity—as indeed Muir knew that they would not—and were lamb-like in their behaviour for the rest of the week.

.   .   .   .   .   .

It was a relief to go out in the mornings. You needed all the air and change you could get after being in that cold yet stuffy ward for twelve dark hours on end. Strange how sleepy you were.

Jogging along westwards in a tram or bus you would find your head dropping forward, and would only jerk back to consciousness as someone pushed past you, or the brisk girl bus-conductor asked you for your fare.

And then, by the time you had got to the Monico, or to the Gobelins, or to the Piccadilly Grill, to meet some boy on leave, it was astonishing how ready you felt for a perfectly normal lunch—even though you had dined at 8 a.m. Sometimes you would be taken to a matinée afterwards, and about half-way through it you would whisper good-bye to your companion, and slip out and back to Camberwell. You had almost got to know the first part of 'Chu-Chin-Chow' by heart, and it was with no regret, really, that you left the spectacle of that gorgeous slave-market, and of all those fat half-naked bodies, and emerged into the street with the tune of 'Any Time's Kissing Time' humming in your ears. You wondered what old Gower would say to you nowadays—for this really was 'the double life'! The night-hut, unlike the hostel, was left unlocked, and although you were supposed to be back in it by twelve-thirty you frequently remained out until three or four o'clock. Perhaps it was not so strange that you were sleepy in the mornings.

· · · · · ·

Colder and colder. It was hardly possible to be so cold. Joan stoked the stove furiously, but it seemed to make no difference. With purple hands she scrubbed out baths in the icy annex, and for the first time was thankful (and rather ashamed of being thankful) that she was not in France.

She had heard from Barbara that conditions there were terrible. Owing, it seemed, to two or three coal-ships having been sunk on their way into Boulogne harbour, there was little or no heat just now in the hospitals. Boilers couldn't be kept up; the men had to be washed in cold water; and the very thermometers were frozen into the little pots of carbolic-water in which they stood. That somehow brought it home. And the vision of Barbara stumbling about at night, in wading-boots, between the tents and huts on the Wimereux cliff, made Joan realise vividly the luxury of her own situation.

.　　.　　.　　.　　.　　.

Men began coming in with trench feet. There was little to be done about trench feet. They were not dressed in the ordinary way. Those swollen blackish lumps, which resembled more than anything else a couple of charred blocks of firewood, were washed in warm water, wrapped in pieces of lint soaked in lead-lotion, and loosely bandaged. As time went on decayed portions of skin and flesh could be peeled off; and there was a certain fascination in seeing the new pink skin forming beneath, and the toes show- ing like little new-born pigs. But these trench feet were foul —there was no other word—foul in appearance, foul in smell.

There was a boy called Murphy, a pretty lad, whose toes had all fallen off except three on one foot; and even these Muir was doubtful of being able to save.

'Oh, Sister!' cried little Murphy, his first night in the ward. 'I used to be a dancer. I shall never dance again. I used to be a dancer on the halls.' The tears were hopping down his cheeks.

The winter of 1917 ground on.

.　　.　　.　　.　　.　　.

Fry came into '31' one night, on her way across to supper, to tell Joan rather an exciting piece of news. Phipps's fiancé was at last coming home on leave; the wedding was fixed for three days hence; and she was asking her special friends from the hospital to come to it. Poor Phipps had been ready for such long months —down to the last ribbon of the last camisole! And now, it seemed, she could hardly believe that her time of waiting was over.

'Lucky for us we're both on night-duty,' said Fry. 'We shall be able to go together and see the show through.'

And see it through they did. The quiet service, in St. Peter's, Cranley Gardens, began at two o'clock; and from their pew— well behind all the relations—they watched Phipps, in her white dress and veil, being joined to Captain Temple, tall in khaki. And as the words were muttered over the bride's bent head there flashed impishly into Joan's mind Phipps's remark, last July, concerning her hairy legs. But Phipps, coming down the aisle (Mrs. Temple now—but you could never think of her as that) looked so transported that all wandering and flippant thoughts were swallowed up in the one main wish for her happiness.

Cake, and champagne, and a hum of talk in a house in Onslow Square. A hand-shake for the bridegroom, a kiss for the bride.

'Oh, you dears, how angelic of you to come! Jack, these are my "mates" of the 1st London. Without them I should have expired. It's to them you owe me in my present condition of comparative sanity.'

'Which isn't saying *much*!' Fry crinkled her nice eyes at 'Jack,' who smiled back at her, and said that it was for him, now, to take charge.

Little Phipps, a flash of blue felt hat, disappeared into a car under a shower of confetti, and it was over. Camberwell would know her no more. She had only stayed on on the understanding that she could leave at any moment to be married. After her brief honeymoon, when her husband had returned to France, she would be living at home and working at some smaller hospital.

Joan and Fry, a little dazed with champagne and emotion, got back about five o'clock and crept into bed. They hadn't noticed Matron, who happened to be crossing the grounds at the very moment of their return.

The result of 'seeing through' Phipps's wedding cost them their freedom—and the freedom of all the other night nurses. From thenceforward the hut was locked every day at twelve-thirty. Any unfortunate girl arriving later was condemned either to go and ask Matron for the key, and incur a strafing, or else attempt a surreptitious entry through the window of the hut bathroom.

.   .   .   .   .   .

When, at the beginning of March, Joan was taken off night-duty she was surprised to find how reluctant she was to leave it. Night-duty in itself was detestable, but she had had her spell of it under ideal conditions. They had been a happy family in '31,' and Muir was the sweetest sister she had ever worked with, or was ever likely to work with.

Chapter Two

JIMMY used to come up fairly often from Woolwich on week-end leave, and if Joan's half-day happened to be on a Saturday or Sunday they spent it together at home.

Jimmy was getting on well. He said he found it interesting being landed in surroundings so utterly unlike any he had known before. He was kept hard at it—from six-thirty in the morning to eight-thirty at night—with drilling, parading, harness-fitting, riding, and lectures. He was getting to know a lot about horses, their management and feeding, and their various diseases; and would amuse Joan by bringing out such words as 'glanders,' 'staggers,' 'lampas,' and 'spavin.'

Contrary to her expectations he was not worried, but was gayer than she had seen him for a long time. The plunge, once taken—although it was into an atmosphere by no means congenial—seemed to have had the effect of raising his spirits.

Sometimes he would bring home his friends Sanderson and Browne (little Carey, being at Sandhurst, would appear less often), and there would be uproarious suppers at which Jimmy would give his famous imitation of the Woolwich grace. It appeared that when all the cadets had filed into the hall, and were standing silently at their places, the cadet in charge of dinner parade would march smartly up to a small table in the middle, stand to attention, and gabble: 'For what we are about to receive—THANK GOD!' The last two words would come in a stentorian shout, like that of a sergeant's 'Slope Arms!', after which everyone would sit down and begin talking. Florence was always convulsed at this performance of her nephew's.

The boys looked rather pets in their absurd red-bordered khaki overcoats reaching to their ankles, and one afternoon Joan took snap-shots of them in the garden. It was impossible to get them to be serious. They clung to each other's arms in lolling groups,

their caps on the backs of their heads, pretending to be 'tight'—
Jimmy, the tallest, in the middle, supporting the other two.

'Now, you alone, Jim-pot,' called Joan, winding her camera.
'Pull yourself together, and you shall be immortalised as the
perfect Gentleman Cadet.'

'Half a tick!' Jimmy dived into the verandah and fetched a toy
Union Jack on a long bamboo, which had been leaning there ever
since the summer, probably left by one of the twins.

'Now!' He stood up very stiff, turning his toes out, and presenting arms. 'For King and Country . . . and all that rot.' A
grin spread over his baby face.

'Portrait of the perfect fool!' said Joan, and privately thought
she had never seen him look so nice.

Military training had not put a damper on Jimmy's love of
music. Whenever he came home alone he would wander into the
drawing-room and start messing about, as he called it, on the
piano. And Florence, if she happened to be out, would find him
there on her return, and experience a pleasant sense of security.
Both the children in England, anyhow. Popping home from time
to time. Long might such conditions last.

.   .   .   .   .   .

'Oh, Betty, I wish I could see him!' said Joan to her friend, who
was on leave.

'You might not like him. He's not really your type.'

'Oh, bother my type! So long as he's yours that's all that
matters. And I'm not nearly so limited in my tastes as you make
out.'

'It's just that Guy might strike you as conventional and reac-
tionary. He's not sound on the Suffrage, you see, and . . .'

Joan made as if to push her friend off the stool she was sitting
on. Then she resumed seriously:

'You're happy, darling? You're really in love with him?'

Betty's slow nod, and the look in her eyes, contented her.

The girls were huddled by the stove in the hall at Beechwood,
and Betty, at long last, had been able to tell Joan 'all about it.'

'You and Colin are the only two people who know. Not even the parents do, yet. You'll be silent as the tomb, won't you?'

'Heavens, yes! Well, you've let me down "good and proper," haven't you? Do you remember how we used to swear to remain free? How we scoffed at marriage?'

Betty nodded a little remorsefully. 'Nobody could have been more astonished about this business than I was, I can tell you. You know, Joan, when it happens you just can't do anything about it—it's very queer—there's a sort of inevitability.'

'So it seems. But, oh, darling, no man will understand either of us as well as we understand each other. They're bound to be-glamour us. They can't know the little funny things, the little awful things, the weaknesses and deepnesses that we know about each other, and which make no difference to our fondness—in fact cement it. There's a sort of unstrained, humorous delicious-ness about the relationship between two women, don't you think?'

'Pet! You'll never lose me!' Betty declared.

Joan wrinkled her nose, then threw her arms round her friend and hugged her.

. . . . . .

The ward in which Joan was now working was in the medical block in the main building. After the cheery, if strenuous, surgi-cal huts to which she had been accustomed she found the atmo-sphere, over here, depressing in the extreme. She missed Sister Muir; her present sister, Sister O'Flannagan, who was also in charge of other wards on that floor, was stupid; the men, poor dears, grumbled a lot, and were mopish and miserable.

Most of them were from Salonika, and were suffering either from nephritis, from trench-fever, from malaria, or from 'flu.

There was a constant going to and fro with drinks and with medicines. There was the filling of hot-water bottles; the taking of urine specimens; the applying of poultices; the arranging of hot packs round patients who had to be made to perspire. All this was not exhausting physically, but you never had the satisfactory feeling of being 'through'—of having, for the time being, done all you could for a man—which followed the dressing of a wound.

In spite of her dislike for medical work, Joan seemed to have the faculty of cheering the men up and of getting them better. Deaths occurred in adjoining wards, but never—while she was on duty—in hers. To Joan this was a mere coincidence, but to the superstitious Sister O'Flannagan there was 'something queer in it.' Nurse Seddon, she thought, might well be one of those people in whose presence 'the spirit cannot pass,' and she took to sending her, from time to time, into other wards to assist with the bad cases.

She sent her one day to a Canadian, whose 'flu had developed into pneumonia, to try whether she couldn't induce him to take some food. Joan fed him with spoonfuls of jelly, telling him it was good and cool, and would make him strong.

'Nothing will make me strong,' said the Canadian apathetically.

Then Joan told him about her brother when he was a little boy, how he had suffered from frequent illnesses, and how strong and splendid he had grown.

'You're rather like my brother in appearance,' she said. 'And you've got to make up your mind to get well. Would you eat some grapes if I brought them you?'

He seemed to think he might. So when she was out she bought a bunch of muscats, and took them to him in the evening, peeling and pipping them, and dropping them into his mouth as she remembered Aunt Florence used to do when Jimmy was a child.

'Nice,' he said, and looked at her, smiling faintly, as he waited for the next bit of grape.

Just before going off duty she came to him again.

'I want you to drink this milk—all of it. I'll put it here within reach.'

He turned on her his wide, pale eyes.

'Stay by me, and I will,' he said. And after he had taken a gulp or two: 'Everyone seems so far away.'

'Do you mean your people in Canada?' she asked, remembering how lonely he must feel.

'No—everyone. Even you seem far away.'

His expression smote her. She went to Sister O'Flannagan, and implored to be allowed to stay on through the night and 'special' him.

Sister hesitated, then refused. Such a thing wouldn't be in order.

'I'm pretty certain I can bring him through,' urged Joan.

At that something seemed to harden in Sister. 'You V.A.D.s think you can do everything!' she snapped.

'It's not a question of that! You yourself think I have a sort of luck, and I know he'd like me to stay.'

'I can't give you permission,' said Sister. 'The night-staff have got to take him over now.'

And Joan returned disconsolate to the hostel.

By morning the Canadian was dead. She nearly cried with rage. Not that she had any sort of belief in her occult powers (had not Hinton died while she was in '31'?), but in this particular case she felt she could have inspired a will to live.

Sister O'Flannagan—which seemed unreasonable—was not more cordial to Joan after this episode.

.   .   .   .

The spring dragged on, and, in spite of the appearance of a few stark and valiant daffodil-buds, seemed merely to be a prolongation of winter. There were hailstones and snow-storms. Nurses coughed and sneezed their way about the wards. There was an epidemic of measles. Civilians crouched over their small fires. Husbands grumbled at the food-shortage; wives made patriotic efforts to be economical, and devised strange dishes of potatoes and beans and maize. Everyone was rather hungry, everyone depressed. 'It will be better later on,' they said, 'when we can start an offensive. This summer ought to see the end.' The Somme was reluctantly admitted to have been a failure, but *this* time . . .

Joan had a letter from Pamela, who was recovering, though

slowly. Her bout of 'flu had left her heart groggy, and there was some internal strain—the result of munitions work—which caused her a good deal of discomfort. She had headaches, too, from weakened eyesight. A bore, these, as they prevented her reading as much as she would have liked. At first there had been continued roarings in her ears as though she were still among machinery. She wished she were working, for then she wouldn't have these empty hours in which to brood over Ian. 'There's no one to talk to here,' she ended. 'Can't *you* have a breakdown too, and come and stay with me? I feel such an idiot, and so ashamed.'

Bad news came from Barbara. Her fiancé, Sam Wyndham, had been killed. Somehow Joan knew it as soon as she saw the envelope. One after the other! One after the other! Barbara would carry on, of course, in those cold tents in France, looking a little whiter, a little larger-eyed. She would nurse till she dropped, or till the war came to an end. Peace might come, but she would never marry now. For Barbara marriage had meant Sam—and Sam only.

.   .   .   .   .   .

Colin came on leave. It was not a very successful leave as far as he and Joan were concerned. For more than a year they had not seen each other, and though fundamentally their feelings had not changed—his love was as deep as ever, her friendship as real— they had both of them been plunged to the hilt in the war, and their young enthusiasms, in all directions, had been chilled. They felt a little strange in each other's company.

Circumstances, too, were against them. They only had snatched hours together. Meetings took place mostly at restaurants. He talked about the trenches; she talked about the wards. Oh, there was plenty to talk about! And sometimes he took her back to Camberwell, and watched her, from the bottom of the road, vanishing up to the hospital in her prim little nurse's coat and hat, and sighed as he turned away.

The one 'half-day' which fell to Joan during Colin's leave they spent together at Beechwood, and there was a glimmer of old times about that day. Florence gave them a fire in the drawing-room, and Joan threw aside her eternal uniform and wore a frock which Colin had been fond of two years ago.

'Isn't it awful? I never read any poetry now,' she said. 'It seems to have lost all meaning—or else I can't concentrate. Sometimes, these days,' she added with a little laugh, 'I feel absolutely suicidal. I find myself wondering which are the most painless poisons!'

'I know—I know just the feeling,' he replied. 'And for me, too, poetry has faded out, but it will come back. We simply can't respond all round, to everything. And I think you and I are rather whole-hoggers, Joan.'

'Perhaps!' she granted. 'In a way it's our misfortune.'

They discussed Betty's engagement. It seemed that Colin had once met Guy, but didn't remember much about him except that he was charming and gay. But he trusted his sister's instinct, and felt that if, with all her fastidiousness, she had succumbed at last, this was probably the right man for her.

'I don't know when she thinks of getting married,' he said, 'but I tell her there's no point in delay once you're sure.'

'No—I suppose there isn't—once you're sure,' said Joan.

She looked at him. His hair was cropped much closer now. It was not becoming to him. He was thinner, and his eyes no longer looked at her with the cloudy passion of the earlier days. She was thankful they did not; and yet vaguely she missed that homage, radiating from his manhood to her girlhood, which at one time had both excited her and been a nuisance. If her emotional being had not sunk to such a low ebb she might have missed it more. And Colin, partly because of her tiredness, partly too because he had so schooled himself into the conviction (expressed one day rather bitterly to Betty) that the modern girl wanted nothing but friendship, made no effort to alter the atmosphere. Love-making must wait—like other things. After the war, when both of them were untrammelled—then . . .

But she was talking of the Russian Revolution. Wasn't it wonderful?—the most hopeful thing that had yet happened. Ancient tyranny overthrown. . . .

Colin, idly battering a piece of coal with the poker, was not so certain. Of course if the Kerensky man could keep them together. . . . The Russians were an immoderate race. . . . Once they'd cast off authority there was no knowing where they might go . . . might even chuck the war. . . .

Joan poured scorn on the notion. She had an enthusiasm for the Russians (derived chiefly from their ballets and their novels), and she believed that having won freedom they would prosecute the war with redoubled vigour.

They argued about it for a while. And then, from discussing the sticking-powers of the different nations, and the various factors, physical and spiritual, that made for 'morale,' they found themselves on the subject of venereal disease. Colin told her that two men in his battalion—not great friends of his, but good officers— had contracted it, and had been sent to hospital.

'Poor devils! Knocked out by *that*—not by a decent wound.'

'But it's possible, isn't it,' asked Joan, 'to become infected accidentally—I mean it may not be a man's own fault?'

Colin smiled with rueful knowledge. 'It was with these two. They got it at the fountain-head all right.'

'Colin,' she asked, suddenly frightened. 'Colin—*you've* never been with that sort of woman?'

He looked at her and slowly shook his head. 'No, my dear. Not drawn that way. The only thing that might conceivably send me off the deep end would be if you were to drop me—cut me out altogether.'

'Colin, I won't—ever. You know that.'

The eyes of each held the eyes of the other in a look that was like the joining of hands. But there was sadness in it.

. . . .

For weeks Joan had been low in health and low in spirits. When Colin had gone her depression deepened. Having lost interest in most other things she now even lost interest in her patients. It was a flat, black, monotonous world. For twenty-four hours she had violent ear-ache—a thing she hadn't suffered from since childhood. Then a stye welled up on her lower eyelid, and, looking at herself in the glass, she decided that, with a face like that, it would be better quietly to pass out.

And then, together with Fry and half-a-dozen other V.A.D.s who had long had their names down for Foreign Service, she was inoculated and sent to the sick-room. She would have enjoyed her two days there, in her little bed next to Fry's, if she hadn't felt so ill. The temperature she ran was at first attributed to the result of inoculation, and only later, when it still remained high, was she discovered to have 'flu.

So Joan stayed on where she was, and the others went to France without her, and she cursed her luck.

A letter came from Betty. Betty had for some weeks now been Senior Lady of the Alexandra—Mother B. having been invalided home.

'Have been having rather a hectic time as S.L.,' she wrote. 'Two of the women workers had to be given the boot—they were so awful. The whole thing made me sick at the time—especially as Bingham was on leave and I had to bear the brunt alone. You know how I *loathe* rows. But as a matter of fact all unpleasantness was well worth while to be quit of those two. They were spoiling the whole atmosphere of the hut. Incidentally they were much older than me! I'm enjoying myself now. Fun being head of a show, and running things one's own way. Roscoe backs me up splendidly, and as S.L. of the hut I have only to ask for things to have them done. Our personal relations, however, have been rather strained of late. Seems to be a bit of an "atmosphere." Can't help feeling he *scents* something, and is vaguely jealous—though what possible right he has . . .! Which brings me to my real news. I heard yesterday that Guy had been wounded—rather badly, but not dangerously. Leg. No details. But oh, my dear, the *relief* of knowing that he's in England—safe! What a queer world it is where one's greatest cause of thankfulness is that a person one loves should be wounded. Everything's easier now—the only snag being, of course, that I can't get over to see him.'

'Good! Oh, good!' sighed Joan. For the time being Guy was out of it. Betty could be at peace. You had begun to feel that a girl had only to get engaged to be almost immediately bereaved.

When Joan was better she was given ten days' sick-leave, and she spent part of it at home and part of it in the country. In sheltered nooks she found a few primroses, but most of the ground was snow-covered. The papers were full of the valour of the Canadians on Vimy Ridge.

When she returned she was restored both in health and spirits, and was rather humiliated to think how much of her recent depression must have been due to the body.

To her delight she was put once more on to a surgical ward.

Chapter Three

WARD 26 was one of the longest huts in the hospital. It contained sixty beds. During this spring of the battle of Arras twelve more beds were crowded in, and looking down its length was like looking down two railway-lines that converged in the distance. Joan used to wonder how many miles of wooden floor one covered in a week.

Convoys came in almost every night. Wounds were, if anything, worse than in the Somme days. Morning dressings continued into the afternoons; evening dressings began at tea-time. There was hardly a breathing-space. Off-times did not exist, or else were thrown at you suddenly when it was found you could be spared. Lucky you were feeling so well. Dog-tired at night, of course, but fresh again in the morning. And, oh, the life *was* worth while! You felt, once more, that sort of spiritual exaltation that came with the nursing of men who were suffering terribly, and were behaving like saints—men whose faces puckered as you moved them in bed, and who looked at you afterwards with great forgiving eyes. Your tiredness of body contributed, rather than otherwise, to your exaltation of spirit, for it was a tiredness that had passed into a stage where it was indistinguishable from strength, and which gave you the illusion of being able to carry on indefinitely.

In spite of the immense size of the ward there were no extra V.A.D.s; and how the men got fed and washed, in among the dressing of their wounds, Joan hardly knew. It was done somehow. But if only Sister Mercer of '26' had been like Sister Ewart of '33' nothing would have mattered. She was not. And Joan realised in person—what she had so often been told by soldiers—the incalculable difference made by efficient leadership.

'26' should have been the best-run ward in the hospital; it was quite the worst. Supplies of all sorts were continually giving out, and were only replaced, if at all, after much delay.

Standing at the top of the ward, Sister Mercer, like a small rodent in pince-nez, would call out instructions and reprimands in a high drawling voice which set the nerves on edge.

'Nurse, I don't think that splint you brought for Johnson will do at all. You'll have to go again to the splint-room and find another. . . .' 'What are you putting a clean sheet on that man's bed for? He had one only yesterday. . . .' 'Surely you've had enough time to boil up those instruments, Nurse? We shall never get through at this rate!' It was nag, nag, fuss, fuss, all the day long. She seemed, during this first fortnight, to have a special down on Joan.

One evening, when Joan was collecting wash-bowls from the lockers, and had paused for a minute to say something to one of the patients, Sister shouted at her from the doorway: 'If you'd talk a little less to the men, Nurse Seddon, and pay a little more attention to me we should get on better!'

Talk a little less to the men? Why, there was hardly time to perform the barest necessities for them. To restrain an occasional smile and a word in passing was not within one's power.

And then quite suddenly, as it seemed to Joan, Sister's attitude towards her changed. Either she saw that Joan was not altogether a fool, or else got tired of the rôle of nagging foreman; anyhow she ceased making herself a nuisance and became quite friendly. As a matter of fact Joan had determined that sooner or later she should. She was proof, now, against bullyings from 'the Olympians.' She had the confidence which comes from knowing one's job.

Sister Mercer had two ruling passions: church services and cups of tea. Joan pandered to both. The tea could be easily produced; and regularly at nine o'clock, at two, and at four, she would bring a tray into the 'bunk,' and receive a grateful, if somewhat acidulated, smile. The services hardly lay within Joan's province;

but she could at any rate arrange that Sister should miss as few of them as possible. She would hear her murmur, looking vaguely through her pince-nez at nothing in particular: 'There's an early celebration in chapel to-morrow which I should very much like to attend, but I suppose . . .' And Joan would say comfortably: 'Well, why don't you, Sister? There's no real need for you to be on till nine.' And on Sunday mornings, especially, Joan would almost push her off to eleven-o'clock matins; for although dressings would be in full swing, and Sister's place was indubitably in the ward, it was so much more peaceful without her that her absence was a relief.

As time went on Joan took over an ever-increasing number of the dressings. She tackled cases which, strictly speaking, she should not have had to undertake alone. While down at the far end of the ward the Staff-nurse—Sister Brown—a coarse, unsympathetic woman, was pounding through her work, Joan, at the top end, went from bed to bed, either with the third V.A.D., or else with 'Jock' Guthrie, a dear stocky man in the Argylls. It was fortunate that Guthrie suffered from nothing worse than septic boils in the neck, and was able to be an up-patient, for he was of inestimable use to Joan. He attached himself quite voluntarily to her, and she accepted his services. After a time he became well-trained, and would stump off with the bucket of dirty dressings, empty it, wash the blood from the mackintosh, and even wash and boil instruments for her between performances. In some ways he was of more use than the V.A.D., for he would lift patients in his strong arms, and hold up limbs while they were being irrigated and dressed, with a steadiness hardly possible to a girl.

There sprang up between them one of those queer friendships— devotion on his side, fondness on hers, with a hint of sentiment behind—which had no counterpart in civil life. The war was their background; the hospital, for the time being, their home; and the mutual help they gave one another was their immediate bond. Guthrie had a native dignity, which not even the grotesque bandage round his neck could decrease, and his eyes were the most direct and honest Joan had ever seen.

In the annex, among bowls and bins and lysol, scraps of discussion would take place, and Guthrie would expound his political views and show a shrewd perception of character. He had summed up Sister Mercer almost from the first. 'Makes an unco palaver about a thing, but leaves others to get on wi' it,' he had once remarked to Joan, but she had shut him up. He might think what he liked about the sister of his ward, but it was her duty to preserve an outward loyalty. On the subject of officers, too, she was aware that she ought not to allow him to talk as he did, but she so deeply sympathised with his feelings that she hadn't the heart to suppress him. What worried Guthrie, and even roused him to bitterness, was the type of officer now being sent out. Lack of efficiency might have been put up with—old soldiers were prepared to give all the help they could to new officers—but there was a manner and tone of voice that were hard to swallow. No man, he said, minded being cursed if he felt that he were also being understood; but many of these little Jackanapes had never used authority before, and their efforts to be impressive were merely irritating and ridiculous.

'You see, the officer class, Jock, is simply becoming exterminated,' Joan would say sadly.

'It wouldna matter so much in peace-time if it wor exterminated, but in war you need gentry to lead you. And that I say in spite of my Socialist leanings.'

The counting of the dirty linen, once a week, was a tedious task. Seventy pillow-cases and shirts, sometimes twice as many sheets, varying numbers of socks, slings and towels lay in a tepidly smelling mass on the floor of the annex—all to be folded, checked and re-checked, before being carried off by the orderly. Here again Guthrie was invaluable.

'I should make a handy man about the house, Nurse, after all this, should I not?' he said to her one day. 'When you marry your duke belike I'll come and be head-housemaid.'

Joan laughed at him over an armful of sheets. 'What makes you think I'm going to marry a duke?'

'Eh, you'll marry some nob,' he said dolefully. 'But don't you forget poor auld Jock.'

And they talked of 'after the war'—if there ever should be such a time. Guthrie was a blacksmith, and he supposed he would go back to his trade. Joan couldn't for the life of her think what *she* would go back to.

Guthrie's boils swelled at intervals and were often very painful.

'Do me dressing for me, Nurse,' he asked her one day, in his guttural voice. 'I canna stand that Sister Brown any more.'

His bed being at the lower end of the ward he came under the Staff-nurse's jurisdiction, and Joan had often seen her (and turned away her eyes from the sight) probing into the back of Jock's neck as he sat on a chair, her thick cow-like face showing complete indifference to his grimly-endured suffering. Yesterday he had almost fainted.

'All right, Jock. Bring a chair in here so that we shan't be seen, and I'll do it quickly.'

When it was over he sighed. 'That's grand, Nurse! Your touch is as different—as different.'

There were about half a dozen cases in the ward which Sister Mercer dressed herself—assisted, of course, by Joan.

One was little Twemlow, a cockney boy of nineteen, with a small vivid face and great brown eyes. He had a wound in the thigh which was liable to hæmorrhage, and his bed was propped up on blocks at the lower end, and a rubber tourniquet kept near at hand. Joan was particularly fond of him. A friend of his, slightly wounded, and now 'up,' told her that Twenlow had crawled out into No-Man's Land one night and brought in a wounded man—the German Verey lights going up all round. 'Such a little bit of a thing he looked too,' said his friend, 'and the other was a hulking great chap. But it wasn't no use, 'e died as soon as 'e'd got 'im in the trench.'

Twemlow was one of those nervously-made and imaginative

people who easily got 'wind up,' and who force themselves to control their windiness. Joan knew this by the eager way he talked, by the intense interest which he took in the dressing of his wound, by his flinchings and his laughing recoveries. 'Aprays la guaire,' he would say, 'me and me Mother's going to run the shop together. One o' them little 'ard-ware shops it is. Shepherd's Bush way. 'Andy for popping into Shepherd's Bush Empire of a Saturday night. Ole lady can't take proper care of 'erself. She needs me, she does.' All this and a lot more he told Joan, as she was washing him one evening. His arms were as white as a girl's.

'Ah, well!' he would say about the war. 'The first seven years is the worst!'

In sharp contrast to little Twemlow was a silent New Zealander, Johnson, who was suffering from septicæmia, or blood-poisoning of the whole system. He had already been in the ward three or four months when Joan arrived, and was still in bed. Rigors, and soaring temperatures, and abscesses forming in different parts of his body would alternate with periods of subsidence. Then everything would start again. Operation followed operation. None but the stoutest of hearts could have stood out. Joan felt, sadly, that there was little she could do for him. He was not responsive or lovable; he was just admirable. There was no one, nurse or soldier, with whom he established any friendly contact. He reminded her a little of Sergeant King in his grim self-sufficiency.

When Sister Mercer had finished off her particular handful of men she would disappear, or else hover in the doorway of the ward, looking down its length with a displeased expression. Her eye lit, one morning, on the third V.A.D. doing one of Joan's dressings. 'Nurse Williams,' she called out in her high irritating drawl, 'what are you doing? Don't you know that Nurse Seddon is the only nurse in this ward whom I allow to do dressings on her own?'

Williams faltered out that she had only wanted to help, and Joan

came to her rescue and took the blame, but Sister was not molli-
fied. Having found one nurse whom she considered she could
trust, she did her the uncomfortable honour of loading most of
the responsible work on her shoulders and treating the others
like idiots.

Gradually Joan found herself in the position of being 'acting
sister' of the ward, as a man might be 'acting captain' of a
company. Not only were half of the entire dressings done by
herself, but various jobs devolved upon her which were not a
V.A.D.'s concern. One of them was 'indenting' for stores. Taking full advantage of her unasked-for position, she would write
on the Dispensary slips her list of requirements (peroxide, lysol,
wool, lint, gauze, bandages, and thermometers), send off the slips
by an orderly, and in due course receive the stuff. The Dispensary was amazed at the increased demands from '26,' and at last
that unfortunate ward began to be adequately stocked.

Taking temperatures had already long been part of her routine.
She would stick three thermometers into three separate mouths;
take pulses meanwhile; remove the thermometers, one by one,
and write down results on the charts. Temperatures normal,
temperatures high. Level or soaring ink-lines. Pulses of 60, or
70, or 80. And afterwards the evening dressings.

Sometimes she was not off till after eight o'clock; and on more
than one occasion she missed even the third home-going 'Tank'
and had to take a tram.

.   .   .   .   .   .

One Saturday morning in June, while the army of weekly charwomen was scrubbing the ward floor, and Sister Mercer was going her rounds with the M.O., Joan became aware of a disturb-
ance among the up-patients. They were crowding to the open
door in the middle of the ward, going out into the grounds,
shouting to each other. She took no notice. There was no time.
Then one of them came back excitedly. 'Say, Nurse, say, Nurse,
they're coming over!' 'Who are coming over?' said Joan, swabbing a large expanse of raw flesh on a man's leg. 'Why, aero-

planes, Nurse! 'undreds of 'em!' 'Do you mean *German* aeroplanes?' she asked incredulously. 'Yes! Come on, Nurse, come
out and look at 'em!'

Quite unable to share the man's excitement, but feeling that
she must put up some sort of a show, Joan, with a bowl in one
hand and a swab in the other, walked nonchalantly to the threshold
and looked up. There, against the blue, were what looked like a
flock of great wild swans flying in the form of an arrow-head.
Puffs of smoke surrounded them; a booming and whirring filled
the air. 'There 'e is! There's Gerry!' cried the men. 'Good old
Gerry! Well, I'll be blowed! Fancy old Gerry!' Joan looked at
their upward-turned faces, devoid of fear, devoid of hatred, then
back at the aeroplanes now slowly disappearing southwards.
'Extraordinary!' she said. 'Daylight too!' And having thus paid
her tribute, and shown—she hoped—a tolerably composed front,
she turned into the ward and went on with her dressings.

Some of the bed-patients were a bit scared. Sister Mercer, to
Joan's admiration, was still going round with the M.O. as though
nothing out of the ordinary had taken place. At intervals down
the middle of the ward stood buckets and scrubbing-brushes; the
charwomen had all fled back to their children.

There were over five hundred casualties in London as a result
of that raid.

. . . . . .

Joan came on duty one morning to find Twemlow looking very
white, and the foot of his bed tilted even higher. He had had
hæmorrhage from his leg in the night. It had been arrested before
much blood had been lost, but it had been a frightening, exhausting experience.

'I don't want to lose me leg, Nurse,' he said. 'I'd rather keep it.
But they say if this happens again they'll amputate.'

Joan tried to cheer him. 'No reason it should happen again,
Sonny. You just keep very quiet, and if there's anything you
can't reach on your locker, call to me. Don't make any unnecessary movement.'

The day wore on. Dressings. Dinner. Evening shift, with temperatures and more dressings. Joan was at the steriliser, wringing out a fomentation, when she heard a cry—a startling—a familiar cry: 'Sister, Sister, it's coming through!'

For a second she stood, the steaming wringer in her hands, then dropped it back into the water and darted to Twemlow's bedside. He was clasping his leg with both hands, terror staring from his brown eyes. 'Oh, quick, quick!' Sister Brown, who had happened at the moment to be passing, was before her; had whipped the tourniquet from where it hung round the bed-rail, and was twisting it round Twemlow's leg, pulling on it with all the force of her stout arms. Joan went for milk and brandy; and five minutes after that first cry for help Twemlow was lying still, panting a little, but with the terror gone.

.   .   .   .   .   .

The following morning Twemlow's mother was sitting beside him. His leg was to be amputated in an hour of two's time. She was a stout woman, with a broad perplexed face, and she was sobbing quietly. Joan, dashing up and down the ward from dressing to dressing, felt sorry for her and furious with her. What a fool! She, who ought at that moment to have been doing all she could to cheer her son was instead being cheered by him.

'Oh, Will, supposing you shouldn't recover?'

'I'm all right, Mother, don't take on so. *I'm* not worrying, you see. It's much better to have it off. I'm not worrying.'

There was a light in his face like the light which must have been in the faces of young martyrs as they encouraged each other before going into the arena. His hand was on his mother's shoulder. Her head dropped to the bed-clothes.

A little later Joan took her away, and Twemlow was put on a trolley and wheeled out to the theatre.

'Good luck, Sonny,' said Joan, smiling at him, while pity tore her heart. 'I shan't be on duty when you come back. See you in the morning.'

.   .   .   .   .   .

By two o'clock she was lunching with Philip Nichol at the Carlton. He had been spending his leave in Somerset. He was going back to France to-morrow. Luck had favoured them, for Joan had not had a half-day off for weeks.

Both for Philip's sake and for her own she pushed hospital anxieties into the background.

She was glad to see him, glad of a good meal, of champagne-cup, of gay surroundings. She had the capacity—useful in those days —of being able to respond swiftly to the demands of the varying moments.

Philip, beyond a certain tension in his movements and an added grimness to his mouth, showed no signs of last year's breakdown. Joan could only guess at the will-power required on his part to dominate disgusted nerves. Men in war-time moved behind a mist. Men you cared for, men you thought you were intimate with—brothers, lovers, friends—all, all, were fundamentally, were pathetically, alone.

She was relieved to learn that Philip had been, for the last few months, on a quiet sector of the Front. But of himself he hardly spoke. He wanted to hear about her and her family—anything that interested her. She told him about Jimmy being at Woolwich.

'That funny silent youngster at Sunday suppers? It doesn't seem possible!' He crumbled his bread. 'The young lot now. No end to it.'

His own brother, the third and youngest of the family, who had always been considered safe, had just fallen a victim to the last Military Service Act.

'He has been rejected, you know, three times, for valvular disease of the heart,' said Philip. 'His last paper was marked "Rejection Permanent," and now the Medical Board have passed him A 1. That sort of thing's going on everywhere. The most hopeless crocks are being passed into the army—not in low grades either. I'm afraid there's real trouble brewing among the working classes as a result of this last imbecility of the War Office.'

After lingering a long while over lunch, they wandered out into the hot streets and along to the Park, where they sat down under the trees. Joan remarked to Philip that he was lucky to have been spending his leave in the country, and so have escaped all the daylight raids of the last month.

'And to think that we *could* have peace!' he sighed, his face tilted upwards. 'There have been German overtures. . . . Perhaps not peace with what's called "honour" though. The warmongering politicians at home make me just as sick as the enemy, these days. I'm sick of them all, and their prating, and their lies, and their bombast. The only people who are tolerable are the soldiers themselves. They're not bellicose. It's only at the Front —and I mean the *Front*, not anywhere behind the lines—that honour's to be found.'

'Philip, why don't you chuck it all and become a conscientious objector?' asked Joan.

He turned on her intent eyes behind spectacles.

'You wouldn't like me to, would you?'

'Me? Well—no,' she admitted. 'But that's hardly the point. I should respect you if you felt you had to.'

He shook his head.

'No. Although I no longer feel we're fighting for "a good cause," although any idealism that there was in the war seems to have faded out, I don't want to chuck my part in it. It's a question of loyalty to one's generation, of loyalty to those wretched men. They're sticking it—I must. And more than ever, just now, they need leaders. I don't believe anyone has a right to be a pacifist, or to say he loathes war, if he hasn't gathered war right into his arms, as it were, and known it through and through. Then . . . then afterwards . . . Well, there's such a thing as a pen.'

But that was Philip's only outburst, and he half apologised for it, assuring Joan, with a smile, that she needn't be anxious—he was no longer 'nervy.' And he referred with gratitude to those days in Hampstead which had so greatly helped to pull him through.

Tea in Kensington Gardens. Friendly, stimulating talk. Books, pictures, history, plays. And then Philip had to go off reluctantly to dinner with some friends of his mother's. Joan had not arranged to dine anywhere. They walked as far as Knightsbridge together; and before they parted he went into a flower-shop and bought her a sheaf of white lilies and of red carnations.

'Good-bye, Joan,' he said on the edge of the pavement, and holding her hand a little longer than was conventional. 'Go on writing to me if you can. I look forward to your letters, you know.'

The setting sun in front of her, Joan jogged along on the top of a bus towards Camberwell, holding the long paper parcel on her left arm like a baby.

At the hostel she had supper, and went up to her room. On the landing she met one of the V.A.D.s from '26.'

'Oh, Williams, by the way, how's Twemlow?' she asked. 'I suppose he was round from the anæsthetic by the time you left?'

'Twemlow? No, he died in the theatre,' said Williams stolidly. 'Awful shame, wasn't it? He was a nice kid.'

In her cubicle Joan slowly took off her hat and coat; slowly undid the flowers and stuck them in her water-jug. Then she found herself sitting on the edge of the bed, crying noiselessly. Mustn't disturb the other girls. Little Twemlow dead . . . 'a nice kid.' Dead. He wouldn't run that shop at Shepherd's Bush now. His poor mother. His voice cheering her. 'Don't worry, Mother—*I'm* all right you see!' His great brown eyes. Soldiers died—they were killed every day—but you didn't know them all, you hadn't nursed them all. And Twemlow was special. He was so small, and so young, and so very very plucky.

Could they have amputated earlier? Useless to think of that. If Sister Brown hadn't been on the spot with the tourniquet, would *you* have been in time? Oh, useless, worse than useless, to think of that.

Her eyes rested, in the fading light, on the white lilies and the red carnations. White flesh of a boy-soldier, red blood of his wound.

Take them away . . . take them away. . . .

.   .   .   .   .   .

Next morning she cast one look at Twemlow's empty bed, and afterwards passed it hurriedly and with averted face. It was flat and tidy like a tombstone. The raising-blocks had been removed from under the feet. The locker was bare.

The morning after there was a new face on the pillow.

Chapter Four

THE July days swung along in hot monotony. It seemed to Joan that she had known no other life but hospital life; known no other smells but lysol and iodoform; no other sounds but the rapid click-click of aching feet on bare boards. She could almost have dressed wounds in her sleep. She was familiar with all their varieties. Dirty-yellow or angry-red, foul-smelling or healthy-smelling, flesh-wound or fracture, she knew them all. Mechanically she extracted shrapnel from quivering muscle; packed holes with gauze; inserted tubes to drain pus; bandaged feet in the 'figure of 8' fashion; adjusted splints.

Familiarity of everything. Arms which had healed, but which in spite of care had shrunk and shortened. Hands stiff and withered because the muscles above no longer functioned. Fuggy smell of sheets as beds were made. Little crumbs of dried yellow skin from feet. Flaccid feel of buttocks rubbed with meth.

Up and down, up and down, up and down the ward. Hoping to get past certain beds without being stopped by calls from their occupants.

'Nurse, Nurse, bring us a drink of water!'

'Nurse, shift me a bit higher up, please.'

And from Curtis, the thin boy in the long splint, 'Oh, me heel! Me heel!'

Stopping to move the heel—a little to the right, a little to the left—for it got sore from pressing always on the same spot.

'There, I'll rub some meth on it. But I'm afraid it *will* be sore.'

Hoping to get past next time without being called. Exaggerating your look of hurry.

'Oh, Nurse, me heel, me heel!'

'You must bear it, Curtis!' Impossible to stop again.

You found yourself yielding to irritation. Pulled yourself up. Yielded to it once more. Felt ashamed. Work was no longer at the fever pitch of the Arras days; and with the lessening of demands on you the spirit's exaltation sank, and you became conscious of your body and of your nerves. Did stupid things, too. Allowed a wringer to burn in the steriliser; broke two thermometers. If it wasn't that Sister left you so much alone you would have been soundly strafed—and would have deserved it.

'You look tired, Nurse,' Guthrie remarked to Joan one morning.

'What's the good of telling me that?' she snapped. 'It doesn't make things easier. If there's one thing I hate it's being told I look tired.'

'I'm sorry,' he said, staring. 'I didn't mean to annoy you, Nurse.'

Remorse flooded her. How disgusting! Where was her early enthusiasm? Where her poignant sympathy with the men, which had carried her through so many thorny places—through the grinding drudgery of hospital work, which but for the men she couldn't have stood?

'I'm fed up to the teeth with everything,' she wrote to Betty. 'And, oh, my dear, I'm getting so *old*! I don't seem to want to do anything silly or young any more. To sleep, sleep, sleep— that is the sum of my ambition.'

She thought with envy of Betty out in France. She and some others, under Dr. Ferguson, were running a Y.M. tent at a Rest Camp by the sea. They had left Boulogne for the summer, and were billeted in a cottage. It sounded delightful.

'A little sunny garden,' wrote Betty, 'with a wall round it, and a white goat! Great place for tea-parties on Sundays. Officers and men come in batches from the Camp. We are on our *own* here, and feel miles away from all the petty Y.M. annoyances.

'It's been awful not seeing Guy for all these months, but there's the satisfaction of knowing that he's in England, and well-cared for. He is ever so much better, and is now convalescing in the country-house of some friends of his. Don't suppose the Camp will close down before autumn, so shan't be home till then.'

.   .   .   .   .   .

Few convoys came in now. There were quite a number of empty beds. An odd man would arrive at intervals—sometimes at night, sometimes by day.

One morning a stretcher-case was brought in. Joan put screens round a bed; the orderlies dumped the man on it and withdrew with the stretcher. The man, whose name was Peters, had come straight through from the line, making only short halts. She undressed him carefully. He was dirty, but as he seemed weak and in pain she didn't worry him with a prolonged wash. The middle of his body was swathed in soiled bandages, and, when questioned, Peters murmured that his wound hadn't been dressed for two days.

Joan took down the dressings in preparation for Sister Mercer. The abdomen was greatly distended, and as she peeled off layer after layer of wool and gauze a stench arose which grew so strong that she had to turn away her head to take in a gulp of clean air. The last layer came off, and behind it, through a long slit-like wound, suddenly bulged part of the man's intestines.

Scared stiff for a moment Joan quickly laid on dry gauze, and went and called down the ward for Sister Brown. Brown was engaged on dressings of her own, and rather grumpily said she would come when she could. A few minutes later, however, not only Brown but Sister Mercer and the M.O. were gathered round the bed with Joan.

It was a horrible dressing. Joan knelt holding basins—handing instruments. Peters bore it all with strange apathy—giving little moans from time to time.

From then onwards he was kept propped up in bed in the 'Fowler' position, pillows under his knees. He had great wandering eyes. He never spoke. Sister Mercer, with Joan to help her, dressed him morning and evening. There was a big tube, now, in the right groin; the wound oozed fæcal matter and a brownish fluid.

It seemed unlikely—even from the first—that Peters would live. He had never become one of the ward; he was apart—alone. On

the third day he lay with half-shut violet-shadowed eyes, breathing faintly. Joan, passing up and down, kept glancing at him.
The ward was warm and quiet, full of dusty yellow light, and the
lingering smell of soap-suds.

Suddenly the eyes opened. There was an expression of suppli-
cation and perplexity in them. The head rolled slowly from side
to side. Before she could reach the bed Sister Mercer, who had
been hovering about, was already there, had taken his hand, was
peering at him, comforting him. Two inconsequent thoughts
flashed through Joan's mind: 'She can be nice to a man, then—
when he's dying,' and: 'Pity it's *her* face he has to look on
last.'

It was over. Screens were round the bed. Dully Joan helped
with the washing and the laying out. Dully she listened to Sister's
subdued but excited chatterings. Noticed her busy hen's claw
hands. Thought how odd it was that the only thing which seemed
to galvanise this woman into life was a death.

'Come along, Nurse Seddon. That's right. Now the wool.
Now the sheet. This is all experience for you.'

Experience! Oh yes, it was that!

The wound was still exuding slightly. Last excretions to be
mopped up from the front—last excretions from the back of the
poor body. Just mess, mess, and smell.

'Hold his ankles, Nurse, while I tie them.'

If only Sister wouldn't be so ghoulish over the job! But she
was amiable too—more so than Joan had ever known her. This
business had been bearable—had been, in comparison, pleasant—
with Sister Muir.

When everything was done, and Joan was clearing up beside
the bed, Sister whispered that she was going to her room for some
candles—there were never enough in the mortuary, and she
wanted to arrange them round the corpse when it had been taken
there. 'I like to show reverence to the dead,' said Sister Mercer.
'Quite,' said Joan, and disappeared into the annex with the pail of
fluid and dirty swabs. Nobody had known anything about poor

Peters. He had been 'the abdominal case,' and now he was a body under a sheet.

In the annex Joan gripped the edge of the sink. She was not actually sick, but she retched as though she were going to be. Her hands were cold as ice.

'Here, Nurse, I've brought ye a chair. I thought maybe you'd be upset.' Jock's kindly voice; his hand on her arm.

'Would ye like a drop o' something?'

Joan, with an absurd vision before her of a peg of Scotch whisky, smiled weakly and shook her head.

'Couldn't swallow, Jock—not even water!'

'She shouldna ha' let ye do it,' said Jock, standing stockily beside her, with disapproving eyes above his bandage.

'It's—it's all experience . . . I mean it's all in the day's work.'

He never knew how near she was to leaning her head against him and giving way.

.   .   .   .   .   .

At about half-past two, on one of her afternoons off, Joan was gazing into Hatchards' window, and had just decided to go inside and spend an idle half-hour flicking over the pages of the new books (they never bothered you to *buy* in Hatchards') when she heard a voice saying: 'Joan again! Well, I'm jiggered!' and looked up to see Thrush beside her—Thrush with a little brown straw hat framing her glowing face.

'Hallo, my dear! We seem destined to run into one another at long intervals!' exclaimed Joan, and she glanced at the man who was standing beside Thrush. It was not the youth of the Chu-Chin-Chow night.

'Captain Wentworth,' said Thrush, introducing them. 'Miss Seddon—an old friend of mine. Used to nurse together, but our paths have diverged.'

'You mean she continues on the stony, while you've adopted the primrose!'

The man's laughing voice, and rather prominent green-brown

eyes, with their look of taking everything in, made Joan uncomfortably conscious of her dingy little uniform.

'Well, Paul, I'm not sure that that's quite a delicate way of putting it!' laughed Thrush. 'But look here, Joan, we've got to meet properly now. Come along to a party I'm giving—oh, when is it?—next week I think. Anyhow I'll send you a post-card. Same old place, you know, in the Fulham Road, but I've got an extra room since you were there.'

'Love to!' Easy enough to accept an invitation that would in all likelihood never be confirmed.

'We may meet again, then,' said Captain Wentworth, and, saluting, moved off with his companion.

He was attractive in a way, thought Joan, as she wandered into the book-shop. And how pretty Thrush was looking. In about another year, perhaps, they might run into each other again.

. . . . . .

Joan's year at the 1st London General was up on July 31st. She had decided not to sign on again, and had made arrangements with Devonshire House to start work, in a month's time, at the 2nd London General, Chelsea. There was doubtless little to choose between one military hospital and another, but the 2nd London had this to be said for it, that it was so much nearer the centre of things. And it was not as though she had any friends to keep her here, now that Phipps and Fry had gone. She could hardly feel lonelier, she told herself, among a completely strange set of V.A.D.s than she had felt at Camberwell all this summer.

To her amazement Matron gave her an excellent report; and Joan smiled as she remembered those early days when she had been told that she had 'no instincts for the nursing profession,' and had fully expected to be dismissed.

When it came to saying good-bye to the men, she minded leaving more than she would have thought possible. Many, whom she had not considered her 'specials,' told her they were sorry to lose her; and she was especially moved when the silent Johnson, who had, for a fortnight now, been wheeling himself about the ward in a chair, and was soon to return to New Zealand on crutches, told her that she had made all the difference to his time in '26.'

Guthrie gripped her hand in the annex.

'Jock, you're to write to me,' she said. 'What I should have done without you I don't know. You won't be here so very much longer yourself, will you? But while you are here I want you to do something for me.'

'Aye, and what's that?' he asked gruffly.

'Help Nurse Williams as you've helped me. She'll be head V.A.D. now.'

He nodded. 'All right. I'll do ma best.'

'Good luck, Jock.'

'Good luck, Nurse Seddon.'

'We're friends, you and I.'

'Aye.'

Her eyes were wet as she turned away.

.   .   .   .   .   .

And so Joan collected her accumulated possessions of a year, and with (as she declared) the perfume of iodoform still clinging to her garments fell into the comfort of Beechwood and Aunt Florence's arms.

'You're to have your sleep out,' she was told. 'Breakfast shan't be brought to you until you ring.'

But Joan woke automatically at six o'clock, and it was only after a few moments' bewilderment that she realised, with a wave of relief, that she wouldn't have to scramble into her uniform, go down to a breakfast of kippers, and climb on to a hospital-bound 'Tank.'

Chapter Five

A LETTER came next day from Pamela imploring Joan to come down. 'I shall go mad if I have to stay at home much longer,' she wrote. 'It was all right while I was still ill, but now that I'm nearly fit again it is unendurable. Yet Mother becomes pained if I mention going off. You know she and I never get on well together for long. I suppose my nature has the chemical effect of turning hers sour. And her perpetual worrying over things that don't matter a damn, and her restless futile activities certainly have that effect on mine. Another thing—though it may be beastly of me to say it—is that I'm pretty sure she is secretly glad about Ian's death—thinks it's the best thing that could have happened. Oh, we never discuss it, never even allude to it, but I can feel her thoughts.

'Do you notice how, in life, everything that happens is always the fault of the young? The old are invariably right and just, and the young selfish and hard—even nowadays. . . .

'Have got schemes brewing. Nursing. Possibly London, possibly abroad. Angel, come and talk things over. Life's damnable, both on its surface and in its depths. I need you.'

So Joan went down for a few days to Wallingford; and in the old garden, or punting about with bare wet arms on the river, she held long talks with Pamela, and cursed the world with her, and laughed with her, and soberly discussed immediate plans.

.   .   .   .   .   .

She would have stayed longer if it hadn't been for Thrush's party on August 5th, to which, after all, she had surprisingly received an invitation, and which had been postponed from an earlier date. She felt that it would be unfriendly not to go, and that Thrush, however little she might wish for a renewal of their old intimacy, might be hurt if this gesture on her part were ignored.

Sitting among a noisy crowd on the floor of Thrush's studio, it was brought home to Joan that life was very gay outside the confines of military hospitals. Girls discussed the newest night-clubs. Dancing, it seemed, had become a mania. During the day you did some sort of war work (unless you were still firmly pursuing your 'art'), and at night you danced. A hectic existence, but men on leave always wanted to dance, it seemed.

A girl with the dark head of a page, and dressed in peacock-blue, was at the piano. Certain groups, from behind clouds of tobacco-smoke, shouted the choruses of the songs she played. Thrush drifted here and there, reminding Joan of a great red camellia. She had matured, and gained poise during the last fifteen months, but something sturdy and lovable had left her. And who were all these people with whom she seemed so much at home? And how was it that she had been able to provide such an abundance of refreshments—even of the unappetising war-time species?

Queer vivid pictures on the walls—Thrush's work, of course. Shabby furniture and hangings; but a tall expensive-looking gramophone in the corner. Flowers. Men in mufti with long hair and thin ankles. Men in uniform with little tooth-brush moustaches. Lolling vivacious girls. A buzz of talk.

'José Collins? Yes, she's wonderful of course, but a bit fat. You mean you haven't seen her in the "Maid of the Mountains"? But how have you escaped?'

'My dear, I was actually *in* the Gaiety when that bomb fell close to! My hair was covered with dust and plaster. Terrified? I should think so, but I didn't dare show it. I was with a boy on leave, you see, and he clutched hold of my arm, and was almost more frightened than I was. Yes, the company carried on with the play—amazing of them! One could hardly hear what they said, though, for the noise of the barrage.'

A young man, who was posted by the gramophone, put on a record. Thrush billowed up to Joan with someone in tow, vaguely introduced him, and left them. 'You must just behave as though you knew everyone here,' she called over her shoulder. 'Can't bother with formalities.'

Joan danced with the nameless youth. Most people were dancing now. Those who were not drew their legs under them, and sat closer against the wall, or else drifted off into the next room for refreshments.

Music; smoke; laughter; the brushing of shoulders. And suddenly, in the doorway, Captain Wentworth.

'Oh, Paul, you *have* managed to come! How noble of you!'

Thrush took his hand, placed it round her waist, and glided with him into the crowd.

Joan thought that in evening clothes he looked slimmer, and rather less exuberant than she had remembered him that day outside Hatchards'. He caught sight of her over Thrush's shoulder and nodded.

The record came to an end. People dropped on to cushions, or huddled amicably on the few pieces of furniture. Paul Wentworth came straight over to Joan.

'How nice to see you! Still nursing?'

'Not at the moment,' she replied. 'Soon shall be again, though.' And she wondered that he should even have recognised her, let alone have remembered what she was doing.

When the music began again, Joan's partner had evaporated, and she found herself sitting in the corner alone with Wentworth.

'Don't want to dance, do you?' he asked.

'Not particularly.'

'I'm no good at it myself. But then, alas, I'm falling into the "sere and yellow"!'

'So I see!' smiled Joan.

'Fact! Thirty next month. Makes one think a bit.'

Well, of course, thirty *was* rather old . . .

'Whereas you, I suppose,' he remarked, fixing on her his warm green-brown eyes, 'are not more than twenty?'

'You suppose wrong. I was twenty-three this summer.'

'And you feel youth's over?'

'How did you know? I do, as a matter of fact. Not just because of being twenty-three, but . . . oh, well, things have been rather grisly in hospital lately.'

He continued to stare at her—not boldly, but with a thoughtful intentness. Then he smiled.

'You baby! Do you know, when I saw you the other day, I thought you looked about seventeen! Sort of school-girl effect produced by that little quakerish coat and hat.'

'Oh, that awful uniform!' she exclaimed. 'Thank goodness I'm out of it for a week or two.'

'It suits you,' he said gravely. 'It suits your personality as well as your face.'

'And what do you know . . .?'

'About your personality? A lot. Cheek, isn't it? About your circumstances, of course, nothing—beyond that you're a V.A.D. And you know nothing of mine. Shall we rapidly tell each other?'

Joan laughed. He was really rather attractive.

When she had given him a sketch of her own life and family he informed her that he had no parents; that he had one brother fighting; that he was in the Machine Gun Corps; had been wounded; was at present working at the War Office; that before the war he had been a dramatic critic and writer of essays.

'And you're engaged to Thrush Shirley,' Joan added.

'Engaged to Thrush Shirley? Good heavens, no! What put *that* into your head?'

'Oh—nothing. I just thought that perhaps you were.'

'Because you saw us together the other day? We'd only been having a friendly lunch at Prince's. And it's true I blow along here from time to time. But *engaged* to her . . .!'

He seemed to find the idea immensely amusing; and Joan, under the odd feeling of relief which she experienced, did not altogether relish that amusement.

'She's a very charming person,' she said stubbornly, 'and at one time we were great friends.'

'That's what's so odd,' he commented.

And then he set himself to dissipate the slight chill that had fallen between them, and for the next half-hour talked so entertainingly about the theatre, about his travels in France and Germany, about actors and actresses he had known, that Joan was enthralled, and felt her mind stirring to life again after its torpor of the last six months. Wentworth, while conversing, hardly looked at her; his eyes were fixed either on his clasped ankles or on the pictures on the wall; but no detail escaped him of the eager face, and wide grey eyes, and rather untidy hair.

For the rest of the evening they were parted. Dancing went on. The crowd began to thin down, and Thrush marvellously produced two jugs of champagne-cup. While she was pouring this out, handing it in small quantities to the circle around her, the youth with whom Joan had first danced pressed through, and whispered something over Thrush's shoulder.

'Oh, not yet, Billy?' she asked, looking up at him. 'Need you? Oh, darling! Well, you must drink this first—and this—and this. Yes, really! If *anybody* needs it . . .'

Embarrassed, flushed, but laughing, the boy tossed off three glasses, then made quickly for the door, followed by Thrush, and by shouts of 'Good luck, Billy, old boy!' from the other guests.

Joan learnt that this was his last night of leave, and that he was catching the early train from Victoria back to France.

Someone put on a tune from 'The Bing Boys.' Music; laughter; dancing; smoke.

Soon after one o'clock Joan and half a dozen others, including Paul Wentworth, were making their way along the Fulham Road. It was as dark as a country lane. The rare taxis that passed refused to pick them up.

'Aren't taxi-drivers insufferable nowadays!' exclaimed one of the girls. 'They do exactly as they like!'

Eventually, after a long walk, a taxi was collared—the whole crowd scrambled into it, and were driven hilariously along

Knightsbridge. 'Last drink at the Junior Turf Club!' cried somebody. And out they all tumbled at Hyde Park Corner, and surrounded the coffee-stall. Steaming cups were handed to them, which they sipped, hovering in their evening clothes among a friendly group of workmen. Overhead, from the stone arch, the long white arms of the search-light swept the sky.

Everyone had been dropped at last. Good-nights had been called from door-steps. And Wentworth and Joan, remaining in the taxi, drove steadily northwards. Although she lived in Hampstead, and he in Westminster, he had insisted on seeing her the whole way home. Her protests had been useless.

Never before, in the company of any man, had Joan experienced this queer nervous excitement. The effect of his eyes upon her, from the corner where he sat, was to send her off into a stream of chatter which quite impressed her with its own brilliance, until she realised that he was paying no attention to it.

'Apropos of Thrush,' he began quietly, in the middle of something she was saying about the Russian ballet. 'You see I happen to be a friend of the man she's . . . of the man who's looking after her. He's at the Front at present. There are some business things to settle. I may be able to wangle him a job at home. As you say, she's a charming person, and I shouldn't be surprised if one of these days she made a success with her pictures.'

Dead silence fell upon Joan. In the darkness of the taxi she felt the slow blood mounting. So that was it? That was how Thrush . . .? She might have guessed perhaps . . .

'Are you shocked?' asked Wentworth, turning a little towards her.

'No-o. . . . She's been very unhappy. She's alone and poor. I can understand it.'

'There could never be anything between her and me,' he continued in the same quiet voice. 'When I was younger, possibly. . . . One's tastes change.'

Joan's imagination took a flight over this man's past, then returned swiftly, and, ostrich-like, buried its head.

'Still,' he resumed, 'for all your broad-mindedness and your loyalty, you don't altogether like it?'

'How can I *like* it?' she exclaimed, wishing that he wouldn't probe her on the subject. 'To live with a man when you love him is one thing, but when you don't . . .'

'When you don't . . .?'

'It's definitely immoral.'

'You darling!' he smiled. 'I adore you to say that. But, after all, who can define "love"? It has so many meanings.'

'I should have thought it was simple enough. Oh, we're almost there!'

At her request he put his head out of the window and gave some directions.

'I suppose it's useless to apologise for having brought you out of your way,' she laughed. 'It wasn't my fault.'

'It's been well worth while.'

He got out with her and said good-bye at the drive gate.

'You'll meet me again?' he asked, holding her hand.

'I—I should like to.'

He tried to pull her towards him, but as she hung back he merely raised her hand, and kissed it in the little hollow where it joined the wrist. Then he stepped away.

The door of the taxi slammed, and her feet went crunching quickly up the gravel.

In her bedroom she shed her cloak, and sat, with arms stretched in front of her, at a little table in the window. Her eyes stared at the outlines of the trees. On her right wrist was a small spot of fire.

．　　　．　　　．　　　．　　　．　　　．

'No, modernity is not necessarily connected with realism,' said Paul. 'Of course it's true that lots of modern dramatists belong to the realistic school, but that's due to a variety of things—to the influence of Ibsen partly—partly to a reaction against excessive romanticism. But the next phase of modernity in the theatre may be something quite else—perhaps a sort of post-impression ism. One can't tell. Modernity is a thing of spirit, not of form.'

'An inspiring banner to fight under!' said Joan.

'A convenient weapon,' said Paul, 'for the younger generation to use in belabouring the out-of-date.'

They had finished lunch, and were sitting over their coffee in a Soho restaurant. It was two days after Thrush's party.

Joan, who had known what it was to listen to good talk, to contribute to discussions, had never felt her mind so throbbingly alive, and at the same time so deferential, as now. Paul was a good deal older, and a great deal more complicated and experienced than any of the men she had hitherto been friends with, and the effect he produced in her was that of an absorbed humility. And although she was sufficiently aware of the state of her emotions to realise that the throb in the atmosphere was not merely intellectual, she found it strangely difficult to get any clear vision of Paul. She knew, vaguely, that his colouring was southern, that he looked well in khaki, that the shape of his nose was good, that his mouth was a little too full, his alert eyes a little too prominent; but actually she saw him through a blur, and she knew that once away from him she would not be able to recall his face.

They smoked and talked until he remarked that he would have to tear himself away and get back to the War Office.

'Meet me at my cousin's house for tea?' he asked her in a casual voice as they left the restaurant.

Joan hesitated, then agreed, and asked for the address.

When he had told her he added: 'My cousin may not be in. She does a lot of canteening, these days, but she always allows me to use the place as my own.'

When they had parted Joan realised that what Paul had suggested was very unconventional. But then, had she not, all through lunch, been giving him the impression that she was emancipated and modern? Besides, where else could they go? Obviously not to his rooms. And if she took him up to Beechwood they couldn't be sure of being alone. No, under the circumstances this was a good arrangement.

She kept her thoughts as much as possible off the coming meeting—hardly knowing what she hoped or expected from it. She shopped. She walked about in the Park. And then, at five o'clock, she rang the bell of the narrow house in Wilton Crescent.

A kind-faced maid showed her to the drawing-room, and one glance round it told Joan that the 'cousin' was a woman whom she would probably like. Tea was laid, and a kettle bubbled on a spirit-lamp.

'Captain Wentworth is expecting you, Miss,' said the maid, 'and Mrs. Muirhead will be back about six o'clock.'

Joan sat down and took up a book. It all seemed very normal and friendly. Why, in that case, should her mouth have felt dry and the palms of her hands damp?

A bell sounded somewhere below. She started; but immediately assumed extreme composure.

And then Paul was in the room and coming towards her.

'Good! I did so hope you'd turn up!' (He had doubted it, then?) 'Will you pour out? I'm longing for tea. But, oh dear, tea's a dismal beverage without sugar, isn't it? The one bright thought about going back to France is that there'll be sweet tea again.'

Joan laughed. How nice of him to be boyish and absurd like this!

'I don't take sugar myself,' she said, 'but everyone at home, who used to take it, has given it up—even Tam, the Airedale. And for him it really *is* a privation. He used to enjoy his bowl of tea.'

They talked away merrily enough, but something told Joan that this safe and silver moment couldn't endure. There came a silence. Paul looked at the toe of his crossed boot; Joan vaguely round at the pictures. And then, with a sudden movement, he rose; lifted the tea-table; carried it across the room; came and sat close beside her on the low sofa, and took her in his arms.

It was all so quietly and so unhesitatingly done that Joan could hardly have resisted even if she had wanted to. But she asked for nothing better than to stay exactly as she was—in this warm dream for ever.

He lifted her chin. For a moment she saw his eyes, immense, like pools. Then he kissed her.

After an eternity she drew away, and put her hand bewilderedly to her hair.

'Do you know,' he said, smiling down at her, 'there's a little brown speck in one of your eyes—only in one of them!'

She smiled back at him—rather idiotically, she felt. There seemed nothing to say. And then came pouring from his lips a torrent of distracting tributes. He praised her eyes, her skin, her smile. He touched her lightly as he spoke; he drew his finger down her 'adorable little nose'; laughed at its freckles; told her she was a baby, an angel; asked her if she had ever been made love to before.

Joan longed to say, 'Yes—often,' but truth could hardly be stretched so far, so she compromised, and said: 'Not in this way.'

'I'm glad,' said Paul.

And suddenly she thought of poor Colin—her friend—her adorer—Colin who knew her so well, and exalted her so high, and who had never, in all the time she had known him, been able to make her feel one-tenth of what she was feeling now. Paul had taken the situation into his own hands; whereas, hitherto, 'situations' had always been in hers. Paul had skill—and he was unafraid. She didn't ask herself, at this juncture, whether he were not also selfish. On her own initiative she held up her mouth, and he kissed her again—long and long.

'Coming alive a little, aren't you?' he smiled, and, at her blush of confusion, added:

'You mustn't be cross with me, little thing! It's all too delicious to spoil. And for me—you don't know . . .' His voice trailed off, while his eyes dwelt on her with a look she couldn't understand—that was half hunger, half remorse.

It was past six, and there was no sign of Mrs. Muirhead. Joan said she must go home.

They arranged for further meetings.

.   .   .   .   .   .

During the next fortnight Joan lived in a state of fever. She hardly gave a thought to the future. The present held such perplexities, as well as such delights, that it required all her attention.

For Paul was not an easy person to be in love with. After moments which were winged for both of them, and from which Joan would emerge radiant, he would suddenly become gloomy, pace up and down the room, hands in pockets, and give vent to little bursts of talk on subjects that seemed quite irrelevant.

She couldn't understand how their physical closeness didn't tend to produce a greater spiritual closeness; yet that swift intelligence which had at first so charmed her became, as the days went on, a source of torment to her. Her experience had hitherto led her to suppose that all enlightened minds marched roughly in the same direction; but here was Paul, enlightened and cultivated to the last degree, straying in the paths of reaction. Joan, at this period of her life, set great store by people's political and literary opinions; and to find that anyone with brains, and to whom she was attached, was unenthusiastic about the Suffrage, indifferent to the Labour Question, and hostile to some of her favourite authors, was disconcerting.

They were discussing different novelists, one day, when Joan made some ardent reference to Meredith. Paul shook his head with a pursed-up smile.

'Don't you agree?' she asked.

'I haven't much use for Meredith,' he told her. 'Too much of the preacher about him. So tiring, all that hearty roaring morality. . . . And oh, God, his style . . .!'

Style, yes, that was it. Paul was an enthusiast for style; and he knew, of course, far more about it than she did. It was possible, she supposed, to be put off by something crabbed and uncomfortable in Meredith's *style*, though even then . . .

'Why don't you read George Moore?' he asked her. 'He's twice the artist.'

She had only read two books of Moore's and had hated them— or rather had hated the leering spirit which she had felt through the beauty of the lines. But Paul, when she tried to explain this, said that in a work of art the spirit didn't matter—it was only the form.

She could swallow that, even laugh at her own possible lack of artistic appreciation, but there were other subjects less easily disposed of.

He was talking, another day, about the mixed camping holidays which had been in vogue, before the war, among a certain section of the advanced and earnest young.

'Men and maidens sleeping in tents together,' he exclaimed, 'bathing together, doing their exercises together; and all perfectly pure—that's what's so comic! All frank and Anglo-Saxon, without a hint of sex!'

'But why *should* there be—on a holiday of that sort?' Joan had rejoined, uncomfortably. 'Isn't it rather nice—I mean, doesn't it speak rather well for this country that men and girls should be able to camp in simple friendship together?'

Paul looked at her as though about to speak, then suddenly smiled.

'When you're perplexed,' he said, 'your eyebrows have an enchanting way of going up in the middle!'

'Have they?' She was not, for the moment, interested in her eyebrows. 'But, Paul, I do want to get this clear. Don't you believe . . .?'

'Oh, does it matter?' he burst out, his hand up to his forehead. 'Yes, yes, I quite believe that it's all very "nice" in a way. But it's only the excessively immature—both among races and individuals—that attempt sexless friendships—or even admire them.'

It was this sort of remark that gave Joan a sense of desolation, as well as of a tiresome crudity in herself; but she continued, in spite of Paul's amusement, to maintain what he called her 'English' views.

One evening they went to the 'Three Daughters of Monsieur Dupont,' then on at the Garrick; and Joan, whose sympathies were always easily enlisted on the side of distressed women, was enthusiastic over the play. She blazed away, in her old style, against the institution of marriage, which, she said, left no choice to a woman except to suffer its restrictions and indignities, or else slam the door like 'Nora,' and take her chance in a hostile world.

'How you do generalise!' said Paul. 'Marriage needn't be like that. It's exactly what you choose to make it. That's the danger of a man like Brieux—he points to one unfortunate case, and says: "That's marriage."'

'Oh, I agree it *needn't* be like that,' retorted Joan. 'But the point is, one doesn't want to be beholden to the caprice of a man for one's happiness. That's why there should be easier divorce, and, for women as well as men, economic independence.'

'Catch-words, catch-words!' he smiled. 'There's nothing wrong with marriage as an institution—if you don't make a fetish of fidelity.'

The noise of the passing traffic drowned the last low-spoken words, which, even if Joan had heard, she would not have allowed to penetrate in their full significance. Under the influence of Paul's smile she frequently construed his alarming utterances in a manner which accorded with her own desires.

And oh, he could be charming! In his happy moods he could carry her along on a stream of tender gaiety which warmed and quickened her so that she was conscious only of the perfection of the world and of her love.

After such times with him Joan felt that nothing he could ever say could worry her again; that henceforth all would be smooth and sweet between them. And Florence, seeing her bright eyes, would admit that London seemed to be suiting the girl, and that the country holiday which she had at first advised was, after all, unnecessary.

Unnecessary! Joan laughed to herself. Unthinkable. Leave London now! Why, every moment spent away from Paul was a moment wasted—a moment filled with longing to be with him again—in spite of the fact that it was impossible to tell whether their next meeting would be one of joy or of wretchedness.

.   .   .   .   .   .

The extent of the change which her whole emotional being had undergone was startlingly revealed to Joan when she happened, one day, from the top of a bus, to see Paul walking with another woman. He had told her, beforehand, that he would be unable to meet her for lunch as he had to take out 'some tiresome relations'; but this woman struck Joan as looking anything but 'tiresome'—if she were even a relation. Very handsome, very well turned-out, she stepped beside her companion, smiling into his face with an affectionate intimacy that it was pain to witness.

That night, for the first time in her life, Joan knew the meaning of jealousy. Hour after hour she lay racked with it. She was utterly amazed at its force. No amount of reasoning, no amount of preaching at herself was the least use; and if any impetus had been needed to drive her still further towards Paul, it was the agonising realisation that he might be getting tired of her. Without his companionship, without his kisses, how was she to live?

It was only after meeting him again, and learning from him that the woman she had seen him with was his sister-in-law, and very seldom in town, that the iron band which had gripped her heart relaxed, and she felt able to eat and breathe.

Casual as she had tried to make her questions to him, and admirably as he had hidden his amusement at them, Joan knew that Paul had seen through her, and he knew that she knew that he had. For the rest of lunch they were particularly detached and intelligent upon a number of interesting topics, and Joan returned home, a little ashamed of herself, certainly, but with a sense of peace inside that was like heaven.

A letter awaited her on the hall-table, addressed in the squiggly pencilled handwriting of Jock Guthrie—a letter which carried her back to another world.

'Many thanks for yours,' it ran. 'I am sure you are enjoying a well-earned rest, and nobody deserves it more than you. You might be angry with me for praising you, but really I think you are the best worker I ever came across. Well, I am doing all I can for Nurse Williams, but I am afraid I have not been working so well this last two days. You see, it is like this; I have not been feeling so well and I will not give in that I am ill. Well, I went to the dentist this afternoon and had all my back teeth out, and I have to go on Thursday and have the front ones out too, and I won't be sorry when he has finished, as my gums are aching a lot at present. I am sorry you are not here, for I know you would have given me the best of attention, as you were the best friend I ever had, and I am speaking the truth when I say so. Well, I forgot to tell you about the massive boil I have got on my leg, and I wish you were here to cut it; I would let you do anything for me, for I know I would have ease after it. Don't be angry with me if I tell you that I don't work so well with Nurse Williams as with you; we seem to get mixed up a bit and don't know what to do next. Well, I will tell you one thing. She don't treat me as you did, she has a different way of using me. She tries to drive me, that one thing you never done; you always led me, and I will be led, but I will never be driven. And she even puts more work on to me and still we don't get through as quick. I think the doctor is going to open my neck again and I hope that will be the finish.

'Yrs. sincerely,
'Pte. J. Guthrie, Argylls.'

Jock! Dear Jock! He recalled a self which already seemed remote, a self, however, which was true for him. Just as another self was true for Paul; another true for Jimmy; and how many more for how many others? Or perhaps one hadn't got a 'self' at all.

. . . . . .

Soon afterwards, in the Wilton Crescent drawing-room, Joan and Paul were again discussing marriage. He was in one of his bitterest moods.

'You can't get away from the fact,' he declared, 'that there's something sacred about it. It makes any other union, however lofty, however passionate, appear shoddy beside it. Oh, I'm old, I'm stained, I've sinned!' he broke out, while she looked at him in amazement. 'I've so many things to regret.'

'But, Paul—darling—you mustn't *regret* things! You mustn't talk about sin. It's as though you were a churchman!'

He gave a short laugh.

'It would be better if I were—if I really did believe in the Christian religion. There'd be a chance, then, of starting again—clean.'

'Paul, you *can* start again—clean, as you call it.' Joan was on her feet now, and her hands were on his bowed shoulders. 'Not in that stupid conventional sense, of course, but in a real sense. I've never asked about your life, you know—your past doesn't concern me, but . . .' her voice faltered, 'your present does, and—and, after all, here I am.'

'Oh, you darling!' he cried, and caught her round the waist, pressing his head against her. 'You child!'

She stroked his hair. It was thick and dark. She loved it. Then he looked up at her, and she saw that his eyes were swimming in tears. Curiously, away behind the immense tenderness which she felt for him at that moment, behind the immense attraction which he always exerted over her, was a flicker of distaste at those tears.

She bent quickly, and kissed his forehead, but he pushed her almost roughly away. 'Go home,' he said. 'Go home now.'

'But, Paul . . .'

'*Please!*'

He got up and walked over to the window. She held out her

arms to him, then dropped them, watched him for a moment, and
went out of the room.

At home her chief sensation was that of a deep relief. He wanted
to marry her. It had been a strange and tortured proposal, but
then there was something strange and tortured about the man.
He wanted to marry her. He had felt suddenly that they couldn't
go on as they were, and now she felt it too. This relief at the
thought of marriage was not, she hastened to assure herself, due
to fear of its alternative—although, with her traditions, the alternative would have been hard; it was due to the fact that Paul
loved her enough to want her for his wife. That, at least, was
clear, and in that lay her comfort. To-morrow he would tell her
everything. To-morrow they would become . . . To-morrow . . .

She slept dreamlessly, as she had not done for many nights.

.   .   .   .   .   .

Next day he was there before her. His greeting was abrupt and
clipped, but there was a light in his eyes.

She sat in a corner of the sofa, and almost at once he came and
knelt beside her, and poured out passionate words.

Her heart raced.

'Tell me you love me, Joan—little darling girl!'

'Oh, Paul, I love you.'

'You *do* love my arms round you?—my nearness?'

'Why, yes—you know it.'

'Then . . . then . . .'

She looked at him, waiting, glowing.

'*Give* yourself to me—all of yourself. Come back with me to-
night to where I live. We'll both be happy. I haven't so very
much longer in England now. Let's make the most of our time
. . . little love . . .'

Staring at him while her world rocked, she sat for a moment
motionless. Then suddenly she pushed him away.

'What are you asking?' she cried.

'Only that you should love me completely! What's the matter?'

She stood up with her hands pressed over her eyes. 'Oh, how horrible! How horrible!'

'But . . . Hasn't it all been leading to this? What did you expect?'

She removed her hands. He was still half kneeling, half crouching on the floor. What did she expect?

'After yesterday . . .' she blurted out.

'Well, after yesterday? You didn't think me horrible *then*! Oh, I see. . . .' He rose slowly and faced her, and his smile was humiliating. 'I see. You wanted to be proposed to—like an ordinary girl? You realise how funny that is—after all your free talk, and your diatribes against marriage? A man listens to all that, takes you at your word, and you freeze up like any little suburban miss who's out for a ring and a wedding cake.'

'Paul, stop! How dare you put it like that! You know it isn't like that! It's because you're offering me something that you yourself despise—that you yourself called shoddy.'

'Well . . . if *you* don't think it shoddy that's all that matters, isn't it?'

'All—that—matters?'

Through a sea of shame that crept up, drowning her, she stared at him. Just because she had been easy, had come with him to an unknown house, had not asked to meet the owner, did he think . . . It wasn't possible! Desperately she fought for her own vision. She had loved him. She had imagined that they could make something beautiful of their lives together. But she had no strength to make him see. All was a blurr, a nightmare. At last, very small, scarcely audible, a sentence dropped from her dry lips.

'You said that marriage was sacred. . . . I'm—not—good enough for it.'

'How literal you are!' he exclaimed. 'Words one just throws off in the mood of the moment. . . .'

Of course—one ought not to believe people's words. One ought to go by one's feeling of what they were like underneath. And deep down she had felt, all the time, what Paul was like.

'Just a specimen to you,' she said dully, 'something fresh. You don't care for *me*.'

'I do, Joan—I do—in my way!' He moved towards her in an attempt to win her back, but he saw by her eyes that it was hopeless.

'Perhaps you do—in your way. I don't feel as though I knew anything. Good-bye, Paul.'

The door was shut between them. On one side of it Joan was going blindly down the staircase; on the other Paul was standing, eyes on the ground, hands in pockets, muttering, 'Damn!'

.   .   .   .   .   .

On the 1st of September Joan took up her duties at the 2nd London General, Chelsea. It was a large building which had once been a college. She was put into the eye-ward.

Chapter Six

'WONDERFUL moon!' people would have said in other years, as the great ball of harvest gold swung upwards nightly over London. 'Ghastly moon!' was now their grim comment. Raids, raids, raids. Nights of broken sleep. Nights of strange vigils in cellars. Nights while the skies detonated. Jangled nerves. Ruined buildings. Deaths.

'What I can't understand,' exclaimed Joan, one evening late in September, at dinner at Beechwood, 'is this exodus of rich people to Brighton and places. I should have thought they'd be ashamed to bolt, however frightened they might feel.'

'How do you manage at your hospital when there's a raid?' asked Jimmy. He had just passed out of Woolwich, and was having a few days' leave before going into camp—a full-fledged second lieutenant.

'Oh, we huddle miserably down to the cellars, with our coats over our nightgowns,' said Joan. 'We're safe enough there, but it's a bore, and one feels a wreck next day. I wish we could be left in our beds.'

'Dickens is an immense comfort on air-raid nights,' said Florence, as she helped Jimmy a second time to maize pudding. 'Cook's getting quite enthralled by *Our Mutual Friend*. I read it aloud to them all on the cellar steps while they knit. Of course now and then it's a little hard to make oneself heard.'

Later on Joan said she supposed she must be pushing off. At the 2nd London, where nurses slept on the premises, it was easy to slip in, and up to your room, at any old hour. All the same it was as well not to be very much later than ten, as there was a risk of being caught by the head night-sister going her rounds.

She began putting on her coat and hat. Suddenly there was the boom of guns.

'There they come! Well, I can't go now, anyhow.'

Florence adjusted her spectacles, and pottered off to fetch *Our Mutual Friend*. 'Come along, children,' she said. 'You'd better join the party.'

'All right, in a minute.' Jimmy wandered to the front door. This was his first real London air-raid, and he was not going to miss more of it than he could help. He had been asleep when those few bombs fell on Woolwich Common earlier in the month.

Joan hesitated, then stayed with her brother.

Wheew . . . *Crump*! Wheew . . . *Crump*! The big anti-aircraft gun by the Hampstead Pond was giving tongue. The air shook.

Jimmy stood on the top of the steps in the open doorway. Joan sat on the chest in the vestibule with her coat hugged round her, the sleeves hanging loose.

Bang! Bang! Bang! A few terrific detonations mixed themselves with the steady firing. BANG!

'That was a near one!' cried Jimmy. 'I should think they were over Highgate.' His face was lit up, but almost guiltily, as though he felt that his tremendous interest in the show were somehow indecent.

'*Must* you go out, Jim-pot?'

Joan sat looking at her brother's taut young figure—now at the bottom of the flight of steps—at his pale young face turned eagerly upwards. No, she couldn't call him back again, couldn't show her own nervousness. The night was still and silvery; the shrubs stood like sentinels; the garden was barred in black and white. The demon-racket going on above had no reality—was yet the only reality.

Wheew . . . *Crump*! Wheew . . . *Crump*! The long screams soared over them and died—soared over them and died. Clatter, clatter, phtt, phtt, phtt. Shrapnel falling on roofs. *Crash!* One couldn't disentangle the noises—which of them came from our own barrage, which from enemy bombs.

Jimmy was walking slowly down the drive now. If she were

really a brave English sister she would join him, slip a hand through his arm. Then came the thought: 'Perhaps he won't so much mind being under fire "out there." ' And then: 'He's still in England—he's left Woolwich, but he's still in England. Lots of time yet.'

Wheew . . . *Crump*! The sounds were getting fainter now. The demons were tiring.

'Seem to have moved off,' said Jimmy, coming in rather reluctantly, his head turned over his shoulder. He took two strides up the steps. Joan allowed a long breath to escape her, gave him a smile of comic unconcern, and slipped off the chest. She had been sitting there nearly an hour.

They stood listening. No—nothing more. And then, in that uncanny silence which succeeded the din, came the tinkle of an approaching bicycle-bell, and a boy-scout's voice—impersonal, faint, but comforting as a fairy's horn in lost woodlands—'All clear! . . . All clear! . . .'

Florence hurried into the hall from the door at the far end. 'Oh, children, how naughty of you! I was getting so anxious, but I couldn't leave the maids. Joan dear, are you really going? Couldn't you stay the night?'

'Not possibly, Auntie,' she laughed. 'But there's no danger now.'

'I think that was about the worst raid we've had,' said Florence. 'I mean the nearest to *us*.'

Joan tubed from Hampstead to South Kensington, and there picked up a late bus which carried her down the deserted Fulham Road.

Criss-crossing the sky in all directions were the beams of the search-lights.

.   .   .   .

After that moon-lit, danger-filled September there were three weeks of peace, and then the raids began again.

On the morning of October 20th, Joan, who was 'off' from ten to one, was waiting outside Swan and Edgar's, where she had arranged to meet Pamela and help her with some shopping. She stared about her, amazed. One of last night's bombs had fallen in Piccadilly, and the street was covered with broken pieces of plate-glass. Within the shop-windows were untidy heaps of goods—nothing to guard them from passers-by but a few hastily erected wooden bars.

'They've cleared things up a bit now,' said a woman who was standing beside Joan. 'But when I passed here earlier the mess was extraordinary. The whole pavement was a litter of hand-bags, and stockings, and blouses, and things. And there was a wax head off one of those dummies lying among it all. Gave me quite a shock for a moment. I thought it was human.'

'Hallo!' exclaimed Pamela, arriving a few minutes later. 'Oh, I *say*! Poor old Swan and Edgar's! Well, that does bring the war home! Come on in, I've lots to do, and we can talk while we're shopping.'

Pamela was staying with Lady Butler in Curzon Street. She was dancing at night and getting her kit together for France in the day. She was off to a military hospital at Rouen at the end of the week.

In intervals of buying necessities she chattered away about last night's raid.

'Darling, it was so amusing—I wouldn't have missed it for anything! You know old Hobson, the butler—face like a large cream cheese? Well, when the guns began he came into the drawing-room and asked us very respectfully to step down to the cellar. Aunt Maud said she didn't think it necessary, but he insisted, saying, "I feel responsible for your Ladyship during Sir Henry's absence." So down we had to go, and there we all solemnly sat, Hobson looking as though he were attending morning prayers, and casting occasional reproving glances at the housemaid who was nervy. There was an elderly lady with us too—haughty-looking, in pince-nez. Nobody knew who she was—she'd just blown in from the street when the raid began, and gone down to the cellar. It seems people do that kind of thing these days. But, my dear, what was so priceless was that she simply wouldn't answer Aunt Maud when she spoke to her—and Aunt Maud was trying to be nice. Just ignored her, and looked up at the ceiling. Bit thick I thought it—when she had taken shelter in *her* cellar. And the guns went banging away, and then there was one terrific explosion—the Swan and Edgar bomb, I suppose—which made everyone duck—though I believe Hobson only blinked—and still the pince-nez woman wouldn't speak. Well, it was over at last, and what do you think? Hobson came in after breakfast with a message from "Mrs. Stapleton, the lady who was here last night, and she tenders her apologies and says that if she had known it was your ladyship she would have spoken." It seems she thought our house was a small private hotel—there *is* one in Curzon Street—and that we were just odd guests, and she wasn't going to talk to anyone to whom she hadn't been introduced! Can you conceive it? An air-raid, and all of us liable to be buried any minute—and these incredible conventionalities still being kept up! How she had learnt her mistake about the house God only knows! And whether she would have apologised if Aunt Maud hadn't been a "ladyship" God still only knows!'

This, and much more, was babbled into Joan's ear during the activities of the morning. It was evident that Pamela was in high spirits at having at last escaped from home, and at being on the eve of a spell of work abroad. But working in a military hospital was no joke, as Joan well knew, and Pam didn't strike her as looking particularly strong yet. 'It's only my eyes,' Pamela assured her. 'I still can't read much; but then, out there, it won't matter—there won't be time.'

No, and there wouldn't be time—that was the chief blessing—for long unhappy broodings about Ian.

France! . . . Joan envied Pam.

·   ·   ·   ·   ·   ·

For nearly a fortnight Jimmy had been in camp near Winchester. His time was spent in strenuous gun-drill, and in riding on the Downs with his friends. He was happy and exhilarated, and wrote of the beauty of the country, and of the misty morning smell of autumn leaves and sweaty horses. As far as he knew he would be there for quite a long time—certainly until Christmas.

.   .   .   .   .   .

Betty came on leave. The Rest Camp was over. But something else was over too—the greatest thing in her life—her engagement to Guy. About a fortnight before coming to England she had had a letter from him breaking it off, telling her he was engaged to someone else, imploring her, if she could, to forgive him, to dismiss him from her thoughts and from her heart. It could hardly have come at a crueller moment, and how she had carried on for that last spell of the camp Betty didn't know.

She was sitting up in her bedroom, on her second day at home. The lovely colour was still in her cheeks—nothing but old age could dim that—but the light in her eyes was dead. Joan gazed at her, sad, furious. It wasn't possible that this thing had happened to Betty—to Betty, of all people.

'Men!' she exploded. 'Why do we ever have anything to do with them! What do they ever bring us but misery!'

To do her justice she would have flung the same senseless generalisation at the universe even if she had not been still raw from her own affair with Paul. It was a cry torn from her by this wrong done to her dearest friend, and by the bitter knowledge that there was nothing whatever she could do to help.

Useless to exclaim that she would like to murder Guy Lovatt, useless to curse him, to point out to Betty his worthlessness—especially as Betty seemed to dislike hearing him abused.

'You see, Joan, what I feel is,' she said, 'that I'm very much to blame myself over this business. He's *not* the rotter you make out. It's been hard for him. If I'd only married him when he wanted me to . . ."

'Lucky you didn't, as things have turned out!' said Joan. But Betty shook her head.

'The point is that if I *had* they would have turned out quite differently. As it is I start the ball rolling in a certain direction, and a sort of ironic fate gives it a series of kicks. First I ask for a long engagement. Then, just when I've brought myself to the point of marriage, Guy gets wounded. Then he goes to convalesce in a house where the daughter was once in love with him. They look after him, give him every comfort. He's weak and ill. He can't tell them about his engagement because of his promise to me to keep it secret. The girl falls violently in love with him again. He's grateful for all she's done. Propinquity. Summer weather. Memories of old times. Me far away, and—and there you are.'

'On the contrary, there I'm not!' cried Joan. 'And there you're not, and it's all the most disgusting muddle. Your defence of him is ingenious, and beautifully like you, but it doesn't in the least exonerate him. He deserves . . .'

'Let it alone, Joan, there's a dear,' said Betty softly. 'You can't know him as I did. You can't do more than see the outside of the story.'

'If there's one thing I do see,' cried Joan, 'it's that girls like us, who do war-work, haven't a chance against the stay-at-homes. What do we see of our men beyond passing glimpses?'

'I only hope that girl's nice,' murmured Betty, not heeding her. 'She sounds all right. There's one good thing—I happen to know the family's well off.'

Joan opened her mouth to exclaim, 'Oh, it is, is it!' but restrained herself. Betty must be left her own curious comforts. There was nothing to be done—nothing. If Guy had been killed she couldn't have felt more unhappy for her friend. That tragedy would have been crushing, but it would have had no sting.

'Thank God nobody knew!' sighed Betty. 'To have had to endure sympathy from one's parents and relations over a thing like this . . .'

Early in November she went back to Boulogne to resume, after the long summer months, her position of Senior Lady of the Alexandra.

.   .   .   .   .   .

Betty had scarcely left England when Joan received a note from

Paul. She had neither seen him nor heard from him since their parting at the end of August, and now he informed her that, after various delays, he was at last leaving the W.O. and rejoining his unit. He asked if he might be allowed to meet her—just once— as the merest friend—before he went out.

Joan had suffered so bitterly over Paul during the past two months that she would have thought it impossible ever again to respond to any sign from him. Yet this note stirred something within her.

Reason warned her that it would be unwise to meet him again; heart urged her to do so, and reminded her that he too, like all the rest, was a soldier and killable.

They dined at 'The Gobelins'—both in uniform—and after the first hand-shake, when he had murmured: 'I don't deserve this,' there had been no allusions to the past. Paul was as charming as she remembered him in the first days of their love; and among the gaiety of lights and diners she could almost imagine that the later, ugly side of him had belonged to another man altogether.

He talked well and vividly, dancing from subject to subject; and the laughter in his eyes held no mockery, no maliciousness, but only warmth. In his company, to-night, Joan began to believe in the possibility of a friendship being re-born between them— different, passionless, sincere. She was quite aware, too, of a tiny priggish satisfaction at the thought that she had perhaps, after all, been 'good for him.'

He drove her back to Chelsea, and outside the high dark wall of the hospital he took her hand.

'Good-bye, little V.A.D.' he smiled. 'This is how I first saw you, and how I shall always think of you. The wheel has come full circle. Good-bye.'

.   .   .   .   .   .

A week later Colin was in London. He was on his way East to serve in the Indian Army. Invalided home in the summer with a slight arm wound and trench fever, he had spent weeks in hospitals and Convalescent Camps in the country. During all this time he had only seen Joan once, but they had, of course, been writing to each other, and towards the end of August she had told him that someone had come into her life who was utterly absorbing her. Colin had long ago made her promise that if such a thing ever did happen she would let him know; and though she gave no details, no name, made no mention of marriage, and though her letter was no less affectionate towards him than her letters had always been, it was enough: there was 'another man.' Colin had his bad hour; and then, with the strength of mind acquired by long iron months of war, and by his own dwindling hopes, made acceptance.

Soon afterwards he had been recommended by a medical board for service in a hotter climate. Nothing could have fallen more appropriately. It looked as though Fate, having dealt him a staggering blow with one hand, were holding out balm to him with the other. A change to new countries, after two solid years of the trenches in France, would anyhow have appealed to him— even though it meant being far removed from Joan. Now—under the circumstances—it was a blessing unimpaired.

'Do a dinner and a show with me, Joan, the night before I leave?' he asked her. And she had managed to swop evenings off with another girl, and had met him at the Savoy.

The Savoy was rather awful in these days—a haunt of 'nouveaux riches' and of rowdy Colonials—but Colin had pre-war memories of it, and he wanted his last night in England to be as typical as possible of old times.

'Do you remember dancing with me here?' he asked, 'one night in July '14?'

'Of course I do.'

How could she forget? He had just begun to fall in love with her, and they had come, a party of six, Betty among them, and danced through the whole programme with a joy in the quivering present, and an unconsciousness of what hung over them, which —looking back on it now—had a peculiar pathos. The favourite waltz of the evening had been 'Destiny,' and Colin had murmured,

as he and Joan glided together, something about the appropriateness of the name to the occasion. It was indeed appropriate,
but not in the sense that he had meant—or that any of the
party could have foretold. Ten days later war broke out,
and a few months after that the two soldier friends of Colin's
who had danced in the party that night were lying dead
in Flanders.

To-night there were uniforms everywhere; uniforms of soldiers,
of sailors, of air-men; uniforms of nurses, of W.A.A.C.s and of
W.R.E.N.s. Of civilian clothes only a sprinkling—but what a
refreshing sprinkling! Joan, who had stuffed an evening dress
into a suit-case, and had changed into it in the ladies' cloak-room,
knew by Colin's eyes that she had been right to do so.

They had a table in one of the windows. Pink-shaded lamps.
Drinks (officially unobtainable). Music.

They talked of many things. Of Colin's Eastern adventure. Yes,
he was looking forward to it—an exciting change—India had
always attracted him.

'And later on you may never have the chance of seeing such
places,' Joan reminded him. 'A good thing to travel while you
can—at the Government's expense. And of course I shall be far
happier about you out there—out of danger.'

'Will you?' he asked, with a curious little smile, looking down at
his plate.

'Well, naturally. I haven't suddenly lost all interest in you,
Colin.'

Hadn't she? She was being very kind, anyhow.

They touched on the Betty and Guy business, but it went too
deep for discussion. Colin merely remarked that if Lovatt were
that sort of chap it was as well Betty hadn't married him; and Joan
agreed, though not so whole-heartedly as she would have done
before her talk with Betty, or—though she would have hated to
own it—before her last meeting with Paul.

She had changed, softened, thought Colin, as he gazed at the far-
away eyes and the pale lamp-lit hair. Never had she seemed to

him so lovely, and never, in spite of her quietness, so deeply alive. That man, that other man, of course . . .

Joan was thankful he didn't question her about her present position. Better that he should go off to India undisturbed, with hopes quenched, believing her happy and absorbed, as she had told him she was in that letter.

Colin—dear, steadfast Colin. She realised that, selfishly, she didn't in the least want him to go. If only there hadn't been this revival with Paul, if only she were still feeling as she had felt after that awful scene in Wilton Crescent, she would have told Colin everything—would most likely have engaged herself to him, here and now—for security—for balm to her battered pride. Even as it was she wondered whether it might not be the best thing to do. No 'security' with Paul.

She looked at the iris-coloured, heavy-lidded eyes, the straight thick mouth. It was a beautiful face, beautiful chiefly for the spirit behind it, a face that showed strength and control. And, yes, there was something to control in Colin; she realised that as she had never done in the past, when she had taken both his love and his control of it for granted. She had learnt so much lately. A great admiration, and a great tenderness towards him filled her; but she was not sufficiently detached from Paul to be carried away on the flood of it. It was still Paul—in spite of everything—with whom she was in love; Paul who had seized her, awakened her, tortured her, thrown her away, and who had now turned and picked her up again. Oh dear, what a pity—what a *pity* it all was! In her present state she could do nothing, hold out no finger. But if Colin, on his own initiative, were now, at the last minute, to go for her— really to go for her . . .

Colin was smiling reminiscently. 'I remember once,' he was saying, 'in the days when I was feeling very emotional about you . . .'

She didn't hear the rest. 'Was' struck on her like a knell. And the question 'Don't you still then?' which had leapt to her lips, was not uttered.

He feels no more for me than friendship now, she thought.

Well, it's all I deserve. Haven't I preached friendship at him for years?

And Colin hearing no question from her, seeing no flicker of dismay on her face, thought how completely she must have gone from him not even to have noticed that deliberately used 'was.'

They couldn't see into each other's minds, and so, because the situation was delicate, and because they both had diffidence and both had pride, they talked of other things, and smiled at one another across the table, while round them people danced, and the Lady Opportunity, who was within their grasp, turned from them with a sigh, gathered her filmy skirts, and floated off.

They went on to a revue, and then Colin said he would see her back to Chelsea; but about this Joan was firm. He was sailing to-morrow, she reminded him; he must get back to Hampstead, and to his parents. It was late enough already.

They walked with the drifting theatre crowd—feeling oddly isolated from it—across Leicester Square and Piccadilly Circus. He saw her on to her bus. Saw her climb to the top, her uniform coat buttoned up over her evening dress, her round straw hat pulled low. Saw her wave to him as it lurched off. Stood for a moment quite still, gazing after her. Then bent his steps in the opposite direction, and his thoughts to 'pastures new.'

.   .   .   .   .   .

Two days later Joan had a letter from Paul. She had had one brief note since his departure, telling her of his safe arrival in France, and thanking her for their evening. This one—she could feel before she opened it—was much longer. Her hands trembled as she took out the sheets. She hardly knew what she expected to find; perhaps an explanation of his feeling for her, past and present, of his conduct to her at the end. Easier to write of these things than to talk of them.

She read it through, sitting on the edge of her little hospital bed, and as she read she grew paler and paler. He told her, after a confused and pointless beginning, that she must not count on him in the future. That she must look upon their 'friendship' (he wrote it in inverted commas that seemed to sneer) as an amusing war-time episode which had coloured some drab days for both of them. That the best thing she could do would be to find, as soon as possible, a decent fellow to be her husband. That as for himself he would always sail through life, interested in its different aspects, taking from it what he could. The great thing was to have a sense of humour. Nothing was worth getting upset about; and whatever adventure one might embark upon, one must be artist enough to finish it off neatly, then cut it out and stick it in the album of one's memories. Albums, of course, were not often opened; but it was sometimes worth doing so for the sensation of gentle regret which arose as one contemplated those queer old photographs. He, Paul, now had a very pleasant and characteristic one of her; he hoped that she had a similar one of him. This was why he had suggested that last meeting—otherwise a little difficult, perhaps, to account for.

If any part of Joan's mind had been able to stand aside and watch her as she laid down this letter it would have been interested to note that 'her hand went to her heart' in the traditional manner of the heroines of old novels. But she was unaware of the gesture; she was only aware that a knife had been turned in her, and that something at last had died.

Walking down the Fulham Road half an hour later she felt light and dry as a reed. It was an odd feeling. Hollow inside. No blood. Only a little white pith, and a hollowness. The wind touched her with friendly fingers. She looked with curiosity and pleasure at the buildings, at some children playing. The outer world was still there. It was so long since she had noticed it. So long since she had noticed anything but herself, and her own aching sensations. Under hospital work, under talks with friends, under the delight of brief meetings with Jimmy, under air-raids, always—always—there had been Paul. Now he had dropped away. She knew that she was free of him, though it was a freedom in which she was as yet too weak to rejoice.

And after an interval there came into her mind a vision of Colin's

ship, very small, rather lonely, ploughing its way day by day
eastward.

.   .   .   .   .   .

Late in November Florence had a telegram from Jimmy saying
that he had had sudden orders for France, and would be home next
day.

'It's too soon, Joan, it's too soon,' said Florence, hovering about
by the stove, large and distressed, holding the telegram.

Joan had come up from hospital, as soon as she was able, after the
news had been forwarded to her.

'Do you remember saying, that day at Stewart's when we got his
letter about Woolwich, that I needn't worry—that the war would
be over long before he had finished his training?'

'Yes, I remember.'

'And here we are, and it's still going on, and it's taking Jimmy.'

Taking Jimmy . . .

'Look here, Auntie,' said Joan, after a silence, 'there's only one
thing you can do, and that's not to let him see how much you
mind. Make to-morrow as cheerful as ever you can for him.'

'I know, dear.' Florence laid a hand on the girl's shoulder.
'You're always scared I shall burden him with my emotions,
aren't you? But I'll be all right, I promise you.'

'Tell him I'll meet him anywhere he likes to-morrow afternoon,'
said Joan. 'He'll probably be shopping. I shall be off from two to
five.'

She kissed her aunt quickly and went.

.   .   .   .   .   .

Joan and Jimmy had an early tea together in Bond Street. His
train, it appeared, went at six next morning. It would be impossible
for her to come and see him off, so this was their last hour. They
made it a perfectly normal and merry one.

'Jim-pot, you're *not* going to France in those boots!' she
exclaimed.

'Why, what's the matter with them?' Jimmy stretched out a long
leg in a boot of the type known as 'trench,' laced up the front.

'But surely, if you're a gunner, you ought to wear field-boots?'

'Not compulsory, you know.'

'Even then, think how much nicer they *look*!'

Jimmy grinned at her.

'I know how you'd like me to be turned out. Like one of those ghastly little T.G. subalterns in soft caps and mauve corduroy breeches. Possibly you'd like me to wear a sword even?'

'Don't be funny. But you've got nice legs, and field-boots *are* smart.'

'They're jolly expensive. These are quite good enough.'

'You were always a miser—even as a small boy. Your money-box used to bulge with pennies!'

'Yes, and who came borrowing them from me? My spendthrift sister!'

She laughed. 'I know, Jumbles. You've always been a darling to me over money. If it was pennies then, it's often been pounds since.'

'Rot!'

'This battery you're going out to join,' she asked casually, 'will it be very near the lines?'

'Not so very. On the other hand, not miles behind. It's a sixty-pounder. Useful sort of battery.'

'I see. Are Browne and Sanderson going with you?'

'No, worse luck! We've all been posted to different places.'

'How sickening!'

It was after half-past four.

'Well, Jumbles, you'll be back on leave soon, I expect. Write as regularly as you can to Auntie—she'll be in a constant state of stew. Write to me only when you feel like it.'

'Rather. I expect I shall have lots of time, you know.

'If you pass through Boulogne, kiss Betty for me. Good-bye, darling.'

The '14' bus from the Ritz. Jimmy smiling at her from the pavement. Wrench of heart-strings. Rumble of wheels. Houses and trees a blur.

.   .   .   .   .   .

'You saw him off, Auntie?'

'Yes, dear. He was very sweet, and didn't try to prevent me, as I was afraid he might. It was almost more awful waking him up in his bed at half-past four than seeing him off by train. He looked such a baby. We had some coffee ready. The servants had got up. I think that embarrassed him rather. He said good-bye to them all—said he'd bring them souvenirs. Then he went and saw Tam in his kennel. He said: "Good-bye, Tam, old man. I'll be back soon." Joan, I can't bear the look in that dog's eyes when either of you children leave home.

'Well, then your Uncle Robert came and fetched us—I thought he'd be a support, and make things more normal at the station somehow. Victoria was seething with soldiers. Some of them were going out for the first time, and some were going back after leave. They all seemed quite calm, and were smoking. Your little brother looked *enormous*. He had all his equipment on him, and his tin helmet, and I don't know how many things. And he got into a carriage packed with other men, and smiled at us over their shoulders. He called out that there was breakfast on the train; and wasn't that "a good egg"! And then the train steamed slowly out, and Robert brought me home. He couldn't have been kinder, and you know how hopeful and cheering he always is. But it was terrible—terrible.'

'Oh, Auntie, I wish I'd been there! But you mustn't worry. He'll be all right, you know.'

'I didn't show anything, Joan. I was quite cheerful. I think you'd have been pleased.'

.   .   .   .   .   .

Back at the hospital. In your bed at night. Staring into the darkness. Where was he? Where was he at this minute? Only eighteen-and-a-half. No friends with him. Travelling towards an unknown unit, in unknown France. The curtain had fallen. Jimmy had been gathered into the war.

Chapter Seven

ALL this time Joan had been in the eye-ward. It was less exhausting physically, but more distressing than any ward she had known. Some of the men had only temporarily lost their sight, some had one eye injured, but the large majority had been blinded for life.

When a man first came in with bandaged eyes he almost always thought the injury was temporary. Sometimes, unless the eyes themselves had been shot away, even the doctor couldn't tell at once. But when it was discovered that the sight had gone for ever, the news would be broken to the patient by Sister Hoarder, a broad-bosomed motherly creature, who would hold his head against her breast saying: 'Face it now, Sonny, and get it over. Face it now,' while he sobbed like a child.

Joan was amazed how soon, after the shock of realisation, the men recovered their spirits. The pluck and the patience of them, although in one way helpful, were in another way more heart-rending to her than if they had given themselves up to curses and despair. In their new darkness the sense of touch and the sense of hearing became delicate and acute.

'Let me feel you, Nurse,' one of them said, before she began swabbing out the red holes that had been eyes. He passed his hands lightly over her bent head and shoulders.

'Describe me,' she laughed.

'Fair hair, grey eyes, and a lovely smile.'

'Quite wrong! Black hair with grey streaks in it, and two teeth missing in the top row.'

'Now, *Nurse!*'

'Don't you believe me?'

'Of course I don't! Why, your voice gives you away. I can tell a lot what people are like by their voices.'

And it suddenly struck Joan that if this man married the quiet

358

pretty girl who came to see him, and to whom he had been engaged a year, he would always have the same picture of her in his mind. For him she would be for ever young.

Why was it, she wondered, as she looked round the ward (a large gloomy ward on the ground-floor of the building) that blind men always tilted their faces at that angle—chin up, as though seeking light, or listening?

'A cigarette doesn't seem the same somehow when you can't see the smoke going up,' one of them told her placidly. And another: 'Sometimes when I wake in the morning I don't know whether I'm properly awake or still asleep. It's funny.'

Jokes were made over glass eyes. When sockets were sufficiently healed, and no longer exuding pus and blood, pieces of plain glass, the shape of an eye, were fitted between the lids.

'But I'll have proper coloured eyes before I get out, won't I, Nurse?'

'Of course you will—these are only temporary. Now what would you like? Blue? Brown? Grey?'

'Well, me real eyes was blue. Supposing I have one blue and one brown? 'Ow would that be?'

'It would make you quite irresistible!'

All through that dim, hopeless autumn men talked of the struggle in the mud of Passchendaele, of huge losses in killed and drowned, of tanks and guns bogged in the slime, of the new German 'pill-boxes,' of our mismanaged futile attacks. The British army was getting mauled to bits to save the French. And the end seemed further off than ever.

A letter came from Jock Guthrie, now back at the Front.

'Many thanks for the parcel,' he wrote. 'I had just come out of wet trenches so the socks I had were soaking and I was glad of a dry pair. Well I must say we are fairly well off at present you know what I mean we could be much worse off, there is not any of it too good this weather. Well it is better to be cheerful for if one starts to lose heart out here and worries himself it puts years

on his life. I have only one thing to worry me and that is the
Biscuits I cannot eat them. You remember they pulled my teeth
out in the Hospital well I have not got them yet, I am afraid I will
have to report sick and get a new set. Some say we are going to
Ypres after this rest and everyone has got wind up in case we are.
I can tell you I am not in love with Ypres. The weather is very
cold. I have no more news at present. It was too kind of you to
put yourself to the trouble of that parcel. I love you a lot for
thinking so much of me. I wonder if you are spoiling your
patients at Chelsea same as you did at Camberwell. Never mind if
you are it is Lovely a Nurse or Sister always Looking pleasant. I
will close now. I keep smiling best I can. I am Yrs. sincerely
J. GUTHRIE.'

Pile upon pile of letters from the Front now lay in Joan's drawers.
Strange-looking letters, unlike any that had been received before,
or probably would be again. Letters written on thin sheets of
paper in indelible pencil. No stamps on the envelope, but instead
two marks: the black circle of the Field Post Office, and the red
triangle of the Censor.

On the surface life was quiet and dull. There were no V.A.D.s
here whom she liked. All her greatest friends were in France.
The only events which came to disturb the monotony were air-
raids, and these, as the winter progressed and they became more
frequent, lost much of their excitement. Matron had decreed that
no nurses need go down to the cellars on air-raid nights unless
they liked, but that if they did go they must be properly dressed.
After this Joan remained in bed, and quite often—such was the
heavy quality of sleep after a hard day—she didn't even wake.
Even the bomb which dropped close to, in the grounds of the
Chelsea pensioners, only half roused her.

Almost every day, in her off-time, she passed the end of the road
where Thrush lived, but she never went to see her. Thrush, she
felt sure, could dispense with her company, and there was no
point in stirring up memories by sitting in that studio.

Food in hospital was fairly good. Haricot beans took the place of potatoes, and on several occasions the nurses were given blue-looking, sweet-tasting beef, which turned out on inquiry to be horse; but there was nothing really to complain of. It was in the houses of civilians that the problem was acute. Meat tickets were collected together to produce a miserable weekly joint. If people went anywhere to stay they travelled with their own small rations of butter and of sugar. Conversation ran almost entirely on food lines. Joan used to become bored by it. Was food after all so very important in view of other things?

And under the dullness of life's surface there was the ceaseless, gnawing anxiety about Jimmy. It was not an acute anxiety; the anodyne of daily work did much to dull it; his short but frequent letters home were reassuring; but always, always, the anxiety was there.

.   .   .   .   .   .

In the first letter Florence received from him, written from a camp, before he had arrived at his battery, were requests for various things to be sent.

'My chief trouble at present,' he wrote, 'is that I have lost one spur. Would you send out the pair I left at home. Also I would like a nice wristlet identity disc, stamped in this manner: 2/Lt. J. B. Seddon, R.G.A., C. of E. I slept very well last night in my flea-bag and my old rug, on bare boards. Love to Joan, Uncle Robert, Tam, and the cousins.'

And then:

'After much wandering I have at last found my battery. It is in rest at present, of which I am glad, as I can get to know something about it before going into action. I am the youngest officer by about two years, and of course, so far, feel rather new to the job, and inferior. However, they are all very friendly and decent to me, if a bit fed up about things in general. I am assistant officer to the Observation party, and have no responsibilities as yet.'

Joan gathered that he was feeling a little like a new boy at school. Jimmy never liked not *knowing* about things.

But as time went on he grew steadily more confident. The battery had been in and out of the line, had been shelled once or twice, but the experience was not half so unpleasant as he had expected. 'There is no heavy fighting at present,' he said. 'The real work only begins when there is a push, and one fires about 800 rounds a day, but I don't suppose that will happen till the spring. The ground in this God-forsaken district is in an awful state. Nothing but ruin and mud and shell-holes. How our infantry ever advanced over it I can't imagine. It was a magnificent bit of work on their part.'

They knew by this, and by other references, that he was in the Salient.

He had been made F.O.O. (Forward Observation Officer), and, strangely enough, liked the work.

'Duty at the O.P. (Observation Post) is not comfortable, but it is exciting and responsible. You have to be watching the country in front of you the whole time, for twenty-four hours on end. You are mostly on your feet, and there is practically no protection. On these occasions I find the Horlicks' tablets a great comfort. Thank you so much for them, and for those new gloves, which are splendidly warm. It was pretty cold last time I was up, and the rain came down all night to the accompaniment of a howling gale. I'm keeping very fit. I will try to write every two days, Auntie, but you are not to worry if I don't. The butter queues at home must be awful. We do much better out here than you, in the way of food.'

His letters to Joan were less frequent, but longer. In one of them, written about Christmas time, he referred to the year which was just over.

'We made the most of seeing each other, didn't we? Me dashing up from Woolwich, and you from your hospital. You are the best and most sympathetic sister a man could possibly wish for, and my love and respect for you are exceeding great—though I don't suppose you would gather as much from my behaviour with you and the way I talk.'

The tears started to her eyes as Joan read this, and she wondered whether the other V.A.D.s, sitting round her at dinner, would think she had had bad news. No love-letter had ever melted her up as these few stumbling words of appreciation from her inarticulate little brother.

If anything happens to Jimmy, she said to herself fiercely, I shall be no use for comforting Auntie. I shall be no use for anyone or anything. I shall be finished.

At the New Year he wrote to her again.

'I hope this year will see the war out. Everyone you meet out here is absolutely fed up with it, and a considerable number think we are fools not to have accepted the last German peace offer. I can't quite agree with these people myself, as the German terms are an absolute 'as you were,' and if we accepted them the whole war would have been a colossal waste of energy. One is very apt to forget what our war aims are—in fact I am not at all sure anybody knows.

'I think the only satisfactory conclusion to it would be a well-organised revolution of the German people, and the consequent deletion of all Germans in any way responsible for it. And I shouldn't be surprised if we had a revolution in England before that happened. Do write to me fully what you think.

'I enjoy reading your letters more than anybody else's, they are so sensible and interesting, and nice. Better not tell Auntie this, as she is so splendid about writing to me every day, and I do like getting her letters, but naturally they are a little incoherent at times, owing to her excessive anxiety about my welfare.

'I am getting to know my men now, specially the telephonists who have been up at O.P. with me, and who are jolly good fellows. Don't worry about me. You'd hardly know there was a war on here.'

And in February:

'I expect I shall get leave about mid-March if all goes well, but will wire when I get to Dover.'

.   .   .   .   .   .

One sunny March day Jimmy loomed up in the door of the eye-ward.

'Jim-pot!'

Joan nearly dropped the tray of dishes she was carrying.

'Didn't you know I was coming?'

'No!'

'I wired to Auntie. She can only just have got it. I had to come and see you before going up to Hampstead.'

He had to come and see her before . . . How fagged he looked —how dim and dusty! But he was there.

'Haven't stopped for a minute since I left the battery last night. Can you come and have some lunch?'

'Come and have . . .? Jim-pot, *darling*, I'm on duty!'

Just then Sister Hoarder waddled past. Joan introduced her brother. 'Just arrived this minute from the Front, Sister.'

'Go off with him, Nurse, go off with him! Take the afternoon, from now on,' beamed Sister Hoarder.

'Oh . . . *may* I?'

Half an hour later they were lunching at the Piccadilly Grill. Jimmy had had a quick wash and brush-up, and was swallowing food with that school-boy hunger and complete indifference to what he ate which had always characterised him.

Joan watched him, hardly able to believe in his presence. They didn't speak much. He looked up at her from time to time, affection struggling in his grey eyes with sleeplessness.

'Depressing place that blind ward must be to work in,' he remarked. And then added growlingly to his plate: 'I do think the way you stick to your uncongenial V.A.D.-ing is magnificent.'

Good heavens! Fancy thinking of *her*! What about himself? There were a hundred things she wanted to know. But she mustn't weary him.

'How's Tam?' he asked.

'Had some awful fights lately. Auntie broke her best umbrella over him the other day.'

'The old fellow doesn't get enough exercise, I expect.'

When they had finished he asked for the bill.

'Certainly, Captain, at once,' said the waiter.

'Why "Captain"?' grinned Jimmy at his sister.

'Form of flattery,' she told him. 'A habit they've got into nowadays of addressing every officer by a rank or two higher than his own.'

'Good idea for getting a fat tip! During my next leave I shall be "Colonel" I suppose!'

They strolled about the Park until it was time for Joan to go back. Jimmy seemed lost in wonder at the greenness and prettiness of everything. He stared at the daffodils, stared at the grass, at a pink almond tree, at the fat hyacinth buds. 'The contrast . . .' he murmured.

'Jim-pot, *sleep* to-night, won't you?' she said as they parted. 'Don't sit up late talking to Auntie.'

'Don't suppose she'll let me,' he smiled. 'I'll go and collect my kit from Victoria now. You'll come up home as often as you can, won't you?'

'As often as I can, I promise you.'

Jimmy's ten days' leave seemed to be over almost before it had begun. He was very tired at first, and slept and slept. He spent hours at the piano. He went walks with Tam. He tried to avoid his Uncle Robert's eager and well-meaning questions about life at the Front. He went to one or two shows with his friend Carey, who also happened to be on leave, and who was now a smart little subaltern in a line regiment. Joan joined the two boys one evening for dinner, and they went to 'The Maid of the Mountains,' and walked afterwards through the dark streets, humming 'There's Honour Among Thieves.'

She had a few talks alone with Jimmy, up in the old nursery, but it was a little difficult to get at his state of mind. The war had not made him more communicative. She gathered, however, that he was not unhappy out there; that he hadn't yet felt fear; that he had made no particular friends among his fellow-officers, except with a certain quiet man called Jones who was 'a bit of a poet';

also that he was burdened with rather too great an anxiety about his men.

His round face was thinner than before he went out, his eyes larger, but he certainly seemed fit, and by the end of his leave he had lost his strained look.

Riding with her back to Chelsea on the top of a bus, on his last day, there was an atmosphere of content about him—almost of radiance. She managed, then, to bring out the question which she had been longing to ask, but had been afraid to.

'Is it worse going back again, Jumbles, than going out for the first time?'

The answer was prompt. 'No, nothing like as bad. You see, I know now what there is to do. I didn't before. I know that I'm up to the job.'

She might have guessed it. With Jimmy things were always worse in imagination than in actuality. His own powers had to be tested before he could trust them.

When they parted at the hospital he gave her one of his wide smiles, and strode off down the road on springing, confident feet.

Next day was the 21st of March. The Germans had begun their great offensive. The British armies were being pushed back. Jimmy had crossed to France.

    •   •   •   •   •   •

Was this to be the end then? After three and a half years of war were we to be defeated? 'Our backs are against the wall,' was Haig's message, and recruiting went up by bounds. It was said the Channel ports might have to go. The country held its breath. Wounded poured over in thousands. The French Government was preparing to move from Paris. 'Big Bertha' dropped her shells daily into the suburbs from a distance of seventy miles.

Every night Joan went to bed with *The Times*, almost too tired to read it, and in her dreams saw the little map with the ink-marked Allied line jumping back, back, back.

One night she was half-awakened by rumbles and bangs. Her instant thought was that Big Bertha was shelling London from

Calais. What was the good of moving though? Might as well be killed in bed. And she dropped off again.

At breakfast she laughed at her fears of the night. Big Bertha indeed! Her nerves must have been in a pretty state.

'Was it a bad air-raid?' she asked one of the others.

'Air-raid? There was no air-raid.'

'But all that noise?'

'Oh, there was a thunderstorm, if that's what you mean!'

So it had only been a thunderstorm—not even an ordinary raid.

Back, back, back. When would we turn and hold them? More killed, more wounded. More names one knew in the colossal casualty lists. One's friends were marching night and day with the tattered remains of their battalions—fighting rear-guard actions on no food, no sleep. Jimmy was out there. Mind swung from numbness to agony. And the bright bleak spring sunshine mocked the inner darkness of those awful days.

And then they were held.

Betty wrote from Boulogne:

'We have been living these last weeks in daily expectation of having to evacuate—the Huns getting closer and closer. Curious. I have never been so much in actual danger from the enemy, and yet it aroused no feeling in me whatsoever! I think I must be devoid of imagination. Most of the permanent English residents have left. Raids of course have been bad. And one night, coming up to my room after a particularly shattering one, I found all the glass broken, and most of the ceiling on my bed! The whole Base has been teeming with soldiers, chiefly belonging to the 3rd and 5th Armies. They couldn't be sent back to their units because no one knew where the railheads were, or even if there were any. The huts, too, have been flooded with Y.M. men evacuated from army areas. Everything an awful muddle. I do hope you have good news of Jimmy. He turned up at the hut—I expect he told you—on his way through in March, and was perfectly sweet. He *said* we cheered him up immensely.

'What I'm really writing to say is, that you've got to come and

join us at a Rest Camp this summer, at a little place called St.
Valery-sur-Somme, near Abbeville. Now, Joan, *do*! You have
nursed steadily for ages, and you're run down. A change of work
will do you good. Trouble is, this retreat has hung up arrangements for a bit. However, as soon as things are settled I will let
you know, and will work your pass with the Y.M.'

This letter of Betty's arrived at the beginning of May, and coin-
cided, strangely enough, with Joan's discharge from hospital.
From Christmas onwards she had been having a series of septic
fingers. No sooner had one healed than another broke out, and
finally the doctor had said that she must have a complete rest from
nursing, and only take it up again—if at all—later in the year.
She was not, he told her, of the type that was 'as strong as a
horse'; and Joan, who had always imagined that she was, was
depressed at the information.

Well, she would join Betty for the summer. The prospect of
that camp was certainly alluring; she would be working mostly in
the open air; and do *something* she must.

She wrote to Jimmy about it. 'Of course you must go,' he replied. 'It will be lovely for you working with your friends again.
And what's the alternative? "Resting" in England, getting more
and more bored and melancholy, and then probably going back to
hospital (if I know you) before you're fit, and breaking down
again. Don't be an ass!

'Well, we've been having a busy time lately, what with night
marches and pulling in and pulling out of position, but I really
think we've finished retreating now. Of course you never know.'

A little later he wrote:

'Am having a top-hole time just now. Lovely weather. Beautiful
country. Moving about France with jingling horses. We are
having awful difficulty with the French civilians. They will barely
tolerate soldiers being billeted on them. You get into a house,
apparently unoccupied, and about two days later the owners
return and begin spinning a tale of woe. As I happen to know the
lingo fairly well I am usually called upon to deal with them.'

How *could* he cope with all these things? thought Joan. Guns, horses, men, billeting. In the ordinary way he would be just leaving school.

By the middle of May her own arrangements were fixed. Betty and some others were already at St. Valery. She was to join them at the end of the month.

. . . . . .

She put away her V.A.D. clothes—feeling a little apologetic towards them—'until next winter,' and went about town collecting Y.M. kit. Her heart rose in spite of her. The wards fell away; winter fell away; weariness fell away. France beckoned. The German advance had been checked. The softness of May was in the air. Hope crept forth like a butterfly from a chrysalis.

And as though to make things even pleasanter, Barbara Frewen was coming with her to the Camp; Barbara still nervy from her months at Dunkirk, where she had been nursing this last winter, and where shells had fallen from land and sea, and where the patients had had to be moved, night after night, down into sand-bagged dug-outs; Barbara with whom she had begun her war-work, under Y.M. auspices, three long years ago.

The last letter she had from Jimmy, just before she and Barbara sailed, brought her a happy impression of him.

'I should love to come out here with you "après la guerre," Joan, and show you the battery position we are in now, and the one we were in before. You could scarcely have a more striking contrast. I should be quite content to stop here for the duration.

'I am sitting out in the sun at this moment, behind the guns, with a telephone near my ear in case of need. One gun is firing leisurely, and life is very pleasant withal.

'There is none of that terrible fed-up-ness and depression which I used to try and fight last winter in that land of the dead which we have left. I think every soldier should go there first, when he comes out, and he will never have occasion to grumble again.

'Good luck to you, old thing!'

PART FOUR

SUMMER: 1918

'Wind of swift change, and clouds and hours that veer.'

Chapter One

IN a ramshackle house which had long stood empty in the middle of the sleepy fishing town of St. Valery, where the Somme ran into the sea, the five girls were billeted. Betty Paley, Barbara Frewen, Joan Seddon, Miss Bingham, and a Miss Duff, rather older than the rest, and known as 'Duffy.'

.At first the life seemed extraordinarily comfortable to Joan. To be able to sleep until eight, instead of only until six, was in itself luxury. And the amount of food! Meat, sugar, jam and butter in quantities that were amazing to anyone just out from meagrely-rationed England. And then no discipline, no sisters, no uniform (beyond blue overalls and head handkerchiefs), no regulations. Completely on your own—a little bunch of friends—with only old Doctor Ferguson over you, and a couple of negligible Christians.

There were two centres of work. The little Y.M. hut in the town, and the great Y.M. marquee at the Rest Camp. The girls took it in turns to work at each; three at the Camp, two at the hut.

The hut was like all other Y.M. huts, except that it was smaller and more congested. The Camp, which was two miles away, up on the cliffs, reminded Joan vividly of Ostrohove. There were the same rows of bell tents; the same thrilling smell of canvas and trodden grass; the same tea-urns on the counter; the same thick mugs. And in and out, in and out, the same khaki crowds of Tommies.

All the men were from the 3rd Army. Every fortnight a batch of fifteen hundred were withdrawn from the line and sent here on rest. And it was a real, not only a nominal rest for them. No fatigues. Absolute idleness. Dead-beat when they first arrived, they would go back fitter than they had been for months.

You were at it all day—either at the camp or at the hut. No times off except on Sundays. Yet Barbara and Joan agreed that once you had known the tiredness of hospital life any other tiredness hardly counted.

If you were working at the Camp you remained up there all day —lunching in a sort of 'dug-out' of packing-cases behind the counter. If working at the hut you lunched at the house.

There was a tall, mild, brown-eyed 'bonne,' called Berthe, who not only did the entire work of the house, but cooked excellently, and never seemed in the least put out however many people turned up to meals. And as often as not there were guests.

'Berthe, il y aura deux officiers pour le déjeuner,' Betty would call through the kitchen door, just before lunch; or: 'Il y aura quatre soldats pour le souper.'

'Bien, Mademoiselle,' Berthe would reply. (It was always 'bien, Mademoiselle.')

You could ask anyone you liked. In fact a certain amount of decorous entertaining was expected of the Y.M. girls. And the roomy old house was admirable for this. The dining-room led out of the 'salon,' and there was a small high-walled courtyard beyond. The furniture was scanty, but sufficient. A long table, a few chairs, some packing-cases and a piano.

For years Joan hadn't felt so buoyant and so free. It seemed a miracle that she should be out here. Pictures were printed on her mind—during that first week of sun and of great winds—which she knew would never be effaced. The changing lights on the Somme's mouth. The stretches of shining sand. The inrushing tide with its horses of foam. The little cobbled streets of the town. The walk up to the Camp, through woods, and along high chalky paths edged with cornfields and poppies. The glare of the great group of bell tents. The dilapidated, ivy-hung walls of their own house. And against all these settings the moving blue figures of the girls.

Yes, we're a *nice* little crowd! she thought, one evening, when they were all gathered at supper at the end of their day's work.

Duffy and Bingham she hardly knew, but liked already. Duffy, a kind and slightly perplexed person, who, because of her Scotch voice and substantial figure, gave the impression of being more capable than she really was. Bingham, brown-eyed, energetic and jolly. Betty, lovelier than ever in spite of the cloud over her. Barbara, her face thinner, more aquiline, but with the same undaunted spirit shining through. Queer that they should be working together again, she and Betty and Barbara, after a three years' separation, and such utterly different experiences.

And it seemed to Joan that over all that last summer of the war—which none of them knew was the last—lay the mild glow of autumn; just as over the summer of '15 had shone the yellow light of spring.

.   .   .   .   .   .

On Sunday morning, very early, the men from the Camp went back to the line. Their fortnight's rest was up. Joan and Barbara, who had arrived in the middle of the fortnight, had already made some friends among them, and were almost as sorry as the others to see them go.

On Saturday night the hut in the town was closed early, and all five girls met at the Camp for the farewell concert at eight. This took place in the huge entertainments tent, next to the canteen tent. The place was packed when they entered it. All available bench room was used up, and behind, as at the back of a theatre pit, men stood in serried rows.

The girls went up and sat on the stage, and Dr. Ferguson, who always conducted these entertainments, gave an address. The soldiers loved Dr. Ferguson—his broad-mindedness, his warmth, his humour. They attended the queer unorthodox services which he held, and they came to him, privately, in every sort of trouble. Curiously enough, colonels and generals liked him too, and any Y.M.C.A. centre of which he was head was certain of success.

The two Christians were also on the stage: Mr. Mackintosh, who played accompaniments excellently; and Mr. Barnes, who did nothing in particular, and lived in a perpetual state of grievance.

The concert ran on the usual lines of soldier concerts, but it was more uproarious than any that Joan remembered at Boulogne.

Two officers sang; several men; then Joan, then Bingham. Joan sang 'Black-Eyed Susans,' and the Waltz song from 'The Maid of the Mountains,' and both were enthusiastically received; so was Bingham's 'Good-bye-ee' which she sang with a full-blooded jollity and lack of restraint that brought shouts and whistles of joy from the men.

By ten-thirty it was over, and to-night, instead of going down to the house as usual, the girls slept up in Camp. There was a tent, standing outside the lines, in a patch of clover-field, that was detailed for their special use; and here they undressed, and crept between brown army blankets on five little folding beds.

It was the queerest night, if it could be called a night, that Joan had ever spent. A gale—the culmination of the high winds of the week—whipped and tore against the canvas. The moon, from behind racing clouds, shed a wan light through the chinks. And if the noise alone had not been sufficient to keep her awake, there was the thought of all those men going back to the Front in a few hours' time. Were *they* sleeping? she wondered.

At 1.30 a.m. an orderly called them—tapping discreetly on the canvas—and brought them two buckets of cold water. They washed, dressed and crept out into the windy moonlight and across to the Y.M. tent. Outside it they split up packing-cases and lit the great boilers. Urns were filled and heaved into position; large trays of biscuits and of cigarettes were placed between; and then the tent was opened. For two hours a stream of soldiers shuffled before the candle-lit counter. Silently they took their cups of tea; silently held out their water-bottles to be filled. Rifle-barrels and ruddy faces appeared for a moment in the circle of flickering flame and passed on into gloom. Outside, the dawn broke, green and wild.

By four-thirty the tent was empty; and by five the column of fifteen hundred men and their officers was marching down the road to St. Valery station—the girls, in a little group, watching them go. Dogged, resigned, bent under their loads the men passed. Guards, gunners, New Zealanders, Jocks—men from every regiment of the 3rd Army. A few cheered; most of them tried to smile; but there was no light-heartedness. Unlike those who used to march off from Ostrohove in 1915, in all the exuberance of their untried spirits, these knew what they were going to.

Tramp . . . Tramp . . . Tramp . . .

The end of the column became a cloud of dust; and the girls turned sadly away, and went back through the deserted tents.

An orderly had prepared breakfast for them, and Joan was surprised to find with what avidity—in spite of the emotions of the last few hours—she fell upon the food.

'When you've had nothing since yesterday tea-time,' Bingham pointed out, munching her ham and eggs, 'and you've been working practically all night, you need a bit of stoking.'

By the time they had finished the sun was brilliant, but the wind still high, and they trudged the two miles back to the house with bent heads, and overalls billowing behind.

The rest of Sunday was passed in sleep and in letter-writing.

.   .   .   .   .   .

On Monday the Camp was full again, and, during lulls in the serving, Joan talked to several of the new men, and noticed how others, too shy to come forward, sat about with eyes fixed in a dog-like gaze on the blue heads behind the counter. A sergeant suddenly got up, lurched forward, and asked for a mug of tea.

'I thought I should have gone mad,' he declared, 'when first I saw you ladies, and heard you talking English.' He was choking, almost inarticulate.

Bingham and Joan had been detailed to dine in mess that evening. Every other Monday Colonel Noble, the Camp Commandant, formally invited two of the Y.M. ladies to dine. He disliked having to ask them, being, as Bingham remarked, 'an old-fashioned stick,' but had been constrained to do so by Dr. Ferguson.

'And of course it's a jolly good idea,' said Bingham. 'It puts us at once on the right footing with the new officers, and makes it easy for us to ask them to the house.'

Joan—never having dined in an officers' mess before, either in peace-time or in war-time—was a little alarmed at first, but she soon found she was enjoying herself very much.

The tables were arranged in the form of a rectangular horse-shoe: Colonel Noble, looking like a sad greyhound, sat at the top, and Bingham, flanked by a middle-aged major, sat on his left.

Joan was round the corner—much more happily placed—between a Captain Warren, dark, thin and married, and a Captain Lee, younger, pink-faced and square. Both had been up at Cambridge a few years ago; both were communicative and extremely easy to get on with. Never had Joan been so bombarded with questions about herself. What was she doing here? What had she done before? What was she going to do afterwards? Where did she live? At last she burst out laughing, and Warren apologised.

'What ghastly manners!' he said. 'You must forgive us. You see, this is the first time we've set eyes on an Englishwoman for over eight months.'

After dinner they insisted on escorting the girls home, and for the whole two miles Warren poured into Joan's ear stories about his wife and his small daughter. Nothing could have shown her so clearly the lonely wretchedness that army life must entail for a sensitive, home-loving creature like this. It was as though a banked-up stream had broken loose.

When Joan and Bingham got in they found that the others had all been back some time.

'We start selling fish-and-chips to-morrow,' announced Betty. 'I've made all the arrangements.'

The fish-and-chip trade had been so successful last summer, at the other camp, that Betty and Bingham had decided to inaugurate it here.

'Nothing like it for keeping the men sober,' said Bingham. 'Makes 'em feel sort of domestic. By the way, can you cook?' she asked Joan.

'No, she can only dress wounds,' said Betty. 'But I'm going to take her under my wing to-morrow and show her.'

'Right you are! And I'll take Frewen another day. These
V.A.D.s, you know . . .! Why did we have 'em out, Paley?'
Barbara and Joan looked at each other and laughed.
'For a rest cure!' said Joan.
'H'm! Wait till you've been out here a month!'
Still ragging they trailed upstairs to bed.

A ray of moonlight lay upon the bare boards of the front bedroom and faintly lit three humped horizontal figures—Betty's
and Bingham's and Joan's; three packing-cases on which were
stuck three stumps of army candle; three trunks with a folded pile
of clothes on each.

On the opposite side of the passage Barbara and Duffy, each in a
small separate room, were sleeping too.

. . . . . .

Next day, after lunch, the tent was closed to the men until
four o'clock; and it was during this interval that the cooking
began.

In the little open-air kitchen, a few yards outside the tent, Betty
and Joan stood over pans of boiling fat, the blue smoke of it
ascending into their faces, the smuts from the iron chimney falling
on to their heads. An old Frenchwoman was there to 'éplucher
les poissons' and help peel potatoes. One after the other, dozens
and dozens of them, the little flat damp plaices went sizzling into
the pans; became brown; were removed, and put to keep warm in
the great wire fish-basket hanging over the stove. At intervals
there was the chopping of wood to be done, and the shovelling
of coke, for it was important that the fire should be kept up, and
the fat never for a moment be allowed to cool.

But from four o'clock onwards, when the tent reopened, Betty
cooked alone, and Joan was kept running backwards and forwards,
between kitchen and tent, carrying the platefuls of ready-fried
fish to the queue of waiting soldiers. As fast as the stuff came from
the kitchen it was bought, carried off and devoured. Six or seven
hundred fish, with their corresponding helpings of potato, were
sold that day.

By eight o'clock Betty and Joan were black with mingled soot, grease and perspiration.

After this initiation Joan was able to tackle the cooking on her own.

. . . . . .

Sunday—a free day. A little crowd of officers to tea—Warren and Lee among them. A trestle table out in the courtyard. Strawberries. Playing and singing in the 'salon' afterwards. Warren showing you snap-shots of his wife and child. An atmosphere of home.

. . . . . .

Some of the officers gave a dinner one night at the Colonne de Bronze. All the girls went except Barbara, who was definitely 'off' festivities. The 'Colonne' was the only hotel in the town, and was considered tolerably respectable now, although until lately it had had a lurid name.

They sat at a corner table in the dingy-mirrored dining-room, and were waited upon by Angèle, the prop of the 'Colonne,' one of those short-legged French *bonnes* with greasy black hair and a beard, the only reason for whose virtue is their extreme ugliness.

The food was good and there was a warmth and friendliness over the little party. When the girls got back, Joan went along to Barbara's room, and hovered in the doorway.

'I wish you'd been there, Barbara, they were all so nice. I believe you'd have enjoyed it.'

Barbara looked up from her letters and shook her head, smiling. 'At one time, Joany. But I just feel incapable of making any social effort nowadays.'

'You do like the life here?'

'*Love* it! And so long as I'm left to myself to work among the Tommies I'm perfectly happy.'

Joan lingered. She thought of David and of Sam Wyndham. She wanted to cry out: 'Barbara, *how* do you carry on?' But what an inane question. People just did.

And as though in answer to her unspoken words Barbara said:

'I don't think, you know, that I realise about them yet—not with the whole of me—only with my mind. The fact that the war's still going on makes me feel that they're still in it—still fighting somewhere. I don't suppose I *shall* realise—until peace.'

That was it. She wouldn't realise—thousands of women wouldn't realise—until peace.

.   .   .   .   .   .

The fortnight came to an end, and once more it was Saturday night, and once more the five girls were sitting on the platform while Dr. Ferguson gave his farewell address. And then there were songs, and at about eleven the tent emptied itself.

Outside, a little group of officers was waiting to say good-bye. 'You don't know what it's meant to us—your house, your friendliness. Never forget.' Warren's face under the star-light was pale and drawn. Lee's handshake nearly broke your bones. Hateful partings . . .

The girls went over to their sleeping-tent and got between the blankets. What a different night from the last up here! No wind. No noise. Hardly a breath of air.

A short while later they were up, had lit the boilers and got the tea-urns ready.

Two hours of handing over mugs, of filling water-bottles, of selling biscuits and chocolates. This lot of men was cheerier than the other had been. 'Had a fine time down here!' 'Don't worry, Miss, *we'll* finish the war for you! They're only waiting for *us*!' And a sergeant thrust over the counter a great bouquet of flowers on which was a label: 'To the ladies of the Y.M.C.A., with the love of two thousand Byng Boys.'

From the side of the road the girls watched them marching away. It was worse than last time—far worse—in spite of the warm bright sun. You knew so many more of them individually.

Chapter Two

AS time went on and the five girls fell into their stride of work, and the 3rd Army Rest Camp became more and more their home, they developed—like different members of the same family —their own special departments.

The counting of the day's takings was Bingham's job. At the end of the day she was to be seen hunched on a stool by the counter, her neat head bent absorbedly among piles of coins and notes, alone, or with a Christian beside her, deaf to her surroundings.

Singing at concerts fell chiefly upon Joan; and she took ever greater delight in it, and in the voices of the gathered men as they roared the choruses.

Barbara—whether at the Camp or, later, down at the house— seemed always to be surrounded by half-done-up parcels. The men would bring her 'souvenirs' bought in the town—frightful cushion-squares painted with pictures of flaming Ypres—aprons —shawls—scarves—which they handed over to be sent to their women-folk in England. They would never have bought half the quantity if they hadn't known that they would be saved the trouble of wrapping up and of addressing.

Duffy had undertaken the flowers, and, with clover, or moon-daisies, or sea-lavender from the fields around, kept both the hut and the tent wonderfully decorated.

Betty did the catering, and this involved endless interviews with all sorts of odd people—French and British—about fruit, potatoes, fish, coke and fat. Neither the Quartermaster-Sergeant at the Camp nor the dirtiest old villager could daunt her, or could fob her off with stuff she considered inferior. Joan was amazed at her practical powers—having remembered her in pre-war days as rather dreamy.

And of the five girls it was Betty who got on best with 'drunks.' Whenever any soldiers 'a little the worse' staggered into the tent, just as it was closing, it was to Betty that they somehow gravitated, and into whose patient ear they poured their confidences.

'I simply *can't* send them away,' she would say to the others, who would be waiting to clean up. 'They're so disarming and pathetic!'

'My dear, I believe you actually *prefer* them in that condition!' Joan laughed, one evening.

A bleary-eyed Jock had just pushed his money across to Betty with a request to her to take all he had and to keep it for him. 'I'll trusht you,' he had said, genially. 'You've got a fashe I can trusht. Ev'ry hair 'v y'r head'sh precioush t'me. Nobody sh'll hurt a hairr.'

It was to Betty, too, that men came telling her she reminded them of their wives. On one occasion a corporal, who had been looking at her attentively for some time, got up and came over.

'You *do* put me in mind of me wife, Miss,' he said, and drew out his pocket-book and produced a photograph.

Betty looked at it with interest. She saw the seated figure of a large woman with spreading hips, a melon-shaped but rather severe countenance, flat black hair and pince-nez. Leaning dejectedly on either side of her, in velvet suits, were two small boys.

'Yes,' she said gravely. 'I think I see what you mean. She's— she's a fine-looking woman, isn't she?'

'One of the best is my Meg! But the nippers take after their father more, don't you think, Miss?'

.   .   .   .

From time to time 'Brass Hats' would descend from their remote altitudes and inspect the Camp. One morning no less a personage than the Deputy Adjutant-General of the 3rd Army strode into the Y.M. tent, and after a glance round came up to the counter. Betty answered his questions and listened to his abrupt appreciative remarks.

'You're doing excellent work,' he informed her. 'Army Head-quarters is very pleased with the Y.M. in this Camp.'

'It's a great privilege to be here,' said Betty, remembering that it was to the D.A.G. that she and her friends owed their presence in the army area at all.

'Colonel Noble behaving nicely to you?' he asked, with the suspicion of a twinkle.

Betty's dark eyelashes flickered, but she made no reply. None was needed. The D.A.G. perfectly understood, and, remarking that the weather was very fine, saluted and strode off.

It was well known that old Colonel Noble resented having women in his Rest Camp at all, and only endured them because, quite obviously, in some queer way, they kept the men amused and reduced the number of 'crimes.'

Another time General S. came round and, escorted by Colonel Noble, made the most thorough investigation into every corner of the Camp. At last he penetrated to the Y.M. kitchen, where Bingham, in a filthy overall, was frying fish. Impressed and amused, he asked her detailed questions as to how many fish were sold per day, where they were bought, how cooked, how served; and when she had satisfied his curiosity he selected one potato chip, fried it himself under her guidance, and put it in a Y.M. envelope 'to take back to Byng,' he said.

'Well,' remarked Joan, when she was told of this, later, 'it's a consoling thought that we're a subject of such interest and mirth at Army Headquarters. Perhaps we do justify our existence after all!'

She often wondered how much of an 'influence for good' the Y.M. really was. Were the men, for instance, who crowded to the tent, who talked to one over the counter, who roared responses to one's songs, the same who hung about a certain fruit-shop in the town kept by two powdered Frenchwomen?

'It's the worst house in St. Valery,' Mackintosh had told her, 'but these women are clever enough not to give themselves away, and so the police have no power to evict them. And mind you,' he had added, 'it's not only the hardened Colonials they get into their clutches, it's the under-aged boys as well.'

Joan, though saddened and sick at heart, was unable to feel so ferociously about it all as Mackintosh, or to join in his pious diatribes against the 'sinfulness' of the troops. It was all natural enough; and a soldier had no need to be especially vicious if, after coming back from months of hell to a period of idleness, he wanted 'love.' The pity was that no better sort was provided. Boys who should still have been at home—still at school—first learnt of it like this. Yet there were people (her Uncle Robert was one) who talked of the 'uplifting influence of war,' and of how it 'made men of boys.' It certainly did. The little Scotch orderly who helped at the hut had been sent to hospital diseased. That was a case she knew of, but there were probably dozens—hundreds —of others.

No, there was nothing to be done, Joan supposed. Nothing but to go on, in one's rather futile way, making that centre of respectability, the Y.M., as attractive as possible.

. . . . . .

Heat, heat. Blinding, the cobbled streets of the town as you went to and from the hut. Blinding, the chalky road as you went to and from the Camp. Corn-fields and clover-fields shimmering in the heat. Shoes thick with white dust. Blue overalls filmed with it. All the little bell tents rolled up from the bottom to let in air. Soldiers sitting about in shirt-sleeves, caps pushed back from damp foreheads. Groups of them interminably playing 'House.' 'Come on, you lucky lads, who'll take a card? Forty-eight. Pheasant's eye. Twenty-five. Top o' the House. Clickety-click. House full.' Droning voices on the summer air. Smell of clover; smell of fish; smell of canvas. Sunsets reflected, red, in the salt marshes as you walked home.

. . . . .

Spasmodic entertaining still went on at the house, but it was often less of a pleasure than an uphill grind, for the 'pukka' officer at this period of the war, was rare. Nothing was more tiring than steering a steady course between friendliness and stand-offishness with little 'T.G.s' who would try to be gallant.

After a particularly difficult fortnight Joan declared that she couldn't be bored with any more of them, and if the next campful were going to be like this one, she would take no part in hospitable lunch-parties.

'But you *must* remember,' sighed Betty, who suffered even more than Joan, for she had a veritable passion for good breeding, 'that, awful as they are, they've had just as bad a time as the others, and are going back to just the same conditions. We *mustn't* only be nice to the nice ones!'

.   .   .   .   .   .

Towards the end of July a burst of rain and wind succeeded the fine weather. The little trenches that criss-crossed the Camp were running rivulets. The chalky dust became white paste. Ragged clouds were blown across the sky.

On one of these wild evenings, just as the tent was being closed, an officer turned up and asked for Miss Paley. His face was vaguely familiar to Joan—square, with mild brown eyes—but even when he told her his name she couldn't place him.

'Someone to see you, Betty,' she called over to the kitchen. And when her friend approached: 'A Captain Pritchard,' she said.

'Lor!' muttered Betty, evidently not at all pleased; then changed her expression to one of amiable surprise, as the officer came shyly forward to greet her.

Joan heard him explaining his presence—something about 'Ordnance Depot'—'Abbeville'—'only just heard you were here'—heard him accept Betty's invitation to supper at the house, and was just moving off to a concert in the other tent when Betty said to her: 'Must you sing to-night, Joan? Can't you come back with us now?'

There was a look in Betty's eyes—a veiled appeal for protection —which made Joan hesitate. But after all the men were waiting for her, and she couldn't let them down. 'I shan't be long,' she said. And Betty turned resignedly off with Captain Pritchard.

When Joan got back to the house at about half-past nine the others had finished their supper.

'Didn't he stay, then?' she asked.

'No, had to get back to Abbeville,' said Betty vaguely.

Later, when they were going to bed, she explained everything. Luckily Bingham was helping Barbara do up parcels downstairs, so that for once the two friends were alone.

'Old admirer,' said Betty. 'Used to hang about just before the war.'

'Oh, *I* remember!' cried Joan. 'I thought I'd seen him before. Pritchard—yes. They look so different in uniform. *Well?*'

'Well, he turned up in Boulogne last winter, and since then he's been writing pretty regularly. I had a feeling that when I saw him next I should probably be "for it," but I wasn't in the least expecting him *here*.

'It was an *awful* walk, Joan. I was cross and tired anyhow, and there was that howling gale in our faces, and though I went as fast as I could, and pretended that I found it difficult to hear what he said, I couldn't prevent a proposal. How he had any hopes I don't know. There was nothing in my letters to encourage him. He was terribly depressed when I said "no." Almost sulked. Wouldn't come in to supper, and got straight on to his motor-bike and rode off. Well, it's over now, anyhow.'

'Oh, Betty, *couldn't* you?' said Joan.

'What, marry him? Utterly out of the question.'

'M'm, I suppose so. But, oh dear, I wish there was somebody. I want you to forget.'

'Can't, that's just it.' Betty was sitting on the edge of her bed, brushing the long ripples of her hair. She looked up, a sheaf of it on either side of her face. 'All the time Pritchard was talking I could almost have killed him for not being Guy. Poor little man —and he's so faithful and good.'

Joan gazed at her. 'Damn!' she said. And then: 'Is he married yet?'

'Guy? Oh yes, six months ago. Saw it in *The Times*.'

Betty extinguished her candle and snuggled down. From over the blanket she saw, with one eye, Joan, still sitting, arms clasped round knees, her hair a halo.

'Darling—I suppose you are—what's called "over" Paul Wentworth now?'

Joan nodded slowly.

'Yes. That was a fever, terrible and blissful while it lasted, but it died. Queer that any man should be able to hurt one like that— have one so completely in his power. Good for one, probably. Good for *me*, anyhow. I'd always been so cold and sure. But I wouldn't not have been in love with him for anything.'

The entrance of Bingham put an end to further intimacies.

.   .   .   .   .   .

There came a letter from Jimmy in which he talked of comfortable billets, of green grass, and of hostile artillery being very quiet. At the end he said: 'I may be able to procure a car in about a fortnight's time, and come over and see you. We are not so very far from one another.'

'Oh,' sighed Joan, 'if he *could* manage to come!'

There was a short letter from Colin, too. He wrote very seldom nowadays. He had taken over two months going to India, as the ship had had to sail far out to sea on account of submarines. He was now a captain in the 2nd/1st Brahmans, and was having an interesting time. 'Although,' he said, 'Anglo-Indians are dried both in body and soul.'

Joan found it difficult to think of Colin out there—found it rather difficult to think of him at all. The present life was absorbing her so entirely, she was giving herself out in so many different directions, that her more personal problems and relationships had fallen into the background.

.   .   .   .   .   .

One night there was an air-raid.

The three girls in the front bedroom were first made aware of it by the voice of Duffy saying: 'I believe they're coming nearer!' and opened sleepy eyes to see Duffy's large behind silhouetted in the window. Duffy, it seemed, had heard the throbbing of the 'planes half an hour ago, and her own window not commanding such a good view she had come over here.

Her wholly unterrified absorption in the heavens rather irritated Betty, who, in any case, disliked being wakened without good cause, and she told Duffy to come in.

'Ourrs or theirrs?' murmured Duffy, ignoring her, while the humming overhead grew louder.

'Whichever they are, for the Lord's sake come away from that window!'

BANG . . .! BANG . . .!

'Well, that's *theirs* anyhow! Of course if you want a bomb on your head . . .'

'Not very near,' said the unperturbed Duffy. 'Over by Le Crotoire.'

Le Crotoire was a village on the other side of the mouth of the Somme where the French had an aerodrome, and it was this place, and not St. Valery, that was the frequent object of enemy bombs.

After this, throughout the first part of August, there were raids almost every night, but only one of them was at all disturbing.

Betty and Joan, who had been working down at the hut, had gone to bed early, and were lying reading, when suddenly the guns began. For a little time they took no notice, and then a series of crashes made them lift their eyes from their books.

'Better come down,' drawled Betty. 'I'm not really brave over air-raids, you know—except when I'm asleep.'

So they put on coats and went to the dining-room. The noise only lasted for about five minutes, and just as they were going upstairs again, thankful that it had been so short a raid, the others came in from the Camp.

'We were caught as we got to the edge of the town,' said Bingham, 'and we sheltered in that stone archway in the old wall.'

'And there was such a kind Tommy with us,' added Barbara. 'He huddled us into a group, and then planted himself firmly in front like a sentinel, and kept telling us not to be frightened.'

'I may say,' remarked Bingham, 'that he was more than half drunk, and would have been perfectly useless if any of us had been hit!'

She was still talking about their adventure when, quite unexpectedly—for the gun-fire had ceased for some time—there was a shattering crash, followed by a kind of windy roar as though all the houses in the town were falling.

'I think the cellar is indicated,' said Bingham, and they all trooped down.

Certainly no one could say they *looked* frightened, thought Joan, as she surveyed the little group crouched on the dirty stone steps, holding bits of candle and reading books and papers. Duffy wore rather a glum expression, but that was not because she was minding the raid, but because she had been that morning into Abbeville, on a visit to the dentist, and had had nearly all her bottom teeth removed. Joan herself was in the frozen condition which always overtook her on this sort of occasion; she was not aware of fear, but she felt that if anything were required of her beyond keeping still she would be totally unable to function.

There was one more resounding crash, a sound of broken glass, the old house shook to its foundations, and then there was silence. After a period of waiting the girls crept up to bed and slept heavily till morning.

It was found on inspection that most of the long salon window-panes had fallen from their frames and were lying shivered outside. Several houses close to had been badly damaged, but, surprisingly enough, no lives lost.

．　　　．　　　．　　　．　　　．　　　．

During the spell of great heat which followed the girls sometimes slept up at the Camp. They found that on these occasions they woke in the mornings with an extraordinary freshness.

One night Joan, with nothing on but her night-gown and a trailing blanket, went outside the tent, and sat for an hour on the grass gazing at the great throbbing stars until she hardly knew where or who she was. Over the water, at Le Crotoire, the little 'planes, like fire-flies, went circling and dropping. The bell tents loomed dimly white. The whole Camp slept.

She went back to bed, and woke to the smell of clover; to the voices of soldiers; to the sound of the cracked bugle calling: 'Come to the cook-house door, boys, come to the cook-house door'; to the stir and radiance of a new morning. Oh, if these days could go on for ever! Dear fields! Dear summer! Dear, dear Camp!

.   .   .   .   .   .

The middle of August brought the best crowd of men and officers that the Camp had yet known.

On the first night Betty and Joan dined in mess, and one glance round was enough to reassure them. Somehow they contrived to sit opposite to one another, and on either side of them sat smiling subalterns—some Scotch—some English—with pleasant faces and pleasant voices. On Joan's left was a very youthful Coldstream Guardsman.

Conversation was as effortless as it was absurd. Joan found herself, at one point, talking about the delights of dressing up and of charades.

'Oh, used you to do much of it?' asked the boy, brightly. 'It must have been a long time ago. I *mean*,' he added, at sight of Joan's mock distress, 'it must have been before the war.'

'It was,' she said. 'I haven't had time since. I suppose *you* were in the fourth form at Eton when war broke out?'

Amazed, he admitted that he was.

'But how did you guess *Eton*?' he demanded.

Joan only smiled.

His name was Foley. She liked him. He was conventional, of course, and would probably, in middle-age, develop a rigidity and narrow-mindedness; but now, with his charm of manner, his youth, and good spirits, he was distinctly attaching. She thought she had never seen anybody look quite so clean.

He, with four or five others, took the girls home, and on the way he talked to Joan about his training at Windsor, and about his very brief experiences at the Front. At the door they all saluted in the moonlight and went back to Camp.

'Nice little bunch!' said Betty. 'I rather feel they'll belong to us this fortnight.'

They did. They blew in and out of the house as though it were their home. They did endless odd jobs. They nailed cretonne on to packing-cases; helped Betty pour oil into the ears of the half-dozen mangy cats she had collected from the village and was nursing back to health; cleared away plates at meal-times. There was Foley, and there was Kilpatrick, and there was 'Scotty,' and there was 'Tufty.' All were under twenty, and all were full of fun. Tufty got his nickname from the tuft of mossy hair upon his forehead. He wore shorts, and was very thin and eager-eyed, and looked about fifteen. 'I can't *think*,' Betty declared, 'how his mother could bear to let him come to the war.'

There was also a Captain Catesby of the Coldstream Guards— 'old Caters,' as Foley affectionately called him—but he didn't come as often as the others. He was large and quiet and fatherly, and had a yellow moustache, and was accompanied everywhere by a gigantic yellow dog, of no known breed, which he had picked up in the village, and was going to take back with him to the Front.

The boys were keen to get up a show at the Camp—some sort of elaborate charade that would be almost a play—and the Y.M. girls said they would be delighted to lend them clothes and props. and give them rehearsal room, but that take part they would not— they had neither the time nor the energy.

'Come down here next Sunday,' they said, 'and stay all day, and we'll help you make things.'

But when Sunday came, Betty and Joan remembered that they had promised to go a joy-ride to Abbeville with another officer; and it was with hearts torn both ways that at about eleven they left a courtyard full of hilarious boys and sped off in a car.

In less than an hour they had arrived; the car was parked; and the three of them wandered off to inspect the town.

About half the houses were destroyed, or partially destroyed.

Piles of masonry lay about, and charred wooden beams. Names of shops could still be read—'Boulangerie'—'Coiffeur'—'Charcuterie'—but roofs had fallen in, and doors and windows were non-existent. They passed one house the whole of whose front had been blown away, but whose floors remained; and beds, dressing-tables and dusty mirrors looked forlornly down on the curious. The church was untouched, but the group of statues in the middle of the square stood headless.

'Not that *that* matters much!' observed Betty. 'It's a hideous group.'

They lunched at the 'Savoy,' one of the doorless and windowless restaurants which still miraculously carried on, and afterwards they drove into Creçy Forest.

Creçy Forest was all that they had expected it to be—a real forest of romance. Long green glades disappeared between gigantic tree-trunks. There was a warm smell of moss and honeysuckle. Wandering about they came upon a beech of even greater dimensions than the rest, and learnt from a little placard that his name was 'Richard,' and that he was three hundred years old.

When they got home the courtyard was still flooded with boys, and everywhere was a litter of string, nails, silver paper, calico and cardboard. Barbara, brandishing a teapot, her eyes starry, her overall full of pins, looked as though she were superintending a party of boy-scouts.

Afterwards there were songs in the salon. Everyone sang—from Tufty, who had a delightful voice, to Foley, who had none. And then the whole crowd departed, shouting with laughter, fighting each other with stage swords, leaping, and reeling up the road, leaving themselves barely time to arrive in Camp for dinner.

Joan, watching them, dared not think of next Sunday when they would be gone. She felt towards them all—towards Foley, Scotty, Tufty and Kilpatrick—as though they had been her own small brothers, and she longed to hug them as she would have hugged Jimmy.

.   .   .   .   .   .

Saturday night came inevitably round, and the farewell concert, enlivened by the charade, was the most successful yet given. The scenes were all, except the last, laid in St. Valery—starting with St. Valery in Norman times, when William the Conqueror had sailed from it, to St. Valery at the present day, dominated by the 3rd Army Rest Camp.

In the last scene Tufty and Kilpatrick, dressed as girls, received home their soldier husbands—Catesby and Foley. The audience rocked with delight at the realism of the stage embraces, and at the lines: 'How long is your leave, dear?' 'Leave, darling? This isn't leave, we're home for good. The war's over!' the curtain came down on a roar.

In the wings, afterwards, the boys were so excited and so pleased with themselves that they could hardly be got to change. They fooled about in their borrowed frocks and hats, and it was half-past eleven before the last good-byes had been said and the five Y.M. girls were in bed in their tent. Poor Foley, to his disgust, was not going off with the others in the morning. An attack of dysentery had rendered him temporarily unfit for active service.

By two-thirty the men, huge in their equipment, were crowding to the counter. This morning, in among the tea-urns, the cups, and the cigarettes, stood great bunches of heather—sent to Duffy, the day before, from Scotland. Each man as he passed was given a sprig. 'To bring you luck, though it isn't white,' said the girls. The success of this heather was extraordinary. If a man had been overlooked in the rush, he came up later and asked for some. One stammered thanks; another blinked back tears; another looked speechlessly at the donor, jerked up his elbow in a hurried salute, and turned away. Great hulking fighters unable to hide their emotion at the sudden gift of tiny sprigs of heather. The whole campful hated leaving. It had been an especially happy fortnight for men as well as for officers.

In brilliant sunshine they marched down the road, the detachment of Guards at the head; Captain Catesby at the head of the Guards, and at the head of Captain Catesby, big Yellow Dog straining at his lead. Every soldier had his piece of heather stuck in his cap or in his button-hole. Every soldier who, an hour ago, in the Y.M. tent, had been nearly crying, cheered as he passed. The whole column was a crash of feet, a roar of voices. The officer boys threw gay salutes. By nightfall they would all have been swallowed up into the offensive. For the 3rd Army had begun to advance.

.   .   .   .   .   .

The first day of the new fortnight was one of such intense heat that it beat all previous records.

The Y.M. tent was seething, and in that atmosphere of sweaty uniforms and of baked canvas the girls worked, stifled. Impossible to keep count of the number of urns of tea and of lemonade that were got through—the number of great cases of cigarettes that were wrenched open and emptied. Noses shone. Faces dripped. Bingham, frying like a maniac, was one besmutted human lump of grease. Joan, dumping down plates on the counter, splashed pools of perspiration beside them. Duffy wilted at the tea-urn. On, on, through the afternoon, until nearly nine o'clock, they were at it, while outside the chalky earth quivered and blistered and the sky was a bowl of hard metallic blue.

'Miss Seddon, will you sing?'

Mackintosh, clean and jaunty, had stepped round to ask her.

'Oh, Mr. Mackintosh—to-night?'

'Yes, specially to-night. The entertainments tent is crowded.'

Row upon row of ruddy-faced expectant soldiers. You had no strength, no voice. Never mind—fake the notes. Force them up into a ring.

The steady deep booming of claps and cheers. Thank God these men, just down from the line, were not critical!

Out into a breathless night, an Italian night. The moon like a great lamp. Little Foley running hatless after you down the road; pouring out his distress at being left behind in Camp; adding hastily that of course there were compensations. 'But my own company going over the top you know—old Caters leading it, and me not there!' Joan agreed it was damnable; loved him for his young and chafing sense of duty; thought what luck it was that he *had* been kept back.

.   .   .   .   .

For the next week Foley practically lived at the house. He was feeling wretchedly ill, though he tried to disguise it, and now that his friends had gone back to the Front he was low in spirits too.

Joan, out of work hours, gave him all the time and sympathy she could, and gradually his interest turned from himself to her. He asked her what she was going to do in the autumn when the Camp closed down. Told her about his home in Essex. More and more he allowed his feelings to show through the beautifully-carved crust of his manners.

'After the war, Joan—I may call you Joan sometimes?—after the war you *must* come and stay with us.'

Foley was referred to, now, by the others as 'Joan's baby Guardsman.'

.   .   .   .   .

The news was getting better and better. The British had taken Thiepval Ridge; were on the outskirts of Bapaume; were forging ahead in the terrible bit of ground between Albert and Arras.

Foley had a letter from 'old Caters' which he showed to Joan. The 2nd Coldstream Guards had caught it hot at Havraincourt. Nearly all the best officers had been killed. Catesby himself was writing from hospital. His right leg had been amputated, and he had been recommended for the V.C. He announced both facts without comment, and added: 'You were well out of it, my son!'

'Well out of it?' Little Foley's pale eyelashes were wet with tears. Joan had never seen him so shaken. 'Kept down here unfit —still unfit—while those fellows . . .'

There was nothing of comfort to be said to him. She thought of old Caters marching out of Camp ten days ago at the head of the column, and now lying maimed in hospital; and then, a little irrelevantly, she wondered what he had done with Yellow Dog.

.   .   .   .   .

During an idle half-hour at the Camp, before the cooking had begun, Joan was sitting in the clover-patch by the sleeping-tent. She looked away across the stretch of salty grass below the cliffs, and there, all in among the pools and up to the edge of the far-out sea, were naked soldiers. Hundreds of white bodies running and leaping in the sunlight—like human beings in the Golden Age. This was right. This was what men were made for; not to blast each other to bits with senseless machinery, but to run and bathe in sunlight and sea—naked, happy, whole.

.   .   .   .   .   .

Early in September little Foley was packed off to No. 2 Stationary Hospital at Abbeville. He was getting no better in the Rest Camp. He said good-bye to everyone. With Joan he had only a moment alone. White-faced and choking, he held her hand; tried to thank her, and turned quickly away.

How people came and went! Just as one grew fond of them it was time to say good-bye. And if, after the war, one ever met them again, how much of the queer unnameable emotion—partly in-love-ness, partly gratitude—which they now felt for one would remain?

Chapter Three

ONE evening Jack Seddon arrived unexpectedly at the Camp, and stood at the counter, slim and resplendent in red-tabbed tunic, while Joan was sent for to the kitchen.

He had been on his Divisional Staff for some months.

'Jacko!' she cried. 'Well, one never knows, does one!'

'Come for a drive? I've got a car here. We might go and dine at Le Tréport.'

Joan's expostulations were cut short by the others, who told her to leave the frying and push off with her cousin.

The drive by the coast to Le Tréport was sheer delight. The car leapt along the roads, and Joan, once seated in its luxurious depths, felt that nothing would be able to drag her out again. Jack, however, called it 'a filthy old bus,' and said that he had planned to bring the smartest car at Divisional H.Q., but had been unable, at the last minute, to get hold of it.

It was good to see Jack again. He had the same gay grey eyes, the same simplicity and charm; but the fresh pink of his cheeks had become a pale, settled tan, and she noticed that between his bursts of laughter he wore a strained expression.

During the quarter of an hour or so that they strolled on the beach before dinner, Joan realised how much he had inwardly changed from the cheerful Jacko of old. Ever since the winter of 1916, when he had gone back to France after recovering from the wound in his foot, he had never been out of the fighting. All his original friends had been killed. He had made new ones, and they had been killed too. The bally old war had been going on too long, he said, and even if we were victorious he didn't exactly see what good victory would do us. There would be awful loneliness —all the best chaps gone. He talked of the March retreat, when, from captain, he had found himself acting colonel to the battalion —or what remained of it.

'The mess, Joan! You can't conceive of the mess! Nobody knowing anything. Thousands and thousands of uselessly thrown away lives. God, our Staff! The wonder to me—specially since I've seen Staff work from the inside—is that we weren't beaten long ago. Of course the fact is we *were*—but didn't know it, fortunately.'

At the hotel where they dined they were joined by two friends of Jack's—a Major Evans and a little captain called 'Bob.' The four had a merry meal together, and afterwards drove back to St. Valery along the darkening roads, a stormy sunset behind them.

The salon looked welcoming and cosy as they entered. A log fire burned in the grate—for the evenings were getting chilly now—and the other girls were grouped around it.

'Hullo, Betty! Nice to see you,' said Jack. Introductions were performed, and the large khaki figures sat down, where they could, among the blue.

The flames licked up the chimney. Voices hummed. Joan talked to 'Bob,' and discovered that he had been at Camberwell, in one of the officers' wards, in July '16. Major Evans said little, but made up for lack of conversation by gazing at Betty. Betty certainly was looking her loveliest. The blue head-handkerchief always suited her, and to-night she happened to be wearing a string of beads that exactly matched the soft dark blue of her eyes. Her cheeks, in the firelight, had a pastel bloom. When she looks like that, thought Joan, I wonder that any man can prevent himself getting up and kissing her!

At about eleven the three men departed. Divisional H.Q. was only about an hour and a half's run away.

'Don't suppose I shall be able to come again, though,' said Jack. 'We just happened to be in rest, but we shall be moving forward now.'

Why couldn't Jimmy have managed to get over? So many people had turned up during the summer, but never Jimmy. And now she could no longer expect him. He had said in his last letter:

'Afraid coming to see you is off now. Quiet times are over. We are moving forward.'

.   .   .   .   .

Soon after this a concert was given by Leslie Henson and his company. It was a company permanently attached to 5th Army Headquarters, and had toured all over France performing to the troops.

They arrived at the Camp about six, all in privates' uniforms, and, as there had been no official preparations for a meal for them, Bingham firmly ushered the whole lot into the 'dug-out' behind the counter and fed them on fish-and-chips. Whether or not they were accustomed to this sort of entertainment they appeared quite at their ease, ate with relish—though silently—and even offered to wash up afterwards.

The concert was at eight, and it was far and away the best show that had ever been given at the Camp. Everyone was good, especially Bert Errol, who, with soprano voice, and dressed in low-cut evening frock and red wig, travestied famous songs from operas. But the success of the evening was, of course, Leslie Henson. He had only to show his funny little face for the soldier audience to bellow. The girls laughed till they were nearly sick. The last turn was a topical sketch called 'The Dis-orderly Room,' in which Leslie Henson was an adjutant with a waggling black moustache, and the rest were Tommies brought before him for various absurd offences. The whole sketch was sung instead of spoken, and the tunes were the popular war tunes of the moment. In its own way it was a brilliant little affair, but would have had no value at any other period.

The company departed in lorries, leaving the Camp enormously cheered by its visit.

.   .   .   .   .

An event which caused considerable excitement, about this time, was the capture of some Australian deserters who had broken loose from their units and had been living wild, for weeks, in the woods about St. Valery, raiding villages and robbing foot-passengers on the road. Things came to a climax when a Jock, returning alone to Camp, one night, was stabbed because he refused to give up his money. He was just able to reel in with his story when he fainted, was taken to hospital, and died next day.

That such a thing should have happened to a man in his own Rest Camp threw Colonel Noble into a frenzy. Search parties were sent scouring the country, and some of the deserters were caught, but many remained still at large. Why the Y.M. girls, walking back at night, unprotected, and carrying the cash-box, had never been molested was a mystery; but from henceforth they were given an escort of Tommies. The precaution seemed rather absurd, because, as Betty remarked, 'If the bandits *had* been going to attack us they would have done so long ago.'

'They must have had a lurking sense of chivalry,' said Joan, rather disappointed at not having been the victim of highway robbery, since such a thing still existed.

.   .   .   .   .   .

October came; and wet tempestuous weather alternated with periods of calm glory that were a reflection of summer.

During the gales, undressing in the sleeping-tent was a shivering process, as the sides were apt to blow right away from the moorings and leave the occupants exposed. The canvas fencing which stretched between the tent and the girls' little lavatory, and behind which they could walk unseen by the rest of the Camp, had sagged so much that it no longer served its purpose. Duffy—ever modest—used to crawl along the ground on her hands and knees, to the intense amusement of the others, who, past blushing nowadays, used to walk boldly erect.

The orderly still called them with buckets of cold water at 1.30, but nobody except Barbara—who would have washed at the North Pole—attempted any ablutions. They hurried into their clothes, wound woolly scarves round their necks, and plunged into the night. Betty never even undressed. Sleepily pushing away her mountain of blankets, she would emerge at the very last second, fully clothed, and wearing about three extra jerseys.

It was pitch dark now when the men tramped off; and the girls, watching them go, held lanterns or torches in their hands.

Supper-parties of Tommies were frequent at the house. Four, five, sometimes six men at a time used to tramp in, heavy-booted, shining-faced, wet-haired, and always touchingly appreciative of the 'home' atmosphere.

Bad news came from home about Jack. He had lost his right arm. Joan couldn't believe her eyes when she read of it. Only three weeks ago he had been driving her in that car to Le Tréport —had been sitting here in the house talking, looking as though nothing could ever hurt him. His job on Divisional Staff had not, then, been the 'cushy' one he had given her to suppose. According to this letter he had been up reconnoitring near the Bosche wire, had gleaned some important information, had gone back to H.Q. to attend a conference about the attack, and had then led a battalion into assembly position, in the dark, right under the Bosche's nose. It had been while watching the attack next day, in order to report progress to H.Q., that he had been hit.

What detestable luck! And however was Jack to manage existence with only one arm?—he whose main delights had been tennis and dancing? Would he in his heart, Joan wondered, have preferred to be killed?

.   .   .   .   .   .

And day by day the miraculous British advance went on. Soldiers lately down from the line talked of the released French villagers, of how they stared and wept at the sight of khaki. Armentières and Lens had fallen. Lille was about to fall. Germany was asking President Wilson for an armistice. It was difficult to believe that these things were true. Was there, people began asking one another, the glimmer of a hope of peace this year?

Into the hut, one morning, came Madame Dupont, a stout bourgeoise of St. Valery who lived on the outskirts of the town, and sometimes sold fruit to the Y.M.C.A. For half an hour, in torrential French, she held forth to Joan and Barbara about the iniquities of the Bosches, and her fear lest they should be granted peace upon too easy terms. What did the English know, she asked, of the horrors of invasion? Easy enough for *them* to forgive. But France! And there followed story upon terrible story about people she knew who had been living in the occupied areas, and who, now escaped, were able to relate their experiences.

The girls listened, repelled and enthralled. This woman spoke of what she knew. How could one blame the French in their bitter hatred of the enemy—in their desire for revenge even?

'Vous Anglais, vous ne comprenez pas—vous ne comprenez pas! La haine des Bosches ne doit jamais mourir—jamais, jamais, jamais!'

And Mme. Dupont, flaming and wet-eyed, swept from the hut.

.   .   .   .   .   .

And then on the 18th of October—a misty, golden, gossamer day—came the most wonderful news of the whole war. Lille had fallen, Ostende had fallen, Bruges had fallen. The 5th Army—shattered under Gough, reconstituted and victorious under Birdwood—had marched into Lille with bands playing, and the inhabitants had gone mad.

That same afternoon Philip Nichol turned up from Sailly-le-Sec, where he was attached to the Artillery School as Education Officer. He had walked and lorry-jumped the six miles to St. Valery, and had traced Joan up to the Camp. Joan managed to take an hour off, and they strolled along the cliffs together, and sat on the short grass.

'I haven't seen you for over a year,' said Philip. 'Do you remember that lunch last summer at the Carlton? I've often thought of it. It was one of the few perfect days of the war for me.'

Joan looked at him in mild surprise.

'Oh, yes, you were feeling rather fit that day—you'd just been on leave in the country, hadn't you?'

'I didn't mean . . .' he began, then was silent, and stared across the marshes to the far-off sea.

She recalled their conversation of that day—how he had told her he must stick the war out for the sake of 'the wretched men.' Well, he had stuck it out—so far. But at what cost? That queer thin face of his had deep lines on it now, and his hands shook a little.

'This Sailly job came just in time,' he remarked. 'I don't believe I could have gone on any more. After the spring retreat I nearly crocked up again, you know—that filthy nerve business. Then the summer was less strenuous, and I hung on somehow, and then I got sent here. Rather fun doing a bit of "educating" again. Good for the mind.'

Joan talked to him about the Rest Camp, amused him with details of the daily life there.

'Have you thought what you'll do afterwards?' he asked. 'For I suppose this *is* the end.'

'Oh, Philip, no, I haven't!' she sighed. She was lying on her back, gazing into the milky October sky. 'And I don't find myself really believing that the war *is* going to end. It's not so easy all at once to shed one's grimly-acquired pessimism.'

But Philip's mind was already moving forward. He talked about 'reconstruction.'

'Nothing will ever be the same again,' he said. 'Out of this mess we've got to rebuild the world. And everyone can help to rebuild —in his or her way. My way must be education.'

And he went on to outline a plan for running a small school of his own on special lines. He thought he would be able to raise the necessary capital to start it. In any case, go back to St. Paul's he would not. This was to be a school where the spirit of militarism and the fear of punishment would not exist, and where learning would be made a delight, and not an abhorrence. English would be the chief subject; and through English literature, and not through a Cadet Corps, the boys would get their love of England. And initiative would be encouraged, and self-development, and self-respect—qualities which our present system did its best to suffocate.

'School life is only profitable so long as it is thoroughly enjoyed,' said Philip vehemently. 'What boys *could* grow up into, given a chance!'

He gave a quick sideways glance at Joan. 'There'd have to be a woman at that school—I mean, I think that for small boys the two influences are needed—the masculine and the feminine. Do you . . . has the thought of teaching ever appealed to you?'

Joan roused herself from a waking dream of Jack, of Jimmy, and of released French villages, to the realisation that she was being offered some sort of post in a Prep. School.

'Heavens, no!' she laughed. 'Besides, I'm not even trained.'

Something came into Philip's eyes and then retreated. 'As a matter of fact that wouldn't matter,' he muttered. 'It's not a question of training so much . . .'

On other occasions Joan had always responded with interest to Philip's discourses. But somehow to-day she couldn't concentrate—she felt out of touch. If peace-time really came, she said to herself, they must have some long talks together.

'You'll join us down at the house for supper, later on?' she asked him.

But Philip didn't think he would. He thought he would be wending back to Sailly.

'Well, you must blow over another day,' said Joan. 'Now that you're so near . . .'

'Of course—if I can manage it,' he said. 'They keep me rather hard at it. Thanks awfully for this afternoon.'

He left her by the Y.M. tent and strode off, narrow-shouldered, in the direction of St. Valery.

He didn't come over again.

Chapter Four

WHATEVER great events were taking place outside, things at the Rest Camp went on exactly as usual. The fish-and-chip business was brisk during these autumn evenings. In the great candle-lit tent the men sat drinking tea, playing chess, playing whist—stolid, brown-faced, philosophical, resigned to peace, resigned to war. The village and the country-side held less attraction for them now than in the summer. The Y.M. was their home. The girls loved them to feel it so—loved to see them happily and crowdedly *there*. And they sighed to think that at the end of the month the Rest Camp would be closing down—for Rest Camps were only summer institutions. And then they would all go home on leave, and then . . .?

. . . . . .

It was the last Sunday in October. Mild sunshine bathed the courtyard. Betty was on her knees on the cobble-stones, stroking the stomach of one of the now sleek cats. Bingham was in a deck-chair deep in accounts. Duffy hovered vaguely with a basket. Barbara, at the dining-room window, was doing up soldiers' parcels. And suddenly it came over Joan that though this was the Present it was already the Past. Curious how certain moments, even as you lived them, seemed to have no reality. Later, when you looked back on them, they acquired their reality. This moment lay in the Past. The ghosts of five blue English girls would haunt for ever, in a sunshine that would never fade, the old ivy-hung court-yard. The life of the village would go on as before, but this house would stand empty, given over to ghosts, its purpose served.

. . . . . .

But during the week which followed, the Present was as insistent as ever. The men were real, the smell of hot fat was real, the cups on the counter were real. And even when the last concert came round it was impossible to believe that there would never be

406

another; even when the last contingent of men marched away in the dark morning it was impossible to believe that no others would fill their place—that this was indeed the end.

Five desolate days were spent by the girls in packing up stores, in seeing the framework of the Camp gradually disintegrate, in taking leave of the Camp staff, in packing their own things at the house, in disposing of the cats. And on November 6th, under grey skies, they travelled back through France.

In Boulogne, where they stayed the night, all was turmoil and excitement, and the girls felt oddly bewildered coming into vulgar civilisation once more after their dream-like and remote St. Valery. 'La guerre est finie!' people shouted in the street. 'Pas encore, pas encore!'

And then the Channel. Fun travelling together in a bunch like this! Then London, and the parting of the ways. Duffy going to Scotland; Bingham to her home in Leicestershire; Barbara to Sussex; Betty and Joan to Hampstead. Same taxi. Betty dropped first.

'Auntie!'

'Joan, dear!'

'*Tam!*'

How small home looked, how cosy, yet how strange.

. . . .

Will they sign? Will they sign? The war was still going on. Jimmy was expected on leave in a week or so. Surely one could count on his safety now? But there was still fighting. It was still the war.

The night of the 10th. The morning of the 11th. The world held its breath. Eleven o'clock. Sirens, and a crash of bells. The world went mad. The Armistice was signed.

. . . . .

A day or two later Joan wrote to Pamela in Rouen.

'I suppose it is even harder for you to believe it all than it is for me, because you are still among wounded soldiers, and to all appearances things are the same, whereas here . . .! Well, nobody who was in London on Monday and the succeeding days could have any illusion that there was still a war on. It was wonderful, in a way, being in those surging shouting crowds, but I wished —oh, how I wished—to be back with the British Army! If peace had only broken out while we were still in the Rest Camp what a time we should have had. But I mustn't think about it. It makes me too home-sick—I mean too army-sick.

'It's queer and dull being at home just among civilians; and this awful 'flu that's raging about makes things still more depressing. Is there much of it in your hospital? And how much longer are you going to stay there?

'Pam, I keep saying to myself: "No more men are being killed! No more men are being killed!" And the fact that imagination almost fails to take in that state of affairs shows how hideously used one had become to the other. Yet only used to it in a general way —never for one's own beloveds. I realise right enough that Jimmy's through.

'Difficult to say things, Pam dear, but don't go thinking that, in my own selfish and immense relief, I've forgotten you. Or that for you—for my friend Barbara, and for how many others?—the ending of the war *can* only be felt, at first, as the ending of a powerful and blessed drug.'

PART FIVE

1919: 1920

'I cannot but remember such things were,
That were most precious to me.'

Chapter One

ON the morning of November 17th Joan had a letter from Jimmy. It was written, as usual, in pencil, but was addressed from a hospital in Havre.

'Isn't this just about the outside edge!' he wrote. 'Down with 'flu, and the battery proceeding through France, in easy stages, towards the Rhine! You know, I don't think I'd have taken my leave yet, even though I was due for it—I'd have asked for it later. This is a bad business, this 'flu that's going about. Hundreds of fellows are down with it, and French civilians too. I'd rather have been wounded any time in the war than be laid low just now. However, it's no good grousing. To use that old phrase of mine, which has always half-amused, half-exasperated you: "It's a great pity, but *un*fortunately it *can't* be helped!" I don't think I've much of a temperature—though they don't tell me—just a bit swimmy in the head, you know.

'By the way, just before I went sick I was inquiring about resignation from the army, and the adjutant said it was no use submitting resignations now, except on extreme compassionate grounds, *i.e.* sole support of a widowed or dying mother, and I *don't* think the Army Council would swallow that from me! But I'm in hopes of being able to send in my papers in the near future, and of getting up to Cambridge by next October term. Meanwhile, as soon as I'm better, and have had sick-leave, a spell of "Wacht am Rhine" awaits me, and I expect it'll be quite fun in its way.

'Good-bye, old thing. The Sister—an awfully nice person—is just bringing me some sloppy concoction to swallow. Love to everyone. There are good times ahead!

'Your bored brother, J.'

'What rotten luck on him!' cried Joan, 'just at the moment when he was either coming on leave or starting on that triumphal progress.'

'You don't think he's bad, then?' asked Florence over the break-fast-table.

'No, or he wouldn't have been able to write,' Joan said. Then added quickly: 'They look after them awfully well in those military hospitals, you know. It's far better he should have 'flu over there—if he's got to have it—than here in London where there's not a nurse to be had.'

'Yes—I suppose so.'

'How like him,' Joan went on, 'to be so philosophical over it. And how like him to have wanted to see the war thoroughly through, and then clear out. He's just taken it in his stride. He's already thinking about the future.'

There was no further news in the morning, and such anxiety as Joan had felt died down. About midday her attention was taken up by her aunt. Florence had been trailing rather wretchedly about since breakfast, and now complained of headache and sickness. She could eat nothing for lunch. Joan took her temperature, saw that it was up, and put her to bed.

The doctor came. It was influenza, but with no complications—as yet. Patient must be kept warm. Milk diet. Four-hourly medicines. 'Watch her carefully,' he said, as he left the house. 'You never know what form this 'flu will take. I'll try and come once a day.'

Doctors were being rushed off their feet just now.

Florence made a good invalid. She knew that the best way to avoid giving trouble was to get well as soon as possible; so, with a woolly shawl round her head, a fire in her bedroom, and Joan in and out attending to her, she submitted with what cheerfulness she could to the situation.

Next morning Annie, the housemaid, succumbed. Two patients now for Joan to look after, and most of the housework to do. Thank goodness old cook still carried on, and the parlour-maid too—though the latter was a silly, inefficient girl, procured towards the end of the war as a 'temporary,' and quite unlike Florence's usual servants. Joan put Annie into a bedroom by herself, with severe orders to keep the windows open day and night. She ran the house as though it had been a ward. She became a V.A.D. again.

Nothing more from Havre. No need to worry in *that* quarter, she thought, as she sped up and down staircases, filled hot-water bottles, and dusted rooms.

Three days after Jimmy's letter Joan was coming through from the kitchen premises into the hall, carrying a tray, when the front-door bell rang. She went to answer it. A telegram. The thin orange-brown paper ripped under her thumb. 'Lt. J. B. Seddon, R.G.A., dangerously ill with pneumonia following influenza.' She stared at the words. 'No answer,' she said. The messenger departed, and very slowly she walked back into the hall. Still she stared at the little pencilled words, '. . . dangerously ill with pneumonia. . . .' Her eyes lifted, and, by chance, fell on the tray which she had put down before going to answer the door. Every detail of it stood out with extreme distinctness. She noticed the white embroidery on the cloth, the flower-pattern on the china. She noticed that on top of the warm milk in the glass a thin skin was forming—crinkle on tiny crinkle.

Oh yes—Aunt Florence's lunch. She must take it up to her.

From one stair to the next she lifted feet of lead.

'Thank you dear, very nice,' said Florence, pulling herself up on her pillows and taking off her spectacles. And then, seeing her niece's face: 'Is anything the matter?'

Joan's eyes widened. 'No, Auntie!'

'You had a broken night, of course, popping in and out on me. Try and get some sleep this afternoon.'

When Joan was at the door she called her back.

'Did I hear the bell?'

'When?'

'Just before you came up.'

'I don't think so. *I* didn't.'

'Oh, well—my stupid head, I suppose. I keep imagining little noises.'

Joan went down to her own lunch and sat in front of it. Now then, what was to be done? She must get over to France, of course—but how?—how? Her mind darted this way and that. A nurse to take her place. But nurses were not to be got. If she hadn't already known it, the doctor had told her so on his first visit. Scarcely a family in Hampstead some of whose members were not down with 'flu. Betty—who would have flown to her rescue—was nursing her own parents. Aunt Rose was in a state of desperation with only one maid fit. No, hunt about as she could, Joan saw no way of leaving home. True, Aunt Florence was not very bad, but she had an intermittent temperature, and at any moment there might be worse developments. The same with Annie.

With a vague idea of letting her decision rest on the result of the two-o'clock temperature Joan went upstairs. The thermometer showed a few degrees higher than it had done in the morning.

'Go to sleep now, Auntie,' she said. 'I'll bring you your tea at four.'

She would have to stay.

'Dangerously ill with pneumonia. Dangerously ill . . .'

She dropped on her knees beside her bed, her face in the quilt.

'Oh, God, don't let him die! God, don't let him die!'

After a while, through no volition of her own, the terror left her and she became curiously calm. She put on her hat, and she took Tam for a walk on the Heath. Everything was bathed in an atmosphere of unreality—but it was not a sinister unreality. People walked about. A number of pale gold leaves still clung to the birches. There was a little mist in the hollows.

Later, as she sat drinking her tea—drinking it in slow sips, and enjoying it—she wondered what she had been so frightened about. Pneumonia, yes—bad, of course. But people recovered from pneumonia. Senseless to allow the wording of a telegram to weigh against her own instinctive and absolute conviction that Jimmy would pull round. He always *had* pulled round, and he had often been ill before. She poured herself out another cup of tea and finished the last chapter of a novel.

During the evening she was fully employed in the two sick-rooms. Florence was flushed and drowsy, and scarcely spoke.

But when Joan had settled her invalids, and was herself in bed, the terror, kept by her subconscious for so many hours at bay, closed down on her again. She fought it off, but it only came and hugged her the closer. She submitted to it, and lay bathed in sweat. At two o'clock and at six o'clock she got up and gave medicines.

Then she fell into a deep sleep until eight.

She was scanning the head-lines of *The Times*, while the parlour-maid cleared away breakfast, when the prolonged 'brrr' of the front-door bell shot through her nerves. With an effort she kept her eyes on a line of print.

'Telegram, Miss.'

The maid, with rather elaborate unconcern, continued to pile her tray, and Joan unfolded the wire ' . . . better night, holding his own, condition favourable.'

Her hands dropped to her lap. Outside, a ray of pale November sunshine fell on the leaves of a laurel bush and lit their varnished green. Joan thought she had never seen anything so beautiful.

When next she went upstairs she told Florence—who was better —the whole position with regard to Jimmy. It seemed no longer possible, or necessary, to keep it from her. Florence took it very quietly. 'I wondered why he hadn't written again,' was all she said. Joan exaggerated her own—quite genuine—hopefulness.

In and out of bedrooms with medicines, food, books. Making beds. Emptying slops. Down to her own solitary meals. Interviewing cook. Joan felt as though she had been carrying on this existence for weeks instead of only for four days. And it was odd how all the familiar inanimate objects with which she was now hemmed in seemed to loom so large—seemed almost to assume personalities. Now, while her inner life was reduced to a tense waiting, her outer eyes were aware, as they had never been before, of the shapes of certain chairs; of the sweet-silliness of the birds and roses on the drawing-room Morris cretonne; of the pompous expression on the face of the hall clock. Sometimes the things were friendly, sometimes inimical. Sometimes they withdrew like neutrals, and watched.

Another night passed—a night of comparative peacefulness.

Coming downstairs, at about ten o'clock, having done the bedrooms, Joan caught sight, on the hall table, of an oblong orange envelope. She stood stock-still. Her hand, icy, felt for the banister. She sank down on to a stair. Somewhere, on the outer edge of her brain, the small voice of reason said: 'The news yesterday was good—the news to-day will be better.' But reason might say what it liked. Her body knew the truth. Her body had already reacted to the contents of that unopened envelope. She leant her forehead against the hand which clung to the banister. 'Oh, please . . .' she whimpered. 'Oh, please . . .'

When, after an eternity, she walked up to the table it was as a corpse, and no longer as a living woman, that she walked.

'Regret to inform you that Lt. J. B. Seddon died of pneumonia following on influenza at 4 a.m. November 22nd.'

.   .   .   .   .   .

For the rest of that day, and for the whole of the next, Joan felt absolutely nothing. She went about her duties. She ate good meals. She slept soundly. When asked by Florence about news from Havre she replied, 'Unchanged,' or 'Maintaining strength.' And the stony expression of her face was put down, by her aunt, either to fatigue or to inward anxiety carefully controlled.

In keeping back the death-news Joan thought that she was acting for the sake of Florence—too weak yet to receive it. And so she was—partly. But it was partly for her own sake as well. An obscure instinct seemed to tell her that, as she still had to carry on with nursing, it would be wise to keep things normal for as long as possible; also that a tragedy unmentioned might yet prove to be untrue.

But on the second morning after she had received the telegram a letter came for her from the Sister who had nursed Jimmy. She read a line or two, then stuffed it back into its envelope. The time for secrecy was over. Nobody could be protected any more.

A fire had been lit in the drawing-room, and Florence, who had already been 'up' in her bedroom, was coming down for the first time. Annie was about again, and was even beginning, feebly, to work. Soon the house would be functioning normally.

Joan rang up her Uncle Robert at his office, and asked him to call in that evening on his way home. She had been keeping him informed about Florence's state of health, but he had so far not been allowed to see her. About Jimmy's condition he knew as much as his sister did—no more.

When he arrived, Joan detained him in the hall, and in a few dry sentences told him everything.

'I just want you to do the breaking, Uncle,' she said. 'I shall be with her afterwards, but I can't do that. She's fonder of you than of anyone—except me and Jimmy.'

Robert, as Joan had known he would, rose to the occasion. He had a strong sense of family, and there were certain things—they might be very disagreeable things—which it gratified him to be asked to undertake.

'My poor Florrie!' he said. 'And you, my poor, poor child! How you've kept up. . . .'

Joan didn't move as, with clumsy sympathy, he patted her shoulder. She watched him disappear through the drawing-room door, and then she fled upstairs.

Sitting on the edge of her bed she took out the letter from Havre.

'DEAR MISS JOAN SEDDON,

It is to you I am writing, as it was you whom your brother so often mentioned during his illness. I would have done so sooner, but I simply have not had a moment until now. Somehow nothing in the war seemed so terrible as this epidemic coming at the end of it. I am bad at expressing myself, so you must forgive me if I sound hard, but truly my heart is full of sympathy for you.

'I did so hope we should get him through. He came in with a temperature of 102°, but he felt quite well in himself, only a little hot and excited. Many cases get better in three days, and it seemed as if he would. But once pneumonia had set in—although there was still hope—it was the beginning of the end. Miss Seddon, there was no pain. He was only semi-conscious, reviving a little when he was being washed, talking a little, then relapsing again. For two hours before the end he was completely unconscious, and passed peacefully away.

'I think I minded his death more than the death of any boy I have nursed, although I only had him for so short a time. He never thought of himself. He used to thank me for everything I did. He often said he hated to see me so hard-worked, and that I was not to bother with him. As if anything was a bother! He found out my name was Joan. He said "Why, that's my sister's name!" and it seemed to please him very much. He showed me a little snapshot of you, in his pocket-book, kneeling on the grass with a dog. "She'll be rather bucked to have me home again," he said. I think he had the most beautiful smile I have ever seen. One night when his head was hot I laid my hands on it. He said my hands reminded him of yours.

'I don't think I have any more to say. Please believe that he had every possible care during his illness. If there are any questions you would like to ask, please do not hesitate to write. I'll always make time. I do not understand God's will in these matters; I suppose there is a purpose. I am very sorry for you and all your family.

'Yours sincerely,
'Joan M. Fowler'

It was upon the last few words that Joan's mind fastened. Grief hovered with grey arms, but it was rage that first possessed her.

'Nor do *I* understand God's will!' she cried. 'And there's no purpose at all in the whole hellish universe!' She was speaking aloud—bitterly—savagely. Her own voice, if she could have listened to it, would not have been recognisable to her.

'You *would* wait till the war was over!' she went on, addressing that God in whom she did not believe, but whom it was her need, for the moment, to curse. 'You couldn't let him be killed decently in battle, while we were all strung-up, and more or less ready for bad news. Oh no! You allowed us to relax, you gave us ten days of peace and breathing-space, and then you pounced on him—like a cat—like the great Celestial Cat that you are! And even then you couldn't take him all at once. You let him creep a little way into health, then clawed him back into death. Me pray to you? But there are people who do. Even after this war, even after this pestilence, there are thousands who do. Much comfort may they get. If I thought for a moment that you existed I should go mad—I should go mad!'

And then the tears came.

Walking about the room, hands touching bits of furniture, long desolate sobs tearing their way through her body, she saw nothing, she knew nothing except that her brother was dead. Piteously she called to him. 'Jim-pot, you shouldn't have died! I do think you needn't have died!' Up and down, up and down. Her face sodden, the outline gone. Tears and saliva mixing on the down-drawn quavering lips.

'Jim-pot, you know I loved you, and you loved me. Don't you think it was cruel to go and die? Because, you see, darling, what am I to do without you? And you liked life. You were going to Cambridge next autumn. You—you——' She stood for a moment, palms pressed on eyeballs, a heaving instrument of sobs; then, into the void before her, flung arms, voice, soul.

'Jim-pot, come back to me! Jim-pot, come back! You haven't been gone so very long. You can't have got so very far. Come back! Come back! Come back! Come back!'

.   .   .   .   .   .

During the days that followed Florence sometimes wondered how much Joan really cared. The girl was gentle, certainly; she was constantly at hand; she answered letters, and she shouldered much responsibility. But there was something which Florence would like to have broken through. This bond of grief which should have united them—which *had* united them outwardly, for Joan had promised not to leave home again—seemed to have separated them more completely than anything had done before. The young fought their grief. The young resented grief. They didn't know how to make acceptance. They knew neither the comfort of God nor the comfort of tears.

.   .   .   .   .   .

Robert had gone over for the funeral. He had only been just in time. It hadn't occurred to Joan that anyone ought to go. She had no desire to go herself. Funerals meant nothing to her—even the funeral of a brother.

Robert came back much impressed. There had been full military honours and the 'Last Post.' As head of the family he was proud to have been there. 'I must say,' he said gruffly, and with an unusual touch of imagination, 'it seemed like a sort of send-off. More like the beginning of something than the end.'

.   .   .   .   .   .

Betty had come round as soon as she had heard the news. She and Joan had strolled together round the wintry garden, hands thrust deep in overcoat pockets. The more Betty felt the less she could ever express; but her voice saying 'Darling' was all that Joan needed—it was as though she had been touched by the petal of a flower.

Jack had come round—in 'civvies' now—his empty right sleeve pinned up. 'Filthy luck!' he had said. 'Good lad, Jimmy. Always seem to see him as a fat little kid in this garden, when we all played together. What you've got to remember, Joan, is that he died in the war exactly like all the chaps that were killed. No difference.'

.   .   .   .   .   .

The letter which came from Jimmy's C.O. showed Joan that

other side of her 'small brother' which she had known, of course, was there, but which she had only with difficulty visualised.

It said, among other things: '"Jim" was undoubtedly the best-liked officer in the Battery, although at times we had to "go for him," as he frightened us with his utter disregard of danger. The men looked up to him and trusted him completely. I would have been ready to recommend him as second in command of any Heavy Battery. *He knew his job*—which is not such a common thing as might be supposed these days. The R.A. has lost a most efficient officer and a brave gentleman.'

Such letters were comforts in that they added to her already crowded and vivid images of him. For all day she saw him—in different attitudes—in different occupations. When she went suddenly into the drawing-room he was at the piano, leaning a little forward, with that absorbed look on his face, the under-lip drawn in. When she sat at her dressing-table doing her hair, he would come clattering down the two steps from the school-room and sit about, making slow comments on her clothes. When she was in the garden he would be standing at one end of the lawn, a ball held high, Tam leaping and barking for it. He was everywhere.

But at night—at night came other pictures. Joan had not worked in hospitals for two and a half years for nothing. That letter of Sister Fowler's might, to the uninitiated, convey no more than a vague impression of a busy ward, and a boy in bed with shut eyes; but to Joan it conveyed every process, every smell. She saw the hollowed face propped up on pillows; smelt the sweaty sheets; heard the breathing—more and more laboured; saw the cylinder of oxygen brought to the bedside; saw and smelt the brandy in the little medicine-glass. Saw—after that—the screens, the dim circle of lantern-light . . . the stretched corpse . . . what was done to it. . . . Started forward with a shriek: 'Not Jimmy! Oh, not Jimmy! Oh, not him!'

And then she would wrench her mind away, and think with gratitude of Sister Fowler, of what a darling person she must be—

rather of the type of Sister Muir, with whom she had worked 'on night.'

But nobody of his own had been there at the end. Nobody to see him off on that last adventure. Young he had set forth on it—young, and quite alone.

. . . . . .

His clothes came home. All his field kit from the Battery. His 'flea-bag,' his tin helmet, the trench-boots at which she had laughed that day just before he went out. A tunic torn, caked in mud. Letters from home, photographs, pocket-books, and strange mathematical drawings and calculations.

Joan had spread them all out in the school-room. Quietly, and at leisure, she went through them—sorting, disposing. His three friends would want something each: Carey, Sanderson and Browne. And she thought of Wirebush—that odd little boy to whom Jimmy had always been so kind—who looked up to him with such adoration—and who had so often been a silent guest at Beechwood. Wirebush would need nothing. If souls lived on, Wirebush would be with Jimmy now. He also had died of 'flu.

Tam pushed his hairy bulk through the half-open door. He sniffed at the clothes, going from one garment to the other, uneasily. Then he curled up on a coat, his brown eyes on Joan.

'We'll keep this one, Tam,' she said, folding up the muddy tunic. 'It's got the mud of Ypres on it, and it's almost worn through. I don't think clothes matter much on the whole, but this one . . . Oh, Tam, *don't* look at me like that! . . .' And she stumbled across to the dog, and clasped his head against her in a storm of weeping.

. . . . . .

The curious thing about misery was the way it rose and fell. Sometimes you felt quite ordinary. You read books; you shopped; the world seemed normal and pleasant. And suddenly, out of the four corners as it were, misery came, and swamped you. You could do nothing about it. You just sat there at the heart of it. Everything else was blotted out—even your personality. You were just a primordial, enduring, suffering nerve. And then—after an hour, after a day—that sea withdrew; and you emerged, if not to life, to something that was tolerable.

People said: 'Time will heal,' but you didn't want time to heal—or rather you didn't want it to heal at the price of remembrance. The one thing you were terrified of was numb forgetfulness. Suffering was atrocious; it was not a thing to be sentimentally hugged; but if it was the inevitable accompaniment of remembrance you would keep it.

. . . . . .

Joan dreamt several times of Jimmy; but two of the dreams although they were quite short, and no words were spoken in them, were of such intensity that they didn't seem like dreams at all.

In the first she was walking down a country lane with high hedges on either hand. Beside her walked Jimmy. He was twelve years old again, and he wore his Prep. School cricket flannels. Her arm was across his shoulder, and his arm round her waist. His large head, with its mop of hair, was bare. His freckled face was broadly smiling. Through the thin flannel of the shirt she could feel his collar-bone. When she woke, the atmosphere of sweetness and bliss which had pervaded the dream lingered on. It faded, and she cried.

In the second Jimmy was grown-up. He was striding up a grassy slope, bare-headed, and about a yard in front of her. She reached her hand to his shoulder to keep him to her level, but he strode on, pulling her up the hill. Again—as in the other dream—she was aware of the texture of his clothes, but this time it was a tweed coat he was wearing. As she walked she looked at the grass, and saw that it was covered with small wild daffodils. 'Spring!' she said to herself. And then just above the daffodils appeared Aunt Florence's face, lying back with closed eyes, very pale, a bit of wispy material floating round it. It was not at all frightening—it was simply there. Jimmy hadn't noticed it—his eyes were ahead. And they walked on together.

Joan felt that if she could dream like that every night, daily existence would be quite bearable. But, alas, such dreams didn't come for the summoning.

.   .   .   .   .   .

The December days dragged on and brought the Christmas holidays. Were there such things as holidays? thought Joan. Were there such things as children?

Her twin cousins, Bill and Babs, fifteen now, had come over to Beechwood on their first day home.

'What we wanted to tell you, Joan,' said Babs, looking straignt at her from round eyes, 'was how frightfully sorry we are about Jimmy.'

'Won't be half the fun coming round here now,' added Bill, with a bluntness that was the greatest compliment to the past.

And Molly Paley, who had come later, her gold plaits done up in a door-knocker, said shyly to Joan:

'You know I liked him awfully. There was something special about him.'

A picture of them dancing together, three Christmases ago, after the ridiculous 'Wipers' charade, came into Joan's mind.

'You dear! Don't forget him—too quickly,' she said.

.   .   .   .   .   .

The doctor ordered Florence into the country for a fortnight. 'It will do *you* no harm either,' he said, looking at Joan, 'to have a change.'

Christmas, anyhow, would have been insupportable at home this year.

.   .   .   .   .   .

Betty, it seemed, was unable yet to unwind herself from the strings of war; and in the middle of January 1919 she went back to France to run a Y.M. hut among some troops that were awaiting demobilisation near Amiens. Bingham and Barbara went with her.

Wistfully Joan watched them go. To be working once more with the B.E.F.—still to be part of a machine—what content!

'How long shall you be gone?' she asked Betty.

'Can't tell, darling. It was you who stuck me into the Y.M. originally. You know how I remain "put!" '

' "Nice, but rutty," ' smiled Joan.

And with a sort of terror she envisaged her own life at home— the life to which she had looked forward for so many war years, and which now seemed to stretch bleakly before her, holding only memories.

She would have to find something to do.

Chapter Two

LETTERS came from Betty. The weather, she said, was raw, cold and unspeakable. The troops were bored, and earlier on had been attempting mutiny; now, however, since the arrival of the Y.M., they were recovering something of their war-time good-temper.

The cottage where she and the others were billeted had no glass in the windows, only oiled calico. Often they went to bed in their clothes. Their rare baths were taken in a wash-tub in the kitchen, the water being heated in a petrol tin.

Occasional expeditions were made into Amiens, and, by now, although the town still presented a ruined appearance, most of the inhabitants were back, and most of the shops and hotels were open.

'We went a drive once,' wrote Betty, 'over the Somme battle-fields, and saw Arras, Bapaume, Albert, Peronne, and the famous Butte de Warlencourt—places which, till then, had only been names read of in papers, spoken of by soldiers, dimly imagined. And there they were—ruined, empty, bleak, and deadly still. Not a soldier, not a shell, not a sound. I had that sort of feeling I used to have long ago on Hampstead Heath on winter afternoons—the light failing, the nurse gone on ahead leaving me to dawdle with cold hands—everyone *gone*.'

At the end of March they left the Amiens area, and were sent to Cologne to run a Y.M. hut for the Army of Occupation.

'Our hut here is enormous,' Betty wrote. 'It isn't a hut at all as a matter of fact, but a converted "Volks Palast" consisting of a number of halls. Rather bewildering, and difficult to run. It is known as the "Central." We have German orderlies—quite excellent—all of whom know English, work like niggers, and stand rigidly to attention when spoken to! I need hardly say we are under-staffed as far as "ladies" go, but a new lot are expected out soon.

'There are strict military orders against "fraternising," but these are difficult to enforce, as the Tommies *like* the Germans—like them far better than the French—and share their rations with the half-starved families on whom they are billeted. "They are kind and clean, these people," they say, "and don't try and make a lot out of you. You can't help feeling sorry for them."

'Our own billet is a large-sized flat close to the "Deutsches Theater," and is kept by a pleasant little dark-haired German woman with a misbegotten war baby.'

Later on, in May, Betty's letters were full of the gaieties of Cologne life.

'We go to the Opera,' she wrote, 'and we go to dances. In fact almost every night, after the canteen has closed, we seem to be dancing. If it's not in one officers' mess it's in another; and if it's not at "Lindenthal" (a sort of country club) it's out at 6th Corps Headquarters. And always, wherever we go, we are sent for in cars. Fetched and wanted and liked and spoilt. And you know, Joan, for the first time in nearly five years I feel able, without qualms, to enjoy myself—knowing that these men can take care of themselves, that their emotions are normal and that the fear of death and the fever of leave-taking no longer hang over them.'

But out of the whole bepolished and beribboned crowd there was only one, Betty said, whom she felt she could treat as a friend. His name was George Davies, and he was always somehow quietly *there*. He was oldish—thirty-seven or eight—and he had the very kindest eyes she had ever seen.

'One of those Infantry officers, you know, who give the impression of having been a schoolmaster, and of having three or four children of their own. As a matter of fact he is unmarried, and a stockbroker! My dear, I asked him once, apprehensively, whether he played golf! To my surprise and relief he said he did *not*. And that led to a talk on different forms of exercise, and *that*

to an interminable walk together in the flat plains round Cologne—
the Cathedral spire ever behind or before us. A bore, you will
say? Well, yes—from some points of view, perhaps—but an
appreciative bore. Barbara says he reminds her of her elder married
brother—and that, I suppose, about sums him up. An epitome of
all elder married brothers—there when required, eternally to be
relied on, occasionally to be confided in, unexacting alike to the
emotions and to the mind.'

'I *wonder*!' thought Joan, as she read this. 'I wonder . . ."

But a letter which came later, after about a month's silence,
showed her that George Davies's chances—if he had ever had
any—were doomed. For Betty had met Guy Lovatt again.

They had met at the 'Simplicissimus,' one of Cologne's gay
haunts, where Betty was supping with George, and, after a
moment of amazement and embarrassment on either side, Betty
had made a sign of recognition, and Guy had left his table and
come straight over to her.

'He was exactly the same—pale attractive face, odd sideways
smile and all. He told me he was stationed out in the country,
and very seldom came into Cologne. He's on the Staff now.
We just talked for a few minutes about nothing in particular, and
then he went.'

The rest of the story, though told briefly and unemotionally,
made Joan sick at heart.

Betty, at a humbly-worded invitation from Guy, had dined out
with him alone at a restaurant, and at first all had gone well. It had
seemed extraordinarily natural to be sitting there with him, and
she had found it difficult to believe that he was married. She asked
him about his wife, and he had talked of her with no constraint.
They lived in Hampshire—a small Jacobean house found by 'Vi.'
He was clearing out of the Army as soon as possible. He had got
a 'youngster'—a boy. Seemed comic, didn't it?

After dinner he had driven her out to Lindenthal, where they had
strolled about the gardens in the soft night air. And there he had
lost his head, and had begun making love to her again. She had

been stupefied, then furious; and he, after a time, wretchedly ashamed.

'It seemed a little hard, all things considered,' Betty wrote, 'that *I* should have been the one to remember "Vi" in England—to feel protective towards her. But when I heard him mutter that he "had made a hopeless mess of things" I had to try and comfort him. I told him that he was happy really, that he was going home soon, and that then everything would be all right. He said "Yes," like a dutiful small boy, and I drove back alone.

'Why, oh, why need he have turned up again?'

After that Guy was never referred to in letters.

Towards the middle of September Betty mentioned that George Davies had been 'demobbed,' and had come for a farewell tea at the flat before going home.

'I had almost forgotten him,' she said. 'Or rather I had only been aware of his presence, all summer, through a kind of mist.

'I asked if he could bear the idea of going back to his stock-broking. He said "Oh yes, why not?"—that he didn't think the war had particularly unsettled him.

'I thought, "No, nothing would particularly unsettle George!" He looked so square sitting on one of the small gilt chairs, khaki legs crossed, holding his teacup, and looking at me out of his crinkled eyes.

'And then I remembered that he hadn't been young even when he joined up, that the change from civil life can hardly have been easy, and that he had made it almost as soon as war was declared.

'I told him I was glad it was over for him at last.

' "When is it going to be over for you?" he asked me.

'I looked vague (as indeed I felt), and said, probably when the last British soldier had left the Rhine!

'When he went he grasped my hand with a sort of large cheerfulness, told me to "take things easy," and said we must meet again in London—some time.

'Work at the "Central" goes on. There are still dances, but now that Peace has been signed and "wives" have begun to come out, the atmosphere of Cologne is changing, and we Y.M. girls no longer have the entire attention of the Army!'

Poor darling Betty—self-effacing, plucky, humorous. Why indeed need that wretched Guy have turned up just as life was growing smooth for her again?

.   .   .   .   .   .

Joan didn't agree with people who said that sorrow 'softened' or 'sweetened' one. She felt far less sweet now that Jimmy had gone; and she knew that as the years went by, unless she could remember him constantly, she would harden. With him she had lost a brother, a son, and half herself. That channel in which a particular set of her emotions had flowed was dammed. There was no outlet for them now; they flowed back, objectless.

She believed that Jimmy's spirit somewhere, somehow, lived on; but that made no difference to the ache she felt for his physical presence—to the fact that she could no longer talk to him, or twist her fingers in his hair, or see his smile.

.   .   .   .   .   .

She had found work to do. Pre-war interests had vanished almost as though they had never been; and the struggle for the Vote, which had been her especial interest, no longer required to be pursued. For the Vote had been 'given' to women—to a section of them, at least—in 1918, as a reward for 'war service,' rather like a chocolate is given to a child who has behaved unexpectedly well under trying circumstances. But the war—officially over—still lingered on. The results of it were all around, distressing, insistent; and the men who for so many years had been heroes were now 'returned soldiers,' a problem to their country, if not a bore.

Joan's work was at the office of the local War Pensions Committee. Every day, from nine to six, she was there, and often later. The office—like most others of its kind during 1919—was daily swarming with men in 'civvies,' just demobbed, come round to see what they could claim.

Interviewing, interviewing; getting the men to fill up forms;

paying out sums for pensions, or for 'treatment allowances'; listening to interminable confusing stories; trying to disentangle the false from the true.

Claims of every sort would be made: some would be granted, others not. To refuse a man his claim was a detestable task, and was often to provoke his fury.

There was a certain man, Beckwith, very nervy, with exophthalmic goitre, who was for ever claiming 'treatment allowances' over and above what were due to him. One day, in the office, he burst out: 'If I don't get my rights I'll get myself arrested, and then it'll all come out in court!' And, taking care first to wrap his cap round his fist, he smashed one of the window-panes.

Another man said he was going to write to the Prime Minister. 'And if 'e don't take no notice I'll write to the Prince of Wales!' he shouted. Joan only wished that his pathetic belief in the power of these personages to help him had a chance of being justified.

All the men seemed to be nervy, and some definitely unhinged. Doubtless they would settle down in time, but their release from the military machine was not, at the moment, beneficial to them.

And the finding of jobs! That also was part of office work. Writing round to people. There didn't seem to be any jobs. Men were sent here and there, and sometimes they found something, but more often not; and sometimes, it had to be admitted, they were not enthusiastic in the search.

It was sad to see men who had recently been, perhaps, smart and efficient sergeants deteriorating, week by week, before one's eyes —either embittered by failure to find work, or loungingly content to do none.

Boys who had gone into the army at eighteen naturally knew nothing of the conditions of civil life, and were unable to adapt themselves. Older men came back to homes which had been running perfectly well without them; to children whom they didn't know; to wives who had been free and well-off on separation allowances, and who resented having to submit once more to male interference, and to perpetual male presence. Was it any wonder that these men took to drink as a self-assertion and as an escape?

There were men whom the war made. There were a far greater number whom it ruined.

Chapter Three

WHEN spring came, and under the sycamore at the end of the garden the pointed daffodil buds showed yellow streaks, the frost round Joan's heart began to thaw.

All feelings became more intensified—agony, and the revolt from agony. And if the longing for Jimmy was greater than ever, there was the longing for life too.

She began thinking—at first only hazily, and then more and more definitely—about Colin. She began associating his figure with that of Jimmy's in the garden. It was ages since she had heard from him; ages, too, since she had written. She knew, from his people, that he had left India, and had been, for over a month now, with his regiment at Muscat in the Persian Gulf; but that was all.

And from thinking of him she got to the point of writing to him. She wrote quite shortly; she only wanted to bridge the gulf, to show him he was remembered. That was about the middle of May. It was not until September that she had a reply.

Colin wrote from the River Tigris, twelve hours below Kut-el-Amara. He was on his way up to Baghdad, and it was August.

'JOAN DEAR,
   How wonderful it was to hear from you again! Your letter took a long time to find me. It seems to have got hung up somewhere, and when it finally reached Muscat I was not there.'

He spoke about Jimmy. He had heard the news, and had almost written, but had thought—stupidly perhaps—that she would rather not be bothered with a letter from him. Would she understand that he knew what the boy's loss would mean to her, and forgive his inability to say all he felt?

He went on: 'You've come so vividly before me again, Joan, in your English home surroundings—never really dim to me—that

433

I feel I must risk boring you by telling you something of my life out here.

'Muscat is the hottest place in the world, very quaint and very filthy, and the capital of a huge Arabian province. Most Englishmen hate being there—I rather liked it, though I'm glad to have left it now. During some of the time I was officiating Consul and Political Agent! Then, in July, I got demobbed, as you may have heard, and through special recommendations got appointed to the Political Service in Mespot (Department of the I.S.C.)—still retaining captain's rank. I am to be, at first, under the Chief Commissioner in Baghdad. Naturally I'm rather pleased, as I didn't know a soul when I came East, nearly two years ago. It is too curious how things have worked out, when I think that at one time I was going into Father's book business!

'Do you remember the Savoy on the night of Nov. 16th, 1917? When shall I see it again? Not for some time, I fear. (This riverboat I'm on vibrates a lot, so please excuse even-worse-than-usual writing.)

'What about yourself? You don't say whether you are still engaged, or whether . . . anything.

'Always yours (yes, always),
'COLIN'

Then he still cared for her!

Out between those funny shy last lines leapt the amazing fact.

Joan's thoughts went back to that night at the Savoy, just before he sailed, when she had had the definite impression that his love for her was dead—that she had kept him dangling too long—had put him through too much. But it wasn't so. She saw it clearly now. He had only held back because he thought she was involved with someone else. And then a few days later had come that brutal little letter from Paul which had dealt her pride and her love-life a very nearly fatal wound, and had set her free. After that she had drifted on, sapless. Then had come the Rest Camp, where life had budded again. Then the Armistice, and Jimmy's death—and night. And all the time Colin had been out there, in those far hot countries, not knowing about her, still loving her, making heaven knew what surmises about her—too proud, too humble, to ask.

Back—back she went to the early days of his love for her; to their poetry-beglamoured friendship; to the way in which, during the war years, he had kept cropping up; to the varying shades of her own feelings for *him*. Always he had been there in her consciousness; and always, without realising it, she had loved him.

'That's it,' she said to herself, with the calm which often accompanies a sudden discovery, 'I love him!'

It was not a question of working herself up, of pretending, for convenience, to an emotion which wasn't there. It was not pity for Colin, or gratitude towards him. It was something quite simple, and final: it was the knowledge that she was his. The 'liking' which she had always felt for him, the mental sympathy, the detached admiration for his beauty of body, were now blended with the hitherto missing factor of in-love-ness.

An extraordinary exhilaration and an extraordinary peace possessed her.

She went to a cupboard and took out some of his old letters. She read them through, absorbed, ashamed. How had she ever been able to resist him? Cold, head-in-dreams little idiot she had been. *Talking* about love. Wasting the years. She was a woman now. He was a man. Would they be shy of one another when they met?

She came upon the little letter which he had written her in April '15—just before going out to France—when he had been in despair about her, and at the same time exalted over the war adventure. 'It was terribly hard not to be unhappy. Not that unhappiness really matters . . .' 'Daffodils are very dear to me now . . .' 'Will the time of roses follow?' 'Joan, if ever you change your mind about me, send me a 'damask bud' in place ot the daffodil'

If ever you change your mind about me . . .

A smile slowly crept into her eyes and round her lips. Here was a means—if she had wanted one—of letting him know. But it would be too sentimental! Besides, he would have forgotten. She herself, until that moment, had forgotten that she had ever given him a daffodil. How young! Flower symbols. . . . No, it wouldn't do.

A little later she was hovering among the stubby rose-trees in the garden. The September crop was in full bloom. She stooped and broke off a 'Hugh Dickson' bud—crimson and velvety. She carried it indoors, and upstairs. Her heart was beating absurdly. She sat down at her writing-table.

.   .   .   .   .   .

Two months later she heard from him.

'ADORED ONE,

When your letter came I was sitting in my little house of baked brick. As always, at sight of your handwriting, I sort of sighed with pleasure. But when I opened the envelope and found that flattened rose-bud . . . ! Oh, Joan, if ever the morning stars sang together they did so then! Because I knew—yes, before I looked at your letter—I knew what it meant. No need for you to have said: 'In case you have forgotten. . . .' Do you imagine that I have ever forgotten, or ever can forget, anything that has happened or been said between us two?

'What do I care what you have felt for other men? What you have done, or nearly done? All that has only made you able to love me more. You have tripped far, 'my pretty sweeting,' but 'journeys end . . .' Don't think me conceited if I tell you that I *felt* ours would end like this. Even when things were at their blackest for me—two years ago; even when my mind saw that it was idiotic to hope, something else in me stubbornly, mulishly, hoped on.

'Forgive me, sweet, for being such a bungling backward lover in those old days. It was impossible for you to love me then. It is a miracle that you should do so now.'

And then he came down to practical affairs, and told her a little about his position. He had every chance, his friends told him, of rapid promotion. The reports which he had to make out were considered good. Did Joan think she could stand life in the East? It would not necessarily be always Mespot. And there would be long home leaves. He was just now administering the district of Diwaniyah. 'Which is, of course, absurd,' he said, 'considering my lack of real qualifications and my poor knowledge of Arabic. But it's fun shouldering such a lot of responsibility, and of such a new kind. And never, darling, as you know, have I been much of a horseman, but now I have to spend days in the saddle—getting into touch with "tribes," and investigating disputes. France and the trenches seem like a distant dream. Heaven knows where my wife ("my wife!") would live, but I'll find out all about that. And in any case I may be moved before long, and in any case . . . Well, we'll talk it all over when I come home—though I'm afraid I shall hardly get leave before the early summer.

'Joan, we'll go to the Savoy! (I don't care how vulgar you say it is!) It saw my hopes born in 1914. It saw them dashed in 1917. It shall see them confirmed in 1920.

'Oh, darling! Anything sweeter than your sending me that rose! You dare laugh at yourself for doing it. It was the perfect gesture.
'Good-night—*mine*!
'Your knight, your lover, your husband, your friend,
'He who wears *both* your flowers.'

To be loved, and to love back! To be in a state of love that was not at the same time a state of torment. To feel herself on a smooth and sunny sea. What did outside conditions matter? The harmony of spirits was all; and the being together. Saddles and heat and sand, or a couple of rooms in London—she didn't care. Her mind —always prone to picture-making—played over a new strange future.

But now there was no Jimmy in her pictures—only a dark spot where he should have been. Now she and Colin would be alone together.

'But, Jim-pot, you're pleased, aren't you?' she asked him that night. 'You'll be there, somehow, with us? You like Colin?'

And Jimmy, sitting on the edge of her bed, having just come in from the garden and changed, said slowly: 'I think he's an awfully decent chap.'

Yes, it was all right.

.   .   .   .   .   .

She wrote to Betty and told her, but she told no one else. Time enough when Colin came home, and they could be—silly but sweet phrase—'properly engaged.'

Through the winter and spring months she worked on steadily at the Pensions Office, tried to acquire some knowledge of Near Eastern affairs, and re-read tracts of English poetry.

.   .   .   .   .   .

April 1920. Colin was coming on leave in June.

Joan did wish she were not going to be twenty-six. That was the queer thing about the war years: in exactly the same way as ordinary years they had added to your age. It hardly seemed fair. You had somehow looked on them as special and apart—not to be counted in Time at all; and had had a vague idea that when they were over you would start again at twenty, or whatever you were when they began.

But this was a small fret in the rising tide of her happiness. And when she compared herself with other girls she had almost a feeling of guilt.

Sometimes, standing in the middle of her room, her hands would go to her throat, and she would whisper: 'Colin, come! Come soon!'

.   .   .   .   .   .

His leave was postponed. There was trouble in Iraq. Curse those Arabs! Or curse our Government's mishandling of them! Joan felt she knew too little about the situation to judge of it. All she knew about was her own sick disappointment. Well, she had waited long, and Colin had waited longer. They could wait another month or two, she supposed.

By June the Arabs were rising against us all over Iraq—both in the towns and the isolated villages. Things looked serious. Was it possible that the corpse of the war, now nearly two years buried, could still send out poisonous vapours which might destroy? Was there to be no safety ever?

. . . . . .

The weeks went on; and one hot evening towards the middle of July Joan heard that Colin had been killed.

She had just come in from the office, and was going upstairs to change, when there had been a telephone call from the Paleys asking her to come round.

She remembered afterwards nothing of the quarter of an hour's walk to their house, and not very much of the forlorn interview which followed.

'It was always you!' said Mr. Paley, his great loose figure towering over her. 'It was always you!' And he blew his nose into a handkerchief that seemed to Joan's stunned apprehensions to be of an extraordinary size.

'We had to ask you to come,' said Mrs. Paley, 'just because he was so fond of you. You did care for him a little, didn't you?'

'But I was engaged to him!' she cried, forgetting, in this nightmare, that they didn't know. And then, labouringly, she told them all.

Their delight astonished her at first.

'He knew—he knew, then, before he died!' sighed Mr. Paley.

Knew . . . ? Oh, that she loved him—yes. Yes, she supposed that was a good thing. They were thinking of everything from *his* point of view, and she, so far, had only thought of it from theirs. She was so sorry for them, and also so overwhelmed by them—in their large, parental, elderly affliction—that nothing else was clear. She wanted to get away. She couldn't bear it. Besides, they might be asking her next: 'Why not before, Joan? Why not years ago?' She must get away.

'Come whenever you can, child,' said Mr. Paley, seeing her off at the door. 'We'll let you know more about—about—as soon as we hear.'

'Well,' said Joan to herself, as she walked home in the slanting sunshine, and felt her own situation emerging, 'that's very funny! That's just about the funniest thing that could possibly have happened now.'

.   .   .   .   .   .

Several weeks afterwards came details from one of his friends in Mespot.

Colin had been sent on July 8th to inquire into a rising at a small village called Khan Jan Mal. When he arrived he found that attacks were in progress against a party of loyal levies, and he decided to send for help. The friend who was with him returned in a motor-trolley, but Colin refused to go, and threw in his lot with the beleaguered force—the only white man there. As soon as the trolley was out of sight there was another attack, and Colin was shot through the head while carrying a box of ammunition to the firing-line. He died instantaneously. Meanwhile his own house at Diwaniyah had been attacked and destroyed, and all his possessions burnt. There was nothing of his—not a pocket-book, not a fragment of clothing—to send home.

Six months later, Colin was mentioned posthumously, in a dispatch from General Sir J. A. S. Haldane, 'For Distinguished and Gallant Services in the Field.'

.   .   .   .   .   .

Betty had got home a few days after receiving the news of her brother's death. She was not going out to Cologne again.

'Oh, Joan,' she sighed, as they were talking together, 'I would have loved you two! Anything more *right* . . .'

And she reproached herself for not having, in her shrinking hatred of interference, done more to help them.

'But for the very reason that I wanted it so much,' she said, 'I couldn't press it.'

'Nothing would have been altered, my dear,' said Joan. 'There was nothing to be done—except by me. I suppose I shall get used, in time, to the company of that unpleasant little pair of words, "Too late!" '

Chapter Four

IT was nearly midnight, and the 'Half-a-Dozen' Club was filling up. At the little tables round the floor-space people sat eating the thick rich sandwiches and the scrambled eggs and bacon which were a speciality of the Club.

New arrivals pushed through the door at the far end; stood looking down the room; waved to acquaintances; called over their shoulders, 'Yes, there's still room!' Went out again to take their things off; re-entered.

Inside, the lights were very pink and very becoming. They glowed on the bare arms and made-up faces of the women, the polished heads and black-and-white clothes of the men; also on jersey frocks and lounge suits, for at the 'Half-a-Dozen' people changed or not as they felt inclined.

On the walls were painted caricatures of actors and actresses— elongated, fantastic, malicious. The negro at the drum, his face tilted, lazily beat out the rhythm of a dance tune. Little waiters in brown Eton jackets darted to and fro.

'Care to push round?' asked Jack.

Joan nodded, and, leaving her half-consumed sandwich and half-smoked cigarette, got up with him.

Her left hand went to the back of his right shoulder. She kept her body tightly against his, and with little pressures of the hand— mechanical to her now—steered their progress His evening coat fitted his flat thin back like a glove. Her low-cut dress filmed out from the waist in petals of Love-in-the-Mist blue which enhanced her fairness.

Throughout this autumn of 1920 the cousins had gone about a lot together; and Joan, with an apparent casualness and an underlying persistence, had lured Jack from merely sitting about in night-clubs and watching other people dance to dancing himself.

With Joan he was now perfectly at ease, but he was still shy of asking other girls to take the floor with him.

The negro drummer banged on his variegated saucepan lids. The saxophone yowled. Feet shuffled, shuffled. The atmosphere became hotter, and laden with the acrid-sweet smell of powder.

The tune stopped on a descending moan; and partners, still half-clinging to one another, went back to their tables.

'No more scenes at home, Jacko, since last week?' asked Joan.

Jack blew up a smoke-ring.

'No. I expect the Pater 'll get sick of them soon. He must realise by now that nothing will induce me to go into the blasted tea business.'

'Poor Uncle Robert! I suppose it is tantalising having his eldest son just lounging about the house, and blewing his gratuity, when that son could be a source of pride and comfort in the office.'

'What chiefly galls him, I think,' said Jack, 'is the fact that *he* had to work when he was young, and why the hell shouldn't I?'

'Quite. And he had to fight when he was young, hadn't he!'

'Oh, well . . .' Jack leant back with a little smile that was both tolerant and bitter. 'I expect he *would* have! But I do tell him I feel I've done about enough for the present. And it's not as though I wanted to earn money—I don't. And that he simply can't understand. I did want to at one time perhaps, but now . . . Well, I mean, what's the point? I've got my pension. Why worry?'

'Why indeed? But I suppose eventually . . .'

'Oh, eventually I daresay something 'll turn up that I can stand the thought of. Something that won't mean grinding in an office with only a fortnight's holiday a year and no fresh air.'

'Hallo, Joan!'

'Hallo, Thrush! How long is it this time?'

'God knows!'

Thrush, with her warm dark eyes and carnation mouth, had suddenly loomed up opposite. Thrush with a couple of shadowy men at her shoulders. She looked round her, frowning.

'No table!'

'Sit at ours,' said Joan. 'There's absolutely no room, but it doesn't matter.'

'May we? All right.'

One of the shadows was dispatched for chairs, and the party crammed up.

'Funny I haven't seen you here before,' said Thrush. 'Are you often here?'

'Whenever we're not anywhere else. Oh, this is my cousin—Jack Seddon. Miss Shirley.'

Thrush's restless eyes fixed themselves in a stare. 'Your cousin? D'you mean . . . ?' And then: 'It's absurd how alike you are, you two!' she went on with animation. 'Don't you think so, Thorne? Same neatly-finished faces—same sort of sea-grey eyes. I wouldn't mind doing a picture of you both, sitting there side by side, and calling it . . .'

'Not at all your sort of subject, my dear—far too Anglo-Saxon,' said the dark young man called Thorne, in a hollow voice. 'When she condescends to paint human beings at all,' he pursued, addressing Jack, 'and not some depraved arrangement of melons and of passion-flowers, she does sad Slav girls or Marseillais fishermen. But perhaps you know her work?'

Jack said, smilingly, that he was afraid he didn't.

'No? Well, I believe she's got a show on just now, at the Munster Galleries—haven't you, Thrush? You ought to look in. You might be amused.'

'Thanks, Thorne,' said Thrush. 'You're a good publicity agent. Now I suppose you want me to tell them about your poems? But I can't, as I haven't read them—anyhow the later ones—only those few about the trenches.'

'Oh, *those!* Very callow efforts. One did that sort of thing in 1917. . . .' He glanced at Joan. 'Utterly *démodé* now, of course. As if anybody wanted even to think about the war!'

'Heavens, as if anybody did!' laughed Joan, stifling the quick hurt within. 'Things change, and the years roll on, and we flap about in an indifferent universe, and nobody tells us what to do, and it's equally unprofitable to remember yesterday or to dream about to-morrow!'

There was a chorus of assent.

'But I'm bound to say, Joan,' added Thrush, 'that as far as outward appearance goes the rolling years have improved you. You're a lot prettier than you used to be—there's more chic about you—more colour——'

' "If God did all!" ' said Joan, sustaining with quiet amusement this volley of comment.

'Whether God did it or the dressing-table,' came Thorne's courteous hollow tones, 'the effect is most agreeable.'

Joan bowed. And then somehow or other they were off on a discussion of Proust—at that time the *furore* of the English intelligentsia. And as they talked Thrush listened, and Jack leant back lazily, and the fair man on Thrush's right kept looking at her under his eyelids, and trying to get her to come and dance.

'All right, Phil, come on!' said Thrush at last, moving back her chair.

Joan watched her up the room—cheek pressed against Phil's soft shirt-front, lashes lowered, a drugged look on her face, her fingers, curled in his, held low at first, and then up to his shoulder.

'Would you care . . .?' asked Thorne, stretching his long neck politely. Joan rose, edged round the table, and slid off on his arm. As she went Jack gave her the merest quiver of a wink, then turned to make a sign to a passing waiter.

'Of course, whether the French themselves appreciate him . . .' she heard Thorne saying, somewhere above her head. (It seemed they were still discussing Proust.) 'Those immense involved sentences. . . . Not in the tradition . . . psychology . . .'

'It is confusing, but then the French . . .'

The music throbbed on; and suddenly, over Thorne's arm, she caught sight of Paul Wentworth sitting at a corner table with a dark-eyed woman in green. Joan gave him a little smile as she passed; and he, without moving, smiled back. There was no emotion in their recognition of each other, no confusion, no surprise even. Joan's only thought was that Paul looked smaller, and somehow *soft*. She noticed too that he was a little bald. Pity some men couldn't always be in khaki.

'Wasn't that Paul Wentworth?' asked Thorne.

'Yes.'

'Far and away the most brilliant dramatic critic in London, I consider.'

'Oh, so do I!' She spoke truth. She read Paul's articles with real enjoyment.

On they danced—sometimes talking, sometimes in silence. The music died; was clapped into life again. Died, and was clapped into life again.

At last Joan and her partner drew up at their table. Thrush—who seemed to have disposed of Phil—was sitting there alone with Jack. Her chin was propped on her hands, and she was looking down, rather pale. Neither were speaking at the moment.

'Well,' said Joan, 'I'm off! It's nearly three. Coming, Jacko?'

Thrush raised blank eyes, then seemed to realise what had been said, and got up quickly.

'I'm coming too. I'm sick of this hole.'

There was no one in the small cloak-room when the two girls arrived there.

'Awfully glad about your picture-show, Thrush,' said Joan, powdering her damp nose at the mirror. 'I saw some good reviews. I was going in this week as a matter of fact.'

'Thank God it's over!' exclaimed Thrush. And at Joan's look of surprise—at her suspended powder puff—added: 'This evening, I mean.'

'Oh! . . . Haven't you enjoyed it?'

'It's been hell! Meeting your cousin brought everything back.'

'My dear . . . But it's not as though you *knew* Jack!'

'No, but he was in Ginger's regiment, wasn't he?' said Thrush brusquely. 'And he wrote me that letter about him. And somehow the poor boy having lost his own arm . . .'

'I didn't think . . .' said Joan. 'It never occurred to me . . .'

'No, why should it? You've always seen me jazzing around with other men, looking as though I were thoroughly enjoying myself —which, mind you, in a sense I am. But I'll tell you, now, that I've never loved anyone but Ginger—not *loved*. And if Ginger were suddenly to appear again I'd chuck the whole lot and follow him anywhere. I'd rather grind an organ with Ginger than have all the success and money in the world with anyone else!'

Joan stared at her, and, in spite of the rather melodramatic phrases, in spite, too, of her own unwillingness, felt forced to believe her. Whatever might be said against Thrush she was honest, and she was not sentimental.

'I'm sorry,' she said. 'I certainly thought you'd forgotten—even hoped you had.'

'One puts up a show,' said the other girl. 'One's got to live. And of course,' she added, more lightly, 'one doesn't always feel like this.' She wrapped her cloak round her and stuck out a hand, boy-like. 'Good-bye, dear. Odd how you're connected with my romantic past!' She turned at the door and added: 'You've changed, you know.'

The next moment she was gone, and Joan heard her voice on the stairs—high-pitched and laughing—mingle with the bantering reproaches of her escorts.

. . . . . .

Pamela was up in town, delivering 'a short sharp offensive,' as she called it, on theatrical managers.

Joan met her for lunch at Stewart's.

'Any luck?'

'None, so far. Was offered a small part in a touring Musical Comedy, but . . .'

'Well?'

Pamela wrinkled her nose. 'I turned it down. Didn't think I could stand it.'

'But, Pam, if you really want to get away from home and earn money, you'll have to stand things—you'll have to squash down that fastidiousness of yours.'

Pamela was silent; and it was born in on Joan that in spite of her friends' dash and sparkle, in spite of the fact that she could screw herself up at times, and carry through with gallantry the heaviest tasks, she would not, in this theatre business, ever achieve what she wanted.

Since the spring of 1919 (and it was now late 1920) she had been coming up, at intervals, for 'offensives'; had pursued them with the same bright determination, only to subside back into Wallingford and be the right hand of that querulous mother who, now that the war was over, was demanding her perpetual service and companionship.

'But it's not only that,' Pamela was saying. 'Not only that I can't face the dustier side of stage life—I *could*—other things being equal——'

'What do you mean?'

'Well, Aunt Maud made me see her doctor the other day, and it seems my heart's weak. You know it went dicky after munitions. It recovered all right, but that bout of 'flu I got at Rouen touched it up again.'

'Pam—I never knew!'

'Didn't know myself till that interview. I used often to get tired—specially when we had a servantless period at home—but I didn't think that meant anything. But the point now is, that a Musical Comedy job, which entails dancing, of course, is rather "off." Ordinary parts in ordinary plays would be all right, but then they're not easy to get, and . . . I've lost so many years.'

Joan could never quite bear it when Pamela's expression of merry wood-nymph became suddenly a tragic mask.

'You *will* get something,' she said, forcing the note of conviction.

'I didn't tell you, did I, that I'd been engaged to my cousin Dickie?' Pamela went on, with apparent irrelevance. 'He asked me when he was on leave once—ages ago. And then, soon after I got out to Rouen, he came to see me there, and we fixed it up. You see, Joan, I'd been so desolate and lonely. And there he was—a darling—and I knew him so well. I got happy again—not in the golden-dream way, of course—but we'd have suited each other, and had quite a pleasant life. However, as you know, he got killed in the retreat, and that was that. He was the last of my lot. There's no one now.'

'Rot, Pam, there are heaps—for a girl like you!' exclaimed Joan. And this time she spoke with real conviction, and also with a little hardness, for sympathy over the past was not a thing which, at this period, she wanted to indulge in, either for herself or others.

The lines began to slant up again on Pamela's face.

'Think so? Well, let us hope! Now look here—I want you to advise me. See these shoes . . .?' She turned in her chair and stretched out a pretty, thorough-bred foot and ankle. 'I want some new ones, the same shape, but in crocodile . . .'

Joan laughed; and 'shoes, and ships and sealing-wax' carried them buoyantly through the rest of lunch.

.   .   .   .   .   .

During the years which followed, Joan's life was full and varied. By day she visited, on her own, soldiers' families in their homes— the War Pensions Committees having ceased to exist as such. By night she danced, and went to studio parties up and down London, and was in all sorts of 'swims.' There were so many people who were interesting, so many new books to be read and discussed. And there were occasional trips abroad. And there was her friendship with Betty.

Betty was now working with her father in the City; and her excellent brains and her flair for the *Zeitgeist* were of ever-increasing benefit to the business.

'You'll be running it on your own in the end,' Joan told her. 'Competent, but soft-eyed and soft-cheeked as ever, you'll run it! And your father will retire and devote himself to research.'

Betty said that if that ever happened, the first thing she would do would be to give herself shorter hours, for at present, when she got home in the evenings, she was really too weary to change and go out, or to do anything but sit. 'Not having your hectic vitality, darling!' she added.

But in spite of her many activities, in spite of her genuine capacity for enjoyment, if Joan had been told, by someone who knew, that to-morrow she would have to leave all this and die, she would simply have said, 'Oh!'

At the roots of her being there lay a vast indifference.

PART SIX

1928

'Daffodil-picker Time took from their lives the glow.'

Chapter One

PAMELA and Joan were gathering apples in the orchard which lay at the bottom of the garden. Lower down, beyond the meadows, the Thames ran sleepily. The willows were hardly touched with gold.

'I think that's enough,' said Pamela, peering among the branches. 'Oh, just this nice russety one!' She dropped it into the basket Joan held.

'Pam, your right stocking!' laughed Joan.

'Oh, down again? It's the fault of the knicker—it's lost its knee-elastic.' She stooped and pulled up the wrinkled stocking over the long shapely leg.

'But you don't trust to your knicker-elastics to keep your stockings up, do you?'

'I do indeed! There's nothing else to keep them up. I tell you I've no clothes, and I haven't time to mend those I have. I'm just kept together with safety-pins.'

She hardly exaggerated. The short plum-coloured stockinette skirt was gathered unevenly round her waist, dipping at the hem on either side; and on her shoulder, under the stuff of the jumper, showed that kind of small hard lump which means that a broken chemise-strap has been pinned. Pamela still bore herself gracefully, but Time had reduced her slimness to angularity; and the small face, although unlined, had fallen in below the cheek-bones.

'I must just have a look at my cuttings before we go in,' she said, leading the way to some frames further up the garden.

She pushed back the glass lids one after the other, and bent lingeringly over the small bits of green in the boxes beneath. There were violets, lifted from the garden and 'divided,' that would be flowering at Christmas; violas and pansies that would be 'put out' in the spring; pentstemons that in summer would be scarlet.

453

'I do think plants are satisfactory!' said Pamela. 'Much more so than human beings.'

'Gardening's a passion with you now, isn't it?'

'M'm. You've no idea how absorbing it can become.' And she went on talking 'garden' with the detailed and intimate knowledge —faintly boring to the outsider ready enough to admire *results*— that marks the real enthusiast. She did a lot of 'showing' at different times, and had won several prizes, but this didn't interest her so much as rearing odd little seedlings for her own delight, and generally pottering.

The basket of apples was taken round to the kitchen-door, and the girls then put on aprons and began cleaning silver at the dining-room table. Spoons, forks, sugar-bowls, candlesticks, salt-cellars received their coating of damp pink powder and were rubbed into brilliance.

'You are an angel to help me with this!' said Pamela. 'I don't feel I ought to let you.'

'Don't be absurd. But, Pam, if it's not too impertinent a question, why do you keep so much silver going? Surely it makes a fearful lot of unnecessary work?'

Pamela agreed that it did, but that her mother liked maintaining old standards, even under changed conditions, and that for her own part she rather agreed with her mother.

'Why should we live like pigs,' she asked, 'just because these brutes of servants refuse to do their jobs properly? I loathe house-work, but I'd rather have things nice than not do it. However, thank God, we've got a cook now who seems likely to stay. The whole of last month I spent in the kitchen.'

And as she talked of the iniquity of the wages now demanded, the appalling difficulty of getting service in the country, and the inadequacy of that service when obtained, her voice became hard and intolerant, and her mouth took on the thin line which Joan, of late, had come to know so well.

'There are occasions,' said Pamela, 'when I feel we ought to sell this place and go into something smaller. It's been more and more difficult, since the war, to keep it going. But then we are all so fond of it—specially Father. We could manage all right, I think, if it weren't that any spare money we ever have has to go to Leo. All those enterprises of his—in South Africa and California and so on—fail, one after the other. It's a perpetual drain.'

They went upstairs to wash. When she had tidied herself Joan came into Pamela's room, and found her sitting at the dressing-table.

'Time you came to London again, Pam,' she remarked. 'Your hair's a disgrace.'

Pamela turned, her whole face lit with laughter, and rounded upwards into the curves of girlhood. At such moments she still looked twenty.

'Little cat!' she said. 'I'm *growing* it!'

"Well, I should keep it shingled. It suits you better.'

'So neat and trim you are, nowadays, aren't you? Talk of the tables being turned!'

Pamela held out two strands of hair, golliwog-wise, from her face. 'Grey on the temples,' she said. 'Do you see?'

'It doesn't show, ordinarily.'

'No, I conceal it. But it will soon. Not that I care!' she added, giving her head a whisk or two with the brush, and rising. 'Middle-age, which looms over us all, my dear, has no horrors for me. Queer how I used to desire things so frightfully—oh, but so frightfully—and now I desire nothing at all. So much pleasanter. Come down to lunch.'

And Joan knew, with a small ache at the heart, as well as with satisfaction, that not merely was Pam resigned to her present life, but that she was perfectly content with it.

As they were sitting down to lunch, Mrs. Butler, faded and pinched-looking, cast a look at the rose-bowl.

'Have these been *done* this morning, Pammy?' she asked. 'They look a little . . .'

'I'm afraid not, Mother,' said Pamela, patiently. 'We were rather busy. I'll do them before dinner to-night.'

'That's right, dear. Your father's sure to notice if they're not fresh.'

The apples in the tart, which appeared for the second course, were almost as hard as when they had been picked. The pastry was like a slab of felt.

'I really don't know, Pammy, whether this cook *will* do,' said Mrs. Butler, helping the tart. 'If she doesn't improve in a week or two I'm afraid . . . You see, your father . . .' She turned with her forced-sweet smile to Joan. 'Things *are* so difficult in the country!'

When Joan went away Pamela kissed her affectionately. 'Nice person! Come again soon.'

The old, dear Pam was always there, not far below the surface.

But as she drove to the station Joan visualised her friend: first as the love-lit girl prepared to follow her man to the ends of the earth, and then, as she had seen her at this time yesterday afternoon, sailing thinly down the field to collect eggs, and making a sudden dive at a brown hen that always somehow got out into the flower border.

Chapter Two

THE October leaves lay damp on the pavement outside Betty's little house in Kensington.

'Hallo, darling!' she said, looking up as Joan came into the nursery. 'I didn't expect you so soon.'

'I know you didn't, but I thought I'd come along a bit earlier and see the infant bathed.'

Betty was sitting, a mackintosh apron tied round her, a towel on her knees, on a low chair by the fire. Anne, aged eight months, was on her back in the water, submitting gurglingly to all that was done to her, and biting a small rubber doll.

Joan took off her hat and sat down on the other side of the hearth.

'I know your theory about not combining friends and babies,' she said, 'but as we were going to have the evening alone together, I thought a bit of "baby" first wouldn't matter.'

Betty lifted the slippery bit of humanity on to her knee and wrapped it in the towel. Gently and systematically she dried it. Face—ears—one fat foot—another fat foot. The head lolled backwards; the doll was still being chewed. Betty looked down at her offspring with a tenderness which she did her best to temper with amusement. Her eyes still gleamed violet through dark lashes, but the peach-bloom of her cheeks had begun to give place to tiny red-mauve veins—less apparent now than usual, because the warmth and steaminess of the room had caused a flush. Generously built, even as a girl, Betty now looked as though six babies on her lap would hardly trouble her.

'There, my pet!' she said, when she had pinned on Anne's nappy and thrust her reluctant arms into sleeves. 'Now you can go to your Aunt Joan for a bit, if she'll have you, while I get your bottle.'

Anne sat heavy, solid and warm on Joan's knee, staring at her with blue-eyed wisdom, cleaner than a sea-shell, and smelling faintly of

457

milk and violets. Joan kissed, once, the adorable nape of her neck, but otherwise made no demonstrations, feeling that the dignity of a small child, unable to defend itself against the onslaughts of adults, was to be respected.

She sank into a state of drowsy, almost consciousless well-being. The fire glowed. Damp towels hung on the fender. Betty, at the other side of the room, was doing mysterious things with saucepans and measuring jugs.

'I wonder if you'll be as pretty as your mother, darling, when you're grown up,' murmured Joan.

'At present I can see no likeness to anyone,' said Betty. 'She's a healthy lump, but beyond that . . . Now then, my funny, come along!'

More and more sleepily Anne sucked at her bottle; Betty, patient, tranquil, tilting it up, uttering little words of encouragement. Anne's eyelids closed; the milky teat dropped away. Betty carried her off into another room.

She had scarcely come in again, a few moments later, when George entered. He was dressed for the evening ('For one of those preposterous Masonic dinners men feel so important about,' Betty explained), but his white tie was hanging loose. He nodded to Joan by the fire, and then stood, chin stretched, while his wife made the bow for him which he could never manage satisfactorily for himself.

Joan watched them. They had been married nearly two years. Betty was thirty-six; George—what would George be now? Getting on for fifty, she supposed. He didn't look it, certainly. But Betty said he had scarcely changed in appearance since Cologne days—except that his hair was greyer, and the crinkles round his eyes a little deeper.

What an extraordinary thing doggedness was! Through all those years that Betty had been slaving in the City George had never abandoned his steady pursuit of her; and in the end he had prevailed. His worth of character, and dearness, combined, perhaps, with the growing lassitude which Betty felt with the life she was leading, had won her. And they were happy—there was no doubt of that. 'In our middle-aged way!' Betty had smiled, when asked. And this little house of theirs, in Edwardes Square, had all that charm of atmosphere and rightness of detail which Joan would have expected a house run by Betty to possess.

'Well, good-bye, dear,' said George, kissing his wife. 'I don't suppose I shall be very late. Good-bye Joan. It'll be a case of "deep calling to deep," I expect, while I'm away! Oh, you girls!' The door shut on his indulgent but understanding laugh.

'What I like about George,' remarked Joan, 'is that he always makes one feel so young!'

Betty was folding clothes and gathering things off the fender. 'Yes, it is rather nice. But, you know, when you're married to him he's a complete baby, really. I suppose they all are. Come on down to my room, and let's brush up for dinner. There are all sorts of things I want to hear about.'

Chapter Three

JOAN was walking rather wearily down the Willoughby Road towards the Robert Seddons', where she thought she might as well drop in for a cup of tea. The November sun was a low red lamp behind the mist. She had been seeing to final—or almost final—arrangements at the hall where, on the following evening, the 11th, a meeting in support of the League of Nations was to take place. She was the secretary of the local branch of the Union. She did hope this meeting was going to be a success. In her own opinion—although she was always congratulated on them afterwards—her meetings very seldom were. Either the speaker was brilliant and the audience scanty, or else the audience overflowing and the speaker poor. She had managed, through a friend, to get hold of someone very well known for to-morrow night. Her chairman was good too, but . . . well, you never knew.

She had arrived at the gate; and there, at the gate too, just going in, was her cousin Babs with her two little boys. Babs, twenty-five, swift of speech, round and pleasant of face, had been married six years, and lived in Hampstead, not very far from her old home. She always knew exactly what she wanted, did Babs, and firmly and punctually brought it about. She had never wavered in her wish—announced long ago as a child—to be married, and to have 'stacks of babies,' and, having achieved the first part of it with ease, she seemed now in a fair way to realising the second. Peter was walking stockily up the path to the front door; John, in his mail-cart, was being pushed through the gate; and the small brother or sister who was arriving in a few months was discernible in the outline of Babs's figure.

'Bringing them to tea with their Granny,' grinned Babs. 'What luck your being here too! When are you coming over to see *me*, you blighter?'

And they went in together.

As Joan was coming out again, an hour or two later, she ran into her Uncle Robert and Bill returning from the office. Bill wanted to persuade her to come in again, but she laughed good-night, said she was late already, and told him he had just missed his sister. It was Bill, now, who was his father's pride. He was doing well in the business—while his elder brother was pottering on a chicken-farm in the country, fairly content, but unsatisfactory. Hurrying homewards in the dark, Joan still saw Bill's round grey eyes—eyes which seemed to contradict his general appearance of dapper young man about town, and which, during the last year or so, had contained an increasing trouble. She knew the cause of that trouble—it was Molly Paley. Molly, lovely scamp that she was, treated him abominably, and—unbeknown to her parents, whose roof she still shared—was living with a sculptor in Chelsea. Curious, Joan thought, how lightly girls took their love-affairs these days. Molly didn't seem to be particularly absorbed by her sculptor, although she admitted that he was 'thrilling,' and that they had 'wonderful times.' Joan was fond of Molly—nobody could help being—and was the recipient of most of her confidences, but she found it difficult at times to gauge the girl's sincerity.

'Is that you, Joan?' called Florence, through the half-open drawing-room door, as her niece let herself into the house. 'Look, dear, I don't believe Mudie's have sent the right books after all. *Are* these the ones I put on my list?' She came forward, a stout figure, her hair quite white, but her face still retaining a certain innocent freshness. 'Surely I've read these?'

Joan looked at the volumes. *The Golden Arrow*, by Mary Webb, and *Point Counterpoint*, by Aldous Huxley.

'No, Auntie, I'm sure you haven't read either.'

'Not *The Golden Arrow?*'

'You're thinking of the *Arrow of Gold* by Conrad.'

'Oh—*yes*. That man you're so fond of.'

'But, Auntie, I don't think I should bother with the other one. You won't like it much.'

'Well, it does look a bit heavy,' said Florence good-naturedly, 'but I daresay I shall get through it. I'll have a try, anyhow. I like to keep up to date.'

Joan smiled, gave her a kiss, and went upstairs to change.

.   .   .   .   .   .

Next morning Joan happened to go into the pantry about something, and saw yesterday's evening paper, which she hadn't looked at, lying on the table. A head-line—'Secret of Shot Ex-Officer'—arrested her attention; and, reading on, a sickness crept over her, and a whole set of long-dormant memories quivered to life. The paragraph ran:

'Letters read at an inquest at Gloucester to-day on Philip Nichol, until recently master of —— School, in the village of ——, who was found shot in a wood with a revolver by his side, included one addressed to "All whom it may concern," in which he wrote:

' "Ten years after the Armistice I find that the world is not worth living in, and that I, personally, have failed to make it better. I cannot face another celebration of that day which seemed to many of us such a radiant dawn. Nowhere have responsibilities been shouldered or promises been fulfilled; everywhere is an undercurrent of despair and shame. I prefer to be with those who died before they knew." '

' Nichol also wrote a short statement, signed but not witnessed, saying that he left what little he possessed to his wife—if she could be found.

' The doctor said that Nichol's wounds must have been self-inflicted.

' A verdict was returned of "suicide while of unsound mind." '

Joan went up to the old nursery and brooded long and long.

Twice only, during all these years, had she seen Philip; and two or three times only had he written. She had known the school was not doing well, and she had known—from that day when he had brought the pretentious little woman to Beechwood—that his wife would be no help, but only a drag on him in his work. When his wife had left him she didn't know; and when the school had finally closed down she didn't know. But she could imagine what his existence had been—the recurrent melancholia—the fight against impossible odds—the final despair—and she felt wretchedly, though unreasonably, responsible. To have married him, which might have saved him, would never have been possible to her. But to have kept a little more in touch . . . Yet, after all, what could she have done? The seed was already sown in him which, helped by circumstances, had produced this end.

For years Joan, immersed in work, and in a variety of friends and amusements, had scarcely given the war a thought—not her own personal war. Now, at the echo of that belated pistol-shot, it rose and faced her. Soon, all over London, would be reigning the two-minutes silence which, whenever she was caught in it out in the streets, roused in her an obscure irritation. For the ceremony was at the same time beautiful, futile, and a reproach. It was also a species of let-off. 'Remember for two minutes; you can then forget, and resume.' As though one wanted to remember—in that fashion; as though one wanted to forget.

But this was different. This 'remembering' was something inward and unexpected—something which broke her completely up, and which there was no resisting. Soldiers, soldiers, soldiers—officers and privates—from those best known, most loved, to those spoken to once, in a camp or hut—they came before her. A ghost world, but more real than any since.

Emerging at last from that living-dream she looked round at the present. Looked at her girl friends—'girls' no longer. At Pamela in that home of hers, accomplishing courageously the 'daily task,' but withering under it—Pamela, who, more than any woman she knew, needed and would have been made by love. At Barbara, running Girl Guides in her Sussex village, doing, in her sweet feudal way, 'good,' not embittered, but growing yearly a little more old-maidish—she, who ought to have been the mother of four or five sons. At Betty, married now, but after how many years?—and not to the man of her heart. At Thrush, dissolute. At little Phipps of V.A.D. days, cheerfully but desperately trying to make both ends meet in a small house at Wimbledon, with a boy to educate, and a husband still suffering from an old spinal injury. At herself, comfortable financially, alive intellectually, a not wholly useless member of society, but . . .

'Joan, can I come in? Your aunt said I should probably find you up here. I just . . .'

A young smooth face, rose-tinted and radiant, was in the doorway. Joan stared at it.

'Molly,' she cried out, 'don't let your young men go to the war! Don't let any of them go to the war! Nothing's worth it!'

'Go to the war, Joan? Are you dotty?'

Joan looked dazed, then blinked, and slightly turned her head.

'No—no, of course—it's different.'

'Joan—*dear*!' Molly laughed, and with an impulsive movement dropped on the hearth-rug. Then, seeing papers lying about, said: 'Oh, Armistice Day? Is that it? Is that what . . .?'

'No,' said Joan, 'that's the merest chance. The *day* means nothing. It was just that I saw . . . My goodness,' she exclaimed, softly, her eyes on Molly's upturned face, 'you are *young*!'

Molly caught the something special in the atmosphere, and became all Joan's—though she had come in full of herself.

'Not so very,' she smiled. 'Twenty-five.'

'Extraordinary . . . Can you believe,' Joan continued, with queer passion in her voice, 'that *we* were all young once? You can't, of course. But we were! Betty and me, and all our generation—all our brothers and our friends. No other generation ever was so young or ever will be. We were the youth of the world, we were on the crest of life, and we were the war. No one above us counted, and no one below. Youth and the war were the same thing—youth and the war were us.' Her voice dropped. 'But why us, specially? That's the unanswerable question. Why just us? The knife cut so close—above and below.'

'How you must have cursed the war,' murmured Molly.

'We did—we did. But looking back, now, I think we loved it too. Oh, it's so difficult to explain.' Joan had risen, and had wandered over to the window, where she stood looking out, unseeingly. 'So difficult not to put one's present emotions back into that period. At the time, you see, the war was so ordinary—it was just our life. Yes, we hated it, and loved it, both. Loved it only because we gave so much to it, and because it was bound up with our youngness—rather like an unhappy school. It was *our* war, you see. And although it was so every-dayish at the time, and we were so sickened with it, it seems, now, to have a sort of ghastly glamour.' She paused. 'Our hearts are there—unwillingly—for always. It was our war.'

Molly, from where she was sitting, looked at Joan. She saw a woman, not tall, with boyish shoulders, and wearing the usual little short skirt and jumper that was the fashion, and with short fair hair. A woman who, if she had been standing with her back to the window, instead of profile on, in that pallid sunlight, might have looked like an attractive page. As it was, her thirty-four years were all too apparent. Those long lines under the eyes that met the fainter downward lines; those little pools of shadow at the corners of the mouth; the hollows and strings in the neck; the flattened figure. Curious about ages. Not for a moment did Molly see *herself* at thirty-four, or as ever looking otherwise than she did just then. She shared with all the young that blessed inability to imagine themselves old. All she was thinking—for it was only mechanically that she noted these outward details—was what a rotten time poor old Joan must have had—she and her crowd. But they never said anything—they always seemed to be all right—and they had probably had fun too. This queer outburst this morning was unique.

From the window Joan could just see, down at the end of the garden, against the wall, beyond the naked sycamore, Tam's grave. She was scarcely aware that she saw it.

'The responsibilities that were on those boys . . .' she went on, almost to herself. 'The conditions they lived under . . .' She turned. 'Has Bill, for instance, ever slept out of his bed for one night?'

'Well—camping, of course,' said Molly, half-apologetically.

'Molly, why don't you marry Bill?' Joan was back by the fire-place now. 'You're an awful little fool not to. What's the good of wasting time?'

'I shouldn't say,' replied Molly, with the glint of a smile, 'that I had wasted it!'

Joan's mouth twitched.

'No—you haven't, in a way. Your lot don't. Still . . .'

'I *shall* marry Bill as a matter of fact,' announced Molly. 'But not just yet. We understand about each other frightfully well, you know. And I'm not just the soulless modern experimentalist that I've sometimes made out to you. Things are complicated.'

'Oh, my dear, don't I know! And, after all—for you—there *is* time.'

A maid came up with a message for Joan that there was someone on the telephone wanting to speak to her about to-night's meeting.

'*What* meeting?' asked Molly, bored at the interruption of their *tête-à-tête*.

'Oh, to do with the League of Nations,' said Joan, hurrying out. 'I'd forgotten all about it . . .'

THE END

Afterword
The Nurse's Text:
Acting Out an Anaesthetic Aesthetic

1. The Nurse's Text

When war is understood as an ideological struggle rather than
strictly a physical or diplomatic event . . . we redefine its temporal
limits. Women experience war over a different period from that
which traditional history usually recognizes, a period which pre-
cedes and long outlasts formal hostilities. Masculinist history has
stressed the sharply defined event of war; women's time more closely
reflects Bergson's concept of *duree*. Military casualties have more
often been recorded in statistics than in studies of the long term
psychological (and economic) effects of gassing or amputation. A
feminist re-vision of the *time* in wartime can make the history of
war more sensitive to the full range of experience of both men and
women. What holds for historical time is also true for the historical
space we record. We must move beyond the exceptional, marked
event, which takes place on a specifically militarized front or in public or institutionally defined arenas to include the private domain
and the landscape of the mind.

Margaret R. Higonnet and Patrice L. R. Higonnet[1]

The 1914–1918 war was just like our civil war, . . . it was a nice
war. A nice war is a war where everybody who is heroic is a hero
and everybody more or less is a hero in a nice war.

Gertrude Stein[2]

467

A kind of melancholy sadness still clings to the title of Irene Rathbone's *We That Were Young* (1932).[3] Even the reprinting of this long-forgotten novel by The Feminist Press and Virago cannot quite dispel the dusty mustiness of its air of a volume found in the sitting room of a seaside boardinghouse, tea stains and tear stains compelling one to recall its *readers* and their nostalgic pleasure in remembering their repressed and forgotten wartime experiences of almost two decades before, almost as vividly as we experience the author, her autobiographical narrator, and her characters. Even the brief preface by E. M. Delafield, an imprimatur, as it were, by an already established writer on women and war, brings no stab of recognition to the contemporary reader, though it is doubly nostalgic in that it marks a brief moment in English literary history when a woman expert is called upon to validate and authorize the realistic "truth" of another woman's narrative. That is, E. M. Delafield was a respected writer on women in World War I, though she has been forgotten, and Irene Rathbone was taking her place in what could be called a "discursive community" of women war veterans who were trying to make sense and art out of war and women's experience of it. World War I, often called, in a way that rings hollow to modern feminists and pacifists, the Great War, has earned a special place in histories of war because of the enormous toll of human life taken in trench warfare. Gail Braybon, one of a new generation of feminist scholars analyzing women's work in wartime, tells us: "In 1914 the population of England, Scotland, and Wales was around 37 million. In the following four years 744,000 men in the armed forces and 14,661 men in the Merchants Navy were killed, and 1,117 civilians died in air raids. Influenza accounted for another astonishing 150,000 deaths in 1918–19."[4] Women died at the Front, too, and on the job as ambulance drivers and nurses in field hospitals. They died horrible deaths in ammunitions factories at home, and they died other kinds of deaths in madness and grief at the loss of so many loved ones. Germans died in similar numbers, and the French and Belgians, on whose land these gory struggles took place, suffered the worst of all. The Eastern Front, on the sea and in Serbia, claimed its share of casualties as well. While the Americans did not enter this war until very late and for them the experience was foreign, many American nurses and ambulance drivers went to help the Allies in France long before their government was willing to risk its troops. Two memoirs of American nurses deserve particular mention because of the brilliance of the writing as well as historical documentation: Ellen LaMotte's *The Backwash of War* (New York: Putnam's, 1916) and Mary Borden's *The Forbidden Zone* (London: Heinemann, 1929).

Irene Rathbone's *We That Were Young* differs from these novels, as well as from Evadne Price's *Not So Quiet . . .* (London: Albert E. Marriott Ltd., 1930), in that it embodies a literary pacifism as well as a political pacifism. Its calm, rational record, in traditional third-person narrative, of a generation's love and a generation's war, is very different from the explosive, angry, fragmented modernist texts generated by her peers. It appears that there were at least two ways for women to write their experience of World War I, both impelled by anti-war sentiments, both shaped by the experience of nursing wounded men. One group chose to open and expose the horrible wounded flesh for all to see, hoping that readers would learn to reject war. The other group—and Irene Rathbone belongs to this group—wrote to heal and soothe the wounds of war, to patch up the body politic, which was seething with generational hatred. She wrote to give the angry, depressed, and suicidal women who had lost their jobs after the war, and with those jobs the self-respect and financial independence that kept them going, a sense of their own history, with its heroism and its hurts.

In *Virginia Woolf and the Languages of Patriarchy*, I outlined the method Woolf used to draw the reader in as co-maker of the text of *A Room of One's Own* along with the voicing of the response of the contemporary audience as speaking subjects. Revising the Bakhtinian notion of the "dialogic" to describe the triangle made in the reading process by the narrator, who has a collective voice, and two different sets of "readers," I called this process a "triologue."[5] Irene Rathbone's *We That Were Young* is also a "triologue." One is continually imagining and filtering one's contemporary response through the misty curtain of the response of those first readers, nurses who were veterans of Volunteer Aid Detachments (V.A.D.'s) and workers at Y.M.C.A. rest camps in France during World War I. Bakhtin claims that the dialogic, or multi-voiced, novel captures history more fluently than a "monologic" text, which operates under the authority of one ego narrating with authority. On the surface, We That Were Young appears to be a traditional, third-person tale in this mode. But Rathbone, sharing Woolf's socialist and feminist desire to dismantle the hierarchies of the history of the English novel and its concentration on the individual heroine, has tried to write the collective novel about a generation. This "readerly" novel encourages us to join the narrator and the contemporary readers in a plot to overthrow the conventional war novel's rigid time frame by stretching its fictional time back through the suffrage struggle and forward through 1920s disillusionment, including the problems of medical care for veterans and the housing crisis, to the dream of a League of Nations.

We That Were Young thinks back through its mothers and fathers and forward to the baby at the end of the book, a baby whose mother is urged to keep it out of war at all costs—but its primary goal is to think sideways through the lives of the brothers and sisters of the generation whose war this was. Critics of modernism have cared about the fragmented texts that reflect the fragmentation of social life in this period. But Rathbone's quiet and calm experiment with a collective subject is equally as interesting. Rathbone's "we" signals not only an attack on the genealogical imperative of the English novel and its narrative enactment of Oedipal struggles between fathers and sons, or the feminist reply along the same model in the mother–daughter struggle, but also the new move of socialist realism of the thirties to collectivize plots and characters. We That Were Young gives a detailed description of women's war work from canteen service to nursing to munitions making, capturing its dailiness and drudgery as well as its dangers, as if anticipating that these lives would never survive in the pages of the histories of this war. However ambivalent the result, Rathbone also tried to write the class text of this war as it intersected with gender and war. We may wince at her characterization of hospital matrons lording it over volunteer nurses and feel that Jock, who follows Joan around the wards, is merely an updated version of the "faithful retainer" who reinforces class differences. But it is a budding socialist conscience, and a humorous one at that, which records the struggle of the canteen workers to learn how to make fish and chips instead of feeding the Tommies tea and toast.

By the time she wrote *They Call It Peace* (1936), Irene Rathbone had learned to disrupt her language as well as her subject, to "break the sentence," as well as breaking "the sequence" to use Virginia Woolf's description of women's fiction. The generation of war veterans in this novel are fighting in the economic war at home, against homelessness, joblessness, malnutrition, infant mortality, suicide, and moving in and out of political groups from the Communist Party to Douglas's Social Credit, and changing the political color of their shirts as they go. This novel uses the now familiar socialist techniques of montage, newspaper headlines, and snippets from the papers which characterize, to take only two of the most brilliant feminist examples, Doris Lessing's *The Golden Notebook* and Elsa Morante's *History: A Novel*. Rathbone's discussion of the Embankment Brotherhood Settlement might be read with profit by politicians dealing with homelessness, an issue of concern now as it was in the late twenties and thirties. *They Call It Peace* is experimental and modernist in its use of several typefaces, italics, capital letters, ellipses. Page 38 looks as if it had been used for target practice, so punctuated is it with diacritical marks exploding the page.

Rathbone also disrupts the temporal movement of the "decade" novel here, sharing Virginia Woolf's desire to "escape the tyranny of the old British week" by structuring the narrative into sections entitled "1914 and After," "1926 and After," "1929 and After," and "1934 and After." Clearly Rathbone joins those experimental women writers analyzed so brilliantly by Rachel Blau Du Plessis in *Writing Beyond the Ending* (Bloomington: Indiana University Press, 1986). It is obvious what a debt Virginia Woolf's *The Years* owes to Rathbone's simultaneous horizontal writing of a generation and her zig-zag vertical rejection of the rigid decade in a new socialist/feminist/pacifist time line. Rathbone calls her novel a cenotaph "for those who died in vain." But in *We That Were Young*, she was still trying to prove, to herself and her generation, that they had neither worked nor died in vain. Did this fiction, which E. M. Delafield called "Miss Rathbone's faithful and unromanticised story of women's war-work," then accurately inscribe the social text of upper-class Englishwomen's war experience? Does it work for us, who are trying to understand the relations between gender, class, and war ideologies? Precisely because it is both radical and conservative at the same time, *We That Were Young* is closer to the experience of Denise Riley's "women themselves," her attempt to free the women of the past whom we study from being named as objects and robbed of their subjectivity. It enacts, painfully, for readers like myself, the battle raging in most women between the desire to nurture and the desire for autonomy, our internalization of the cultural script which casts us as "natural" nurses, preparers of food, and waitresses, as workers biologically capable of extraordinary feats of labor for the sake of our families, our children, our country. The heroic day and night work stints, which are the centerpiece of the novel, descriptions of double and triple shifts in the ammunitions factory, on the hospital ward, and in the canteens, while meeting the personal demands of loved ones when off duty, will be read by women with little surprise. Whatever the definitions of theorists (e.g., Julia Kristeva et al.), the real definition of a woman's time is that it adapts to the needs of those around her. Women's time is OVERTIME. And Irene Rathbone records the heroism of daily work, women's "overwork," which we are trained to expect of ourselves and other women and to devalue in relation to the "glory" of men's killing and being killed in wartime.

It is perhaps the ungendered and impersonal (inhuman?) *that*, rather than *who*, in the title *We That Were Young*, which first alerts the reader to the fact that Rathbone's novel concerns a generation that was young during the Great War, a generation of men and women rather than individual characters. While women's work experience is her subject, women are always the sisters and lovers of men, constructed by these relationships in primary identities. War work is, as many historians have observed, however enthusiastically shouldered by competent young women, experienced as temporary, *"only for the duration"* of the war. Scholars continue to observe with surprise the speed with which women took up the burden of nursing, ambulance driving, munitions making, as well as any number of other traditionally male occupations on the Home Front, as well as the seemingly uncomplicated "retreat" from the labor force when the men returned.

It seems to me that this is a convenient ideological fiction which reinforces the notion of women as the willing and passive victims of historical forces, and that we would do well to study works like Elizabeth Robins's *Ancilla's Share: An Indictment of Sex Antagonism* (London: Hutchinson, 1924), which chart women's anger at being summarily discarded, as well as documenting, with figures, England's displacement of large numbers of skilled women workers back into the home with a "pronatalist" social policy which defined women as mothers only. Arthur Marwick has demonstrated in *The Deluge: British Society and the First World War* (New York: Norton, 1965) that union leaders and Labour Party representatives actually sat down with the government and agreed to what they called a policy of "dilution," which guaranteed both the factory owners and the men in the labor unions that women workers would be dismissed from their jobs in the munitions factories as soon as the war was over. As Gail Braybon demonstrates in *Women Workers in the First World War* (London: Croom Helm, 1981), women's productivity and performance in these dangerous jobs far exceeded men's. Thus, it was all the more important for the government to maintain the fiction that women workers were silly and idle, weak and irresponsible, or they would have had a social revolution on their hands after the war and might have had to keep women in the work force and pay them decently as well. The government knew, even better than modernist novelists, how to exploit the idea of suspended time in wartime, repeatedly suspending laws and contracts "for the duration." The use of the word "dilution" in relation to the exploitation of women in the ammunitions factories suggests the way whiskey was watered down during the war.[6] Women's "adaptability," as psychologists like Alice Miller have argued, is not only a strength but a weakness. Repressing her own needs for freedom and work in favor of serving the needs of family, community, and state earns a woman, of course, the praise of the men for whom she sacrifices herself but also, Elizabeth Robins insists, gains men's contempt for her spinelessness, a double bind which allows men to demand from women even more self-sacrifice.

E. M. Delafield praises Irene Rathbone for "remembering," noting that for the thirteen years between the war and the production of this novel, women have not forgotten but "put away the memory of their side of the war."[7] I cannot help but wonder at the function of this fiction in British culture. It certainly provided a plot around which women could fix their own memories. The novel is structured as a fiction which "makes sense" of the years from 1915 through 1928 in terms of women's work. Is Rathbone playing the traditional role of woman as culture-bearer by attempting to bridge the gap caused by the war? Is We That Were Young also a victim of cultural "dilution," watering down the horrors which surely filled the pages of her diary as she made it into a novel? I am not making a moral judgment here. It is impossible to move into an objective position from which to observe one's own collusion with a cultural ideology. As we now can see from the publication of the original diaries, Vera Brittain obviously ignored her own worst self and feelings when she rewrote her diary for publication as the now famous pacifist tract Testament of Youth (London: Victor Gollancz, 1933), the classic woman's text from this war. In her introduction to We That Were Young, Lynn Knight, who has had access to the Rathbone papers, suggests that the diaries recorded many unpleasant experiences which did not survive translation into fiction.

Certainly she weaves together the story of English culture as a seamless web, a whole fabric in which the holes made by the war are mended. Some French literary theorists have excluded women writers from the modernist canon on the grounds that their grammatical correctness, old-fashioned narrative structures, and polite language are merely monologic imitations of the nineteenth-century novel. But, as Celeste Schenck has shown in the work of the poets Charlotte Mew, Anna Wickham, and Edith Sitwell, great works of art often slip through the cracks of literary history in the arbitrary categories of literary historians. Shari Benstock has revived the work of Gertrude Stein, Djuna Barnes, and a large number of "lost" modernist women writers and shown how they were lost despite the fact that their writing fits all the modernist requirements.[8] A case can be made for Irene Rathbone on literary grounds in the way she straddles both of these positions. She wants to be the woman artist as nurse, healing a wounded society, making historical continuity out of prewar, war, and postwar time, but Joan's unconscious dreams the nurse's writing arm as a grotesque and phallic German sausage, a phallic enemy inside the woman's body.

An almost invisible subtext of the novel, but one which works as a "political unconscious" is the construction of Joan, the heroine, as reader, as the audience for culture and political ideas. She and her friends date their experience (and judge their men) on the principles of feminism and their involvement in the women's suffrage campaign. They discuss plays and books. They dance and go to the music hall and the Russian ballet when on leave. (See Edith Sitwell's 1916 poem "The Dancers," which figures a gyrating world dancing on "floors slippery with blood" in *Scars upon My Heart*.)[9] Joan sings for the troops and enlarges her repertoire to include popular songs and music hall routines, as she learns to cook and serve fish and chips instead of tea and biscuits. On one level, she caves in to a sentimentality that would have been bad taste for a woman of her class before the war. On another level, we ask whether the "highbrow" adoption of popular culture is merely a "democratic" effort as "temporary" as women's war work, which may mean that a unified culture exists only as a patriotic duty "for the duration," a cultural policy of "dilution," which will disappear when class and gender polarities reappear after the war. Poetry and politics continue to be produced during the war, and Nurse Joan continues to be both the audience and the embodiment of the unbroken line of English culture.

What began in suffrage ends in work for the League of Nations. Both are calmly and genteelly espoused. No passionate pronouncements of either feminism or pacifism ruffle the pages of this book. Perhaps this is because, as Delafield notes, the interest lies in detailed descriptions of the work at the camps and in the hospitals, rather than in the characters. Joan, Betty, Pamela, and Barbara slide into one another as a composite portrait of their generation. Only Thrush stands out as an individual—and she is not *quite* of their class. Joan's brother Jimmy and the individual men and their wounds are far more lively creations.

The continual third-person narrative with its slight privileging of the character of Joan Seddon maintains a discreet distance from the inner lives of the young women. Controlled (and controlling), the narrative stance perhaps allowed readers to distance and depersonalize their experiences in ways that a first-person narrative could not. The difference between this text and the first-person narrative of Evadne Price's *Not So Quiet . . .* is enormous.[10] Under the pseudonym Helen Zenna Smith, Price wrote a series of shockingly modernist novels, whose rough, crude language enacted the linguistic masculinization of the women ambulance drivers. Her texts, torn apart by ellipses and dashes, hallucinatory outbursts, dreams, soliloquies, and dramatic re-enactments, are an explosive commentary on the war's effects on women workers. Fear, anger, and loathing find their voices here in a discourse directly produced by the war and its gender anxieties.

Rathbone, despite her realistic descriptions of wounded men and the especially graphic scenes of the dressing of wounds, remains detached and disinterested, injecting the reader with a narrative aesthetic meant to function as a soothing anodyne to the reader's memories, rather than to arouse one to social action against war. *Rathbone's writing is an exact mimesis of nursing.*[11] The qualities of reserve and self-control, cheerful good breeding, the acting out of woman's role as the representation of civilization and culture, drown individual pain at the loss of so many loved young men in a general anaesthetic of a generation. *We That Were Young* operates under an *aesthetic of anaesthesia*, choosing to numb consciousness rather than to prick the conscience. The use of anaesthesia was a fairly new medical practice in Edwardian and wartime England. It was a godsend to victims of battle and also urged by public policy writers for women in childbirth, not so much out of concern to ease their pain, but to decrease the infant and mother mortality rates, which were exceptionally high. The nurse herself became a figurative painkiller. While *Not So Quiet* . . . explodes in red and khaki, raw and realistic, *We That Were Young* blurs the bloodstains and the deadly telegrams into national collective loss, for which the appropriate response is two minutes of collective silence on Armistice Day. During the seventieth anniversary of the Armistice, modern readers can understand why Rathbone chose this pacifist literary method, which she derived directly from her nursing experience and its rigorous training in the repression of the nurse's own personal feelings and the depersonalizing of the patients', a necessary act since so many thousands died. She was acting in the interest of her women readers in the thirties, who were still mourning, still demoralized, and feeling suicidal.

We That Were Young is not only the Nurse's Text, it speaks in the Nurse's voice, the impersonal discourse that speaks *for* the patient in the first-person plural of "We feel better now, don't we?" The reader, like a good patient, develops a stiff upper lip, a forced smile of suppressed pain. Even the deaths of so many young husbands, cousins, lovers, fiances, and brothers are spooned out in doses, so that one blurs into another, none assuming individual tragic dimensions in the massacre of a youth of a generation— except for the pointless death from influenza of Joan's brother Jimmy after the war is over and the heartbreaking death of Thrush's lover Ginger, because she so recklessly flings herself at life in order to forget him. Irene Rathbone's "we" is caught between its political status as the perfect socialist pronoun and its narcotic "opium of the people" status as the healing patriotic pronoun. Joan tells the reader quite clearly that she learns nursing as previously she learned the lines of a play or a poem. It is the only role for a woman artist in wartime. When she in turn adapts the nurse's art to writing, it appears at times to patronize the reader as patient (as popular representations of the nurse figure often mock the distance, control, and depersonalization which allow her to efficiently carry out her duties). But we are left in no doubt here about the origins of women's art in women's work.

In "Discipline and Cleanliness," the chapter on the professionalizing of English nursing in *Independent Women*, Martha Vicinus quotes Florence Nightingale: "Nursing is warfare, and the nurses are soldiers." The enemy was disease, degradation, and degeneration, and "lady" nurses were going to reform the whole of society, purify the filth from bodies in the hospital and bodies in poverty, drink, and sin in the outside world.[12] Joan and her sister nurses spend a great deal of time as upper-class charwomen in their hospital work, as inheritors of Nightingale's dream of an army of genteel scrubwomen on their knees, as well as a great deal of time fuming at the outmoded authoritarian behavior of their matrons. They blame the class of the matrons, below their own, for the strict discipline, but the real problem, according to Vicinus, was that the "Lady with the Lamp" was looking for dust in the corners and couldn't imagine a woman's profession with a feminist and egalitarian structure. The military model was the undoing of nursing. The V.A.D. nurses were less the carbolic disinfected nun/sisters of previous generations than ghostly figures who brought the blessed relief of pain to their soldier patients.

Klaus Theweleit's powerful and controversial *Male Fantasies* studies the writing of German Freikorps men in the years following World War I. They killed "Red Nurses," communists, and fantasized about the pure sister figure, the white nurse:

> In a historical sense ... the white nurse is an emblem for the bourgeois woman's renunciation of her female body. The nurse's is a dead body, with no desires and no sexuality (no "penis"). She unites in herself the opposing poles of mother and sister, burying all of

their dangerous enticements inside the fiction of a body, which men
need in order not to feel threatened. All of that is signalled, in the
end, by the nurse's uniform. "White" signifies untrodden ground . . .
the nurse is a blank page. . . .[13]

Male fantasies about the nurse in war fiction make clear that she
is not only a healer but a killer, not only a virgin, but the robber of
his virility. What happens when the nurse herself becomes a speaking subject? Can she write her role, her work, her experience outside of the powerful cultural scripts written for her, see herself
differently from the posters and the ballads and the newspaper ro-
manticizations? If she is a blank page, how can she write herself?

One thing she can do is to *write under anaesthesia, the needle
her pen.* That is what Irene Rathbone does in *We That Were
Young.* E. M. Delafield finds the novel sentimental, a fault she for-
gives, shrewdly observing that "sentimentality is one of the most
powerful narcotics in the world." The sentimentality is cinematic,
constructed in scenes. It works with the anaesthetic aesthetic in the
Nurse's Text precisely in the pictorial representations of the alter-
nating work scenes and love scenes, accompanied by scraps and
bits of popular wartime songs which trigger the insistent displacement of war's tragic losses by romantic (and eternal) losses in love.
That is, Rathbone's "women's time," a war narrative which goes
from 1915 to 1928 instead of stopping at 1918, diffuses the spe-
cific events of war into an extended adolescence of the generation
who were young at the time—Joan is thirty-four when the novel
ends. What is interesting to trace is the move from Joan and Colin
quoting poetry at each other, the poetry which connects love and
war, to the text's reluctant quotation of music hall dance tunes
and popular love songs. The sentimentality sheds its class colors
and becomes generalized and figured as a national broken heart.
The songs serve as a conservative "political unconscious" which
erases the possibility of a serious political analysis of war and its
capitalist and imperialist aims. (While Frederic Jameson uses the
term "political unconscious" to make canonized texts acceptable to
radical readers, I reverse his process here to note the hegemonic

cultural discourse beneath the text of a radical writer).[14] War, then, in We That Were Young becomes a natural disaster in which young women are cast in the poetically romantic and "timeless" role of abandoned women, a nation of those who have lost their lovers. (Helen Zenna Smith in Women of the Aftermath casts them more realistically as women who have lost their *work*, and Norah James in Sleeveless Errand, as Angela Ingram has pointed out, casts them as superfluous would-be suicides after the war.)[15] Thrush is the only character who insists on retaining her private personal pain at the loss of Ginger. She is angry and maintains her subjectivity. She refuses to be a blank page or to write the nurse's painkilling text. While the other young women recognize and embrace a collective loss of selfhood, Thrush joins a group of *avant-garde* artists, takes several lovers, and begins to paint. At the end of the war she is successfully showing her work. It is also significant that Joan does not go to see her friend's paintings, a woman's *individual* expression of feeling. For the novel is ambivalent about Thrush, about self-expression when the nation is at war, and it is this ambivalence which suggests reality to the reader, who says to herself, "Yes, this is what it must have been like, to be torn between self-sacrifice and the need to create. It was a time of deferred gratification for women in more ways than one."

2. The Safety Curtain

War is more like a novel than it is like real life and that is its eternal fascination. It is a thing based on reality but invented, it is a dream made real, all the things that make a novel but not really life.

Gertrude Stein[16]

It is a standard characteristic of women's World War I novels to figure the war as scenes in a drama, a way, one thinks, of imagining an end to suffering. The war is a theatre, and the response to the ideological call for female self-sacrifice is sketched as role-

playing—acting (as in war work), a *temporary* role for the duration of the war, as in Shakespeare's "nonce roles." Rathbone's
novel participates in this rhetoric of the theatre of war. In fact, she
articulates her own anaesthetic aesthetic of the Nurse's Text in the
metaphor of the theatre by describing Joan's V. A. D. nursing in
Ward 33 of the First London General Hospital as requiring her to
let down a "safety curtain" of the mind in order to perform her
duties:

> Every night during the first week Joan dreamt about the wounds,
> saw them floating before her eyes, almost had the stench of them in
> her nostrils. It was inevitable this should be so, for, during the day,
> sensibilities had to be hardened, quivering disgust controlled, and
> head and hand kept steady for the sake of the sufferers themselves.
> *With unconscious wisdom she let down a sort of safety-curtain be-*
> *tween her mind and the sights before her, keeping them at bay, pre-*
> *venting their full significance from penetrating* [italics added]. If she
> had not done so she would have been useless. The nights were reac-
> tions from this discipline, and the safety-curtain no longer function-
> ing the horror rushed in on her in the shape of dreams. . . .
>
> A fervent emotion—whether towards a person, a country, or a
> cause—may be able to express itself in a poem, or at any rate some
> form of words. Happy if it can. But it may also have to be ex-
> pressed in ways more indirect, and less glowingly satisfactory. Joan's
> feeling of almost weeping admiration for the men had to show itself
> in the severest practical form—and this was not easy for her. Men-
> tally she was on her knees to them; actually she was on her feet
> twelve hours a day, sweeping, washing, bed-making, moving down
> one long line of iron bedsteads and up another with the wheeled
> table on which were the appliances for the dressings. It was her
> pride, while getting ready this table in the morning, not to forget
> one single necessary article. She learnt them by heart, as she might a
> poem, and with a corresponding fervour. And though for the first
> few repetitions she occasionally forgot a line she was soon word-
> perfect. (195)

The construction of "remembering" the correct objects for performing the work of dressing wounds as an art akin to memoriz-

ing the lines of a poem or a play enacts itself the repression of the artist in the nurse. The bandages and sterilized instruments become words or lines with which to write the Nurse's Text, on the bodies of wounded men. The play must go on in the theatre of war. The learning of the script of nursing is not real; it will not lead to a career. Joan and her fellow upper-class V.A.D.s are "playing nurse." They will be no threat to "real" nurses once the war is over, like Barbie dolls in nurse's costumes. The fascinating question here is how did this language of "play-acting" "for the duration" of the war move from official government policy into the consciousness of women who accepted it and, like Irene Rathbone, wrote it?

3. In Parentheses

What is there inside one that makes one know all about war.

Gertrude Stein[17]

Tempted as I am to name this writing of women's suspended or bracketed time "In Parentheses,"[18] as my section title suggests—an anaesthetic numbing discourse which directs women into unpaid exhausting labor for the state with no thought of work or a career which might upset the labor market after the war, as a *language*— I take heed of the caution expressed by Denise Riley. She points out that if we speak about an official rhetoric of state policy and study its effects on women measured as compliance or resistance (women are then to blame or else heroically cynical), "we obscure the fact that there are no completely naive or completely knowing linguistic subjects." Further,

> Rather than simply identifying "a language of" something, we need to inch toward some sense of the effects on our lives of ways of talking and reading and being always represented. How to assess, for instance, the impact on "women themselves" of their continually being described as mothers, girlish employees, docile mother-

workers? Especially when these "women themselves" may not have access to a contrasting set of descriptions, how does the language *work back* on the consciousness of its ostensible subjects? For sometimes one must speak and act within a language one may feel half-consciously uneasy with, unsatisfied by: *there may be no choice of words.*[19]

Riley is speaking of the "overfeminization" of social policy rhetoric regarding motherhood in Britain in World War II. This overfeminization was clearly already present in the rhetoric of women's roles in World War I. If the culture does not construe woman as a speaking subject, it can call upon her as an actress to mime the role of speaking subject (for the nonce) while men are at war. To emphasize the temporary nature of her authorization to speak, she must acknowledge that she is playing a role, that she is not a nurse, but *acting as* a nurse, *acting as* an ambulance driver. The language of anaesthetic numbing of consciousness, which I identify here as written in the Nurse's Text over a decade after the war, participates in the bracketing off of the war years as a space of time between the acts of a continuous drama which is English culture and civilization. To what extent does *We That Were Young* as a fiction participate in government rhetoric? Can it be said to represent the reality of Irene Rathbone's experience or that of her generation? What is the relation of Joan, Betty, Barbara, Pamela, and Thrush to "women themselves" in this period?

Motherhood is not an issue here (as it is, complicatingly, in *Not So Quiet . . .*), but heterosexuality is. Each of the women loves and is loved by men who die in the war. In fiction as in life, there are no completely naive or completely knowing linguistic subjects, but the third-person controlling narrative acts as if there are. It pulls down a "safety curtain" between the reader and the characters that is not present in a first-person narrative. When Joan Seddon names the objects on her nursing tray as "words" she will memorize as she memorizes a poem, she is letting her "work" as a nurse speak for her. The novel is written to remember what is inside the historical parentheses, a time when women were working/speaking subjects. Nostalgic and sentimental as it is, *We That Were Young* also documents in great detail the actual work done by volunteer women, as well as Pamela's experience in a dangerous munitions factory. It is ironic, given the structure of "acting" that controls the women's consciousnesses, that Pamela's ambition and talent to be a *professional* actress is thwarted, and she returns after "acting" as a war worker to play the "daughter at home" to her aging parents. Woman's wish for self-expression is deemed selfish in the ideology of war, though Pamela's failure is described as laziness, a class inability to accept the physical hardships of stage life, though she certainly has shown her mettle in war work! The chapter that describes her work in the ammunition factory is a frightening tribute to the "art" of making bombs and the real-life melodrama of the thrill of dangerous work. The theatre could never compete in emotional excitement. Staged deaths could never compare to the real deaths in factories. Certainly for the reader, the scalping of a woman whose hair gets caught in her machine is as gruesome as any battle scene. Pamela could never work as hard for herself as she does for her country is presumably the message. Acting as a worker during the war has cured her of her desire to escape downward from the nonworking class.

The temporary bracketed nature of women's war work is also present in the novel in a critique of works of art produced by the war, also "in parentheses" as temporary entertainments that will not survive. Joan's sophisticated lover Paul mocks her feminist pleasure in the performance of plays by Brieux in London when they are on leave and judges the works to be too moral and topically political to survive as works of art, because, like her beloved Meredith, they lack style. Perhaps anticipating the eclipse of her own novel, Rathbone describes a concert given by Leslie Henson at the Y.M.C.A. Rest Camp in St. Valery in the summer of 1918: "In its own way it was a brilliant little affair, but would have had no value at any other period." (400) This is a strong statement from the usually reserved narrative voice, especially when the soldier audience is described as bellowing with laughter and "the girls laughed until they were nearly sick." Is the comic different in war and peace? The content of the sketches is clearly topical and meant to allay wartime anxieties about *gender identity*, *authority*, and *class*. Bert Errol "with soprano voice, and dressed in low-cut evening frock and red wig, travestied famous songs from operas." In a musical sketch to popular war tunes, Leslie Henson in "the Dis-orderly Room" plays an adjutant with a moustache dealing with Tommies who have committed "various absurd offences." (400) The narrator is equally critical of the popular romantic songs of war time, while their lyrics seem especially appropriate to the reader. "Of all the lyrical atrocities produced by the war," she writes of "Broken Doll," "this was about the worst; yet it was extremely popular in the summer of 1916." (238) Joan is in hospital herself, being treated for an infected arm "now swollen to the dimensions of a nightmare German sausage," which, in her fever she thinks must be her leg:

> From the gramophone in one of the officers' wards below came the strains of "The Broken Doll." Over and over and over again that inane and vacuously sentimental song droned its way up through the windows.
> "And when you go away,
> You'll be sorry some day,
> You left behind a bro-ken do-oll". . . .
> That ghastly broken doll—half-waxen, half-human—stumbled its way in and out of Joan's dreams. . . . (238)

She was herself a broken doll, a toy, an object to be thrown away and abandoned. The broken doll is terrifyingly close to her role as temporary speaking subject. This tune alternates with "The Only Girl in the World" as a chorus to her rising fever. She thinks of suicide, since most of the young men of her generation are already dead: "Something laughed inside her. 'The only girl!' Yes— *if!* But being one of thousands—of millions—she could well be spared by the country. Quite a good thing really to pop off—equal up the sexes a bit." (239) But these occasions when the "safety curtain" of anaesthetic discourse is raised are very rare. At the end of the novel in 1928 Joan bursts out to her young cousin Molly, "Don't let your young men go to the war!" (464) but soon recovers her nurse's composure.

4. The Daffodil Dream

The other unmediated moments in *We That Were Young* are Joan's dreams of her brother, Jimmy. The dreams are "quite short, and no words were spoken in them; . . . of such intensity that they didn't seem like dreams at all." (423) The sentimental "picture" of twelve-year-old Jimmy playing with his dog, Tam, at the beginning of the book, the perfect specimen of the English schoolboy, good at sports and math, has carried a good deal of the emotional weight of the novel. When his clothes are sent home "his 'flea-bag,' his tin helmet, the trench boots at which she had laughed that day just before he went out," she breaks down:

> "We'll keep this one, Tam," she said, folding up the muddy tunic. "It's got the mud of Ypres on it, and it's almost worn through. I don't think clothes matter much on the whole, but this one . . . Oh, Tam, *don't* look at me like that! . . ." And she stumbled across to the dog, and clasped his head against her in a storm of weeping. (422)

This would be the perfect ending of a *Masterpiece Theatre* series on women and war. In fact the whole novel seems already scripted for these instant nostalgia programs, with the interlocked lives of Betty, Barbara, Pam, and Joan, and all the men who figure in their lives, in scenes of bliss and parting, home wounded on leave, in the hospitals and camps, in France and London.

Clothes, Joan says, don't matter much, and yet in her two dreams, Jimmy is not in his khaki tunic; he is twelve years old in his cricket flannels, and later in a tweed coat. In her dreams she restores him to civilian clothes—"through the thin flannel of the shirt she could feel his collar-bone." (423) Under the safety curtain she divests him of his military uniform. And, in fact, there is a great deal of discussion in the novel about the value of uniforms

for V.A.D. nurses as well as the demilitarization of clothing for the
women munitions workers, and patriotic descriptions of the Scots
regiments in their kilts. The clothes are important and they signify
as the *costumes* of *war as theatre*. Having played her part, Joan
wants her brother back as he was before he was a soldier, as a boy
and the young man she teasingly but truly claims is the one she
really loves. The daffodil dream is quite moving in a text which
has repressed the women's subjectivity so successfully. The daffodil
figures in the poems she and Colin read to each other in 1915 and
comes to symbolize her inability to *feel*, the "white glitter" of her
role as "frost princess." But that young Joan is the image of the
Joan of Arc appropriated by the suffrage movement to spiritualize
the women's struggle as virgin soldiers on a crusade for women's
honor. Her chastity and integrity of body were formed by feminism and then, ironically, ripe for reinscription as the white nurse
to the male imagination. In the second dream, Jimmy

> was striding up a grassy slope, bare-headed, and about a yard in
> front of her. She reached her hand to his shoulder to keep him to
> her level, but he strode on, pulling her up the hill. Again—as in the
> other dream—she was aware of the texture of his clothes, but this
> time it was a tweed coat he was wearing. As she walked she looked
> at the grass, and saw that it was covered with small wild daffodils.
> "Spring!" she said to herself. And then just above the daffodils ap-
> peared Aunt Florence's face, lying back with closed eyes, very pale, a
> bit of wispy material floating round it. It was not at all frighten-
> ing—it was simply there. Jimmy hadn't noticed it—his eyes were
> ahead. And they walked on together. (423)

Behind the safety curtain of the nurse's text is the repressed
dream of forbidden love, the incestuous wish to exchange the life
of the brother for the death of the mother. (Aunt Florence has
raised the orphaned Joan and Jimmy.) Somehow the most vivid image in this very pictorial text, with its scene crowded upon scene
of intensely realized portraits of factories, camps, marching soldiers, hospital wards, and English country houses, is Aunt Florence's face in the field of daffodils. It is one moment in which the

488 AFTERWORD

anaesthetic text reaches out to the complex of emotions on the motherhood/war axis which fuels the energy of *We That Were Young*'s sister fictions of World War I like *Not So Quiet*. . . . The daffodil dream also reminds us of the theme of the lost beloved brother that runs through so many women's war narratives from Vera Brittain's diaries to Katherine Mansfield's stories to Virginia Woolf's *Jacob's Room*. In a paper given at the Feminist Theory Conference in Dubrovnik in 1988, Margaret Higonnet argued that the literature of nationalist wars enforces heterosexuality as politically correct, while Civil War narratives allow incestuous themes to emerge. What is interesting about *We That Were Young* in this regard is that the daffodil dream writes the other insistent formulation of World War I literature, both male and female, English and German, prose and poetry—of the Great War as war between generations: the Old who made the war and the Young who fought it. The dream's invocation of "Spring," its resurrection of the dead brother over the head of Aunt Florence on a platter of daffodils, recalls Christian exegesis of the beheading of John the Baptist as a herald of Christ's predicted arrival. That is, the foretold death becomes hallowed because it is not read as a death but as an event leading to Christ's coming. Jimmy's collarbone is a wishbone which in the dream exchanges one head for another. His soft civilian shirt collar replaces the stiff collar of the uniform that stiffened the faces of V.A.D. nurses as well as soldiers. Diana Cooper, who also served at Guy's Hospital, complained of the collar's sharp grip, which toughened her neck "like the man they couldn't hang, though they tried six times."[20] The generational conflict rewrites the nationalist drama as a civil war. The daffodils of *We That Were Young*, first used to signify the "virgin soldier" aspect of Joan's generation of young women war workers, come to signify the youth of their brothers as well. Prewar and war literature celebrated a violent and demonic "rite of spring," frenzied preparations for a bloody sacrifice of a generation instead of one vegetation god. The loss of spring is the theme of Richard Aldington's *Death of a Hero* (London: Chatto & Windus, 1929), which influenced

Irene Rathbone. In her dream, Joan is a Joan of Arc whose sword severs the mother's head to save the brother's virile spring.

Joan's intense identification with Meredith's *Diana of the Crossways* connects the daffodil to Diana's phallic crocus, the "chivalrous knight" aspect of her character, which Joan and her friends had already experienced as soldiers in Christabel Pankhurst's army of strong and pure young suffragettes. The "we" in Irene Rathbone's title doubtless also refers to Meredith's caution to his readers about Diana's status as an *individual* heroine. He argued that women would not be free until they "learned to say not 'I' but 'we.' " Surely Rathbone's collective of heroines is meant to enact his prescription, including their brothers and lovers as well.

Yet it is unclear to me as a reader whether the socialist, feminist, and pacifist ideals of Irene Rathbone are fully realized in her anaesthetized text. Its stretching of the war experience out of the parentheses of strict battle time, 1914–1918, in which standard male history encloses the period, does make clear, however, how much training in suffrage organizations and demonstrations prepared these young women for their war work. Extending the novel to 1928, the year in which Englishwomen got the vote, also records the work of the same class of volunteer women, shouldering the heavy burden of social responsibility for finding jobs for veterans, resettling their families, and mending the fabric of wartorn society. What strikes the contemporary reader most forcefully is the power of the state to exact so much *unpaid* and necessary labor from a class of people not even accorded the basic rights of citizenship. What has also become clear is that the government maintained a clandestine class warfare by hiring upper-class women to do overtime work in the munitions factories and used the volunteer nurses so they would not have to pay the wages of trained nurses, though, of course, women like Irene Rathbone and the characters in her novels did not know this at the time.

An explanation seems to lie in Denise Riley's caution that women are neither fully naive nor fully knowing linguistic subjects in relation to the discourse of public policy and state propaganda regarding their roles. Perhaps this numbed and numbing Nurse's Text is, after all, more representative of the ambivalence of the historical subjects, "women themselves," than the radical, passionate anti-war novels of Ellen LaMotte, Mary Hamilton, or Rose Macaulay. The soothing and healing effect of the depiction of heroic, smiling canteen workers and nurses caring for unfailingly courteous armies of soldiers displaces any social or sexual ugliness onto an interestingly constructed group of outsiders and scapegoats, the "Christians" of the Y.M.C.A. camps in France. These men are invariably characterized as lazy, skulking, good-for-nothing creatures who are shirking their duty to fight, fools in love and of an ambiguous social class, neither gay, courageous officers nor "darling" Tommies. These shadowy unwholesome men, of course, act as the agents of the women's representation as "ladies," as Mother England herself, the "home" that the men are fighting for. The working-class professional nurses, the "matrons" under whom the V.A.D. nurses serve, are also demeaned in class terms, overbearing and brutal to their underlings because they are unused to authority.

We That Were Young may also be more representative of women's ambivalence about the war because, despite its graphic descriptions of wounded men, the reader's outrage is controlled by corresponding passages that glamorize and eroticize the war experience in descriptions of handsome bodies of marching troops, the girls' responses to the knees of Scottish warriors in their kilts, the way the women change into evening dresses to dance in London clubs with uniformed soldiers. This tug between the glamour and horror of war was real, and it also appears in the work of May Sinclair and the letters of Vera Brittain, part of the brother/sister incestuous "we" of the narrative of the generational war, often accompanied by the wish of the New Women, liberated by the suffrage movement and already trained by that movement to think of themselves as part of a righteous army, to be soldiers themselves and fight alongside their brothers.

The repressed wish to be one's brother or an androgynous approximation of him lurks behind the safety curtain of women's

war dramas. The incest plot lurks beneath the surface of nationalist war writing. English poetry by men in this period is homo-
erotic. Women writers mourn the loss of their suffragette-soldier
selves in the deaths of their brothers. They mourn the loss of sis-
terhood in political struggle, their own hopes for autonomy and
freedom, for that is what they really sacrificed, in mourning the
men of their generation. *We That Were Young* compensates women
readers for the fact that the Nurse's Text will be a blank page in
the history of the war. The nurse-writer must anaesthetize herself
and her own desire for physical action (even the wish to kill?) before she writes the sentimental war novel as the opium of the
women survivors. Certainly some things escape her narcotic, like
Joan's dreams.

The opening scene describes Joan and Colin as radiant and pathetic, like "some favourite Watts or Burne-Jones picture." Joan
has "eyes like a boy-angel's," (1) an androgynous profile she re-
tains at the end of the novel, at thirty-four in 1928, when her
"boyish shoulders" and "short fair hair" make her look like "an
attractive page." (465) She confesses to her young cousin Molly:

> We were the youth of the world, we were on the crest of life, and we
> were the war. No one above us counted, and no one below. Youth
> and the war were the same thing—youth and the war were us. . . .
> Yes, we hated it and loved it, both. . . . It was *our* war, you see. And
> although it was so every-dayish at the time, and we were so sickened
> with it, it seems, now, to have a sort of ghastly glamour. . . . Our
> hearts are there—unwillingly—for always. It was our war. (464–
> 465)

Though Joan rushes off to her League of Nations meeting, the
pacifist effect is muted by her honest outburst about the ghastly
glamour of war. The same is true of the feminist effect. Joan and
her friends are introduced as serious suffragettes (committed but
afraid to go to prison), but she is sexually aroused only by the
misogynist anti-feminist, Paul. The socialist effect is similarly
muted. The young people talk at the beginning of the novel about

their idealist hopes for social progress. They reject social Darwinism and the belief in an "unchanging human nature," yet the novel mocks the "Christians" of the Y.M.C.A. and the matrons in the hospitals. In the way that it undermines its own intentions (this is obvious linguistically, when Rathbone uses military language like "strafing" and "bombarding" to describe civilian activities), *We That Were Young* is, perhaps, a more historically interesting women's war text than those war writings that espouse a pure pacifism or a righteous anger after the war. It is steeped in the kind of ambivalence the New Women must have felt about war, sex, and death. Irene Rathbone saw herself as a woman torn between timidity and bold visions of a just society, full of convictions but lacking courage. So is her text, and that is why the woman reader, who, if she is like me, often finds herself in the same position, will deeply enjoy this novel. The daffodil dream is all the more effective because of the numbing narrative around it which has repressed much that was unpleasant or ugly in nurse/soldier relations. Aunt Florence's head is the repressed woman warrior's dream trophy—she has metaphorically killed that stepmother, the Home Front, and the patriarchal family for the preservation of which wars are fought, to merge the maiden with the brother. Is the wispy bit of material which floats around her head the uplifted "maiden's veil" in the epigraph poem that begins the book? That poem also recalls the laughing schoolboy in a tree, the Jimmy whose senseless death is the most emotionally powerful scene in the book.

The Nurse's Text has given the reader-survivors a picture album of their war work. The most vivid for me is of the young woman being scalped by her machine in the munitions factory because she cannot bear binding up her long hair in a cap.[21] Equally memorable is Joan's feverish dream that her infected arm has become a grotesque German sausage. Inflamed by the wounds it has probed and cleared of shrapnel and bullets, the arm, the agent of her healing power as a nurse, becomes the enemy, German, phallic, the nightmare of the guilt male writers also projected upon the disturbing figure of the nurse, who is blamed in men's writing about the war for wounding or emasculating those whom she heals. Her capacity to bear this survivor's guilt, to hallucinate her own arm as the enemy's gun and to *repress* it, recovering and continuing the work of patching up bodies and culture, is a testament to her generation's incredibly successful ability to bear the burden of cultural representation, to wear the nurse's uniform, to be the blank page, but to write on its starchy surface the record of her work.

Jane Marcus
Oberwolfach, West Germany
June 1988

Notes

1. "The Double Helix," *Behind the Lines: Gender and the Two World Wars*, ed. M. R. Higonnet, Jane Jenson, Sonya Michel, and Margaret Collins Weitz (New Haven: Yale University Press, 1987) p. 46.

2. *Wars I Have Seen* (1945; London: Brilliance Books, 1984) p. 77.

3. First published by Chatto & Windus, London, 1932. Lynn Knight in her introduction to this reprint claims that Irene Rathbone wrote to congratulate Richard Aldington on the brilliance of his novel, *Death of a Hero*, and that he was instrumental in getting hers published. They had a brief love affair while he was engaged in liasons with other women. Susan Friedman in her studies of the poet H. D. has analyzed the literary uses H. D. made of the fact that she, too, was abandoned by Aldington. See Friedman's "Exile in the American Grain: H. D.'s Diaspora" in *Women's Writing in Exile*, ed. Mary Lynn Broe and Angela Ingram (Chapel Hill, N.C.: University of North Carolina Press, 1989) and her "Modernism of the 'Scattered Remnant': Race and Politics in H. D.'s Development" in *Feminist Issues in Literary Scholarship*, ed. Shari Benstock (Bloomington: Indiana University Press, 1986), pp. 208–232.

4. *Out of the Cage: Women's Experiences in Two World Wars* (London: Pandora, 1987), p. 2.

5. Jane Marcus, *Virginia Woolf and the Languages of Patriarchy* (Bloomington: Indiana University Press, 1987); Mikhail Bakhtin, *The Dialogic Imagination* (Austin: University of Texas Press, 1985).

6. Elizabeth Robins, *Ancilla's Share: An Indictment of Sex-Antagonism* (London, 1924; Westport, Conn.: Hyperion Press, 1976). For a discussion of pronatalist policy in Britain, see Denise Riley, *War in the Nursery* (London: Virago, 1983) and "Some Peculiarities of Social Policy Concerning Women in Wartime and Postwar Britain" in *Behind the Lines*, cited above. While Riley is especially concerned with World War II, her methodology in the analysis of the rhetoric of social policy should prove enormously useful for literary critics engaged in cultural critique. She argues that war work was permeated with gender in order to define any woman's work except for motherhood as temporary. "Women *when named as sex* by the formulations of social policy cannot escape being the incarnation of gender as strange or temporary workers; nor can they escape being seen as hovering on the edge of maternity. . . . Rhetorically, women were overpersonified as mothers and desexed as workers." (*Behind the Lines*, pp. 260–261). For a devastating account of the sufferings of the wives and children of working-class soldiers and sailors during the war, see the articles from *The Women's Dreadnought* by Sylvia Pankhurst reprinted in *Suffrage and the Pankhursts*, ed. Jane Marcus (New York and London: Routledge and Kegan Paul, 1988).

7. Irene Rathbone (1892–1980) was the author of seven novels: *Susan Goes East* (1929), *We That Were Young* (1932), *The Gold Rim* (1933), *October* (1934), *They Call It Peace* (1936), *When Days Were Years* (1939), and *Seeds of Time* (1952). *We That Were Young* is based on her own experience in the war. Born in a family of Liverpool progressives, she was educated at a boarding school, and before the war she acted in the Frank Benson Shakespeare Company. Jimmy is based on her youngest brother, Ben, who died in the Army of Occupation in Germany in 1919. Her other brother, Reginald, became a Brigadier. She wrote *Susan Goes East* in a flat in Chelsea after the war, which she shared with

several women friends, from the letters she wrote while visiting Reginald in China and India. A friend of Storm Jameson and Nancy Cunard, Rathbone was an early suffragette, a socialist, a pacifist, and deeply upset about fascism in Spain. She nursed her aging parents until they died in 1952 and 1964, then returned to London, where she was active in PEN.

8. These essays by Celeste Schenck and Shari Benstock will appear in Broe and Ingram's forthcoming collection, *Women's Writing in Exile,* cited above.

9. *Scars upon My Heart: Women's Poetry and Verse of the First World War,* ed. Catherine W. Reilly (London: Virago, 1982), p. 100.

10. *Not So Quiet . . .* has also been reprinted by The Feminist Press and Virago Press. See the afterword and notes to that volume for further bibliography on women's writing of World War I. Neglected novels worth study are Rose Macaulay's *Non-Combatants and Others* (London: Hodder, 1916) and Mary Hamilton's *Dead Yesterday.* Most of these novels are not included in Cyril Falls's annotated *War Books: A Critical Guide.* For a discussion of the banning of women's war books under DORA (the Defense of the Realm Act), see Angela Ingram, " 'Unutterable Putrefaction' and 'Foul Stuff': Two 'Obscene' Novels of the 1920's," *Women's Studies International Forum* 9, #4, 1986, 341–354. Claire Tylee's response to Sandra Gilbert's interpretation of World War I literature (*SIGNS* 8: 422–450) in a paper adapted from her forthcoming book on women and World War I, "Maleness Run Riot: The Great War and Women's Resistance to Militarism," *Women's Studies International Forum* (vol. 11, #3, 1988, 199–210) is perhaps the best introduction to the controversies in current critical debate about gender and war. See also Claire Culleton's study of the popular cartoons of the bodies of women munitions workers in which their wombs and breasts are figured as bombs in *Women's Studies International Forum,* vol. 11, #2, 1988, 109–116.

11. For another discussion of the representation of nursing in World War I literature, see my "Asylums of Antaeus: Women, War and Madness" in *The Differences Within: Feminism and Critical*

Theory, ed. Elizabeth Meese and Alice Parker (Amsterdam and Philadelphia: John Benjamins, 1988), pp. 49–81. In "Liberty, Sorority, Misogyny" in *Virginia Woolf and the Languages of Patriarchy*, the patriarchal use of the image of the nurse is discussed in relation to fascism, an analysis instigated by Maria Macciocchi's "Female Sexuality in Fascist Ideology," *Feminist Review*, #1, 1979. The discussion of the figure of the nurse in the male imagination and from the German point of view appears in Klaus Theweleit's *Male Fantasies* (Minneapolis: University of Minnesota Press, 1987). A controversial history of nursing in England is Martha Vicinus's *Independent Women: Work and Community for Single Women 1850–1920* (Chicago: University of Chicago Press, 1985). Vicinus's negative portrait of the class snobbery and rigid authoritarianism within the nursing profession as due to the internalization of male models in the original institution-building process has come in for criticism from feminist historians. See Blanche Cook's review in *The Women's Review of Books* and Carroll Smith-Rosenberg's review in *SIGNS* (Spring 1988, 644–649). See also Eva Gamarnikow, "Sexual Division of Labour: The Case of Nursing" in *Feminism and Materialism: Women and Modes of Production*, ed. Annette Kuhn and Ann Marie Wolpe (London: Routledge and Kegan Paul, 1978) and Celia Davies, ed., *Rewriting Nursing History* (London: Croom Helm, 1980).

12. Vicinus, *Independent Women*, p. 92.

13. Theweleit, *Male Fantasies*, vol. 1, p. 134.

14. Obviously, this usage of the term "political unconscious" to signify a conservative subtext in a work by a radical writer is not in keeping with Frederic Jameson's usage of the term in *The Political Unconscious: Narrative as a Socially Symbolic Act* (Ithaca, NY: Cornell University Press, 1981) to signify a radical subtext in a conservative novel. Jameson's methodology, while claiming to be Marxist, often in fact reinforces the literary canon by finding subversive subtexts in the classics. Reversing the process is enlightening in revealing the strong conservative elements in texts considered "radical."

15. *Women of the Aftermath* is a sequel to *Not So Quiet*... by Evadne Price under the pseudonym Helen Zenna Smith. Angela Ingram discusses Norah James's *Sleeveless Errand* in " 'Unutterable Putrefaction,' " cited above. See also her discussion of the important and neglected pacifist novel by Rose Allatini, *Despised and Rejected*, published in 1918 under the pseudonym A. T. Fitzroy. Ingram's work on postwar literature continues in "Un/Reproductions: States of Banishment in Some English Novels after the Great War," in the forthcoming *Women's Writing in Exile*, ed. Broe and Ingram, cited above.

16. Gertrude Stein, *Paris France* (1940; New York: Liveright, 1970), p. 138.

17. Stein, *Wars I Have Seen*, p. 9.

18. Parentheses or brackets set off words in a sentence both to highlight them and to hide them. They "set off" the phrases and function in the Nurse's Text like the screens the nurses put around their patients when they are dressing their wounds. They are also psychic "screens," like Joan's "safety curtain," which represses her feelings. See Winifred Lett's poem "Screens" in *Scars Upon My Heart*, p. 62.

19. Riley in *Behind the Lines*, pp. 270–271.

20. Diana Cooper, *The Rainbow Comes and Goes* (London: Century, 1985), pp. 166–167. On the relation of war to spring see Charlotte Mew's poem "May 1915," *Scars Upon My Heart*, p. 72.

21. Gail Braybon's study of interviews with those who had been munitions workers in *Out of the Cage* reveals that some women took on their husbands' jobs and found they were not as difficult as the men had claimed. For a time it was fashionable for upper-class girls to take jobs as munitionettes as Pamela does in *We That Were Young*. Braybon also says that many women interviewed changed jobs often as the women in the novel do. One upper-class woman who became a writer of genius, Sylvia Townsend Warner, worked in a munitions factory and wrote an article about the work for *Blackwoods Magazine* in 1916. She was a relief worker, stamping out cases for shells, and in her article she pointed out

that she was paid sixteen guineas for writing, while the wages at the munitions factory were six shillings for an eight-hour day including the bonus. A newspaper then asked her for another article, saying they wouldn't offer her any payment since she was helping the workers by writing. She couldn't understand why her not being paid would help the workers and did get paid in the end. This experience contributed to making her into a dedicated communist. Only later did she realize that she had been a "blackleg," part of "a dilution scheme, devised to avoid the payment of overtime to the regular workers. . . . The conditions were bad, there was an incessant shortage of small tools, there was no canteen and the sanitation was an outrage." (Cited in Wendy Mulford, *This Narrow Place*, London: Pandora, 1988). For further descriptions of women munitions workers, see the three essays by Rebecca West in my *The Young Rebecca West 1911–1917* (Viking, 1982; Bloomington: Indiana University Press, 1989).

The *Feminist Press at The City University of New York* offers alternatives in education and in literature. Founded in 1970, this nonprofit, tax-exempt educational and publishing organization works to eliminate sexual stereotypes in books and schools and to provide literature with a broad vision of human potential. The publishing program includes reprints of important works by women, feminist biographies of women, and nonsexist children's books. Curricular materials, bibliographies, directories, and a quarterly journal provide information and support for students and teachers of women's studies. In-service projects help to transform teaching methods and curricula. Through publications and projects, The Feminist Press contributes to the rediscovery of the history of women and the emergence of a more humane society.

New and Forthcoming Books

Black Foremothers: Three Lives, 2nd ed., by Dorothy Sterling. Foreword by Margaret Walker. Introduction by Barbara Christian. $9.95 paper.

Get Smart: A Woman's Guide to Equality on Campus, by Montana Katz and Veronica Vieland. $29.95 cloth, $9.95 paper.

Islanders, a novel by Helen R. Hull. Afterwork by Patricia McClelland Miller. $10.95 paper.

Library and Information Sources on Women: A Guide to Collections in the Greater New York Area, compiled by the Women's Resources Group of the Greater New York Metropolitan Area Chapter of the Association of College and Research Libraries and the Center for the Study of Women and Society of the Graduate School and University Center of The City University of New York. $12.95 paper.

Lone Voyagers: Academic Women in Coeducational Universities, 1869–1937, edited by Geraldine J. Clifford. $29.95 cloth, $12.95 paper.

My Mother Gets Married, a novel by Moa Martinson. Translated and introduced by Margaret S. Lacy. $8.95 paper.

Not So Quiet: Stepdaughters of War, a novel by Helen Zenna Smith. Afterword by Jane Marcus. $9.95 paper.

Ruth Weisburg; Paintings, Drawings, Prints, 1968–1988, edited and curated by Marion E. Jackson. With an essay by Thalia Gouma-Peterson. $15.00 paper.

Sultana's Dream and Selections from The Secluded Ones, by Rokeya Sakhawat Hossain. Edited and translated by Roushan Jahan. Afterword by Hanna Papanek. $16.95 cloth, $6.95 paper.

We That Were Young, a novel by Irene Rathbone. Introduction by Lynn Knight. Afterword by Jane Marcus. $10.95 paper.

Women Activists: Challenging the Abuse of Power, by Anne Witte Garland. Foreword by Ralph Nader. Introduction by Frances T. Farenthold. $29.95 cloth, $9.95 paper.

Women Composers: The Lost Tradition Found, by Diane P. Jezic. Foreword by Elizabeth Wood. $29.95 cloth, $12.95 paper.

For a free catalog, write to The Feminist Press at The City University of New York, 311 East 94 Street, New York, NY 10128. Send individual book orders to The Talman Company, Inc., 150 Fifth Avenue, New York, NY 10011. Please include $1.75 for postage and handling for one book, $.75 for each additional.